I0525381

Midwinter in Mexico

Midwinter in Mexico

CALLEY CLOVER

Copyright © 2025 Calley Clover
All rights reserved.
ISBN: 979-8-9986818-0-6

DEDICATION

To Tyler. For always ensuring I have whatever I need.

ONE

I took one look at my cringey passport picture and then stuffed it into my sling bag along with my wallet, lip balm, earbuds and phone.

I'd dyed my hair blonde last year much to the reluctance of my stylist. It had been fun for the first two weeks, before the roots grew out and it became painfully obvious I'd paid an exuberant amount of money trying to look good. Since then, and at the behest of my boyfriend, Eric, I dyed my hair back to its natural chestnut brown that matched my chestnut eyes. The unfortunate thing though, was that I'd needed to pose for a passport photo during that blonde era. A small part of me worried I'd be held up in customs for it.

I looked down at my packed luggage and then lifted my eyes to Eric who was standing at the other side of my bed rifling through his own luggage one last time to make sure he had everything. He caught me staring and gave me a half smile.

"You get everything to fit in there?"

I huffed a laugh. "Shockingly, yes."

Seemingly satisfied with his belongings, he let the lid fall shut and then pushed it down with his large hand as he worked the zipper closed. "I was wondering if all five pairs of your shoes would make it in."

"Oh, come on." I rolled my eyes, but a smile of amusement graced my lips. "I need flip flops, sandals, hiking boots, water shoes, and a nice pair of high heels for each and every excursion and or event we have planned. Five shoes make perfect sense. What are you bringing?"

"A decent pair of sandals," Eric said with an air as though that made all the sense in the world.

"Well don't come crying to me when you get turned away at the club for your attire," I laughed, picking up a pillow and playfully tossing it towards the stupid smirk on his face.

"It's an all-inclusive resort nightclub, Molly. They can't turn me away—I've already paid." He lugged the sizeable suitcase up and off the bed, setting it down on its wheels with a clunk against the vinyl floor of my basement apartment. Eric was staying the night since my apartment was closest to the airport.

Eric had his own place about a block from my work—I was the head teller at the local community bank. Eric worked as one of many accountants for a local law firm that was situated in a strip mall across the street from the bank, and he'd become a regular of mine when he frequently came in to deposit client checks into the law firm's account.

We'd been seeing each other for only two months when my best friend, Gracie, and her boyfriend, Ben, begged us both to book an all-inclusive vacation with them, and Ben's twin brother, Alan, and Alan's boyfriend, Cam. My closest friends.

I'd never been on an all-inclusive vacation before. Neither had Eric. We'd been a few cocktails in when Gracie and Ben cornered us in their dining room in the house they'd moved into together the year prior and shoved a laptop in our faces. Riding off the buzzes of alcohol and the still-sweet honeymoon phase of our budding relationship, Eric and I had said *what the hell* and booked the tickets that night.

By the next day, Gracie had called with news that Alan and Cam had purchased their tickets and even our close friend Colter—who'd been drinking beers with Alan and Cam that night—snagged a ticket to join us all. I'd given an excited *whoop* that all of us were going to be able to make it.

I hauled my luggage off the bed and rolled it over to sit beside Eric's. Stepping up in front of him, I looked up with an excited smile. "Think we'll get a wink of sleep tonight? I'm so excited, I don't feel tired at all."

Eric bent down and kissed me. "I'm sure we can find a few ways to tire you out."

My toes curled at the implication. "Is that so?"

~

Forty minutes later Eric was already snoring as I checked and rechecked the alarms for the next morning. One for 4 a.m., another for 4:30 a.m., and then one more at 5 in the morning for an oh-shit-get-your-ass-out-the-door-now alarm. Our flight was scheduled for 7:30 a.m. and we had to be to the airport two hours in advance to get through baggage and TSA.

I struggled to fall asleep, still too excited about the upcoming week-long vacation and simultaneously nervous for the flight. I'd been on a plane. Once. Ten years ago, when my parents flew us out to California for a great uncle's funeral whose name I couldn't remember now. I'd been terrified then, but it had been a pretty easy-going ride, and I knew this time shouldn't be any different. I'd flown once before; I could pull on my big girl panties tomorrow and do the same again.

When I did finally fall asleep that night I had a nightmare I'd slept through the alarms and arrived late to the airport having to watch as the plane took off without me. Just me alone. Wasn't sure where Eric wound up in that scenario. Regardless, I woke with a jolt to the very first alarm at 4 in the morning.

"Eric!" I half-shrieked. "Babe—wake up. It's time. It's time!"

Eric groaned as he rolled away from the playful shoves I was landing against his shoulder. "Snooze it for ten minutes," he mumbled as he tugged the top blanket up to his chin.

"I'm going to start coffee!" I threw off the covers, not bothering to make my side of the bed—as I so often *didn't* do—and raced to the small kitchen.

I didn't bother keeping quiet. My raucousness would help wake the 'sleeping' bear I'd left still pretending to snore in the bedroom. I filled up a water bottle for myself and for Eric, tossing them into the refrigerator to chill then set to work on coffee.

I'd been pouring two thermos mugs to take with us when I heard the shower turn on and I let out an excited squeak, happy that Eric finally had dragged his butt out of bed.

Leaving the lid of my thermos on the counter, I blew on the surface of my coffee as I scurried back to the bedroom to start wheeling the luggage towards the door. Eric had his suitcase up on the bed once more and opened as though he'd forgotten he'd needed something out of it. Likely something from his toiletries for the quick shower he'd jumped into. I walked to his side of the bed, bringing the hot cup of coffee to my lips and took my first sip as I investigated his belongings.

When I jumped with surprise at what I saw, I'd spilled more coffee into my mouth than anticipated, burning my tongue. I swallowed the hot contents down before they could do any more damage and brought my fingertips to my lips.

Condoms.

He'd packed a brand-new box of condoms.

An innocent and sensible precaution to some. It would have been an acceptable precaution to me too…if Eric and I *used* condoms. We'd been together for a year now and I was on the birth control shot. It'd been some time since we worried ourselves with using a condom. So long that I couldn't even remember the last time we'd even bought them.

My brain wanted to nitpick, but I heard the shower turn off and, panicking, I bit my lip, closed the lid of his suitcase and hurried back to my side of the bed where I pretended to mess with my hair in the mirror above my dresser.

The door to the bathroom across the hall opened and I stared at myself in the mirror, then at Eric through the reflection. He'd shaken out his still-wet black hair and had a towel wrapped at his waist. It was a sight that would've normally had my knees going weak. Yet, as I watched him flick his gaze up to me and smirk at me through the mirror…my stomach hollowed instead.

Somewhere in the deepest part of my consciousness, distant alarm bells were ringing. My gut was not happy. Even if my brain was coming up with every nonsensical excuse it could think of for why he'd decided we'd need condoms on our vacation.

Like...maybe he intended to have such an ungodly amount of sex that condoms would be an extra precaution should the shot fail? Maybe he'd picked them up for Alan and Cam? Who, for obvious reasons, didn't need them. Or maybe they were for Gracie and Ben? Who were adults who could buy their own condoms without an issue...

I kept my eyes on Eric as he walked to his side of the bed and tossed his bottle of bodywash haphazardly into his suitcase. Evidently he hadn't noticed he'd left it open, and that I'd shut it. Or he didn't care. "If you keep looking at me like that Molly, we're going to be late for our flight."

So, he thought *that's* why I was staring. I forced out a breathy laugh and then brought my coffee up to my mouth to busy myself. After another too hot sip, I wiped at a spill at my lip and then left the room, crossing the hallway, and closed myself into the bathroom for a quick shower.

I shakily removed my clothing and my hand slipped on the wet shower faucet as I clumsily turned it on. My heart—my love for Eric—was screaming at me to let it go. The condoms were obviously for us. Stop overthinking things. Don't make a big deal out of nothing. My heart had stuck its stubborn fingers in its ears and was obnoxiously singing *la la la la la*. I didn't even turn the shower hot. I blasted myself with cold water to clear my mind.

~

The car ride to the airport had been painfully quiet. Though, Eric seemed none the wiser. He happily hummed to the soft music on the radio as he drove his sensible Chevrolet Malibu to the long-stay parking ramp. We'd just passed through the rising arm of the gate when my cell phone rang.

I hurriedly answered the phone, relieved for the distraction.

"Gracie!" I chirped a bit too excitedly—I could easily blame the vacation excitement for that, though. Eric looked at me and smiled politely as I gave him an awkward thumbs up.

"Hi! You guys here? Ben and I are still driving in circles looking for a spot. This place is packed!" she replied with equal enthusiasm.

She was not wrong. Row after row of vehicles packed nearly every space for the next three levels we drove through. She'd ended the call abruptly with a command to meet her and Ben at the very top where several spots right next to one another were still available.

"*Damnit.* The top?" Eric groaned.

"The top." I nodded, giving him an apologetic smile.

Eric loosed a curse as he revved the engine and swung the vehicle rather harshly up the next ramp to the top. He was muttering something about not wanting to have to unbury his car at the end of the week. Apparently, a couple of snowstorms were in the weekly forecast while we were set to be in paradise.

Chewing on my lip, I watched out my window for any sign of Ben and Gracie. Eric continued with his quiet rant. The crisp winter sky would have probably been lit with stars if not for the surrounding harsh lights of the airport runways in the distance. At least it wasn't snowing yet.

I caught sight of Gracie up ahead at the same time she noticed me, recognizing Eric's car. "There!" I straightened in my seat. "They're right there!"

"Yeah, I see them," Eric bit out. Apparently even the promise of sun and fun wasn't enough to turn his sour mood around.

I ignored his bad temper, there was no reason to let him bring me down. Instead, I reached over and patted the top of his hand as he pulled into the spot beside Gracie's SUV and threw his car into park. He had the decency to at least turn his hand over, clasp mine, and give it an encouraging squeeze. I smiled a little and then so did he. The tension eased off some.

Gracie ripped open my car door before I could even grasp the handle and she practically pulled me out by my shirt collar into the frigid Michigan winter air as she pulled me into a jumping hug.

"Ah! I'm so stupid excited! Aren't you?"

I leaned away from her, smiling. "Very!"

Ben greeted Eric on his side of the car with a firm and friendly handshake. "Need help with the luggage?"

Eric shook his head. "Nah man, I've got it. Thanks though." Ben just nodded in understanding and then rounded the vehicle to peel me from Gracie's grasp.

"Grace, babe. You're going to kill her before we can even get to Mexico with that death grip," he teased.

Gracie and I laughed as she let go and Ben enveloped me in one of his spectacularly awkward hugs. It always made me laugh a little inside. One of the many quirky things about him.

Greetings were paused as Alan's familiar car pulled up. While Ben and Gracie made their way to say their hellos, I met Eric at the trunk and steadied my luggage on the concrete as he set it down and then reached in for his own.

"I can't wait to get out of this frigid weather." It was truth, but still, it felt a bit weird to be discussing *weather* with Eric. Something was still ringing off inside of me.

Another round of excited shrieks from Gracie meant Alan and Cam had exited their vehicle.

"Agreed," Eric sighed, forcing a smile to his lips.

I kept my face cheerful even as something in me sagged. That was it then? One-word responses. I supposed maybe I was throwing off a more obvious vibe than I thought. To compensate, I wrapped my arms around his waist and pulled him in for a kiss.

Thankfully, Eric softened into me and responded by gripping my hips, kissing me back. Fervently.

From somewhere down the ramp, tires screeched against pavement and an obnoxious thumping of a vehicle's radio came blaring. The sounds grew louder as the vehicle neared, cresting the top of the ramp.

The burnt orange Jeep Wrangler's engine revved as it passed us, the sound so offensive that I pulled away from Eric in a flinch. The Jeep swung a left before its driver yanked the wheel on a hard right and sent the vehicle directly into a parking space three spots down.

"He drives that thing like it isn't his daily driver," Ben's voice carried over.

Colter.

Of course, he'd make a loud and chaotic entrance. Anything but just wasn't his style.

I turned out of Eric's arms to find Gracie, Ben, Alan and Cam approaching. I gawked as I looked between Ben and Alan. Identical twins, both with their deep brown skin as smooth as silk, their same honey brown eyes, the same wide jawline, and even the same crease in between their eyebrows like they'd spent their whole lives making the exact same facial expressions, too.

"Mol, you're looking incredible," Alan exclaimed as he playfully shoved Eric aside to get a look at me. "Did your boobs get bigger?"

I barked out a laugh. "No, you kiss-ass."

"God, Alan," Ben grumbled with a roll of his eyes. Gracie just giggled, squeezing Ben's arm affectionately.

"Well, of course I have to kiss ass. It's been way too long since I've seen you," Alan said, pulling me into a hug that was about the only thing wildly different from Ben. Alan knew how to hug and hug well. Warm and affectionate like a big teddy bear.

"Bruh, it's been like three weeks," I replied as he let me go.

"Yeah, well, when we used to be up each other's asses every Friday and Saturday night for the past five years straight, three weeks apart is a long time," he argued.

It was true. Our gaggle of friends had either attended the local community college or had forgone higher education altogether to venture into the trades, meaning we'd all remained within ten minutes driving distance of each other after high school. We've spent nearly every weekend together over these many years.

Cam pinched the bridge of his nose beneath his glasses to hide the flush on his cheeks. "Sorry guys—he's drank like an *entire* pot of coffee to himself already this morning."

"Oh, hush it." Alan waved him off.

As if on cue, Colter's Jeep engine cut out along with the obnoxious thumping music. The eerie quiet had us all looking over to the dark windows of his vehicle.

"What's he doing?" Gracie asked, eyes squinting.

We all watched as what appeared to be a lighter flicked, briefly illuminating the front seats. Then we watched a cherry flare. I could see his figure leaning to reach into the back seat and snatch a large duffle bag with one hand. Then he was out of the car, momentarily disappearing behind its tinted windows, then reappearing in the middle of the parking ramps two-way lane…

Looking like absolute sin.

Ben hissed an amused curse. Gracie's jaw dropped open. Beside me, Eric stiffened. Alan and Cam went silent.

Colter sauntered our way and reached up to finish the drag on his cigarette that had been hanging from his smirking mouth. He'd sucked it so hard he'd already created a decent ash build up that he nonchalantly flicked to the pavement, letting the smoke billow tantalizingly past his lush lips.

"Good evening everyone," Colter crooned, flashing a lazy half smile, his eyes hidden behind sunglasses. At five thirty in the morning. In January.

The t-shirt he wore was pulled loose at the collar as though he'd had a woman tugging on it all night. Maybe it was the shadows in the light, but I thought I might have seen what looked suspiciously like a hickey on his neck too. His jeans were low on his hips and he had a gray hoodie thrown over one of his broad shoulders. I could see the goosebumps rising on his exposed arms from where I stood.

"It's five in the morning, jackass," Giving voice to my thoughts, Gracie playfully scolded him, smacking a hand to his large chest.

Colter laughed and gingerly placed the cigarette into his lips, speaking around it. "In that case, good *morning* everyone."

Gracie shook her head but enveloped him in a hug that he received with a friendly one-armed squeeze. Ben was next, clasping his hand and pulling him into one of those manly half-handshake-half-hug maneuvers.

"Good to see you, man!" Ben said, the authenticity prevalent.

"Yeah, you to, man. I'm ready to get my ass on the beach." Colter moved on to Alan, giving the same embrace he'd given his twin brother. Then the same with Cam. The four boys back together again.

"You smell like the bar," Cam noted, scrunching up his nose.

Colter pushed the sunglasses up into his sandy brown hair, revealing his blue-green eyes, heavily lined with thick eyelashes that had most women envious. "That would be because I just came from one." He was definitely still buzzing given the cheeky smile he unleased on us all.

I'd been watching the whole ordeal with wide eyes.

Three months. It'd been three months since I'd last laid eyes on Colter. He'd left at the beginning of fall for a temporary, out-of-state job in Tennessee. And he was back now. Back and somehow a bit more rogue than when he'd left. Older. Sturdier. Definitely tanner. Whatever he'd been working on down there, it'd obviously been partly outdoors.

He was almost four years into his field of being an electrician, and last I knew, he'd been studying to test for his Journeyman's license. A license he could take to fourteen other states within the country. And Colter, I thought, was exactly the kind of person to take that special little certification and run as far away as he could from here. From home. From us.

Colter drew closer and I felt the smile grow on my face with each step he took.

"Hey, you," he said, opening his arms welcomingly.

"You know you're not supposed to smoke here, right?" I said wryly, burying my face into his chest as he drew me into a hug. I caught the whiff of the bar Cam noted...and what suspiciously smelled like women's perfume. But underneath it all I smelled *him* and instantly felt better.

"*Hello Colter, so nice to see you,*" Colter mimicked my voice. We rocked on our feet together for two beats as I laughed. Then he let me go abruptly, taking another hit off the cigarette. "Come on, Rockstar. Since when do I follow the rules?"

Rockstar. The nickname he'd dubbed me after my twenty-first birthday when I'd finally drank enough vodka to think I could work the mic at karaoke night at one of the bars we'd hopped.

I'd chosen *I Love Rock n' Roll*, of course.

Britney Spears's version, of fucking course.

I still felt the sharp twinge of embarrassment to this day any time I recalled that memory, no matter how many times my friends reassured me I'd *killed it*. Yeah, killed their eardrums with such a horrendous song, more like it.

"Ah yes, how silly of me," I whispered under my breath as I watched Colter offer his hand to Eric. Eric gave him a polite, tightlipped smile and accepted the handshake. From where I stood right next to Eric, it appeared as though the two of them had each other in an iron grip. My brows pinched together in confused alarm. Noticing Gracie watching me, I relaxed my face and shook it off.

"Let's get on with this rodeo," Gracie chimed in, bending over and smacking her hand twice upon the face of her luggage. "I have a margarita with my name on it waiting at a swim-up bar."

"Let's do this thing!" Excitement suddenly clawed at me once more with a vengeance. Vacation mode was set to activate.

Colter, Alan and Cam led the way, followed immediately by a skipping Gracie who had her pink-painted fingernails wrapped around her beau's arm. Ben threw his head back laughing at whatever wicked little thing Gracie had whispered into his ear.

Eric and I brought up the rear and I watched my friends from afar with a soft look as a bubbling feeling of warmth washed over me. God, I loved them all so much.

My knuckles brushed up against Eric's and I looked up at him. Immediately, that warmth dissipated as I saw the way he was watching my friends: narrowed eyes, forced smile, jaw set.

With that, the memory of this morning washed over me.

Condoms.

TWO

I slowed my pace as my anxiety built. Eric hadn't even noticed me slowing down. He was still trailing after them as I came to a stop. My friends rounded a corner towards the covered bridge that would take us into the airport and it took a few more steps before Eric realized I wasn't beside him.

He spun around. "Mol?"

I hadn't wanted to bring it up. Not before our much-anticipated vacation. But as I stared at him in the harsh lights of the parking ramp, the word vomit came up before I could stop it. "Why did you pack condoms?"

Eric blanched. "What?"

I dared step toward him. "I saw it. Packed in your luggage this morning while you were showering."

An answering scoff. "I don't know what you're talking about, Molly. It's probably just an old box from my toiletry bag that fell out when I got in there to snag my bodywash." With that, he gave me his back and kept walking. "Come on, we need to check our bags and get to our gate."

I opened my mouth to request he stop his retreat and talk to me, but from somewhere further down in the ramp Ben's voice carried, "Hey! You two get lost? Hurry your asses up!"

"We're coming!" Eric shouted back, then he flashed me a look over his shoulder. One I'd never seen him level on me before. He looked angry. Riled. As though daring me to say

12

something further. I swallowed and kept my mouth shut. Picking up my pace, I passed him and caught up with Gracie, linking my arm in her free one.

She flashed me a winning smile. "Cozumel, here we come!" My returning smile was shaky, and she picked up on it immediately. "Babe, what's wrong?"

I had never thought so quickly on my feet in my life. "Nothing. Well," I sighed heavily for theatrics, "my nerves are a little wonky...*flying*, y'know?"

She bought it. "No worries, my dear. We'll visit the airport bar as soon as we make it through TSA. Calm your nerves."

~

True to her nature, Gracie rapped her knuckles twice on the bar top inside the airport bar nearest to our departure gate. "Can we get a couple of Screwdrivers?"

The bartender smiled knowingly and offered one silent nod as he set to work making our drinks. The boys had hauled our carry-ons off to the gate while us girls stopped for a drink.

"I thought you've flown before?" Gracie hiked herself up onto the stool.

I followed suit and twisted in my seat to face her. "Yeah! Once. Ten years ago."

She gave me a look that said, *Ah ha*. "Well, don't worry. We'll get a couple drinks in you and you won't even feel it as we take-off."

"Yeah, okay." Heavy on the sarcasm.

"That'll be thirty for the two of them," The man said, placing the drinks down in front of us.

Gracie feigned a gag. "Fuck. Would you like my arm too?"

The bartender put his hands up. "Hey, I don't make the prices. I just make the drinks."

Regardless, Gracie fished out cash from her wallet and slapped it onto the bar. I raised my brows at her, shocked she was prepared to stiff the guy. I gave him an apologetic look as I fished some cash from my own wallet and slid it to him while she wasn't looking. He gave me a discreet head-bob of appreciation.

"Thanks for the drink," I said to Gracie, holding up my glass to toast a cheers.

"Anything for you, dear," she cooed, clinking her glass to mine. I tipped mine back and then gawked as I watched Gracie down nearly half of her drink in one go.

"What?" she laughed. "Don't look at me like that. We've only got thirty minutes until boarding. We've got to make quick work of things." A wink, and then she prepared herself for another chug.

I laughed, shrugging my shoulders as if to say *oh what the hell* and brought my drink back up for a hefty slug.

"Slow down there, you two. Or the boys and I will have to carry your passed-out asses off the plane at our layover."

Gracie and I lowered our glasses to see Colter striding across the short expanse of the airport bar.

"Oh! Please tell me you've come to drink with us and keep us company and have some fun." Gracie was nearly jumping in her seat as she held the "n" in fun for a few seconds too long.

"G," Colter crooned to her, knocking his sunglasses out of his hair and back onto his nose with one fluid bob of his head. "*Fun* is my middle name."

I choked on the drink I'd been taking, laughing, "Your middle name is Gerald."

"Okay, Suzanne, calm down," he retaliated…with my middle name.

My nostrils flared. "Touche'."

Colter ordered a vodka Redbull. Apparently he was not holding back this morning either. When his drink arrived, he held it up for a cheers. I clinked mine off his first then we all laughed when we realized Gracie had already finished off her first one and she clinked her empty cup. With twenty-seven minutes to spare until boarding.

Colter bought the next round: mimosas. And I noticed he'd tipped the bartender generously. It appeared he'd been paid well in Tennessee. He caught my look of appreciation and gave me a reassuring smile that made me feel warm. Or it was the screwdriver finally making its way through my bloodstream.

Halfway through our mimosas a voice over the intercom at our gate alerted that, lo and behold, our plane was ahead of schedule by some air-traffic-control miracle. Boarding for first class was beginning now.

"Shit—we've got to go," Colter said as he rose from his seat and slammed the rest of his mimosa. It was impressive...for a grown man with a girly drink. He was already halfway out the bar as Gracie and I attempted and failed to chug our drinks as effortlessly as him.

"Let's go." Gracie grabbed my hand and pressed a fist to her chest. She belched and blushed. "The bubbly makes me gassy."

I stifled my snicker, and we hightailed it after Colter. The three of us looked like quite a sight as we bolted through passersby. We passed gate seven. Then eight and nine. And like bats out of hell, we burst into gate ten with giddy grins on our tipsy faces.

The three of us keeled over, heaving in breaths and laughing through it as we cooled down. I lifted my gaze to the rows of seats, searching for the rest of the party. Ice hit my veins the moment my eyes connected with Eric's. While he didn't look angry, he also certainly did not look happy as he watched us from afar. If Gracie or Colter noticed my sudden change, they didn't mention anything about it. Once we sobered up from our laughing fit, we made our way through the lined-up crowd and stood before our friends.

"Drinking at seven in the morning." Cam's brows inched up his forehead. "I think that's a new record for you three."

"Don't pretend like you won't be doing the same thing at breakfast tomorrow at the resort," Gracie snapped as she moved around him to latch herself to Ben's side.

"She's right. We all know you love to sneak a splash of whiskey in your coffee when you're on vacation," Alan said through a mouthful of sunflower seeds, the torn-open bag in his hand.

"Fair point," Cam conceded, his cheeks turning ruddy.

The next seating class was called out.

"That'll be us!" Ben tugged Gracie into his side tighter as he gripped both their luggage handles in one of his large hands and made to get in line. Seeing as they orchestrated this getaway, they'd bought their tickets first and had chosen seats up near the front of the plane.

I slowly shuffled my way through the boys until I came to Eric's side. He was already wearing one earbud and beginning to plug in his second, when he paused with his hand halfway to his ear. "How are you feeling?"

The ice thawed by a fraction at the pleasant tone he'd given. "Good. Actually, I think Gracie was right. A little drink or two has helped with the nerves." Satisfied with my answer, he popped the other headphone in. "W-what are you listening to?" I asked, increasing my volume so he could hear me over whatever it was.

"You don't have to shout, nothing's playing yet." Amusement in each word.

"Oh," I whispered, smiling weakly.

"I'm listening to a podcast." Vague answer.

I nodded and looked at my feet. A beat passed. "Which one?" I asked conversationally as we fell in line.

"What?" Eric half-shouted as he pulled out the earbud closest to me, leaning in. Guess he'd hit play already.

"Nothing, never mind."

He popped that earbud back in like it was nothing and kept up with the fast-moving line.

I fell in step behind Eric, trying to convince myself that there was nothing weird about what strikingly felt like a sudden dismissal from him.

Condoms—no. I'm not going to get hung up on that. Think about the happy vacation with our friends—

Maybe if I hadn't been so lost in thought I'd have sensed how close the mouth at my ear was when it whispered, "He's awfully charming this morning."

I jumped and nearly knocked my face right into Colter's as I whirled on him. "Don't do that!" I hissed, readjusting the sling bag I wore across my chest. All I got in return was his low chuckle of amusement.

I was left in silence as Eric led us through the boarding bridge and onto the waiting plane. Colter had started into a story about the previous night's escapades with Alan and Cam behind me. I stared at the back of Eric's black head of hair. Down the slim aisle we went. When we approached Gracie and Ben's row, I reached out my hand to her and she squeezed it back, mouthing *It'll be okay*. I didn't have time to inquire about what exactly would be okay as I was swept down the aisle with the boarding passengers.

The flight. She had to be referring to the flight. It would be okay. I *knew* that. But it didn't stop the sudden pang of panic that pressed against my chest that had nothing to do with the fact we'd be wheels up in minutes. I slowed to a stop. A wall of muscle hit my back.

"Oof, sorry Molls," Colter chuckled. "What's holding up the line?"

My eyes caught the back of Eric's head again. It bobbed as though he was listening to music. I thought he was listening to a podcast...

Condoms. Planes. Flying. Take-off. *Condoms*.

I whirled on Colter. "Sit with me."

A demand. Not a request.

I was so close to him that I watched as his eyes flashed with surprise, then immediately soften with concern. "Molly?"

"Please, Colter. Switch seats with Eric." I averted my gaze, suddenly feeling incredibly vulnerable. "Sit with me?"

"Hey Rockstar." Colter's warm fingers touched my chin as he brought my eyes to his. His tone was shockingly gentle. "I'd ask if there's trouble in paradise but...we haven't even made it to paradise yet." I gave him a deadpan look. He dropped his touch and looked up the aisle toward Eric then back to me. "Okay, stupid joke. Sorry."

Somewhere down the queue someone shouted for the line to move along. Colter rubbed the back of his neck. "Molly, are you sure? You know I'm happy to do whatever need of me, but...don't you *want* to sit with your boyfriend?"

Condoms.

"No. I don't want to. Not right now." The truth of that rattled me as much as it seemed to rattle Colter.

Another increasingly annoyed shout to keep moving from down the line.

"Whatever you need." Colter nodded once. "Do you want me to say something to him?"

"No!" I said, taking a step backwards down the aisle. "I'll talk to him."

Colter's eyebrows rose. "Okay," He sighed, "Tell him I'm Row twenty-two, seat C. Right next to Thing One and Thing Two." He jerked a thumb over his shoulder at Alan and Cam who I hadn't realized until now had been watching and listening to our conversation. The look of concern that flashed across their faces prompted me to smile, to reassure all three of them that—as Gracie had mouthed—*it'll be okay*.

Eric must have been so wrapped up in his podcast-music-whatever-it-was that he hadn't even noticed he'd walked right on past our row—I always snagged the emergency exit row for the extra legroom it allotted. I rolled my eyes in annoyance at his behavior and tucked my carry-on away. I eased myself into the window seat and watched Colter lift his bag next to mine in the overhead compartment. The stretch caused his navy-blue t-shirt to hike up, and a thin stretch of taut, tan skin peeked out from above his pant line. I wasn't sure if I was more shocked that I'd caught myself staring at it or more shocked that it caused a flush of warmth through me, surely alcohol induced.

I looked away before anyone could notice and cleared my throat. "Alan?" Alan immediately stopped to look at me, waiting expectantly. My voice seemed so small. "Can you—"

"We'll snag Eric. Don't worry about it," Alan said, reaching over to pat the top of my hand clutching the armrest.

Colter settled into the seat beside me and I called a *thank you* over his shoulder to Alan and Cam's retreating backs. I flopped back into my seat and dropped my head to the headrest. A sigh escaped my lips and my eyes slid closed.

"You good?" Colter asked softly from beside me.

I looked over at him and smiled, humming, "Mhm."

Colter just nodded once.

Our third-seat row companion was a sixty-something year old woman named Etta with a blonde bob and sparkling blue eyes, who was flying down for her daughter's destination wedding. She was recently retired from her job as a mailperson with the United States Postal Service. She lost her husband, George, ten years ago to a heart attack—heart issues ran in his mother's side of the family. Her daughter was named Tori and her groom's name was Archer. They'd been together for five years.

And this was all before we even began taxiing the runway.

Colter smiled charmingly at her stories. And I lost myself to the words she said, clinging on to them to distract me from the nerves that threatened to flip my stomach. I watched Colter as he listened to her. He treated her with a shocking amount of charisma and kindness. I admired him all the more for it.

And then our taxiing plane turned, getting into position for takeoff. I straightened, pressing my back into my seat. Colter caught the movement in his peripheral and turned to me.

"Still good?"

"Mhm," I squeaked to the affirmative, but involuntarily shook my head to the negative.

Etta wiggled into her seat, unaware of my fear. "Takeoff and landing are my favorite parts!"

Colter and I both leaned forward in our seats to look at her as though we hadn't quite heard her right. We had. Etta was cozily leaned back into her seat with her eyes softly closed and a peaceful smile on her lips.

Then the pilot worked his magic as the plane started forward, increasing in speed at a rate that sent my heart pumping into overdrive.

"Oh God," I breathed, plastering myself to the seat back once more. I couldn't have closed my eyes if I wanted to. They were peeled open wide to the scene out the window as the runway, the grass, the airport and sky beyond all blurred. My stomach dipped at the sensation of wheels-up, a dizzying feeling that made my eyes nearly go cross-eyed as I watched the ground leave us. Or we left the ground, rather.

So quickly, too quickly, everything outside the window began shrinking, and the plane banked to the right. My shoulder pressed into Colter's. That was when I noticed I'd reached across the armrest to grab his left hand at some point during takeoff. As if noticing my stare his other hand joined, sandwiching mine in between his. His hands were warm, big, and calloused. I should have pulled my hand away—it wasn't his job to baby me. And yet, I didn't move. Him holding my hand was the only thing that relaxed me enough to remember to breathe as my ears filled with pressure at the change of altitude. Bless him, Colter had the decency to look unperturbed and even avert his gaze to save me from the embarrassment of my, albeit minor, panic attack.

It took longer than I remembered to get to altitude. Colter didn't let me go until the seatbelt lights shut off and the pilot announced the refreshment carts starting momentarily.

"Oh, thank God," I breathed, slumping against the window, my hand now surprisingly cold without his warmth. I slid it between my knees and clamped down. Down below the earth was just a checkerboard of various agriculture fields.

"Handling it like a true Rockstar," Colter quipped. I softly nudged him with my elbow. He chuckled.

When the flight attendant reached our row, Etta ordered a vodka cranberry. It piqued my interest, and so I ordered the same. But made it a double. And Colter ordered a rum and coke.

"If I'm headed to the Caribbean I might as well do as the pirates do," he joked.

Then he proceeded to pay for mine and Etta's drinks as well. Etta had gone adorably red in the face and pressed a hand to her chest with an outpouring of gratitude. She was laying it on thick, but I didn't dare judge her. I'd probably be doing the same if I were a widowed older woman with a good-looking young buck charming me up too.

The three of us cheered to a successful takeoff—and a hopefully equally successful landing—and shared continued conversation over our adult beverages. I'd been having so much fun that I didn't even feel nervous for the landing in Atlanta two hours later.

~

The layover was short. We had thirty minutes to get ourselves to the next gate at the other end of the large airport.

We'd bid out goodbyes to our lovely row companion, Etta, and then ran once we met up with the rest of our crew at the arrival gate. Who knew I'd be doing so much running on my vacation.

I'd naturally found myself at Eric's side. We'd shared a glance and a smile that seemed to insinuate he wasn't in his bad mood anymore. Neither was I. Not after the last two hours of cocktails and Etta's life stories: she'd been doing an exorbitant amount of traveling since her late husband's death and this would be her third trip to Cozumel. She had a bichon-poodle mix, for which she hired a beloved long-term dog-sitter to watch over. His name was Buffet. After Jimmy Buffet.

I was shocked when I felt Eric reach down to clasp my hand in his, pulling me along faster beside him. I couldn't help the laugh that came out next. Our racing was silly and thrilling. Or, again, maybe that was the vodka in my system.

When we boarded our next plane our group was spread out again. Ben and Gracie at the front in row seven, Eric and I—now sitting together—at the emergency exit at the wing, and Colter, Alan and Cam at the back. The third passenger in our row turned out to be a tall, well-built businessman in a suit. Eric had immediately struck up business-like banter with him. I'd overheard bits and pieces of their conversation as I watched those still putting their things away in the overhead compartments, shuffling down the line to their seats. A young couple with two small children filed into the row behind us.

Eric used a quiet moment in his conversation with Mister Businessman to whisper in my ear, "Great. Now we'll be listening to screaming and crying the whole flight." Without thinking, I snapped my gaze between the seats to the family behind me, connecting eyes with the mother who'd gone still and a blush crept to my face. I smiled at her, hoping she wasn't too offended by Eric's not-quiet-enough remark. I looked away before I dared to see what kind of expression she offered in return.

I breathed through the takeoff, diving into a fantasyland where I was indeed a world-renown Rockstar who flew all over the globe, all the time, as Eric kept up his shop talk with Clive. That was Mister Businessman's name. When the refreshment carts came along sometime later Clive and Eric both ordered a coffee. I opted for a chamomile tea this time around. It was obvious my row was no longer the fun party row, but the business-casual row.

As the men chatted about financial planning and estate legalities and the business meeting Clive was to attend as soon as we landed, I began to sober up from the mornings metabolized alcoholic beverages. Exhaustion and a slight headache set in. And despite Eric's slightly rude remark from earlier, the children behind us were absolute angels. I fell asleep within the first hour of the flight.

Laughter. Haughty, male laughter is what woke me. Not crying children. Not turbulence. But Eric and Clive as I realized they'd struck up a rather chummy little friendship during the—I checked my phone—nearly *two-hour* nap I'd just had. My headache was gone, but I felt a bit groggy still.

I'd tried to ignore it, but after ten minutes of distracting myself with the plane brochures in the seat pouch in front of me, I couldn't deny that I needed to use the bathroom. I excused myself and made the awkward shuffling out of my row, not failing to notice how Clive only now seemed to realize I'd been tucked away in the window seat the whole time. Seeing as I was going to head to the bathrooms that were closer at the back of the plane, I'd given Eric and Clive my front. And as Clive's eyes soaked up their fill of the front of my body so close to his, a hollowing feeling in my gut made me wonder if giving him my back would have been any better...or worse. Eric either didn't seem to notice, or he adored his new friend so much that he didn't even care. Okay, then.

Heading to the back of the plane, I caught sight of the boys in their row, laughing and huddled around Alan who sat in the middle showing Colter and Cam something on his phone that had them all grinning. As I brushed by, I had the urge to reach out and pinch Colter's shoulder. But I let him be and focused on my bathroom business. I hated airplane bathrooms. Not even for the cramped space but for the silly ways the designers tried to camouflage everything to look like a generic part of the plane. I wasn't sure if I was grabbing toilet paper, tissue paper, or paper towel by the time it came to needing it. It all looked the same. I supposed it didn't really matter though, either way.

I checked myself out in the small mirror and frowned. During my nap I'd smudged my eye makeup, and I had the faint stain of what appeared to be drool at my lip. I got to work righting myself and brushed my fingers through my hair. I didn't have enough room in here to fluff it out like I wanted, so I opened the door to exit into the larger space of the hall. I bent at the waist, raking my fingertips over my scalp, enjoying the soothing massage until I heard the sound of someone clearing their throat. I shot up straight, tossing my dark hair over my head and spinning around.

"Sorry—oh!" I nearly fell back a step as the first small bit of turbulence we'd yet felt on this flight jostled the plane under my feet. Colter was there, throwing out a hand to catch and steady me at my elbow.

"It's okay. I just wasn't sure if you were bent over to stretch or vomit...but primping makes more sense for you." Amusement danced in his blue-green eyes as he made to squeeze past me toward the bathroom I'd just finished with.

I smirked, pulling my elbow out of his grip. "Says the pretty boy who's probably on his way to do the same thing." We were face-to-face and inches apart as we shuffled out of each other's way in the hall. I could almost *feel* his responding laugh.

"That's how us pretty people stay that way." Colter winked.

I snorted a laugh and left him behind as I made my way back to my seat. Passing Alan and Cam, this time I did reach over to pinch. Alan faked a yip and shooed my hand away as I giggled to myself.

When I squeezed my way back into my seat, I gave Clive and Eric my backside. Something about the way the little hairs rose on the back of my neck told me that this was possibly worse than giving him my front. But at least this way, I didn't have to look at him. I jumped when I felt a slight squeeze to my backside then flooded with relief as I realized it was Eric. Who hadn't even bothered to look up at me whilst fondling said buttocks. I huffed a soft laugh and rolled my eyes at no one as I resituated into my window seat.

CALLEY CLOVER

I distracted myself with a movie on the built-in screen in the chair ahead of me for the remainder of the flight.

THREE

The door to the shuttle slid open bringing with it a glorious ocean breeze that feathered against the beads of sweat at the nape of my neck and cleaved through the scent of sweat and decades old cigarette smoke. Somehow Gracie and I got jammed into the very back of the stifling hot shuttle ride that took twenty minutes from the airport to the resort. Short, but hot. Gracie regaled me with her story of how she and Ben had snuck each other a couple of handies on both flights. I dubbed it the *Half-mile High Club* and high-fived their efforts...then grimaced at my hand...

"Let me out of this furnace!" Gracie groaned as she pushed her way out of the shuttle, cutting between Cam and Ben who just exchanged amused looks.

Last but not least, I scooted my way to the bright airy opening and looked out to find Colter waiting there with his luggage—lucky guy had been the first one out. I peered through the vehicle's windows looking for Eric and found him at the back tugging on our own luggage bags.

I climbed out and wiped my sweaty palms on the front of my jeans. Outside the shuttle was definitely breezy but not necessarily any cooler than inside the van.

"Holy hotness," I murmured and then I fell silent as I took in the resort all around us.

The entrance was a huge thatch-styled roof that was supported by wide red and gold painted columns. The lobby was open straight through to the pool and tiki bar and then the ocean beyond. Several white couches in circled groups dotted the marble floors that were accented with woven, chunky jute area rugs. The flowers in large crystal vases on every end table were incredible. Huge flowers in varying shades of pinks, reds, and yellows that I'd almost forgotten existed after spending the last several months in the midst of a bleak Michigan winter.

A beachball caught my attention as it was sent flying in the air from the pool area. A net had been strung across the pool and a game of volleyball was in play. *That* looked like fun. I felt the smile spread across my face.

"¡*Bienvenidos a* Coral Rojo Resort!" A silky feminine voice greeted. We all must have been too enthralled with the view to notice her approach, so we all had to spin as one to our female greeter.

"¡*Gracias!*" Gracie replied excitedly.

The woman held a tray of tropical drinks and damp, rolled towels.

Gracie did not waste time snatching a glass and a towel. "Oh, thank the good Lord baby Jesus—it's chilled." She shook out her small hand towel and flung it over the back of her neck.

I stifled the moan of gratitude as I made my way to the tray for some cool relief as everyone else followed suit. Eric handed me my welcome drink and I sucked it down. Flavors of coconut and pineapple tingled on my tongue. It wasn't alcoholic but it was carbonated and blissfully refreshing.

Eric took off the sunglasses he'd put on in the shuttle and wiped his whole face down with his cool cloth. I snaked mine over the back of my neck and then down over my collar bone and to the swells of my breasts. Goosebumps erupted all over and I closed my eyes, sighing through my nose. Indeed, we'd reached paradise.

Our greeter's name was Imelda, and she was a striking beauty even while wearing her resort issued white button-down blouse and sky-blue pencil skirt—all curves and luscious locks of dark, wind-swept hair. She chatted with Ben and Gracie, our unofficial group leaders for the week, as she led us all to the reservation desk. We broke off into groups down the line of receptionists waiting behind the counter: Ben and Gracie, Eric and I, Alan and Cam, and poor lonely Colter by himself at the end. Though, as I grasped the counter's edge and leaned back I noticed it was the curvy greeter, Imelda, that had personally rounded the edge of the counter to serve him herself. She offered a flirty smile as she leaned her elbows onto the counter. I had no doubt Colter was in the perfect position to see directly into that white button down of hers. I bit down on the inside of my lips to keep from laughing. Good for him.

The clerk behind the desk offered Eric and I a winning smile as I refocused my attention.

"*¡Beinvenido!* I would ask if you're here for business or pleasure but by the looks of you two I'd bet my *dinero* on pleasure." The charming man with the straightest and whitest set of teeth I'd ever seen in real life was handsome and he gave Eric a knowing wink.

Eric laughed and handed over his identification required to claim our room key. "Pleasure, definitely."

I hoped to snag Eric's eyes and give him a meaningful smile, but he never wound up returning my gaze as he continued with checking in. I played it off by pretending I was simply peering out at the ocean beyond the lobby and took a sip from my drink.

"Room *trescientos dos*." The man said as he handed Eric the room keys. "You'll stay to the right of the pool and follow the red brick path to the north wing of the resort."

"Got it! Thanks, Javier," Eric said, tapping the room cards on the top of the granite countertop.

"It's been my pleasure. Enjoy your stay!" Javier waved us off.

Eric and I were the first ones to finish at the reservation desk so the two of us wandered over to the pool.

"I'm so ready to get in the water." I rose to my tiptoes to get a better view of the ocean. I could see a row of mini catamarans on the beach edge and wondered if they were for guests or for some kind of add-on boating excursion.

"I'm ready for some food." Eric dropped into one of the white couches and hooked both his arms across the back. He stretched his legs out long, crossed his feet at the ankles and dropped his head back. Spread out like that, so at peace and surrounded by paradise, he looked incredibly delicious.

"Why don't we go to our room and make a meal of each other." I'd slipped my tone into a sultry one that had Eric picking up his head to look at me with an intrigued expression. "And then, when we're finished, we can go get a real bite of food to eat."

A low whistle from directly behind me had me whirling and blushing. The rest of our party was standing there with their luggage and knowing smirks on their faces...like they'd heard every word.

"Atta girl." Gracie winked as she made to walk by me, tugging Ben along. She landed a playful smack to my ass as she did so, too. I could hear her mutter to Ben something along the same lines I'd offered Eric and knew I wouldn't be seeing either of them until dinner.

Alan and Cam were already over it as they followed Ben and Gracie down the red brick path, their wheeled luggage clunking along behind.

Colter stepped up to pass me with a lazy smirk on his face. "Maybe no trouble in paradise after all?" he whispered so only I could hear.

I didn't bother with a response, but I also couldn't hide my smile of amusement as I turned back to Eric who had risen and crossed the small distance to me. He planted a kiss to my forehead. "Let's go get *settled in*, Molly."

~

The room wasn't nearly as fancy as the rest of the resort, but I didn't care so much about that. I was here to enjoy the beach, not the hotel room. The room did have a wonderfully soft king-size bed, though, that Eric and I wasted no time testing out.

In fact, we tested it out so deeply and thoroughly that I knew it was his silent apology for how he'd been acting all day.

I was riding a vacation and post-sex high that had me giving him my silent acceptance of said apology as I watched him get dressed.

I appreciated the way his biceps flexed as he brought a fresh t-shirt over his floppy head of black hair. It never failed to make me giggle any time I realized how much he looked like Prince Eric from The Little Mermaid. It's like his parents just *knew* they would have to name him Eric. And sign him up for the swim team. It was hysterical, really. Eric had been his swim team's captain in high school and even went on to swim for the University closest to our hometown. I'd met him a little over a year ago when he first landed his job at the law firm that would eventually bring him into my path on a regular weekly basis. And here we were, a year later.

"What?" he laughed as he tied the drawstring of a pair of casual beach shorts.

"Nothing." I smiled coyly. "I'm just happy we're here." Eric nodded in agreement as he zipped up his suitcase and tossed it to the floor. Feeling particularly cheeky, I unleashed a mischievous grin. "Would you still love me if I had a fish tail instead of legs?"

Eric tipped his head back and groaned exasperatedly, "Not this again." I broke out into a fit of giggles, as he whined, "I thought we were past the whole Prince Eric joke." I hadn't noticed him pick up his pillow before he walloped me with it. I smacked it out of the way before it could hit me in the face.

"Well, that wasn't very princely," I continued to tease.

"For the love all things holy," he grumbled as he disappeared into the bathroom, then shouted. "Get your butt up and out of bed. We need food."

I rolled my naked ass out of bed. "Yes, your Highness!"

~

After dressing in a black wrap dress and my nice pair of sandals, I texted Gracie that Eric and I were incoming. All of us had snagged rooms on the same floor and in line with each other: Colter was in the jungle-view corner room in 300; Gracie and Ben in room 301 with the ocean-view corner suite;

Eric and I, and Alan and Cam were next in rooms 302 and 303…pool views. Again, I couldn't care less—I was here to be inside the pool, not staring at it from my room.

We exited our room and into the open-air hallway of the hotel floor. We walked a few short paces before I reached out for Eric's hand. He looked down at our joined hands then up to me. We smiled at one another as we reached Gracie's door. Eric's smile was friendly, but I thought it maybe wasn't quite reaching his eyes—

The door swung open, sending the air around us whooshing. "Who's ready for a margarita?!" Gracie leapt toward me, and I dropped Eric's hand to catch her in a full-on excited bear hug. Ben appeared in the doorway, laughing and smiling at his woman with a dreamy, far off look in his eyes. They must've made good use of their king-size bed too for him to be giving her googly-eyes like that.

"I'm thinking some much-needed grub that isn't plane snacks or airport vending machine food is needed first," I countered, surprising myself with how sensible I was sounding.

"Sure, sure," Gracie said as she started to lead me towards the open staircase to the main level.

There was one elevator in this wing of the resort, and it was at the opposite end of the building. I had no complaints, though, for we learned on the way up that a lot of tropical birds could be found perched within the wrought iron designs that enclosed the stairs. It was whimsical, beautiful.

"After we got your text, Ben called Alan and he and Cam will be meeting us down in ten. Is it okay that I told them to meet us at the Mexican restaurant?"

"Of course!" I'd been rifling through the restaurant menu in the welcome book back in our hotel room while I'd been changing and already knew exactly what I was going to order. We made it down the first flight before we came to a pair of green parrots perched in the iron that we spooked. We all watched as they flew off into a nearby tree filled with more of them.

"Yucatan Amazons," Ben informed. "Did you know a flock of parrots is called a pandemonium?"

We all paused to stop and stare at Ben now.

"Since when did you become a bird enthusiast?" I softly asked as I playfully squeezed Gracie's arm into my ribs.

Gracie and I had a running joke that a boyfriend started to become hubby-material as soon as he started into his old-man phase: the phase where cutting the grass became a neighborly competition, when they began to trade in their expensive Nike's for sensible New Balances, and most definitely when they started to not only take an interest in birds but also be able to identify and recite facts about such birds. Gracie's laughter was silent, but I felt her jiggle with it beside me, knowing she was thinking exactly what I was thinking. She squeezed my arm back.

"I studied a bit about this place before coming here." Ben shrugged his shoulders and stuffed his hands into his pockets. "We booked this trip nearly a year ago...I've been so excited and needed something to pass the time."

"Yeah, yeah." We started back down the stairs. "I get that, but I mean...I spent the time looking up what kind of excursions are available around the island. Y'know, like a normal person." I winked at Ben, and he scoffed a laugh.

It took the next flight of stairs before something tugged at me. "Did anyone talk to Colter?"

"No, I figured you did." Gracie stopped and looked at me expectantly.

I backed up a step. "Why would *I*?"

She smiled sheepishly. "Well Alan had said you two have been buddy-buddy all day, so I just assumed..."

"Why would he say that?"

By now Ben and Eric stopped their descent and turned to look up at us, waiting and wondering.

"Didn't you sit next to him on the flight into Atlanta?"

"Well, yeah, but..." I trailed off, not sure why I could feel a warmth flushing the skin of my chest. "We've not been buddy-buddy."

"Okay," Gracie held the world, long and slow. "Well, do you want to call him?"

"I didn't bring my phone."

"Me neither."

Eric took one step up toward us. "Why don't you just go knock on his door, Molly? It'll be quicker than going back to the room to call him first."

Sounded reasonable enough. "Uh, yeah ok. I'll meet you at the bottom."

Gracie nodded and continued down to meet back up with Ben. I waved to Eric who waved back with a small smile. As I rounded up to the next flight of stairs I noticed the parrots returned to their perch in the stairwell. I walked slowly and steadily hoping not to spook them off again. They immediately noticed me, but they did not make any moves to fly. I took that as a good sign as I crept around them, giving them their space. They watched me with their beautiful beady eyes.

"Hi, pretty bird," I cooed.

Laughter cascaded down the stairs from above. "Getting a head start on your crazy bird lady era?"

I glared up at Alan and Cam as they descended—and successfully scared the parrots away once again. "Rude! I was admiring them."

"They'll be back," Cam assured. "Where is everyone?"

"Keep going, you'll find them at the bottom of the steps waiting," I instructed, throwing a thumb back over my shoulder. "I was sent to retrieve Colter."

"Oh?" Alan simpered, clasping Cam's hand tenderly.

I paused. "Yes…"

Alan composed himself and tugged Cam down another step. "Good luck with that, then. See you down there!"

And before I could ask what the hell that was about the two men disappeared around the next bend in the stairs.

"What the what?" I murmured to myself as I finished the climb. My sandals smacked on the polished concrete of the hotel floor and the walk to Colter's door was laughably short. I shook off the weird vibe Alan had thrown at me and rapped my knuckles to the door of room 300.

"Colter! It's Molly," I called out.

Silence. More silence. Enough silence for me to start feeling awkward.

"Colter? Are you in—"

The lock was thrown and then the door cracked open. Complete darkness and an icy chill spilled out from the opening and Colter appeared. Shirtless and blocking his blue-green eyes with a hand over his brow from the bright daylight. He was wearing a towel around his hips, and I realized then he must've been sleeping. In the nude. I took a reflexive step back.

"Hey, Rockstar." His smile was lazy, sleepy. And utterly adorable given how genuinely happy he appeared for someone who'd likely just been so rudely awakened.

"I'm sorry. Were you sleeping?" I crossed my arms over my chest to warm myself against the frigid air of his cranked-up AC unit that was pouring out the door.

"Uh," Colter shot a dazed look over his shoulder and then turned to me with a crooked smile. "Yeah. Sleeping."

"Sorry I woke you."

"No! It's fine, Molls," he assured.

"Colter?" a third, singsong, lilting voice drifted on the chill air that still seeped from his blackened room.

My eyes popped wide. Colter winced.

"Sleeping, huh?" I bit my lip to stop from laughing. Before he could answer, the realization of who that voice belonged to struck me. "Oh my God, Colter…is that…is that…"

"Imelda," he supplied with a boyish grin, then he called back over his shoulder, "Un momento, por favor."

I mouthed a big *wow* as his eyes returned to mine.

"Don't give me that look." Colter dragged his hand through his mussed sandy brown hair. "It's not like this isn't exactly what all you couples were just doing."

He had me there.

"You right, you right," I conceded, digging the toe of my sandal into the floor. I sucked on my teeth. "Well, once you've finished…working up your appetite…we'll be having an early dinner. At El Sombrero. That's the Mexican restaurant we passed. On the way to our rooms. The one by the pool. It has the little…sombrero…on the sign." *Why the hell was I rambling.*

"I actually think I'll skip dinner. I wasn't lying when I said I'd practically arrived at the airport straight from the bar. I had barely two hours of sleep last night so I'm going to take a *siesta* and I'll meet up with you guys later for drinks." Colter rubbed the heel of his hand into the spattering of blond hair on his chest, drawing my eye. Before I knew it I was staring at his pecs. More defined since I'd last seen them months and months ago this past summer. Then I was staring at one of his dusky nipples, comparing it to the other.

"Molly?"

I swallowed and met his eyes. "Yes?"

"Did you hear me?" He had one brow raised and that crooked smile was back.

"Yes."

"So…I'll see you later?" Colter slowly started to close the door.

"*Sí.*"

"Bye, Molls."

"Bye."

The door softly clicked shut. I spun on my heel and cringed deeply. I kept my face scrunched up in that cringe as I wobbled back to the stairs because fuckity of all fucks, one of my closest guy friends just caught me ogling his nipples. His *nipples*, for goodness' sake.

FOUR

Three sips of a fresh margarita and half a bowl of chips and salsa later, I sat at the head of the table with Gracie on my right and Eric on my left. Gracie sipped her margarita and zeroed in on me, even as she held Ben's hand on the table, resting them between their place settings. Ben was talking to his brother who sat beside him, still spinning off facts about those parrots.

Cam sat beside Alan, across from Ben and at Eric's other side and had Eric's full attention as they discussed the latest legal and finance podcasts they were into these days.

Gracie gaped at me. I'd just whispered discretely to her the scenario I'd interrupted with Colter and the muck up I'd just made. Unsurprised by Colter's little rendezvous with Imelda, Gracie focused on the important things...

"His *nipples?*"

I nodded with a grimace. "His nipples."

Gracie looked away for a moment wearing an expression that said she was currently considering how male nipples have made her feel in the past and settled with a look that read, *meh,* and nodded.

"Okay. Well, that's not so bad." She took a sip of her margarita and crunched a piece of ice in her teeth. "At least he answered the door with a towel on. Can you imagine if you were caught staring at his di—"

My knee jerked, slamming into the underside of the table and rattling the ice in my own margarita.

Eric whipped his head in my direction. Everyone at the table did, actually. "You okay, Mol?" Eric asked, his brow creased.

"Fine. I'm fine," I promised as I hid myself behind a shaky sip of my margarita as filthy visions of Colter's manhood invaded my thoughts.

Unbothered to press me on it, Eric turned back to Cam. Beneath the table, I felt a pinch on my thigh. I glared at Gracie.

"Hey," I warned.

"You good over there? Awfully jumpy."

"Well, when your friend forces images of another friend's dick into their minds…you'd be jumpy too," I snipped back, forcing another sip of my margarita, hoping the tequila would kick in any minute now.

Gracie scoffed and smiled at me incredulously. "Oh please! People imagine what their friends' bodies look like. I've wondered what every dick at this table looks like before." She had the audacity to hiss it at me as if I were a prude. A *prude*. This did not go unheard by Ben's ears. He snapped his head to Gracie, snagging her attention as he mouthed *what the fuck*.

She leaned into him, still keeping her voice hushed to the rest of the table. "Before we were a thing baby, don't worry."

"You met Eric a *year* ago. We've been together for three," he countered with a fake scowl. The teasing edge in his eyes was my only proof that he wasn't actually mad at her.

"Yeah. Well," She stumbled for the words. "It's not like you haven't pictured what it would be like to see Molly's tits so. Drop it." Teasing, playful banter. Gracie smirked at Ben as his dumb laugh gave him away. "Exactly my point." She spun back to me. "It's human nature, Mol. Besides, he probably loved it. Stuff like that inflates a man's ego. They eat that shit up."

Regardless, I wished I could undo my wrap dress right at this table and rewrap my head into it like a cocoon and hide from the world. Those *nipples* belonged to my friend. My very platonic, practically-my-brother, *friend*. Those male nipples should not have a hold on me.

My eyes searched out Eric. I studied the right profile of his face as he talked to Cam. My eyes scanned lower to his jaw, down his neck, then down to where his nipples would be if I could see them through his shirt. *Lord help me.*

Food came out then and all nipple talk and thought were washed away. I gorged myself on chorizo and oaxaca cheese.

~

Hours, a walk on the beach, and several margaritas later we stood in line outside the one nightclub the resort had on the premises. There was a second nightclub at the sister resort next door, but it was a family resort and not an adults-only and we were set on avoiding children at all costs for this vacation.

The evening was going perfectly. The atmosphere, the drinks, the island music; it was truly paradise. I felt light, weightless and I rocked my hips back and forth against Eric's front. He laughed softly in my ear as his fingers dug into the flesh at my hips.

"Who needs a nightclub for dancing. We can start our own party—" I slithered against him, lifting my arms and pointing at the ground, "—*right here.*"

Gracie squealed with laughter and pressed herself to my front, dancing along with me and Eric. Ben snagged Gracie's hand and twirled her into him effortlessly.

"You girls better pace yourselves or you're going to crash and burn on the first night!" he joked. Gracie reached up and pulled his mouth to hers.

When they finally came up for air she gave a hoot of laughter. "Let me burn, baby. Let me burn!"

She spun and Ben took the lead, spinning her around and around, then he pulled her close, caging her in his loving arms. That glimmering dreaminess was back in his eyes. Boy, did he have it bad for her. As he should. As everyone *did*.

Gracie was a petite and spunky beauty, with naturally platinum blonde hair and ass for days. She was my exact opposite and I one-hundred-and-ten percent believed that was why we'd had such a gravitational pull to one another when we met in gym class of freshman year. Both of us pissed the

P.E. teacher off to no end for either half-assing our mile runs or flat out refusing them altogether. We've done a lot of maturing since then. Well, Gracie still won't run, even if her life depended on it. But we both could admit we'd been stubborn brats and had eased up a bit since.

Where Gracie was petite, I was tall and filled out. Where she was blonde, I was chestnut brown. Where she was spunk, I was sly. And while I had no complaints about my backside, she definitely wore the crown in that department. It all leveled out decently with the gorgeous breasts genetics gifted me. Even I stared at and fondled them from time to time. Just because.

In fact, thinking of them now made me want to touch them. So, I leaned back against Eric, still writhing and dancing and grasped my breasts seductively for him. He was slow to notice, but when he looked down and saw what I was doing he just chuckled and shook his head.

And then two hands circled my wrists, pulling me away from myself. Shocked, I stiffened and looked straight into blue-green eyes.

"Colter?!" I half-shouted. *When had he shown up?*

He looked pissed: eyes narrowed as a muscle feathered in his clenched jaw. "Don't do that, Molly."

I wrenched myself from his grasp. "What—"

"Easy, Colter. She's just having fun," Eric interrupted.

Colter leveled those hard blue-green eyes on Eric, and if I hadn't been so astonished at Colter's behavior I would've felt scared for Eric.

"You wouldn't be saying that if you had any sense of situational awareness," Colter snipped. That silenced Eric. And confused me. Colter read our expressions and gave a sigh of exasperation through his nose. "There's a group of like five drunk, feral dudes behind me that have been eye fucking your girl in a way that would have me defending what's mine if I were you." Colter backed off, dragging in a deep breath in through his flared nostrils. "Protect your girl."

The line moved and Colter stalked off as he, Alan and Cam entered the club. Stunned, I stood there, staring stupidly at Gracie who looked equally shocked at what had just happened.

Ben was trying to play it off with a nonchalant scratch behind his ear, but the way he tucked Gracie even closer into his side said he'd seen the guys long ago and had done exactly as Colter had suggested. He'd protected his girl.

"The fuck was that about?" Eric laughed it off passively. He took my hand and pulled me after him as he moved to the front doors of the club. I stumbled after him, giving Gracie a shrug. It wasn't Eric's fault. I was the dumb tipsy girl fondling herself in public. My cheeks warmed with embarrassment, and I couldn't deny that a huge part of me was grateful that Colter had stopped me from making a bigger fool out of myself than I already had. My face was set in a frown.

Inside, the loud music of the club and the strobing, colored lights fractured the darkness, dancing all around, welcoming us. Colter, Alan, and Cam were already lost in the crowd. Gracie caught me as I strained my neck searching for them.

"Let's take a shot, yeah? I don't know about you, but I could use a pick-me-up after that," Gracie laughed, trying to make light of the situation.

I wanted to. Because I had felt the same way not five minutes ago. But I couldn't deny that there was a sour tang to the idea of getting wasted now. Especially as I looked up and noticed the group of guys that Colter had been talking about make their way into the club. Darkened eyes glued now to Gracie's ass.

"Molly?" Gracie stepped up in front of me, demanding my attention.

"Sorry. Yeah, let's do it."

Gracie took my hand and weaved us through the crowd up to the bar. "Don't get hung up on it. Those guys look too wasted to even do any real harm, I'm surprised they were even let in."

I knew she was trying to ease my concerns, but that was not helping. I just nodded my head and turned back to where we'd left Eric and Ben behind. Ben was watching us, and he gave me an encouraging wave. Eric was eyeing the crowd, craning his neck around as though looking for something. Or someone. Hopefully not Colter. Even I could admit that they'd need some time apart after that brief pissing match.

"Can I get two shots of tequila, a saltshaker and a bowl of lime wedges?"

I spun back around to Gracie. "A whole saltshaker? Not just a packet?"

Gracie shrugged. "Oh, come on, it's not like we're only going to do *one* shot. This way we streamline things."

"Gracie—"

"Molly!" She cut me off with a frustrated laugh. "We are young. We are hot. We are in Mexico. On. Vacation." The bartender served up our shots and Gracie slid a tip to the man saying, "Gracias." He tipped his head in an appreciative nod, but she hadn't noticed as she licked her hand and coated the wetness with salt. Gracie impaled a lime wedge to the rim of my shot glass and handed it to me. "We. Shoot. Tequila."

Before I could say another word, she clanked her shot against mine, licked the salt, downed the shot and bit into her lime. I blinked in surprise as the tequila she'd knocked out of my shot dripped from my hand to the floor.

She spat out her lime. "Your turn," Gracie said with a harsh voice as though the alcohol and the acidity of the lime torched her throat.

She was right. This was the very first night of vacation. I couldn't hide in a shell already. That was for night five when the fun of tequila wore off.

"Okay! You're right." I pulled my big girl panties on and licked my hand.

"Yes!" Gracie shouted way too happily as she salted my hand. "That's my girl."

"Cheers to being in Mexico!" I saluted, raising the shot in the air. I brought my mouth to my hand and licked the salt. As my tongue collected the crystals, my eyes flicked up and connected to ones of blue-green across the bar. My heart threw itself against my ribcage as Colter watched me take the shot and suck on the lime. His nostrils flared and I just knew he was still pissed about what had happened outside. But as the tequila warmed my belly, I was reminded that this was a time for fun and revelry, not worry. So, I gave him a wink and knocked on the bar top, requesting another.

Blissful blackness embraced me. Soft sheets skated across the bare skin of my arms and legs as I turned onto my back. The sound of a door softly latching had prompted my eyes to open. The room was dark but backlit by the lighting of the controls on the air conditioner unit on the wall. From the bathroom, the shower turned on. I pushed up to my elbows and winced as a tequila-induced headache slammed me between the eyes.

"Damn," I whined as I rolled my head to the side, reading the bedside alarm clock. It read 3:23 in the morning. Certain I couldn't possibly be reading that right, I blinked my eyes several times and tried again. Yup. 3:23 a.m. *Damn*. Suddenly aware of my bodily needs, I threw my legs over the bed and hissed at the simultaneous sensations of a growing headache and the chill of the cold floor on my bare feet. I shakily straightened to standing and realized I was still wearing my black wrap dress. *At least I took off my shoes before falling into bed.*

I padded across the tile floor, keeping a hand on the wall as my guide, navigating in the dark to the bathroom. I tried the knob, and it was unlocked so I let myself in—then internally cursed at myself for the onslaught of the bright light hammering at me from within. Rubbing my eyes, I dragged my feet to the toilet and wiggled out of my panties altogether, abandoning them to the floor. I kept my eyes closed as I did my business and yawned. After I washed my hands—eyes still closed—I fell back into bed and reached out to Eric's side. It was cold. Then the shower water turned off, reminding me of where he was. I fell asleep knowing he'd be beside me again soon enough.

~

In the morning, I woke up to the soft light of day filtering in from underneath the hem of the blackout curtains. I rolled over and found myself alone in bed. Figuring Eric was in the bathroom I crossed the room and drew the curtains wide.

The morning sun had everything either illuminated in its welcoming glow or cast in long, cool shadows. I knew it couldn't be too early in the morning given the fact that there were people already saving their chairs down at the pool.

My brows furrowed as I made my way back to my side of the bed and picked up my phone. I had a message from Gracie letting me know she and the boys were meeting for breakfast at 9:30 a.m. My phone clock read 9:17 a.m. I hurried to the bathroom to brush my teeth and comb out my hair, only to find that Eric certainly wasn't in there. He wasn't anywhere in the room. I wondered if maybe he'd left for the gym. It was usually where he'd run off too on the mornings I woke up at home alone. But he usually left a note. Or a text.

I didn't bother with creating a cute outfit for the day, knowing I'd be coming right back after breakfast to shower and slip into my bathing suit. Toeing on my flip flops on I shot a text out to Eric.

Good morning. Didn't hear you get up this morning. I'm meeting everyone for breakfast. Will I see you there?

I snatched my room key off the nightstand and briefly wondered how I'd been lucid enough to have even remembered to set it there given I didn't have any recollection of last night after Gracie and I started into the fifth round of tequila shots on the dance floor.

Halfway down the stairs a ding alerted Eric's reply. I read it as I carefully descended.

I'm at the gym. I'll meet up with you at the room after.

Well, that settled it then. I slipped my phone into the pocket of my yoga shorts and carried on my way, feeling slightly bummed the parrots were nowhere to be seen this morning.

I smelled the breakfast dining area before I saw it. It smelled of bacon and maple syrup. And coffee. Glorious, fragrant coffee. I let my nose do the leading.

The place was packed and as I scanned over all the groups at their tables. I'd started to pull my phone out to call Gracie so I could find them, but before I could get it out I heard her shouting and waving her arm like a lunatic, "Right here!"

She calmed down when she saw me notice her. I walked to the table, noting that it wasn't only Eric who was missing today. Apparently Colter was MIA as well.

Ben looked up from his coffee he'd been stirring cream and sugar into, "Morning!"

"Good morning my favorite people," I sighed as I dropped into the empty chair.

"You look like you got ran over by a train," Alan teased as he leaned over and swiped his thumb under my eye, apparently wiping away a smudge of last night's eye make-up.

"Feel like it to!" I laughed and a server stopped at our table to offer coffee. "*Si, por favor. Muchas gracias.*"

The coffee was steaming and dark and smelled of divinity. I cradled it in my hands, and I brought it to my face just to *sniff.* "I'm not going to lie, Gracie. I think I'm going to have to steer clear of the tequila today. I was so blacked out last night I don't even remember Eric and I leaving to go to bed."

Gracie laughed. "Maybe because Eric didn't take you to bed last night." When she noted the confusion on my face she elaborated, "*Colter* did."

I carefully set down the piping hot coffee. "What?"

"You got a little too drunk soon after we got there—I will admit that it was my fault—but Eric wasn't ready to leave. God," She barked out a chuckle. "I actually don't think I've ever seen him so drunk in the year I've known him, Molly. It was hilarious. He'd somehow got himself coaxed to the dancefloor by a bachelorette party. You were cracking up. I'm kind of sorry you don't remember it." My lips twitched into a smile, but it was a reflex thing. In my belly, my stomach flipped. "Anyway, you started to get the spins. Colter had been with you when he could see it on your face. He'd left you with Ben and I while he went to find Eric, but after like two minutes he came back and just whisked you off. Apparently, Eric had gotten roped into a dance battle with the bride-to-be and Colter was tired of waiting—wait... Eric didn't tell you all this himself?"

I blinked a couple of times as I forced an air of nonchalance. "He'd left for the gym before I woke up this morning."

"You're kidding me." Gracie gaped. "He's working out on his vacation?"

Alan pinned her with a look. "Colter's off doing the same thing, Grace. And you didn't find anything weird about that."

She waved him off. "Colter isn't *working out*. He's swimming in the ocean. It's just different."

As the rest of the group argued about what constituted as a workout and what didn't, I'd realized breakfast was served buffet style. I quietly excused myself and headed to the line. On the way, it was hard not to find the bachelorette party from last night near the windows. The bride-to-be was still wearing her gaudy sash and a white t-shirt emblazoned with gold lettering that simply stated, *I'm getting married bitches.* Classy. I ignored the loud women as I focused solely on food for the next twenty minutes.

After breakfast, and after I'd washed myself down in the shower, I was finally feeling completely hangover free. I struggled into my aquamarine bikini—it stuck to my damp skin—and sent out another text to Eric who was still nowhere to be seen, as I tied a purple fringe-edged shawl around my hips as a cover-up.

Where are you? Gracie and I are about to head to the pool for a few hours.

It took only seconds to receive his reply.

Shit. Sorry babe. I was starving after my cardio, so I stopped for breakfast real quick. I'll meet you at the pool.

I'll save you a chair.

K thanks.

Wrong.

Wrong, wrong, wrong.

We never used *K* with each other.

But my brain refused to acknowledge it. This was vacation after all. I didn't want to spend it fretting over Eric's off-the-wall behavior. Honestly, it was probably nothing. I'll bet if I checked my phone calendar, I'd be starting my period next week and that's why I was overthinking everything. I snagged my sling bag and double checked that I had everything I'd need; wallet, lip balm, room key, phone, bottle of SPF. Good to go.

Seconds later I was out in the hall, standing before Gracie and Ben's door about to knock. I froze halfway when a hair-raising moan from within slid out from under the door. Then another moan, louder this time. "Uh…"

"Molly."

I whirled around at my name, knowing that voice. Colter was at the top of the stairs with his hand still on the railing. He was wearing black swim shorts with a teal accent at the hems and had a damp hotel beach towel slung around his neck. Thankfully it covered his nipples, though it left a tantalizing amount of washboard abs peeking through. "Hi Colter. Good morning!"

A third, even louder moan followed by an equally loud thump from room 301 had my eyes going wide as saucers. Colter straightened as he heard it, too.

"Are you *listening* to them, Rockstar?" he asked in a scandalized tone, unleashing a mischievous grin. "This is a new and interesting side of you I've never known."

My hands wrung the strap of my sling bag as I gritted my teeth. "Ha. Ha. No, I'm not *listening*. We had plans to meet to go to the pool, but I guess…I guess they got sidetracked."

From the other side of the door Gracie called out Ben's name and I was done after that. "Okay!" I exclaimed, dragging out the word. "I guess I'll go by myself and wait down there." I made a move to pass Colter on the steps.

"Wait, Molly—about last night…" He struggled to find the words.

"Thank you," I interjected softly, genuinely.

His brows furrowed as he turned to look down at me from one step above. "For what?"

"For bringing me back last night. I'm actually a bit embarrassed at how drunk I'd been. I don't even remember you bringing me back but thank you." I turned to leave and then stopped, adding, "Thank you for what you did before, too. I wasn't even that drunk at that point in the night, so I have no excuse for my behavior but…honestly after you pointed them out, those guys were giving off bad vibes and, well…I'm just glad you had the nerve to say something. Anyway," I was rambling again. "I hope you'll be joining us at

45

the pool today? I noticed a cool volleyball net across the pool yesterday and was hoping to strike up a game. Could use you on my team! Y'know…if you're not already water-logged?"

"Uh," Colter paused to look down at himself and then laughed, "Yeah, sure thing, Rockstar. Whatever you need. I'm just going to rinse off in the shower really quick."

"Ok! I'll save you a chair."

"See you down there."

As I made my way down, I was happy to notice the parrots were back. And this time I was able to pass them without spooking them.

FIVE

I fell into a bit of luck when I arrived at the pool and was able to find seven lounge chairs in a row. I'd snagged a handful of towels from the kiosk at the entrance of the pool area and set to work laying out the towels to lay claim to our seats. I left my flip flops at one end and planted my bottom in the far end, hoping that was enough to deter anyone looking to scoop my prime piece of poolside real estate away from me.

We were equal distance from the swim up bar inside the pool as we were from the tiki bar between the hotel and the beach. We would have options when it came to our drink and food choice for the day.

I sat and people-watched as others began swimming or sunbathing. I sat for about three minutes before I realized there wasn't a volleyball net strung across the pool. Jumping up, I headed to the recreation station close to the lobby. Inside I was surprised to find Javier examining a clipboard.

"Ah! *Buenos dias.* You are Molly, *si?*" He made a cute scrunched up facial expression as he gambled with his guess.

"*Si!* Thank you. *Buenos dias* to you too!" The fact he remembered who I was in a place as chockful of people as this was rather flattering.

"What can I do for you this beautiful morning, Senorita Molly?" Javier carelessly flopped the clipboard onto the desk behind him and crossed his arms over his broad chest as he leaned back against the counter. He flashed that uber white smile.

"Yesterday there was a volleyball net in the pool. I was wondering if that could be put up again? I was hoping to strike up a game with my friends." I leaned against the door frame, mimicking his relaxed stance.

Seemingly pleased, he clapped his hands in front of him. "Aye! Si, you've come to the right place. You see, here at Coral Rojo I am Director of Fun. I can certainly get the net up for you. Give me, oh about *diez minutos, bueno?*"

"Bueno! Gracias Javier," I sang, spinning on my heel as I all but skipped back to my chair.

My smile grew when I noticed Colter hovering around our seven chairs, staring at my flip flops. He looked like he was working really hard to remember if he'd seen them before. His hair was still wet and pushed back like he'd combed his fingers through it. The white t-shirt he wore was a nice contrast to his black swim shorts and his golden tan. I stealthily snuck up to his side. "Yes, those are mine. And yes, those chairs are for us!"

Colter didn't startle like I'd been hoping for, but he did chuckle nervously as he massaged the back of his neck and said, "I figured as much. New shoes?"

I slid the flip flops further under the chair with my periwinkle-painted toes. "Yes. I bought them to have brand new ones for this trip." They were a pristine white and not something I would have regularly bought back home knowing it wouldn't take probably more than two wears before they got so dirty there was no saving them. But I knew they would make the tan of my feet pop, especially with the pretty blue color of my polish, so I'd decided what-the-heck and bought them.

Not expecting him to want to discuss shoes for a second longer, I plopped my butt into the chair. "Javier's bringing out the volleyball net in a few minutes. Have you heard from Cam or Alan?"

"They said they were a few minutes behind me." Colter followed my lead and sat down on the side of the chair to face me. He rested his elbows on his knees. "Where's Eric? Didn't he come down with you?"

"Uh…" A bolt of alarm swept through me. *Where* was *he?*

I paused to check my phone. No unread texts. "No, actually, he's been at the gym all morning. Thanks for reminding me, though. I'll see where he's at." I didn't look up from my phone as I opened our conversation in my messages.

Hey. Coming down to the pool any time soon? Javier's setting up the volleyball net for us.

I tucked my phone back into my sling bag and laid back comfortably in my lounge chair.

"He should be down soon," I said, smiling briefly at Colter before I closed my eyes and faced into the pleasantly warm sunshine. There was a beat of silence that pricked my awareness, and I was about to open my eyes out of curiosity when I heard Colter shifting, the plastic of his lounge chair squeaking as I presumed he also got comfortable.

The ding of my phone rang out and I peeked at Colter before I checked the message. Colter indeed had laid back and had one eye opened, watching me as I unlocked the screen and read;

Don't think I can make it. As soon as I got back to the room to shower my stomach flipped. Not sure if it's something from last night's dinner or maybe I accidentally drank the tap water but I'm going to lay down for a while and see if I can't sleep it off.

Halfway through reading his text I'd sat up straight, my face falling into a grimace of concern.

"What's up?" Colter asked from beside me. I looked up to see he'd opened both his eyes now, but he remained relatively relaxed.

I started to collect my flip flops from under the chair as my thumb hovered over the phone button, ready to call Eric. "It's Eric. He's not feeling well. I'm going to go check on him."

"Drink the water, did he? He knows those little water bottles all over the hotel room are for him to use instead right?" Colter's light, humorous tone had me giving him an eye roll.

I hit Eric's number to initiate the call. Pinning my phone between my ear and shoulder, I pulled on my flip flops. It rang only once.

"Hi," Eric croaked from the other end.

"Hi hon. I'm on my way up. Can I bring you anything?" I was up and gave Colter an absent-minded wave good-bye as I rounded the foot of his lounge chair. He offered me a halfhearted wave in return then tucked his hands behind his head.

"*No*, Moll. Don't worry about me. Stay. Enjoy your game of volleyball. Like I told you, I'm just going to be sleeping. There's nothing for you to do." I slowed to a stop just as I hit the covered walkway to our hotel wing. I looked up just as Gracie, Ben, Alan and Cam were walking in, smiling excitedly as they spotted me. Their smiles instantly fell when they caught whatever concerned look must have been evident on my face. I held up a hand to let them know I'd acknowledged them as they passed, and I leaned a shoulder into the wall.

"Eric," I sighed in protest.

"Molly." His tone turned exasperated. "Seriously. I'll be fine. I was already almost asleep when you called. Give me some time to rest. I'll call you later to meet up with you guys wherever you're at."

I wanted to convince him otherwise. I could find him some Pepto, or crackers, or *something* to help settle his stomach. Then I heard a humored yelp followed immediately by a splash and turned to see Gracie and Ben popping up out of the pool water, beaming at one another.

"Are you sure?" I tested one last time.

A responding sigh on the other end. "Yes."

"Ok. Well, I love you. Call me if you need anything. I mean it, Eric."

"Will do. You, too." And he hung up.

I looked down at the phone as it blinked *Call Ended*. Chewing on my bottom lip, I couldn't shake the lingering weird feeling I'd been sensing from the beginning of this trip. But I could understand Eric's attitude if he truly wasn't feeling well. I wouldn't want someone fussing over me like that while trying to rest. Well, that was a lie. I'd eat it up, but I'd feel loads guilty for being a burden on someone else's vacation time. I figured if he really did need me, he'd have been honest with me. I sighed through my nose, tucked my phone away and turned to meet back up with my friends.

Javier was there, standing at the side of the pool and staking one pole of the net into a base. I noticed the defined back muscles of someone in the pool carrying another pole, slowly unrolling the net as he hopped backwards through the water. I continued staring as I walked up to the base, ready to help. Then I noticed the hair. Colter.

He reached my side and turned to look at me just as I was realizing who I'd been—once again—ogling at.

"Hey, Rockstar!" He smiled, surprised to see me.

"Hey." I forced a smile and held out my hands for the pole. "I can take it."

His eyes flicked to something behind me for a hot second. "Sure." Colter's smile turned wicked, mischievous.

And it was at that moment I knew I'd messed up. I didn't have even a second to back away as I felt someone reach around to unbuckle my sling bag, slipping it off my shoulders as Colter clamped down on my arm and pulled me forward. My shriek of laughter was eaten up by the pool as I tumbled in.

Goosebumps erupted at the pleasant sensation of the lukewarm water on my skin. I broke the surface as I stood up and splashed the biggest wave at Colter I could muster, laughing, "You jerk!" He tried to move out of the spray of water but failed and giggled—*giggled*—as he took the force of my water just as he and Cam placed the pole into the base to erect the net. "You, too!" I jokingly seethed as I pointed a threatening finger at Cam's face. My sling bag dangled in his free hand, so I didn't dare send a splash his way.

"Should've known better, Molls." Cam shrugged. "You only have yourself to blame for that one."

Begrudgingly, I silently agreed. The boys had always pulled this shit on me since way back at the beginning of junior high when our elementary companionship solidified into real, true friendships. The same could be said for Gracie when she moved into town and started attending our school freshman year of high school. The boys treated her like one of them.

Well, everyone except Ben. Looking back on it now, it was obvious they'd wind up together; he'd immediately switch from boyish mischief to proper gentlemanliness whenever she came around. It was no shock when they started dating immediately after graduation.

The real surprise was Alan and Cam. Who, apparently, had been keeping their love for one another secret since junior year when they were sentenced to weeks of after-school detention after pulling a prank of racing in and out of classrooms near the end of a particularly hot spring in nothing more than speedos and gorilla face masks. They'd been barred from going to Junior prom that year.

It had taken another year before they took their relationship officially public, and after the initial shock, we all had to admit that we should've seen it coming too. Alan and Cam had always had a special closeness growing up. All in all, nothing about our friendships changed a whole lot after that. We'd settled into a new and better norm as we all admired the fact that most of the friends in our group were happy and in love.

I personally had dated regularly throughout college and even our rowdy Colter had found a brief love interest in a girl he'd met at a music festival three years ago. They hadn't lasted more than three months, but none of us were astonished. Sophie—I think her name was—grew to hate the way he beat up his Jeep every other weekend at the two-tracks near the edge of the farmer's property behind the school. ORVing wasn't for everyone. Even I tired of getting my head slammed against the roof of a car every now and then. It'd been over a year since I've done anything like that, though. A part of me missed it.

Thinking back on old times, I freely smiled as I closed my eyes and leaned back to float, enjoying the feel of the water sluicing over my legs and belly. I gently waved my arms to help keep afloat.

I sensed someone looking at me and opened my eyes to find Gracie standing above me. Water dripped from the ends of her hair, splattering on my forehead. I blinked and straightened, hovering in the water up to my shoulders.

"What are you doing?" I laughed.

She'd found a pool noodle and wrapped it under her thighs as she sat down into it like a floating chair. "Everything okay?"

Gracie...ever the observant and nosey friend. I loved her. "Yeah, I'm fine."

One of her astute eyes narrowed on me. "Yeah? Because Colter told us you were headed back to the room to care for a sick Eric. But we'd just seen you having what looked like an unpleasant phone call on the way in and...here you are. *Not* with Eric."

I raised my shoulders out of the water briefly. "He asked that I let him sleep. Told me to enjoy my pool day." I frowned. "Insisted on it, actually."

"Well, that's...selfless of him, I guess." Gracie cocked her head to the side, analyzing me. I gave her a tightlipped smile.

"Let's get this game started!" Alan shouted as he ran and jumped into a cannonball that drenched Gracie and I in the splash. We shrieked again with laughter, and I was secretly grateful for his distraction from the conversation Gracie was trying to have. I had a sinking feeling she was going to start nitpicking her way into a narrative that I didn't want to hear.

Unsurprisingly, Ben, Gracie and Alan struck up a team on one side of the net—keeping it in the family, I supposed— while Cam, Colter and I spread out on the other side. When it came to competition, the brothers always teamed up, and it worked to their advantage with whatever twin magic they pulled out. They were always a force to reckon with where games and sports were involved.

Colter waded through the shallow water, holding out his arms and motioning with his hands for Cam and me to huddle in and we obliged. He set us in his stern gaze. "Ok, so we already know their MO. Tweedle Dee and Tweedle Dumbfuck are going to be too tuned in to each other to utilize their strongest player; Gracie." True. "So, we're going to do the opposite." Colter slung a warm, wet arm around mine and Cam's shoulders. Cam and I embraced each other in the same manner, holding back our laughter at how serious Colter was taking this. Colter zeroed in on me. "How's your muscle memory, Molls?"

I smirked. Colter was right; Gracie *was* her team's ace up the sleeve. Just as *I* was mine. Where the twins never competed against one another, Gracie and I...we thrived on it. Despite our loathing of mile-runs in gym class, we'd dominated at volleyball, making JV team our sophomore year. Neither of us continued regular playing after high school but we occasionally joined co-ed beach volleyball tournaments at the lakeshore once or twice a year.

I hummed as I rolled out my shoulders underneath his and Cam's arms. "Admittedly, a little rusty. But once I've warmed up I'll be good."

Cam and Colter both gave me one curt nod of acceptance, then Colter turned his eyes to Cam. "You and Molls will take setter positions, I'll defend the back. And you and I will set Molls up for her wicked spikes every chance we get, got it? Knowing Alan and Ben they're going to work together to set each other up for spiking."

"Smart," I praised. "Gracie's a strong server, so keep an eye on where her eye is focusing before she serves. She has a nasty habit of giving it away." Colter and Cam both nodded once.

"Alright amigos!" Javier shouted from the pool's edge. We broke apart to look up at him and get into positions. "Are we ready?"

We all vocalized our agreement. I peered through the net, and just as Colter had suspected, the twins hovered just below the net's other side.

"Shall we do a coin toss?" Javier suggested as he fished around in his shorts pocket.

"Why don't we let the girls duke it out?" Ben proposed with a barely concealed sneer of a smirk. "Serve up a spike and see who comes out on top."

Gracie narrowed her eyes on me as she swam up between the twins. "I'm up for it if you are, Molls."

Competitive mode engaged. "Just like old times."

She and I paced in unison on opposite sides of the net and Javier raised the ball, shouting, "On the count of three!"

Gracie and I got into position—shoulders back and legs loose. "*Uno. Dos. Tres!*" Javier tossed the ball up in a perfect parallel with the net. Gracie and I locked in on it as it neared and we both shot up at the same time. I drew back my readied arm and swung.

Lightning fast, Gracie swiped down, smacking the ball with enough ferocity the slap echoed off the walls of the surrounding hotel. Javier let out an awe-struck whistle. The ball came splashing down into the water just outside of Cam's reach.

I'd eaten net.

I snapped my gaze at her, shocked. "Looks like you've been practicing," I commented, a fire igniting inside of me.

Gracie was ready to play—and play *dirty*.

She wagged her brow at me. "Use it or lose it."

"Mhm," I hummed, sucking on my teeth.

I turned to my teammates. Colter and Cam looked at me with wide eyes of equal shock and amusement. "She's going to give us hell. But don't worry," I promised as I rolled out my neck. "We're going to kick ass and take names."

Colter emitted a low, deep chuckle as his eyes flashed at me. "There she is."

"Who?" Cam laughed.

"Our murderous Molls." Colter smirked at me with an air of pride.

"Don't you forget it." I remarked, giving him my back. "Into position Cam!" I ordered, snapping my fingers and pointing to the spot as I watched Javier, who'd retrieved the ball, toss it to a ready and waiting Gracie. Over my shoulder I connected eyes with Colter's blue-greens. "She's little, but she packs a punch. Get ready."

"You got it, Rockstar." He winked and gave a two-fingered salute.

A thrill bolted through my veins.

SIX

Gracie had started out strong, but as we'd predicted, the twins got it into their heads that they were the MVPs of the game and Colter, Cam and I clawed our way to victory. As the twins sobered up from their strange twin connection, Ben realized his mistake and vowed to Gracie an evening's worth of making it up to her. She'd melted in his hands, happy to accept his groveling at the loaded promise.

We dried off and decided to break for lunch. As the gang left to snag a table at the beach bar, I took it upon myself to go check in with Eric. I'd left them with strict instructions to order me a piña colada so it was ready and waiting for me when I'd soon return. Gracie pinky promised. *Child*. Still, I wore a silly smile on my face as my friends and I went our separate ways.

The parrot pandemonium was nowhere to be seen at midday, so my birds were not waiting for me at the stairwell. I needed to remember to take a photo of them the next time they came back. I rounded the landing, using the rail to swing myself around and almost crashed into a stack of folded towels.

"Ope!" I called out compulsively as I steadied myself.

"*Senorita* Molly! Please excuse me!" Imelda poked her head out from around the towels, her big brown eyes were somehow even bigger in surprise.

I rested a hand over my racing heart and let out a breathy laugh, "No! It's okay! I was not paying attention—my fault."

Imelda leveled me with a smile that said she begged to differ, yet didn't dare disagree. I pointedly looked at the stack of towels in her hands. "Greeter, receptionist *and* housekeeper, eh? You stay *mucho* busy here, huh?"

She laughed and if I didn't know any better I'd have said something about it rang false. "Ah, no, *Senorita* Molly. A guest called the front desk for extra towels." Imelda suddenly perked up as though an epiphany washed over her. "But! It seems I've mistaken myself for the wrong floor. Pardon me."

She made a move to step around me. "Oh, yeah. Sorry. *Hasta luego!*" I sidestepped out of her way and gave her a silly little wave. Imelda tipped her head at me politely in passing. Continuing on my way, I retrieved my room key from my bag. Once at my door, I carefully and ever so gently let myself into the room. As expected, it was blanketed in darkness. I delicately closed the door and tiptoed my way in, hoping not to wake Eric if he was sleeping soundly. My flip flops smacked softly on the tile floor, and I was halfway to the bed when I heard a rustling. Then Eric spoke, "Back already, *hermosa?*"

I smiled and bit at my lip. Well, that was promising if he was well enough to start using sweet nicknames. "*Si, mi amore.* How are you feeling?"

Silence.

I made it to the edge of the bed and sat down. My eyes adjusted enough for me to make out his shape. I reached out and ran my fingers through his hair.

Eric made a sound as though he was stretching. "Feeling okay. I think maybe I should try to get some food in my stomach and see if I can keep it down."

"Oh good, we're just now ordering lunch at the beachside bar if you want to join—"

"Nah, that's okay Moll." His voice had pitched. "I'll probably just order up some room service. Still feeling a bit…shaky."

He couldn't see my shoulders as they sagged, or the frown that took over my face. "I'm so sorry, babe. There's always that one person on a group vacation that gets sick. It's too bad it wound being *you*."

A light chuckle. "Maybe not. You did come down here to be with *your* friends. If anyone should have to wind up sick it might as well be me."

I balked. "I came down here to be with *you*. And they're your friends too, y'know."

He rolled over onto his back. "Sure, sure."

It was all he said in return, but he didn't sound upset, so I just pursed my lips and rose from the edge of the bed.

"Well," I sighed, smacking my hands on my legs, "I probably have a waiting piña colada with my name on it that's melting in this heat, so I'll let you continue resting. Try to get that food down and hopefully you'll be able to join us at the pool later or come out to watch the sunset at the beach or something."

"Yeah! Sounds good. Hey—before you go, will you grab me a water out of the mini fridge?"

Overly eager to be some sort of help, I jumped up excitedly. "Of course!" I crossed to the fridge and quickly did as he asked, even going so far as to open the bottle for him on the walk back. I went to set it on the nightstand by his head when my foot hit something that was sent skittering under the bed.

"What was that?" I mused under my breath. I went to bend down but gave a start when I felt Eric reach out for me, clasping my wrist. He pulled me down to him and placed a sweet kiss to my forehead. My chest squeezed.

"Thanks, Molls," he said tenderly. I straightened, but he still held on to my wrist. "Have a piña colada for me, will ya? And don't worry about me—because I know you will—just enjoy yourself, okay?"

I giggled a little then, "Yeah. Okay."

"Promise?" I could hear the smile in his voice.

"Promise."

As I left I could have sworn I thought I smelled a light floral scent in the sheets. Most likely the laundry detergent they washed the bedding in. I wouldn't have remembered from sleeping in it considering how sloshed I'd gotten last night. But it was nice. Pleasant. I might ask Javier to find out what brand it was and buy some for home.

~

Like the true friends they were, they'd ordered my piña colada and even ordered a giant plate of fries to share as they waited for me to return before placing their orders in. The sweet and salty combination of French fries and piña colada was interesting, but surprisingly good. I had ordered a cheeseburger and a second piña colada and was full and happy. Javier had even stopped by our table to invite us to a casino-themed party at the pool this evening and everyone was enthusiastic to reply yes.

After lunch we'd all made our way to the beach and the boys left to see how far they could make it on a walk down the shoreline before being turned around, while Gracie and I happily spread out towels in the sand to lay and bake in the island sun.

"What should we wear tonight? I know he said it's a pool party, but a casino night sounds too fancy for swimsuits," Gracie said as she turned over to lay on her belly.

I rolled over as well, digging out small pockets in the sand beneath my towel for my breasts. I'd been mulling over my answer when Gracie noticed what I was doing and snickered.

I grinned. "Shut up."

"Big titty problems," she murmured.

I ignored her comment and refocused on her previous question. "I don't know. I'll probably wear a nice dress. I don't think my body can take any more swimming today." I reached around and untied the straps of my bikini top. Tan lines were no fun.

"Yeah I was thinking the same thing." Gracie pressed her cheek into her towel and closed her eyes. "You should come to my suite to get ready with me! You haven't seen it yet, it's really cool, and the view is incredible."

"Okay, sure. Sounds fun." I closed my eyes too, blissfully relaxed. From somewhere back in one of the beachside restaurants a live steel drum performer began playing. "Perfect," I moaned, smiling like a Cheshire Cat.

I awoke abruptly to the sensation of a cold spray at the same time a shriek rang out beside me. Gracie and I jumped at the same time, and I'd thankfully had the quick sense of mind to slap my arm over my bare breasts as I sat upright on my knees, shielding my eyes against the blinding sun. "What the hell was that?" I shouted over the raucous laughter nearby.

Gracie was already on her feet shouting profanities as she took off toward the water. Then everything quieted down as I blinked my eyes quickly to adjust my vision. As I stood and looked to where I'd last heard Gracie yelling, I found the culprits.

The boys were back, standing in the crashing waves of the shoreline and all but Alan were staring at me with mouths gaping. "Did you guys seriously splash us? Bunch of children," I grumbled. I glared...and they stared.

No one moved until Gracie noticed Ben staring and whacked him in his abdomen with the back of her hand. Then, snapping out of it, Ben whacked Cam, who whacked Colter— a domino effect of gut smacks. Alan broke out in a cackle as I looked down at myself, realizing they were gawking at *me*. Gracie and Cam included. "Yeah, a bunch of *immature* children." I rolled my eyes and turned to bend over to retrieve my bikini top.

Someone choked a cough, and I peered over my shoulder as Alan clapped Colter supportively on his bare back. Gracie scrunched her face. "Yeah, Molls—you're *really* not helping your case bending over like that."

"Oh, for fuck's sake," I sighed, stomping my foot defiantly as I faced them all again. Another staring contest. "Anyone care to help?" I asked with annoyance as I motioned to the towel still on the sand.

Gracie clutched onto Ben as though she'd need to stop him from assisting me. Cam closed his eyes and shook his head like he was talking himself out of it, reminding himself that he, in fact, liked men. Alan was still in a fit of laughter as he shoved Colter in the shoulder toward me. Colter stumbled but caught himself quickly and threw Alan a wide-eyed smile over his shoulder as he started into a soft jog my way.

I flashed Colter an unimpressed, tightlipped grin and he blushed.

"Do you always sunbathe topless?" he asked, bending down to snatch the towel, giving it a firm whip to rid it of sand. He held it up, angling away from the resort and our friends so the heavily wooded jungle was behind me.

"Thank you," I muttered, "And no. Not always." Even with the towel up between us I turned my back to him and collected my hair, twirling it into a rope, pulling it over the front of my right shoulder. "But the sun down here is strong. And it takes only a few minutes for me to develop a tan line. And the two swimsuits I brought are the same style, just different colors, so if I'm not careful, I'll leave here with a one-inch strip of white around my back." I quickly tied the knots at my neck and then around my back and rested my hands on my hips as I turned around. "Thank you," I muttered again but Colter's eyes were near watering as he intently stared at something interesting in the tree line behind me.

The humor of it all finally hit me, and I laughed, "Colter, I'm decent."

"Yep," he said, still averting his gaze.

"For the love of God, Colter. Are you having a stroke? It's not like you haven't seen my boobs before." It was true. Things like that tended to happen when you've known someone as long as we have.

Colter's brows jumped as he cleared his throat. "Well, Molls. That was ten years ago. You were fourteen and a lot more...different."

"Ah, so you do remember," I quipped as I turned and walked away.

Colter fell into step beside me. "A boy never forgets his first real glimpse."

I stopped in my tracks. "Wait...that night in your hot tub was the *first time* you'd seen boobs?"

"I said *real*," he emphasized with a crooked smile he offered to the sand. "As in, not a picture."

"Ah. I see." I took up walking again and we met back up with everyone else.

"Valiant effort, soldier—going into the trenches like that." Alan joked as he grasped Colter's shoulders, he continued through everyone's laughter, "Brave soul."

"Oh my God…" Gracie groaned but she was smiling as she pinched the bridge of her nose.

"What?" Alan snapped, "Moll's knockers almost had my *very gay* boyfriend switching sides."

Cam rolled his eyes and pulled Alan into his side.

I sighed through my nose. "Can we stop talking about my boobs?"

Colter raised his hand as he fell into step with everyone. "I second that."

"I third that," Gracie laughed as she stepped to my side, leaving Ben behind with the boys as she linked her arm in mine. She leaned into whisper, "In Cam's defense, those babies almost had me switching sides too." I threw my head back and barked out a laugh that turned into a yelp as she landed a good-humored smack onto my ass cheek.

One of the boys let out a whistle.

"Enough!" Ben shouted, playfully scolding his woman. We sniggered mercilessly.

~

The birds were back as we climbed the stairs to our rooms, but our large group was too boisterous and so they flew away, startled, before I was able to snap a picture.

"So, we meet out here in an hour, right?" Gracie reiterated the plans we'd made on the walk back from the beach.

"Yes! Where we'll enjoy a lovely meal together before I clean out all your wallets at the roulette table." Alan smirked.

I brought my hand to my mouth to cover up my smile.

"My dear, sweet love of mine," Cam sighed. "Let me gently remind you that Javier explicitly informed us the games were played for fun. Not real money."

Alan's eyes could not have rolled any further back into his head. "And let me remind *you*, my sexy but insufferable know-it-all darling, I don't care." He pointed at Colter, "*You're* going in on real money with me under the table, right?"

In front of Cam, Colter had the audacity to play innocent, "Yeah—the monopoly money Javier said we'd all be playing with."

Alan's face fell blank. "How dare you."

Cam snorted. "Alright, come on."

Alan was herded back into his hotel room as he whined about all of us being absolutely no fun.

Gracie leaned her shoulder into Ben's, whispering loud enough for Colter and me to hear, "He knows he's a god-awful gambler right?"

Ben smacked his lips. "I wish I could say yes but he's as clueless as they come."

Colter chuckled and clapped his hands once, loudly enough for the rest of us to turn to him, "I'm going to get cleaned up. See you back here in an hour, guys!"

We all murmured or waved our goodbyes, and I was left the third wheel with Ben and Gracie. I decided now was a good a time as ever to let Gracie know I'd changed my mind about getting ready with her. The guilt about leaving Eric behind all day had eaten away at me and I just knew I needed to spend some time with him.

"Hey listen—"

"I already know. I can read it all over your face." Gracie said waving her pink-tipped finger in front of my nose.

I chuckled lightly, "Always so observant."

"Yes, I know." Gracie leaned in to give me a parting hug. "You're welcome to come on by if you change your mind." I went to pull away, thinking the hug was over but she held me just a little longer.

"Ok, ok. That's enough," Ben jested as he pulled her off me, the three of us snickering.

"I'll see you soon." I waved them both goodbye as they retreated into the privacy of their room.

When I opened my own door I'd half expected to be greeted by stark blackness once again but was pleasantly surprised to find that the blackout curtains had been pulled back and the sunlight was pouring in from the floor to ceiling balcony door.

"Hey babe! You feeling better?" I called out, closing the door behind me and toeing off my flip flops.

No response.

"Babe?"

Silence.

"*Eric.*"

I checked the bathroom just to make sure, but it was confirmed; he wasn't here. I plopped down to the edge of the bed and pulled my phone out of my bag. No missed text messages or calls. I sighed through my nose and tossed my phone onto the blankets. I knew I could ease my mind by simply calling him, but I couldn't deny the fact that I just...didn't *want* to. I was getting mad. If I didn't know any better I'd think he'd been avoiding me all day.

This was my first adult, out-of-country adventure and there was an ever-growing ominous cloud of doubt and confusion in the shape of Eric raining all over the parade. I looked around the big, empty hotel room again, as though he'd pop up out of thin air. Alone and feeling vulnerable, my self-doubt began nitpicking away at me. Had I not done enough to try being with him today? He was the one that snuck out first thing in the morning for the gym without so much as a note. He's the one that skipped breakfast with us. Granted, he'd fallen ill, that much was true, but he was the one to insist I let him rest. He's the one who told me to enjoy a piña colada for him. He'd been pushing me away all day. Well, not counting the sweet moment when he'd pulled me in to kiss my forehead...

I remembered that moment, enjoying the stir of warmth it ignited in my chest. Until I remembered what had happened right before it. I'd run into something small and featherlight that went sliding under the bed. Like a candy wrapper. I straightened. *Like a condom wrapper.* I slowly rose to my feet. A bristling feeling erupted on the bare skin of my arms as I slowly made my way to Eric's side of the bed. My breath became shallow, and my ears began ringing. I stared down at Eric's nicely made side of the bed. Then the floor.

Feeling a little dizzy, I slowly lowered to my knees. I sucked in a sharp breath when I saw...

Nothing. Absolutely nothing was underneath the bed. It was perfectly clean down there. A wave of relief hit me so hard I almost started to feel nauseous.

Stupid. I was so unbelievably stupid. I let out a nervous laugh, "Imagining things..."

As my heart rate slowed back to normal, I rested my hands on my hips. Was I imagining things though? I had hit *something*. Hadn't I? Whatever it was it had been enough for me to actually ask 'what was that' *out loud*. Which means Eric would have had to have heard it too. But he...

He'd stopped me.

The nauseous feeling worked its way back into my belly. Quick panting breaths started all over again and like a moth to a flame, my eyes zeroed in on Eric's suitcase sitting atop the entertainment center. My brain was telling me—no, it was *screaming* at me—to go to it. To find that supposed *old* unopened box of condoms to see for myself if one had gone missing.

I'd taken a few wobbly steps toward it, my hand stretched out for it—

The door opened.

I tucked my arm to my chest wicked fast as I whirled around. "Eric!" I exclaimed with a pitchiness to my voice. It was obvious he wasn't expecting to see me here as he looked up at me, his eyes going wide. I tried to look natural as I rested my hip against the entertainment center, folding my arms over my chest.

"Hey, what's going on?" he asked with a casual coolness.

I blinked stupidly. It seemed like such a dumb thing to ask considering everything, so I ignored it and moved on to the question that was on the tip of my tongue. "You look like you're feeling better."

Eric strode the short distance to his bedside as he tossed his phone next to mine on the bed. "Yeah," he agreed as he slipped the room key into his back pocket. "I think whatever it was has worked its way through my system."

"Where were you?" I hoped that sounded as casual as I'd meant it to.

"Out for some much-needed fresh air." Eric crossed his arms over his chest. "Went down the beach about a half mile or so. Picked up some shells."

"Shells?"

Eric reached into a front pocket and pulled out several small white seashells. It struck me as such an uncharacteristic thing for him to do, but the proof was literally in his hands.

I swallowed and finally pushed myself up to head to the bathroom, knowing I was supposed to be getting ready. "Pretty."

"I thought so," Eric agreed as he tracked my movements.

Feeling him out, I stopped beside him on the way and planted a tentative kiss to his cheek. "I'm glad you're feeling better." It wasn't a lie.

"Me too."

"We're all planning to go to a party tonight. It's casino-themed. Can I expect you to be joining us?"

"Yeah," he drawled, and I was admittedly surprised he wasn't conjuring up some kind of excuse not to go, until he continued, "Maybe. After I go sit down for a real meal. I'm starved."

Anger began a low and slow swim through my blood. There it was. His excuse. I'd heard enough out of him, so I walked off and headed into the bathroom for a shower, not even bothering myself with a response.

Inside the bathroom, I turned on the rainforest showerhead and with a striking vengeance a blurred memory popped into the forefront of my mind. I'd woken up in the middle of the night last night to Eric showering. At nearly 3:30 in the morning. For what reason would he need to shower in the middle of the night? There was a suggested answer from a nasty voice in the back of my mind that I kept smothering.

By the time I finished washing away the sweat, sunscreen, sand, and chlorine from the day, I was fuming. I'd wrapped a towel around myself and stepped back into the room to start into an argument but found Eric sprawled on the bed with the TV on. Asleep.

"Un-freaking-believable," I mumbled, gaping at him. I turned back into the bathroom and angrily collected my toiletries then stomped to my suitcase to tear out a nice dress and my nice pair of wedge sandals. I'd almost walked out without my phone, until I passed by the foot of the bed and saw it sitting there next to Eric's crossed ankles. I snatched that too, cradling all my belongings in my arms and, still wrapped in nothing more than a towel, I stormed out of the room.

SEVEN

I pounded a fist on Gracie and Ben's door. "Grace? It's Molly!" I waited a good handful of silent seconds before I pounded again, this time a little harder. "Gracie!"

Behind me, the door across the hall opened. "You just can't seem to keep your clothes on today can you?"

I stiffened. Any other day, I'd have been laughing at his quips, but I was barely containing my annoyance with Eric, and if Colter wasn't careful he was going to get the full brunt of my inevitable breakdown.

"Not now," I bit out, not bothering to turn around.

"Whoa. Molly, is everything okay?" Colter's tone had taken a nosedive into such genuine concern that I almost felt guilty. Almost.

I was saved from having to answer as Gracie finally swung open her door. "Molly?"

Something about seeing her deflated some of my anger. I hated how sad my voice came out as I asked, "Can I still get ready with you?"

"You don't have to ask, of course!" She reached out her hands and pulled me inside by my shoulders. "Come in."

Ben had appeared from the balcony with a look of curiosity as Gracie, sensing I needed time alone with her, guided me to the bathroom, announcing that she and I were going to spend some girl time together.

Gracie was one of those gifted people who knew when and when not to ask questions. Instead, she took my demeanor in and decided whatever I was stuck in my head about needed a little bit of pampering to counteract. She'd placed her phone into one of the bathroom plastic cups and started an old school music streaming station for something uplifting. When she asked what I was thinking of doing with my hair, I'd shrugged and said something along the lines of the same old same old. But she clicked her tongue at me and insisted I let her curl it. So, I let her.

And damn if she didn't do a beautiful job. She'd curled the long lengths and then worked it into a voluminous ponytail of cascading chestnut waves and even pulled out some pretty wisps of curls to frame my face, kissing my cheeks. It was the exact kind of look I'd always dreamed of but could never seem to perfect. Whenever I'd tried something similar in the past I wound up looking like I'd just stepped off a roller coaster. No, what Gracie did...this was impressive.

"You're hired." I was only half-joking as I leaned in closer to my reflection to investigate exactly where she pulled out tendrils, taking notes. She just snorted a laugh as she started to work on herself.

Ben then poked his head into the door frame. "This is your fifteen-minute warning ladies."

"Shoot." Gracie hissed around the bobby pin she had clamped between her teeth.

It was then I'd realized that her doing my hair had eaten up most of her own getting-ready time. "Oops. I'm sorry, girl."

A scoff. "Don't be silly. You look fantastic. I'm not sorry, so you shouldn't be either."

Easier said than done. But then she so expertly slicked her own hair back into such an elegant low bun at the nape of her neck with such effortlessness that I didn't even feel bad anymore. Being so naturally talented should be a crime.

"You're a wizard," I said in a jokingly awestruck tone.

She cackled, "Oh please. You can do this too, you just have to have a little more confidence."

Ben's floating head returned. "Ten-minute warning." He disappeared again.

I struggled to hold back my giggle. "Does he always do this before a night out?"

"Oh, most definitely." She gave me wide eyes through the mirror. "If he didn't we'd be late to *everything*."

"You've trained him well."

"Or maybe he's trained me well." She countered as she slicked a lip stain over her bottom lip.

"True," I conceded.

We both used the last few minutes to make any last touch ups and finally get dressed. Gracie looked smokin' in a white bodycon dress. She was the sexy angel to my demure devil as I slipped into my off-the-shoulder red sundress with a neckline that had a cute little drawstring that tied into a bow at the cleavage.

At the three-minute warning, Gracie snagged my attention in the mirror. I stilled and held her gaze. I knew at that second that she wasn't going to keep quiet any longer. "Will Eric be joining us for the party tonight?"

I bit the inside of my lips, taking a short pause to consider my reply. "Honest answer?"

"Always."

"I'm not sure I care whether he does or doesn't."

She kept her face calm, but I could tell by the way her eyes flared by a fraction that she was shocked to hear that come out of my mouth. "I see."

~

The party was in full swing as our group entered the pool area, sans Eric. Again.

In the time since we'd left the pool sometime after lunch, the staff had strung up lines of decorative flags and festooned lighting all over the place. The poolside lounge chairs had all been moved out of the way for a dozen various casino game tables. Lanterns hung over each one casting everything in a soft, warm light. The moon was a sliver in the distant sky above the softly rolling waves of the ocean and beyond the streamers and flags the stars were a force to be reckoned with.

A band played music beside the bar and there was a double-line buffet of an assortment of finger foods.

As Gracie, Ben, and I had left their room, I'd felt guilty enough to send Eric a text that we'd all be down at the party and to join if he felt up to it after his *meal.* I had no idea if he was still sleeping, but there was no way I wasn't going to at least let him know where he could find me should he change his mind.

Cam, Alan, and Colter had already been standing out in the hallway ready for us. They all looked beach casual in their shorts and crisp short-sleeved buttoned-down shirts. Colter had even gone so far as to wear a fancy looking watch I'd never seen before. It was a nice touch.

Alan wore a pair of sunglasses, even though the sun had already set and we'd all given him crap for it, but he insisted it completed his look. Truth be told, he was right. Cam's shirt was my favorite—black with a pink floral Hawaiian print.

But as we now entered into the buttery glow of the lantern lights, I had to admit Colter's khaki-colored button down, cream shorts, and white sneakers against his enviously tanned skin were eye-catching. He looked like he belonged on a *GQ* cover.

Like kids in a candy store, everyone in our group split up to their most anticipated games; Cam had beelined it for a Blackjack table, it was no surprise that Gracie dragged Ben to the roulette wheels, and Colter had set off for another poker table. I, on the other hand, hit the bar.

I'd sidled up onto a stool and ordered a blackberry mojito. As I indulged in the first sweet sip, I spun the stool around to people-watch and keep tabs on my friends.

Alan weaved his way through the crowd and closed in on me. "Not into the games?"

"Into the games just fine. Just into the alcohol a little more at the moment." I regretted the bitterness of my words as soon as I said it.

Alan promptly planted his butt in the seat beside me. "Talk to me, Connors." When Alan started using surnames, he meant business. I mentally kicked myself and took a long drink off my mojito. "Would it have something to do with a certain gentleman not in attendance tonight?"

I shot him a look as if to say, *isn't it obvious?*

Alan simply nodded as he paused our one-sided conversation to order a drink. He'd patiently waited to prod any further until his drink arrived and he'd taken his first refreshing sip.

"Whose fault is it?" Alan questioned as he too spun his stool around to lean back against the bar top and scan the crowd.

"His." Then I thought about how I'd held back my questioning about the condoms until we were in the airport parking ramp. That'd been cowardly. I thought about how I'd basically kicked him out of his seat on the flight into Atlanta. That'd been inconsiderate. I thought about how I'd let him talk me into spending the entire day having fun in the sun while he slept off his illness all by himself. That had been selfish. "Mine," I amended with a sigh. But that didn't sound exactly right either. "Both." I settled on. *Yes, both.*

"Yeah, can't say I'm surprised." Alan leaned deeply into the bar top to crack his back and took another nonchalant sip of his beer.

"What?" I knew I leveled him with an unattractive look as my brows furrowed together.

Alan shrugged. "He doesn't seem himself. Hasn't this whole trip." I opened my mouth to add my strong vocal agreement, but Alan turned to pin me with a look, silencing me. "And honestly, neither have you."

I recoiled. "Have to!"

"You have not," he drawled, then inclined his head. "Something's been bothering you. Did you really think none of us would notice it the second you asked Colter to sit with you instead of Eric?"

Like a well-rounded, mature adult, I tipped the remainder of my drink back, down the gullet, and crossed my arms defiantly over my chest as I crunched on ice. After far too much time passed, Alan nudged me in the arm with his shoulder.

"He packed condoms," I finally mumbled as I glared into the throng of partygoers.

A beat.

Then, thoroughly confused, Alan offered, "Good for you?"

I slowly rolled my head to look him in the eye. "Eric and I don't *use* condoms." Alan's eyes immediately flared with understanding. "Haven't used one in *months*," I added as I returned to scowling at all the stupid, happy people. While Alan processed what I'd just said, I looked over my shoulder and flagged down the bartender, gesturing for another.

Alan looked at me, then at the bartender, then back at me. He threw up a hand at the bartender to halt him. "Wait! You're not pregnant—"

"No!" I shouted almost too loudly above the noise of the party. I cleared my throat and tried again, this time softer. "God, no. Alan! Do you really think I'd be drinking if I were?"

"Well—no! But you did just tell me you and your man don't use protection. Can you blame me for jumping to that conclusion?"

"I'm on birth control, you dummy," I chided as I turned to the bartender who'd been watching and listening. "Please. Another mojito."

"Coming right up," he said as he walked off, a flustered look in his eyes.

"So why did he pack them?" Alan inquired tentatively.

"Well, when I asked him that same question, he said they must have been an old pack that have been in his toiletry bag that he'd forgotten about."

Alan went quiet as he considered it. After some time, he finally said, "Well. I guess that's plausible. But you said you were both at fault. What did *you* do?"

The inevitable question.

The bartender clanked my new mojito on the bar top, and I greedily sucked on it, giving myself some time as I accepted the truth about myself. "Alan, I—I almost *snooped* through his stuff. I was seconds away from sneaking into his suitcase to see if he had used any of those condoms. He almost caught me." There was more I could have fessed up to. For instance, if I wanted to be honest, I'd been finding myself repeatedly ogling our dear, mutual *friend* since the moment he'd made his grand entrance back home in the airport parking lot. But this was neither the time, place, nor person that I wanted to dissect that disturbing notion with.

"Molly!" Alan hissed in reprimand.

"I know, I know!" A blush of shame worked its way to my cheeks.

"Do you have any reason to believe he did?"

Just then, I caught Colter as he parted through the crowd, heading straight for us. "Just drop it, ok?" I asked Alan hurriedly as I tried to act calm, sipping my drink coolly. Alan looked to where I'd been staring and—bless him—immediately got the hint.

"You two going to just keep those seats warm all night? I thought you were gung-ho for a night of gambling," Colter joked, directing the last part to Alan.

Colter was graced with one of Alan's famous eye rolls. "Please. This is not gambling. This is children's carnival games." And with that, Alan rose from his seat. "And I'm going to go find my lover now and see how he's enjoying his carnival game. See you two around!" He was gone before he'd given either Colter or I a chance to say goodbye in return.

I offered Colter a weak smile as I sucked down the entirety of my second mojito. Colter leaned his elbows onto the bar top. "I was just about to hit the craps table. You should come with me. Do something other than sulk about."

I took offense to that. "I'm not sulking."

I was.

"You are."

He was right.

I froze for just a brief moment to consider my predicament. I was definitely sulking on a beautiful midwinter night in Mexico with a party in full swing going on around me and my friends scattered throughout, no doubt enjoying themselves. I gave Colter a sidelong look. He wagged his eyebrows at me, goading me. Clicking my tongue I nodded my head. "Fine. But I need another drink."

"Aha! There she is." Colter winked. "I need one, too."

We flagged down the bartender and I switched things up for my third drink of the night. A lemon drop martini. Colter had opted for a whiskey neat. Mr. Fancy Pants McGee.

He offered me his arm as we rose from the bar, and I accepted it with a proper nod of appreciation. I was certain we looked like the picture-perfect casino royale couple about to do some damage—that is, if we weren't playing with fake money.

I'd never played craps before, but I wasn't interested in actually playing anyway. I was happy to be a silent observer. Javier was manning the table when we arrived, and he eagerly handed over the dice to Colter as everyone placed their bets. Colter cupped the dice in his hands to scramble them, and just as he was about to launch them down the table Javier stopped him.

"Amigo, *wait*. Now, wait!" Javier made a theatric show of waving his arms in an X. "You don't want to roll those dice before your lady can blow on them for good luck."

Javier darted his eyes to me and pinned me to the spot with a wild look. Realizing he was talking about me, I flushed and turned to Colter who was grinning at me with barely restrained amusement. I let out a breathy, shaky laugh. It wasn't the first time people thought we were an item. I was pretty sure even Etta—our flight companion—had eluded to the fact that she thought we were together. I had every intention of correcting Javier's mistake, but before I could do so Colter's open hand rose before me, expectantly cradling the dice.

I looked into those churning, blue-green eyes for only a second. That was all it took, and I tucked my cares away, deciding I just wanted to let go and have fun. I let Javier make of it what he would as I leaned in and softly blew on the dice in Colter's outstretched hand. I may have been willing to play along with Javier and Colter's little game, but that didn't stop me from averting my gaze as soon as Colter wound up to toss.

A rush of the island heat washed over my skin igniting goosebumps. At least I thought to blame it on the island heat. Or the mojitos.

Colter rolled the dice, and as they both came to a bounding stop, the players around the table erupted in cheers. Regardless of the fact I had no idea how the game was played, the excitement around the table was contagious. I lit up as Colter celebrated by throwing his arm around my shoulders, smacking a kiss to my temple.

Gathering his 'winnings', he gave me an awestruck grin. "You are staying *right by my side* the rest of the night."

I rolled my eyes in humor. "It's not real money, I don't get what everyone's so excited about."

"Sure, but you see these chips?" Colter asked as he placed them into the grooves of the table in front of him. I nodded, following along. "These chips can be turned in for chances at winning draw prizes. The more chips the more likely the chance of winning."

My brows flew up. "Wait, what?"

"Were you not there when Javier explained it earlier today?" he laughed, as he withdrew three of his chips, flipping one of them between the knuckles of his nimble fingers like he was used to handling them.

I racked my memory from earlier today of Javier stopping by our table during lunch, then internally laughed at myself. "I'd kind of been distracted by my cheeseburger, so admittedly I did not catch every part of that conversation."

"That explains it," Colter chuckled as I playfully shoved my shoulder into his. "What bets should we place next?"

I balked. "You do know I have absolutely no idea how to play this game, right?"

"No worries, Rockstar." He placed his chips on the table and Javier handed over the dice once again. "We're just looking for this roll to either be a seven or eleven, got it?" I nodded. Colter then said, "Alright Lady Luck, you're up."

He held his hand out to me for another good-luck blow. Still riding on the excitement of the first roll's success, I was eager to oblige. Only this time, I grabbed him with both hands—one gently closing around the side of his forearm, the other cupping his hand from underneath. As I slightly bent, I flicked my eyes up to meet his and he watched as I blew softly into his palm.

Colter's eyes swam with an intensity of wildness I'd never seen before. My eyes lowered as I watched his throat working on a swallow. Then his chest rose on a deep inhale as he half-smiled, then let his dice fly on the exhale.

If I'd thought the first roll was a cause for celebration, it had nothing on the whoops and cheers that burst forth as the dice landed in a one and a six. There was our seven. A thrill shot through me—it apparently shot through Colter too as he turned to scoop me up into a celebratory hug, lifting me clear off my feet. I let out a shriek of laughter.

I caught my breath as he slid me down to my feet once again, our bodies still pressed together. A bolt of electricity raced through my veins as we caught each other's gaze. I felt it then. The alarming feeling that he was going to…kiss me.

"*Muy bueno*, Colter."

The female voice was a jolt to my senses as I looked over Colter's shoulder and saw Imelda standing there, waiting. Colter let me go as he angled himself by a fraction so he could see her from over his shoulder. "Thank you," he replied simply. Politely. It would have been a normal, passing compliment until Imelda grasped his shoulder from behind as she leaned herself into his body to reach up and plant a celebratory kiss to his stubbled cheek.

Something ugly stirred inside. Imelda leveled me with her deep brown eyes and gave me a sweet smile, "I was watching from the other table. You certainly *are* Lady Luck incarnate tonight."

Imelda laughed at her own stupid quip and even went so far as to gently grasp my upper arm, pulling me in for an out-of-pocket half hug. I let her hug me, not wanting to seem rude. As her soft hair brushed across my cheek I smelled something that immediately had my chest tightening and my stomach roiling. I stiffened.

Imelda backed away and whatever she saw in my eyes, made the pretty smile she'd been wearing slip right off her face. She gulped. I could see it clear as day in her eyes…

She knew I knew.

Anger bubbled, so strong and so fierce that I couldn't even hide the fact that I was taking another sniff of her perfume wafting in the air between us.

Yes...*that* was the scent I'd picked up on in my bedsheets. Imelda's eyes flared wide and her lips twitched into a nervous smile for a fraction of a second before she mastered herself. "Excuse me." she said, lowering her face to the ground as she abruptly shuffled along to the next table.

My knees felt wobbly as I turned in the direction of our wing of the hotel. My eyes scanned the levels until I reached the third floor, and I found my balcony. Behind the drawn curtain, a light was on. Eric was in there.

Fuming anger mixed with a gut-wrenching sensation as I took one step. Then another. And then I broke into a fast pace as my one-track mind took over my body. I couldn't tell for sure, but as I'd stomped off, I thought I heard Colter calling after me. But his yelling was muffled by the sound of the blood rushing in my ears.

I couldn't think about it. I couldn't think about anything other than getting back to my hotel room. And getting back there *fast*. Because if I dared think—if I dared entertain the notions threatening to swamp my head, I was likely to have a meltdown right here, right now.

I didn't even remember the dark walk back, I just suddenly found myself at my hotel room door, fumbling with my keycard as a rush of nerves threatened to turn me into a ball of shakes. The green light blinked as the latch slid unlocked. And without taking a moment to steady myself or even take a breath, I entered the room.

And what I saw was my undoing.

EIGHT

Eric froze halfway through slipping a condom into his wallet. There was a stretch of silence and about a million miles between us as we stood there, both coming to grips with the situation. Left to swing on its own, the door latched shut behind me and the sound echoed in my head for an eternity.

Then Eric moved to face me fully, opening his mouth to finally say something, but I took a step forward and shook my head. "No."

His lips thinned as he struggled to keep quiet, as he struggled to watch me advance with each and every slow step, knowing full well there was nothing he could do to stop the fraying that was happening.

"No," I repeated dumbly. I was so at a loss for words that it was all I could get out.

Eric finally worked up the nerve then to finish his task of stashing his condom as he folded his wallet and slid it into the back pocket of his shorts. My knees finally gave out and I dropped my ass to the edge of the bed, clutching my waist, praying the counterpressure would ease the hollowness being carved out there.

"You said that was an *old* box." I started, my voice hardly above a whisper. Eric was smart enough to keep his mouth shut. "You made me believe you had no idea they were even in your luggage." I snapped my eyes closed with shame at just how long I'd been letting myself live in Delulu Land.

"Molly—"

"Don't," I warned, holding up a hand to ward him off. I reopened my eyes to take him in. "You were angry with me for even *asking* you about them. You intended to *shut me out* on the flight. You…" My gut wrenched a little more as my brain walked me through the last two days, "You *fucked* me when we arrived here and then—" My voice broke then, and I had to stop for a moment to regain my composure.

The pain was coming in waves, ebbing and flowing as my rage battered against it. "Oh my God…" I whined as everything started to fall into place, "You stayed at the nightclub while Colter walked me home. I'd ask what time you got in that night, but I already know…because you were in the shower washing away whoever's fucking body must've been all over you!"

Rage won.

I rose to my feet, yelling, "Did you fuck Imelda last night or was it just today while you were pretending to be sick to avoid me? Or no…fucking unbelievable..." I ran my hands down my face as I watched Eric wince. "Duh, the *bachelorette party*." I barked out an ugly laugh, but I was beyond caring. "Tell me, Eric. Exactly how many people have you slept with in the last *forty-eight fucking hours?!*"

Eric's jaw set in a hard line as he looked away.

"Don't worry, I can figure it out for myself." I spat as I pushed past him, throwing open the lid to his unzipped suitcase. There it was—the damning box of condoms, the seal ripped open. In the pack of ten, only seven remained. Including me, and not counting the one he'd put in his pocket, that was as many as three women.

The weight in my chest felt heavy enough to crack bones. A small, silly little part of me had been holding out that there was a reasonable, logical explanation for all of this. But this was the final nail in the coffin.

Like a switch had been flipped, I emptied of everything. All fight, all emotion. I was a husk of a person as I focused solely on packing my stuff. It was a small mercy that my toiletries were still in Gracie's bathroom from earlier. Eric watched in silence.

I'd set the wheels of my luggage onto the tile floor with a clunk and then looked to Eric who was watching me with grave, bloodshot eyes.

"Am I allowed to speak yet?" he asked in a voice so low and severe it conjured up feelings of disgust within me. I wanted to tell him no. But then I looked to the bed beyond him. I looked to the nightstand where the opened water bottle he'd asked me to retrieve—a distraction, I now realized—still stood, untouched.

I frowned, "It was a condom wrapper I'd kicked under the bed wasn't it?"

"Yes."

"Imelda?"

"Yes."

"You thought I was *her*…that's why you called me—or *her*, rather—*hermosa*."

No response, but I didn't need him to give one anyway, silence was all the confirmation I needed. I was going to be sick. I headed for the door, unable to hear another word.

"Molly, where are you going to go?" Eric asked with the audacity to sound sincere with his concern.

I turned to face him then and answered as I threw my room key at him, "Anywhere but here."

Then I grabbed the doorknob and walked out without even saying goodbye.

~

Like the omniscient she was, Gracie stood across the hall from the door, leaned up against the railing, the wide island jungle expanse cast in shadows behind her. She had her head held high, waiting for me. The door shut on its own once again behind me and I'd embarrassingly startled at the jarring sound. We locked eyes and hers narrowed slightly. Evaluating.

"You heard." It wasn't a question. I hadn't been particularly quiet while digging into Eric.

Gracie cleared her throat as she pushed off the railing. "I did." A pause. Her eyes scanned my face. "Come on." She reached out a hand to me, coming forward. Gracie wrapped her arm around my shoulder pulling me into her side as she let us into her room.

I'd managed to hold it together until the door shut. Then I stumbled into the bathroom, falling into a crawl by the time I'd gotten halfway to the toilet. And I heaved, vomiting, as angry hot tears finally slipped free. I broke.

~

Gracie had stayed by my side for what *felt* like hours as I cried, and spat, and cursed Eric's name. She'd softly played with the ponytail she'd given me, and she just nodded along, listening. I couldn't look her in the eyes as I told her everything from the beginning. The whole ordeal probably lasted only ten minutes, but the ache in my knees against the hard tile floor felt like I'd been shaking there forever.

"He's such a fucking asshole," Gracie cursed under her breath after I'd finished. I finally looked up at her, resting my cheek against the arm I had slung over the toilet seat. The heartbreak and anger in her eyes rekindled feelings of my own. And she immediately softened her features…into something akin to pity. I groaned, turning away in shame. "Come on, Molls. Let's get you off this floor and get you some water."

I let her help me up. The bathroom smelled like vomit and blackberry mojito, so I was ready to get out of there as much as I was sure Gracie was. Arm in arm, she walked me to the side of her king-sized bed, and I dropped down onto my ass with a humph. While she stepped away to get a water bottle out of her mini fridge, I turned my swollen eyes up to the ceiling and proceeded to flop down onto the bed. Like a lady.

"Fucking asshole," I whispered my agreement to Gracie's earlier statement. The sound of the seal on the plastic cap breaking snagged my attention. I propped up to my elbows and reached out for the opened water she held out for me. "Thank you."

"You'll sleep here with us tonight." The demand hung in the air between us like a ticking bomb...she wasn't going to say what was probably ringing around in both our heads; *for how long?*

"But—"

"Don't, Molls. Let's just take things day-by-day, okay? We don't need to borrow tomorrow's problems, you've got enough of today's to worry about." Gracie sat down beside me on the bed and patted the top of my thigh. "I know you're hurting right now. I know it probably feels like the world is ending..." She sighed as she looked up to the heavens as though searching for an answer. "But you're surrounded by people who love you. In paradise. You are going to be okay. Okay? I promise you...everything will be *okay*."

I nodded as I sipped the cool water, more tears silently slipping down my cheeks. Gracie let out a deep sigh and she set to work getting ready for bed. As I watched her dig through my luggage for something for me to sleep in a little piece of reality slipped into my head. "How did you know to come for me?"

Snagging an oversized t-shirt, she answered as she set back to task in search of bottoms, "Colter. He'd come looking for me, saying you'd stormed off with a crazed look in your eye that troubled him. He was smart enough to realize that whatever was happening...it required a girlfriend's touch. Not a guy friends. He was worried about you, Molls. It was sweet."

My chest tightened. "I'll remember to thank him in the morning." I said as Gracie turned to me, finding my pajama shorts. She bundled the items of clothing and tossed them to me.

"Go brush your teeth and wash your face," she ordered like a clucking mother hen. I obeyed without a fight.

I'd already passed out in Gracie's bed by the time Ben had finally called it a night and returned to the room. I never heard or saw him come in. Later, I'd woken up at some point in the middle of the night, and once I realized it was Gracie who had an arm around me and not Eric, the pain reignited and I cried silent tears until I fell back asleep, listening to her and Ben's breathing.

~

I woke up to the sound of hushed talking. Rolling to my back, I wiped the sleep from my eyes. I stretched out my arms and legs, surprised to find that I was alone in Ben and Gracie's bed. It was their voices I was hearing.

"You know I love her like my own sister," Ben said from behind the drawn curtain that blocked off my view from the balcony. "But this is a special vacation for us babe."

"I know." Gracie's reply was strained.

"She can't stay here."

"I *know*."

Humiliation slammed me right in my gut. I closed my eyes together tightly, fighting back the tears of embarrassment as I realized the situation we were all now facing. I hated being the downer on my friend's tropical vacation.

Their hushed conversation continued, but I'd heard enough. I couldn't stay in this bed or this room a second longer. It'd been hard enough to crash the happy couples party already, and the conflict I was forcing between the two was a weight I couldn't bear on top of everything else. So, I rose out of bed, silently slipping on my flip flops, and I snuck out the door without a word. I didn't even bother bringing my phone. I craved solitude.

As I hit the steps, only one of my beloved parrots was sitting in the rail fencing. I analyzed the lone bird as I passed, fearing it was some kind of too late omen. "We're both waking up alone this morning I see... At least we have each oth—" The bird shook out its wings and took flight out of sight. "Or not."

"Are you still talking to birds, Molls?" Alan's amused voice echoed off the concrete walls of the stairwell.

I spun around to face him and the immediate look he registered on my face had his smile disappearing. "Fuck. What's wrong?"

Anger sliced through the sorrow. "Turns out, the issue between Eric and I wasn't my fault," I said as I leaned against the rail, needing the support as I divulged. For the shortest moment I could see Alan struggle to remember what I was talking about, but when it hit him, his budding anger was almost palpable. I continued, "It was his fault. And the two other women's that he's fucked since we've been here."

Alan threw his head, looking away abruptly as though the news physically hurt to hear. "*Rat-fucking-bastard,*" he hissed under his breath. Alan turned his sorrowed gaze back upon me, "Molly, I'm so s—"

"No, please don't," I half-begged. "I've been getting enough pity from Gracie and Ben."

"Do you want to talk?" he asked as he took a couple cautious steps down toward me.

I backed down a step as he approached. "No. No, Al, I appreciate it, but I just need to some alone time to process shit before I have to force myself to enjoy another day in fucking paradise. Please?"

Alan's face scrunched up, rather pained, as if he was asking if I was sure in my decision. He sighed, shaking his head. "Fine. You know where to find me when and if you need me. At any time. No matter what."

The watery-eyed smile I gave him was genuine. "I do," I breathed. "Thank you." Alan let me leave without a fight, without another word.

I wasn't sure where I was going or for how long I intended to walk, I just put one foot in front of the other. Unsurprisingly, I found myself at the ocean. Blessedly empty, given how early in the morning it was. There was an old couple walking along the beach and a single kayaker just off the shore. And me.

I sat directly onto the sand, not giving a damn where sand wound up, considering there was no need to worry about someone *chafing* it anymore. At that acknowledgement, I groaned, curled my arms around my shins and rested my chin in the vee of my knees. Just staring at the soft lulling of the ocean waves.

As I contemplated how I'd found myself here, I watched the old couple as they came closer and closer, hand-in-hand. They seemed so at peace. So safe in each other's tender love. I wondered how long they'd been together, the kind of life they'd shared together through the years. My ruminations led me back to thoughts of Eric and our relationship over the past year. I tried to think if there had been anything that looking back on it now would have been a sign, or some sort of red flag that I'd been too blind to see—hindsight was twenty-twenty, right? But no. There was nothing. He'd given me no indication he was capable of hurting me like this. And that, for some reason, just made me angrier with him…

With *myself*.

But the more I watched that couple, the more I thought about it; had I ever seriously considered what kind of future Eric and I had together? If I was being honest with myself, the answer was no. I hadn't given much thought to the next steps in our relationship. I'd been content with where we were at. I'd never had the chance to picture myself growing old, walking the beach hand-in-hand with Eric, so I'd never put him on that pedestal.

That thought alone was the only one that offered any kind of hope that I would be alright. Still stung like a son of a bitch, though…

"Hey Rockstar."

His voice sent a pang of emotion through me. I had no idea how he found me. I fixed the frown on my face, morphing it into a tired smile as I peeked up and over my shoulder.

"Hi Colter."

He gave me an early morning's half-grin as he dropped his belongings—a towel, his sandals, and his phone—in the sand beside me. "What are you doing out here?"

"Enjoying some fresh air." It was only a partial lie. Trying to remain casual, I asked, "What are *you* doing out here?"

"I come out here for a swim in the morning." Colter turned his gaze out to the ocean and pulled his shirt up and over his head, shaking out his hair as he tossed it to his pile. The way my breath caught was entirely inappropriate, uncalled for. And a bit jarring. My eyes roamed over his pecks dappled with golden chest hair, his abs and the lower muscles that formed a vee that faded beneath the band of his swim shorts. This was wrong, this blatant perusal. Somewhere deep inside, my better judgement was screaming at me that I was mentally and emotionally unstable right now and this—*this* was my best friend.

Colter's low chuckle knocked me back into reality. "Molls."

"Mhm?" I said, whipping my face back to the ocean, a blush burning my cheeks. *What in the* actual *fuck?* I couldn't stop the wince. And he must've seen it.

"Molly, what's wrong?" Cautious. He was now approaching me with too much gentleness.

The question only served to throw my lingering pain and sorrow back in my face. And shame for how I'd just so flippantly eyed my friend like I wanted to *taste* him. Somewhere between my vomiting and my crying last night, I'd crossed some important wires in my head. Because I was losing it. But, like I'd done with Gracie and Alan, I figured getting it all out now in a rush was better than holding back. We were all stuck together on this island for the next five days, I wasn't going to be able to hide my heartbreak or the obvious fact that I was without Eric for long. And I...I didn't want to.

"Is it about last night?" Colter dropped into the sand beside me, so close our shoulders brushed. The contact issued an unwarranted tingling sensation that shouldn't have had an effect on me. But it did. And it wasn't what I was expecting given how I'd just been eyeballing him not two seconds ago. No, instead of rousing, it was calming. Grounding.

"Yeah. It is." I could see Colter shift beside me in my peripheral, but I couldn't look at him. So, I just glared out into the ocean as I went on, "Eric cheated on me with one of the women from the bachelorette party at the nightclub the first night here." I took a pause to breathe and keep myself calm.

"Fuck—"

"—I'm not done."

"*Fuck.*"

"Then he pretended to be sick all day so he could avoid me...and sleep with *Imelda.*" As soon as I said it, a glaring realization drew the air out of my lungs; Colter had been with Imelda on day one. *Fuck, fuck, fuck.*

Colter went deadly silent. I bit my lower lip as I realized what I'd just done. I had held nothing back as I laced Imelda's name with every ounce of revulsion I was capable of.

"Eric's a *fucking idiot*," he said darkly.

"Sorry," I whispered weakly, "I know you were with her only two days ago—"

"*Sorry*? You do not have to apologize. That is not even remotely important right now, Molly," Colter warned. He ran his hands down his face and spoke from behind his palm as he massaged his temples, "Where is the fucker?" His tone was full of wrathful promise. "I'd like to have a few words with him," he added, mumbling under his breath.

My eyes bulged. "Absolutely not."

"How did you find out?"

I regaled him with the story of how it'd been a series of little moments that accumulated to one big moment as I caught the scent of Imelda's perfume that had been haunting me while at the casino party. I told him what I'd walked in on. And how I'd so quickly and easily walked right back out.

"So yeah," I sighed, laying back on my elbows. "I slept with Gracie and Ben in their room last night and now...now I don't know what to do. I guess, I'll see if I can check into another room," I mused.

Throughout the entire thing, I'd focused solely on the waves crashing against the shore, but when I was met by silence, I finally looked over at Colter who was sitting there, almost frozen except for the way his chest heaved with steady, deep breaths. His eyes met mine and there was a flash of something there as he opened his mouth, "I have an extra bed in my room. Stay with me."

Awareness swept over me, all the way down to my toes buried in the sand. "What?"

"My room is a double queen. It was the last one available on our floor when we booked the trip. The extra bed—it's yours," Colter explained all too simply.

That was a very kind offer...but had he really thought that one through? "Oh, I don't know Colter. That doesn't sound like the best idea."

"Why not?" This time he turned his whole torso toward me as he leaned over to hear exactly what I had to say.

A nervous laugh escaped me. "Well for starters, it's kind of hard for you to be having *fun* on your vacation when there's another woman sleeping in your room. Doubt you'll find any potential *lovers* willing to share your space."

"To use your words; *for starters*, you underestimate my game." The nerve of this man. Still, I couldn't help but crack a smile as he continued, "And lastly, there's no way I'm going to let my friend fend for herself for the rest of the week. Save your money. Now…what other excuses do you have?"

How about the fact that I was heartbroken woman, who's no doubt bound to have a few more cry sessions before the end of this vacation? How about the fact that I'd already been struggling to keep my eyes in appropriate areas while looking at Colter himself? "I don't want to have to share a bathroom."

Lamest. Excuse. Ever.

Colter laughed. "Molls…we've known each other since we were seven. I'm perfectly aware of, and used to, all your bodily functions—"

"Okay, stop," I groaned.

"It's not like we haven't shared bathrooms before…I mean that one week when my parents took us all camping in high school for that one music festival—"

"Colter!" I laughed. I *actually* laughed. "I said stop. Fine. I'll stay with you. Please just stop."

"You had to go so bad in the middle of the night and were too afraid to get out of the tent alone, so you dragged Al and I with you—"

"I'm going to go drown myself now, 'kay? Thanks." I stood up, brushing the sand off my damp backside. Colter laughed and I knew he'd jumped up after me as I heard his footsteps thud across the beach. I waded into the water until my legs disappeared under the churching of saltwater, sand, and seafoam.

Colter's splashing steps from behind silenced as stopped he just shy of beside me. "I'm sorry, Molly."

He didn't need to say what he was sorry about. We both knew he was talking about Eric.

I couldn't vocalize a response, so I just nodded my head. I let a few more silent minutes go by as Colter sidled up next to me, his arm brushing mine once more. His touch was comforting. So was his silence. And there, standing in the turquoise water of the island of Cozumel with my oldest friend beside me, I almost felt a little bit like maybe the world hadn't just fallen apart at my feet.

NINE

After several attempts, I'd managed to convince Colter that I was fine. I'd only just talked him into completing that swim he'd come down here for in the first place, by promising I'd sit my butt back down by his stuff and keep vigil until he was done, where we then planned to both head back up to his—our—room to get my stuff settled in. I watched him, and the waves, and the fading backs of the old couple for about ten minutes before I laid flat on my back in the sand, staring at the clouds.

Turning my head, I saw Colter's shirt laying there and reached over, shaking it out, and then rolled it into a ball to place under my head to spare my hair. It smelled like him, like his cologne and his skin and the ocean breeze we'd been surrounded in over the course of two short days. Even a faint smell of his terrible smoking habit lingered, though I had yet to see him smoke while we were here. But it didn't stop my toes from curling into the sand as I pressed my bent knees in together. His smell was familiar, comforting. Reminded me of home.

I'd just been about to slide my eyelids shut when I caught sight of something above. Two parrots, flying side by side in the sky. I smiled to the heavens, listening to their calling as they landed in the tree line behind me.

The bird's freedom, the fresh air, and the smell of home; it was just the thing to remind me that life would move on. That I would move on. That, as Gracie promised, everything would be okay.

~

From what I could tell, it was nothing in particular that had woken me. I just sensed the world beyond my closed eye lids, first hearing the sound of the ocean. My eyes opened as birdsong rang out in the background. I looked up and blinked against the sunshine.

"How was your nap?" His voice was soft and carried an edge of amusement.

I turned my head, shielding my eyes against the higher morning sun. "Colter?"

I sat up first to my elbows and scanned my surroundings, then rose to the palms of my hands and faced him just as he was taking a drag off a cigarette. He drawled, "Morning Rockstar."

I frowned. "How long was I out?"

Colter shrugged one casual shoulder as he blew out smoke. "Maybe twenty minutes from when I first saw you lay down."

He'd been watching me?

"You could have woken me up," I noted as I twisted to grab his shirt. I shook out the sand and offered it to him. He set it beside his hip on top of the wet beach towel he sat upon.

"Figured you could use the rest." He flicked off his ash.

"Where did you get that?" I asked, running my fingers through my hair to fluff it out.

"My pack was wrapped in the towel," Colter said as he reached beside his opposite hip and then tossed over the opened pack of cigarettes. I stared at the pack, then his mouth. My jaw set in a hard line.

"Hasn't anybody told you that those things are bad for you?" I scolded. I slipped my hand over his towel and snatched the box. Turning it over in my hand, inspecting it.

Colter emitted a wry, close-mouthed laugh. "Several times, yes…and I have a feeling somebody is going to tell me again right now."

I whipped my head at him and tried to force away the smile, biting down on the inside of my cheek. "Yeah, well...that's because it's true."

He froze with the cigarette halfway to his mouth as we looked at one another. "I know I should quit."

I raised my brows as if to say, *ya think?* "So quit."

"That easy to you, huh?"

I bounced my shoulders. "Sure it is. You just decide that's what you want. And you do it."

Colter made a humming sound of contemplation as he narrowed his eyes on me, calculating.

Heat and awareness crept up my chest and neck to my cheeks. "What?"

"How about," he started, taking another long, heavy pull off his cigarette. He held in the smoke as he said around it, "we make a deal."

He exhaled as he paused to let me consider.

Colter had that look on his face that said his gears were turning. So, I was treading carefully as I slowly asked, "What kind of deal?"

He snuffed out the cigarette in the sand and pocketed the remnants. I recoiled with surprise—he hadn't even smoked half of it yet. "I will promise not to smoke for the rest of this vacation...if you promise to try to forget about Eric and just have some fun. You're in Mexico with your friends. Enjoy yourself...there'll be time for tears when we get back to the frigid ice hell of Michigan." He bit his lip as his smile turned mischievous, and as he spoke the next words, I knew why, *"Just decide that's what you want. And do it."*

Eric. Holy shit. Up until he'd mentioned his name, I'd already forgotten about Eric. Now having him brought back to the forefront of my mind, the broken animal inside me rattled its cage. Did Colter really think it was that easy to just forget? But he'd so expertly turned my words right back on me. *Decide that's what you want. And do it.* Sitting here next to Colter with his deal still hanging in the air, I threw a metaphorical blanket over that caged animal and pressed my lips together in determination. "Deal."

The crooked smile he flashed me in return lit a thrill of excitement in my bones. Just like that, I was smiling again. Only mere hours after having had my heart trampled on.

~

I stood outside of room 301 and had the strangest reaction as I lifted my hand to knock. Something felt a little nerve-racking with Colter standing at my back as I prepared to ask my friends to grab my stuff so I could move in with him. I forced a deep breath into my lungs and followed through on the almost too-loud knock. *Calm down. He's your best friend. It's not a big deal.*

But, as Gracie opened the door, pleasantly surprised to see me standing there with Colter as I explained the rooming situation he and I'd agreed on, she seemed completely unsurprised by the idea. If she didn't see anything wrong with Colter and I shacking up—even after the nipple debacle—then I didn't see why I had any reason to feel nervous about it. Actually, she—and Ben, especially—seemed rather relieved to not have had to deal with the messy situation of kicking me out of their room so they could enjoy their vacation in privacy.

I'd collected all of my things from the bathroom that were still sprawled out all over the place like a bomb had gone off in an Ulta store, and was just heading for the main area when Gracie passed the bathroom doorway, wheeling my luggage directly into Colter's waiting hand.

"Thank you Colter, for being such a good friend." Gracie emphasized the good friend part, and I halted in the door way, wondering if my ears had picked up on that correctly.

"Whatever Molly needs." He gave her a tightlipped smile.

They noticed me watching in the doorway and shifted to give me space to exit as they wiped the peculiar looks off their faces. Gracie beamed at me for a brief moment before she remembered why we were in this situation in the first place. "It's going to be okay, Molls. I'll be here whenever you need to talk, okay? I love you."

"Of course. I love you, too," I said as she pulled me into a warm hug. I went to let go, but she doubled down, squeezing me a little tighter and my heart clenched in my chest. God, I loved her. Then I felt a hand softly pat my back. Ben.

"We all love you, Moll," he said, and Gracie finally let me go as I turned to face him. My heart softened as I walked into one of his spectacularly awkward hugs, returning the sentiment.

I straightened and turned to Colter, flattening my palms on the thin fabric of my pajama shorts to straighten up my appearance. His smile was soft, warm. His blue-green eyes were bright as he'd watched me with our friends. "You ready, Rockstar?"

"Yes," I sighed, yet it was with a smile. Side by side, Colter and I made to cross the hall to our room, but Gracie stopped her door from clicking shut.

"Hey!" she called out after us, and we both turned toward each other and looked to her. "Meet for breakfast in twenty? Afterwards, Ben and I have something exciting planned for the day! Wear your swimsuits under your clothes." She let out a giddy shriek of secretive excitement as she slammed the door before either Colter, or I, could say another word.

We moved toward his door, and I eyed my luggage. "I can take that."

Colter huffed a laugh. "It's fine, I've got it."

I pursed my lips as he stepped between me and the door so he could unlock it. A dizzying sensation hit me as he swung the door open and angled to me to let me pass through first. A half smile pulled at the corner of my lips as I passed under his arm.

The balcony drapes had been pulled back to reveal the day's sun and the wide expanse of the trees beyond. It wasn't an ocean view, but it didn't matter. It was still incredible, and I absent-mindedly dragged my flip-flopped feet across the tile floor as I gawked in awe. There was a jacuzzi tub tiled into the concrete balcony that overlooked the sun-kissed leaves of green below and as I slid open the glass door, still precariously balancing all of my haphazardly stacked toiletries, I realized that, perhaps, Colter had had the best view all along...

The pandemonium was back, and from our perch, you could see the bright green of the birds as they chattered about, socializing, flying, walking sideways along their branches and ruffling their wings.

"My birds!" I whispered excitedly as I admired them. "Wow."

I turned to shoot Colter a look of excitement and found him smirking as he leaned his shoulder on the doorframe of the balcony's sliding glass door, arms crossed over his chest. The posture drew attention to the muscles in his arms, and I reflexively tightened my grip on my belongings. My hairbrush was squeezed out and clacked obnoxiously to the floor.

I'd made a start to pick it up, but Colter beat me to it. He swiped it and took a step in front of me. A very close step in front of me. I froze.

"Why don't I put these away for you," he offered, as he plucked my toothbrush from my fist.

"You don't have to do that, I can...do it..." But he continued pulling item after item out of my arms.

"I've got it, Molly. Enjoy your birds. It's not like I haven't noticed how much they fascinate you."

Really, I thought, as he stacked my things in his capable arms; my hair straightener, curling iron, toiletry bag, toothbrush and make-up bag. He made it look too easy. I'd opened my mouth in protest, but he simply winked at me and backed away into the room then through it, disappearing into the bathroom. My gaze dropped to the beds. The one closest to the door was untouched, the one closest to the balcony was unmade, disheveled.

I wondered if the sheets smelled as good as his t-shirt. The thought sent a bolt of equal parts longing, shame, and downright confusion through me. I shook the thoughts and feelings from my head and rounded the tub to get to the railing of the balcony so I could get a better view of the Yucatan Amazons. I rested my elbows on the wrought iron and basked in the sun that warmed my face.

I hadn't heard him sneak up on me as Colter suddenly entered my peripheral, slinging his wet swim shorts over the railing. I spun to look at him so fast I gave myself a small case of whiplash. I slammed my eyes shut and I *wanted* to blame the wince of pain on the whiplash. But Colter would never know it was because I'd caught the shortest glimpse of him in nothing but a towel tucked around his waist, far, far too low on his hips. The knot of the towel was a few mere centimeters from where a dark blond dusting of hair disappeared beyond.

"You alright?" Colter asked, his tone much too innocent in comparison to the pictures I was trying to burn from my head.

I turned my face back into the sun. "I'm fine. Maybe a little hungover from last night still, is all." *Lie.*

"Well then let's get into the shower so we can make it to breakfast and feed that hangover." He clapped his hands together as I shot him a look. He smirked. "You want to go first or should I?"

I was white-knuckling the rail. "You look halfway there. You go first."

"Promise not to use all the hot water," he assured as he squeezed behind me, grasping my upper arms as he did so.

My knees felt weak, but I held myself together as he passed, finally letting me go, once again disappearing into the room. When I was certain I was completely alone as the shower water began, I took a deep breath into my mouth and exhaled out of my nose.

Something inside of me was waking up and for the love of all things holy I needed to smother it the fuck down with a fierce vengeance. Because I knew what was going on. I was thirsting after Colter after a few short *hours* of being released from the longest relationship I'd ever been in. And that was wrong. So wrong. It was unfair to me, and it was certainly unfair to Colter who was innocent in all this. I couldn't understand the chaotic mix of emotions that the last forty-eight hours had unleashed on me.

Colter was a rock in the ever-changing flow of my entire life. He'd been there since we were kids, always pushing back against me as we navigated adolescence. He'd been there for me during past breakups, but it'd never been like this. It'd never been like this because Colter and I had never felt this way towards the other.

We were strictly platonic friends. That much had been absolutely clear from the moment I turned twelve and overheard him at a football game saying he wouldn't touch me with a ten foot pole to a particularly rough group of friends he'd started to hang out with during junior high. By high school, he'd come to his senses and found his way back to Ben, Alan, Cam, and I, ditching the group that we would later learn broke apart as half of them wound up in jail for a slew of offenses that ranged from minor to felonious.

I never told him I'd heard him say those things about me. At the time they'd hurt me, pissed me off, sure, but I'd been too young then to maturely understand that he found me— the girl who was practically his sister—completely unappealing and unfit for his attention.

And boy oh boy, if giving his attention hadn't become quite the problem once we'd hit high school. There was hardly a girl in school who hadn't been vying for his attention after he grew five inches over the summer after freshman year. Colter had never had any serious girlfriends throughout that time, but he definitely had girl *friends*. And it only escalated in junior year when he'd bought himself that obnoxious Jeep, squealing tires every Monday morning with a new coat of the weekend's off-roading mud all over it. The girls at our school had loved his rugged wildness. I'd found it annoying. Especially because I was the only girl who knew just how much that wildness was a mask. Colter was a sweet, kind boy as a child. And when it was just the two of us, he still was. Yet, he'd paraded himself around like the Class A bad boy so much that by the time we graduated, it was who he'd actually become. I'd learned to love him through it all the same, even if it still sometimes annoyed me to this day.

After he'd made it a couple of years into his apprenticeship with the electrical company, he'd started to settle down some. But not much. Looking back on it now, it wasn't until his mom passed away half a year ago that he'd seemed like he might throw away the fast life altogether. That was until he'd taken that out-of-state job in Tennessee. Then our friend group chats were filled with the proof of revelry in all his wild escapades in Nashville every weekend.

To be fair, after I entered college, I'd finally found my wilder side and could pretty much wholly understand why he nose-dived into the lifestyle. There was something about being a young adult, unleashed on the world, which welcomed all to let loose a good-time monster from within. I'd quickly learned which alcohols would make me happy, which ones would make me sad, and which ones turned me into the Rockstar like that fateful birthday night. Funny thing, it was tequila that brought out the most wildness in me.

And here I was, in tequila's motherland.

"Alright, Rockstar. It's all your yours." I hadn't even heard Colter turn off the shower or leave the bathroom as I'd lost myself in thought. I turned to face the room and found him in just that damned towel again as he lifted his suitcase to the edge of the bed to rifle through it—except this time, his body was dewy with the shower's steam. I swallowed.

"I shouldn't be long," I managed to say as I gave him a wide berth on the way to the bathroom. He'd only absentmindedly nodded in response, solely focused on his task at hand.

The bathroom air was thick with the steam of his shower that smelled like his bodywash. I shut the door behind me and leaned against it as I breathed the scent in deeply. Fuck, I was in trouble. A tightening in my chest came so fast and so hard it almost *hurt.*

I pushed off the door and wiped a clear streak through the steamed-over mirror. It was the first time I'd looked at myself since washing my face last night after having cried my eyes out for hours on end. I looked thoroughly haggard. Completely bare without an ounce of make-up on, every freckle, every blush of color, every line of worry about my behavior was stark as I looked at my reflection. I'd never been the kind to compare myself to other women, at least not in a self-conscious way, but as I looked at myself it became so painfully clear that I was no Imelda. I would never pull two different guys in the span of twenty-four hours—that thought alone flipped my stomach as I reminded myself that I didn't *want* to. Ok, well that wasn't exactly honest because one of those two guys had been my boyfriend at the time and I would have certainly been open to sleeping with him.

Colter, on the other hand…

Busying myself, I stripped and jumped into the shower.

TEN

Ben and Gracie most definitely had something fun planned, we realized, as the six of us stared at the four brightly colored Jeep Wranglers that sat parked at the entrance of the resort. Javier popped out of the first one—it was a bright baby blue with black accents.

"*Buenos dias, amigos!*" he exclaimed, flashing that bright smile at us, his eyes shielded behind huge sunglasses. He wore an equally bright blue shirt tucked into khaki beach shorts and a matching blue lanyard of the Jeep's keys hung around his neck. We all offered our hellos in our own way as he rounded the front of the vehicle. He reached into the Jeep's open passenger window and pulled out another three brightly colored lanyard sets of keys.

"Today, you're scheduled for a Jeep tour of Punta Sur Eco Beach Park. It will be about a half hour drive, and I will be your guide. Each couple will have a Jeep of their own, so who wants the first beauty?" Javier explained quickly as he walked up to the second Jeep in line. It was a candy apple red.

"Ours!" Gracie piped up, bounding forward to collect her key.

Javier laughed at her eagerness, Ben—always in a permanent state of awe with her—smiled.

"And the *amarillo* one?" Javier dangled the lanyard in the air enticingly.

"Seeing as the last one is orange," Alan started as he walked forward, shooting Colter a look from under the lip of his straw sunhat, "I already know Colter's going to fight for that one. So, yeah. We'll take the yellow."

I giggled, sneaking a glance at Colter over my shoulder as he gave Alan a look that said, *you're damn right you will.*

Gracie appeared at my side then, startling me. She gave me an apologetic smile and then lowered her voice so only I could hear, and probably Colter, who was still close behind me. "One of the Jeeps were for you and Eric. Colter was supposed to go with Alan and Cam but seeing as there's probably no way Colter's going to pass up driving a Jeep around today, you're more than welcome to ride with me and Ben. Or you can stick with Colter." She shrugged nonchalantly.

Apparently she had not spoken quiet enough as Javier sidled up to drop the orange lanyard into Colter's outstretched hand. "Or the *dama bonita* can ride with me."

That seemed more fun than third-wheeling it with Ben and Gracie or being trapped in a tin can with Colter while in my fragile state of lunacy. I opened my mouth to agree but Colter swung past me, snatching my hand in the process and led me towards his orange Jeep. "Not a chance. Rockstar's with me."

I threw a look over my shoulder at my friends. Alan and Cam were already in their vehicle, Ben still had his googly eyes on Gracie, but Gracie and Javier both looked at me with smiles of what seemed like deception. As we slowed and Colter opened my door for me, I had half a mind to question if this little scenario had somehow been orchestrated.

~

The drive to the beach park was actually really nice. We'd rolled all the windows down and Colter had blasted the radio to a lively Spanish music station, and we spent the whole time vibing and laughing. It was perfectly innocent and wonderfully enjoyable.

At the first meeting point, we parked the Jeeps in a row and grouped at the tailgate of Javier's.

"Good to see everyone's made it," he announced jokingly,

"The Punta Sur Eco Beach Park is as the name implies—it is an ecological park. Here you will find a wide variety of island wildlife, including our first exhibition…crocodiles." Looking at all of our faces as though noting we were all in fact in attendance, Javier set off on a brisk pace backwards toward a boardwalk entrance across the white gravel parking lot where people were funneling in and out of. "Right this way, *amigos!*"

Our crew fell in line, Ben and Gracie at the lead, Colter and I in the middle, and Alan and Cam bringing up the rear. We rounded the back of a vehicle that was parked in the entrance, and I wasn't paying attention as I stepped out a little too far beyond it. I hadn't realized another tour group of Jeeps was barreling through and I gasped.

Colter's hand snagged around my hip bone as he came from behind, pulling me out of harm's way. We stumbled a few steps, and he grasped my hips with both hands as we steadied, my feet clumsy between his, my back pressed firmly against his front. The adrenaline rush of the almost-catastrophe mixed with the rush of warmth at his tight grasp. "Holy shit," I said through a breathy laugh.

"You alright there, Rockstar?" Colter's mouth was right at my ear and a zing of sensation hit my neck as his breath caressed it.

I clapped my hands on top of his and pried them off. "Fine. I'm fine. Thank you."

Javier, Ben and Gracie hadn't noticed anything, thankfully. But as I casually sneaked a glance at Alan and Cam behind me, I knew they'd seen what just happened and each wore different facial expressions. Cam looked at me like I was just a plain ol' idiot for not being aware of my surroundings. I stuck my tongue out at him. He stuck his out back. But Alan…Alan's narrowed eyes darted between Colter and I, the ghost of a smirk across his open mouth.

My nostrils flared and I faced forward, straightening my spine and picking up my pace. The mangroves rose high on each side of the narrow boardwalk, creating a branchy tunnel. We fell into single file as we passed those on their way out of the boardwalk, and several times Colter slid his hand around the small of my back to maneuver back and forth from being at my side and then behind. I would have yelled at him to quit it if it wasn't such a natural Colter thing for him to do. He'd always been a handsy person. It'd never bothered me before and it felt out of place to start being bothered by it now. But I was bothered by it. Hot and bothered.

By the time the mangroves parted into the wide lagoon, and we entered the large deck that led to a scenic tower, I was flushed, shoving towards the open air to get some much-needed space. Ben had been the first to spot a croc and everyone followed him across the deck to catch a glimpse. I held back to collect myself.

The lagoon *was* incredible. Flat and wide, it was obvious the nature preserve stretched on for miles. I walked off to the left to hang on to the wooden rail. Below in the water I could see the sandy lagoon floor and a spattering of tiny jellyfish that had attached themselves to the bottom. Where the mangroves reached the water, small crabs skittered across the exposed roots.

"Well, hello little *Rockstar*." Alan rested his elbows on the rail beside me, pressing his shoulder into mine.

I took a deep breath and involuntarily rolled my eyes at this pointed use of Colter's nickname. Only Colter called me that. It felt silly coming from Alan's lips.

"Hey," I replied coolly.

"You're looking a bit *flushed*. Too much sun? Have you been drinking enough water? Do you need to borrow my hat?"

"*Alan*." The warning in my tone was evident as I stole a glance over his shoulder to make sure the rest of the group was far enough away.

"If I didn't know any better, I'd say this newfound proximity between you and Colter is having an effect on you. I'm just trying to decide if it's a pleasant or an adverse reaction."

I stifled a grumble. "Alan, I just split with my long-term boyfriend. Last. Night. And come on. It's *Colter*."

"Ah." Alan grimaced. "So adverse reaction, then?"

"No." I said it before I thought better of it. Alan's jaw dropped. "Shut your mouth before you accidentally swallow some endangered insect or something," I hissed as I nudged in his shoulder.

He chortled. "So the big bad wolf is catching the attention of the Rockstar. Never thought I'd see the day. And so fast after coming off of Eric—girl you are one crazy—"

"I'm going to feed myself to the crocodiles now. *Bye*." I pushed off the rail forcibly.

"Molly!" he called after me, laughing. But I was already halfway to the group who were waiting at the bottom of the stairs for people to finish their descent from the scenic tower. I skirted past the outgoers and slid to the front of my group, slipping my arm through Gracie's.

"Hey you!" She perked up at my presence.

"Hi!" I was a little too cheerful. Her eyes widened with her smile.

"I was beginning to wonder if you and Alan we're going to hop in with the alligators," she teased as she looked back down to where Alan was just beginning to take a step up the stairs.

"They're crocs, baby," Ben corrected with a wink from her other side.

"Right!" It wasn't often I'd catch Gracie being the one to make doe eyes at Ben, but here it was, in the bright light of day. I was beginning to wonder why on earth the two of them insisted on inviting all of us a year ago when we booked this trip, if they were so smitten with each other. Why wouldn't they have just enjoyed each other's company alone? Not that I was complaining. Though, I realized, a part of me could get away with a complaint or two these days…I did just catch my ex-lover with at least two other women…that I knew of.

We reached the top of the scenic tower, and the view confirmed my earlier musings. The park stretched for miles. It was amazing. I walked to another edge to check out the view of the ocean just a few hundred yards in the distance. A large white lighthouse with a bronze roof rose high above, even higher than the scenic tower. I wondered what *that* view must look like.

"We're headed there next." Ben suddenly said as he approached my side. I looked around, expecting to see Gracie in tow, but she was still standing by Javier, Cam and Colter. Alan finally reached the top of the steps and took off toward our group. It'd been a while since I'd talked to Ben one on one.

"Oh yeah?" Excitement flooded my tone.

He nodded as his eyes narrowed against the wind and sun that flooded in from that direction. "How are you doing, Moll?"

Well. I'd expected to get a talking to at some point today, but my bets hadn't been on Ben. Yet, a part of me was glad it was him. He was the least judgmental of all.

"I don't really know." The admission hung between us as a seagull screeched through its flight path overhead. "When it gets quiet, the...the pain is there. The humiliation."

"I feel like there's a *but* coming," he prodded, hopeful.

"But it could be worse," I mused. "I could be back in the dread of midwinter in Michigan, soothing a broken heart. But I'm here. In this beautiful place with beautiful people." I looked him in the eyes then. My smile was real—the small spark of happiness inside—it was real. He mirrored my smile, and I noticed something about him today seemed extra...handsome. He'd shaved. His hair was styled nicely, especially for a day roving around in a Jeep. I took in the soft pink polo shirt he wore. It matched Gracie's pink sundress that was flapping delicately in the wind. It brought out a brightness in his deep drown eyes. "Beautiful people," I said again as I placed my hand to his cheek.

"Okay, now," he laughed nervously, shoving my hand away gently. "You haven't even had a drink yet today and you're getting all emotional."

Feigning offense, I playfully swatted at him, "Just take the compliment, you butthead."

He shocked me then, pulling me in for a surprisingly warm hug, coming from him. "Fine." A pause. "There's something I need from you."

"Ah, so that is why you're being so nice," I teased.

He rolled his eyes as he let me go. "When we get to the lighthouse, can you round up the boys and distract them in the museum? I'd like to take Gracie to the top, just her and I."

My curiosity rocketed. He saw the question forming in my eyes.

"Mm. Nope." He shook his head. "No questions. Can I just…can I count on you?"

"Of course you can," I assured. But it didn't stop me from eyeballing him as if something on his person was going to show me all the answers.

"Stop that."

"Stop what?"

"Analyzing me like that. Just please," he took a step away, "babysit the boys for me?"

I noticed it then. Their *matching* outfits. Her freshly manicured nails. His nervous fidgeting. The skip in her step.

Holy shit, I mouthed.

His eyes bulged and he brought one finger to his lips, begging me to shut up.

I spun around and looked at the lighthouse. "Holy shit," I whispered aloud.

~

I was still squirming giddily as Colter and I hopped back into the Jeep ready to start our convoy to the lighthouse.

"What's gotten into you?" He sounded happy to see me so…joyful. Colter started the engine, and the noise started another leap of excitement in my chest.

I smiled sweetly. "Nothing." One brow of his slammed down, skeptical. "I just…really like crocodiles. The baby ones are so…cute."

Amused incredulity; that was the adorably hilarious look he gave me then. He put one hand on the back of my seat and used the other in one fluid spinning maneuver as he backed out of our parking spot—the action took over my full attention, making me forget what we were even talking about for a brief second. *What was it about that move that made girls go stupid?*

"Whatever gets you smiling again, Rockstar," Colter said as he watched over his shoulder.

I had to look away then as that one line had a trembling affect over me. That was…that was incredibly sweet. And it weighed heavy on my heart.

Thankfully the drive to the lighthouse was a short one. In a handful of minutes, we'd parallel parked our Jeeps in a line beside a bathroom facility—the lighthouse towered on the other side of the open area, the nautical museum offset to the left.

I'd taken a deep breath to announce, rather loudly, that I would like to go see the museum and they all should join, but Gracie snagged me. "Come to the bathroom with me?"

I glanced at Ben who subtly nodded, but his eyes said everything; *Keep it together. Don't say a word.*

Everyone else chimed in, agreeing that now was a good time for a bathroom break and we split our separate ways.

The bathrooms were open and airy with all the windows propped open. We quickly claimed our stalls and I sat to do my business.

"Isn't this place wonderful?" Gracie chatted from her stall beside me. She'd never been bathroom shy. Neither had I.

"This is really cool!" I agreed with overenthusiasm, smiling secretively to myself. "And it's just such a *beautiful* day."

"Oh gosh, I know!" Her toilet flushed. "Honestly, you seem happier today than I thought you would be. I'm so glad."

I flushed my own and stepped to the sink beside Gracie's as we continued talking through the mirrors. "Why wouldn't I be happy? I'm with the people I love." She shot me a soft, pitying look. "Oh *don't.* I already promised Colter I'd forget all about Eric for the rest of the trip. I can cry all I want when I get home."

"Colter got you to promise that?" She sounded impressed.

"Yes. We made a deal." She leveled me with a look that begged I go on. "If I try my best to have a good time with my friends, he will not smoke another cigarette while on this vacation."

Gracie finished washing her hands and turned to look at me straight on. "He made that deal with you?"

"You sound surprised."

"Uh, yeah. Colter's been an on-again-off-again smoker for nearly a decade. He only quits when he's with a girl he likes who doesn't appreciate the habit. And even then he dumps them by the time he's jonesing for another one."

"Well, he's only got to hold out another five days."

"Mhm." she hummed as she passed, flicking at me with her dripping hands.

I scoffed as I followed after her, ripping off a piece of paper towel to wipe away the water from my arm. Gracie hurried out the door without another word about it.

The glaring sunshine blinded me as we stepped out of the bathroom. The boys were already outside waiting as we exited.

There was a lull in their conversation and now seemed as good of a time as any to get the ball rolling, so, making a show of it, I bounded up to Javier's side. Oddly enough, he had somehow procured a drone in his hand, and it was then I realized he must be playing a role in this. "Javier, what's that little building there?" I already knew.

Javier played along. "That is the Nautical Museum. It's a neat little place if you want to learn about shipwrecks, pirates, and sailing knots, among other things."

I laid it on thick, "Oh, pirates? That sounds cool. Come on guys, let's go check it out!"

It worked so well that even Gracie had started to follow after me, but Ben gently took her hand, stopping her. He whispered something to her, and she nodded. He addressed the group as we walked off, "Hey we're going to hit the lighthouse first. Meet up with you guys in a few, okay?"

The boys didn't notice a thing. Alan had just raised a lazy hand as if to say *yeah, yeah, whatever.*

I schooled myself facing forward, giving Gracie and Ben my back, and stayed at the back of the group, because if either party saw my face they'd probably be worried about my sanity. Regardless of my bruised heart, I was over the freaking moon with excitement for Ben and Gracie as they made their way to quite literally climb the steps to the next phase of their stupidly wonderful little love story.

Inside the museum was surprisingly dark and cool. Ocean breeze blasted through the wide-open doors and windows. The knick-knacks, ropes, miniature boats in glass bottles and sail diagrams everywhere were interesting enough on their own, but as our smaller group wove in and out of the exhibits, I stuck to the walls where I could steal a glance at the lighthouse beyond through every window we passed. If Gracie and Ben were up there now, I wouldn't be able to see them from where we were at. I frowned as I looked at the beach and noticed Javier at the bottom of the lighthouse, his head straight up in the air, keeping a hawk's eye on the drone that flew circles around the top.

I couldn't be certain, but I thought I maybe heard a feminine scream of delight over the sound of the waves crashing into the breakwater beyond the lighthouse.

"What're you looking at?" The voice was close to my ear, and I jumped, knocking my knee into a display table of old Captain's logs from centuries past. Straightening, I backed away from the window I'd nearly been sticking my head out of. Colter chuckled.

"Nothing. Well—the lighthouse. I'm about ready to ditch this place and go climb it myself."

Colter crossed his arms over his crisp, white t-shirted chest—again, the contrast of the white against his deeply tanned skin was eye-catching, distracting. "So parrots, crocodiles, and lighthouses. Those things get ya going, do they?" He was thoroughly amused.

I wrung my hands behind my back and took a step backward so I could keep an eye on the lighthouse through the window as I carried on. "Not just any parrot. Specifically, the two Yucatan Amazons that frequent the stairwell at the resort. And it's *baby* crocs. And the lighthouse...well yeah, lighthouses are just cool by default."

He followed in step as I continued blindly walking backwards through the museum, making agreeable facial expressions to all my little corrections to his previous statement. He kept pace.

"And how do you feel about bindings?" Colter asked, his eyes darkening, his voice low and packing a punch that sent the muscles in my belly jolting tightly.

"W-what?" I stammered, my breath hitching as I forgot all about the lighthouse. Even as the wind gusted through the open windows, it suddenly felt like it was a thousand degrees in the tiny museum. *Where were Alan and Cam?*

"Knots. Ties. Restraints," he rattled off a multitude of

examples, his voice somehow growing darker with each one.

"Why would you ask something like that?" I breathed shakily as Colter suddenly lengthened his gait, swallowing up the distance between us with his long legs.

"Because you're about—" Colter shot forward, wrapping both his arms around me, pulling me into him as he bolted us down to the spot. "To crash into a display case full of them."

The amount of liquid fire that had shot through my veins had my heart pounding, my skin prickling, and my palms sweating. It was *that* instantaneous. I leaned back a little in his embrace to peek over my shoulder and almost smacked my face into the glass. Sure enough, there were about two dozen examples of rope in nautical knots arranged on a tier within the case with little name tags denoting each one. "Holy knots!" I gasped.

I could feel the rumble of the laughter in his chest all the way to my traitorously curling toes as he looked down at me, "Holy knots?"

I loosed a breath I'd been holding and wiggled in his grip, trying to unlock my pinned arms. "You can let me go now, Colter." My voice pitched as I realized I'd effectively rubbed my breasts into him.

"What's the magic word?" he murmured darkly as he brought his lips to my ear, his breath dancing along my cheek.

A shudder took over my body and I blushed because I knew he felt it too. My brain quit working, skipping along several different words that shot through my head that made absolutely no sense; *knot, parrot, mangroves, dice, cigarette, lighthouse, lips, bodies. Pressed together. Holy knots. Holy fuck!* My knees gave out— *What had he asked me?* —my eyes searched around for something, anything as I pled my mind to say something that wasn't wildly inappropriate. I looked to the heavens praying for help, "Sail!"

Colter—who had taken my weight after my knees gave— set me gingerly on my feet. He let me go, his hands hovering around me to make sure I was steady before he studied my face, my body language. I couldn't stop my eyes from darting between him and the ceiling, where a small old boat sail was strung up like a canopy overhead. *Sail?! The magic word I thought to come up with was* sail*? Good Lord almighty…*

"I mean," He paused to chuckle as he eyed the sail, his head tipped back, his neck stretched long as I watched his throat work, "I was looking for *please*, but…I guess sail will have do."

He looked back down at me then, amused and seemingly unbothered by whatever the fuck that was that just went down. This…this was becoming a repeat occurrence. This wasn't right. Colter was my friend. Anger locked into place, and I clenched my teeth. The anger was with myself for being so weak, so incredibly stupid to be so affected by Colter out of left field. To be so reckless with my head and my heart—and my fucking *vagina*—as they all warred to take control.

"Molly." The amusement was gone. The dark and sultry tones—gone. He'd felt and heard and seen all he needed to, to know damn well exactly what he was doing to me was overwhelming me. My anger spun on him, latching on.

"Can you please move." Structured as a question, it was anything but. It was a clear, concise command. And Colter, the smart guy he was, immediately obeyed as he side-stepped away from me.

"Moll." He followed after me as I hurriedly worked my way back out of the museum from the way we came. "*Molly.*"

I burst through the entrance of the museum, practically throwing myself into the onslaught of the island sun and heat. I prayed it burned me alive.

"Hey Molly!" The excitement in Alan's voice as he came barreling towards me knocked me back into my senses. "Oh my God—you will not believe it—wait, where's Colter?"

"Here," Colter said as he finally caught up. I whirled around as I watched him saunter out of the museum, his hands shoved into his swim short pockets, a forced smile on his face.

"Oh good. Fucking *guess what*?" Alan beamed.

I had a decent guess. The reminder of why I'd dragged everyone into the museum in the first place flooded through me, clearing my ire. Alan didn't wait for us to ask *what* as he opened his mouth—

"Ben proposed!" Beating Alan—rightfully—to the punch, Gracie's shrill of excitement echoed between the concrete walls of the lighthouse, the bathroom, and the museum as she suddenly appeared from behind him. "And I said yes!"

Cam, who'd by the looks of it had been chasing after Alan in a sprint to stop him from blabbing his brother's good news, slowed to a stop at Alan's side as he heaved in steadying breaths. Ben and Gracie, who had been a few paces behind caught up and the two of them slammed into me for a double hug that ignited a fire of sheer joy. Even if I'd known it was coming, it didn't stop the rush of delighted shock that bound through me. "Oh my God!" I cried—happy tears this time. As we let each other go, I repeated, "Oh my *God!*" as Gracie flashed me the ring.

It was a gorgeous, solitaire cut, whopper of a diamond. It looked elegant on her dainty pink tipped finger. I leveled a look of shock on Ben. "Did you pick this?" He nodded. "Well done, Ben. I mean it." Like a magpie, I examined the pretty, shiny thing as I twisted and turned her hand to catch all the dazzling sparkles from each and every angle.

The rest of the group took their time offering hugs and congratulations to the happy, newly engaged couple. Honestly, the happiness of it all lifted my mood enough that I offered a small smile to Colter who held it as though he was skeptical of its authenticity. I looked away, deciding I didn't care if he believed it or not.

Ben asked Gracie to go see the museum now with her— true to his nature of being the nerd he was—and she about swooned at the idea of following him around anywhere he wanted to go at this particular moment. Javier appeared shortly after that, explaining how he'd captured the whole thing on video, and he requested my phone number so he could send me the link for the drone video and a few snapshots he'd be sure to cut from it later.

As he stashed his cell into his back pocket, with my phone number newly added to it, he motioned to the lighthouse. "I can take pictures of the rest of you guys, if you'd like! Might as well use it while we're here!"

"Yes! Immediately yes," Alan said as he threw an arm around me, nearly dragging me toward the door to the lighthouse. I didn't dare look, but I knew Cam and Colter followed us as we passed the front desk and ducked our way through a vaultlike metal door that led to the bottom of the lighthouse's spiral staircase.

"Where did you and Cam go, I thought you were with us in the museum?" I pressed, climbing the stairs rather hurriedly so I could create some space between Colter and I, hoping I sounded casual.

"I got bored real quick, so Cam took me outside to see the lighthouse breakwater," Alan explained simply. "Javier flagged us down to point out Ben and Gracie's celebration after she'd said yes. I about shit myself."

I choked on a laugh. "I'll bet."

"How was it in there with Colter?" The question was innocent. At least, I thought it was. Yet, my hypothalamus was pumping hormones that had me replaying—and warming to—the brief, heated exchange I'd had with him. Why had Colter talking about knots sent me into such a tizzy?

"Fine," I replied shortly. Too short, I realized, as Alan glanced quizzically at me. "I like the…sails." *Oh, for fuck's sake.*

"Yeah," he laughed under his breath. "Sails are cool, I guess." Alan shot a look down below us where we could see the tops of the boys' heads through the wrought iron steps. He leaned into whisper, "Colter still getting handsy with you like he was on the boardwalk?"

Seriously, for fuck's sake. "I don't know what you're talking about." I became a wall of stone for the rest of the climb up.

At the top there was a hatch to crawl through. Alan went up first. While I waited, Cam and Colter caught up with me.

"I didn't know I was coming to Mexico to work out," Cam groaned as he leaned against the concrete wall of the inside of the structure. The space up here was narrow, and his words echoed around in the tube like buckshot. I offered a soft laugh and rubbed his arm encouragingly. He reached up to pat the back my hand before I slipped it away.

Colter and I locked eyes. I read everything I needed to know in his gaze. He knew he'd struck a nerve, and he was most definitely regretful of it. I almost felt guilty for my snappiness earlier. Colter and I didn't do this whole cold-shoulder kind of thing. If we were standoffish with one another it was usually in a teasing manner. This hit different.

"You guys coming?" Alan's voice carried down through the hatch.

"You're up, Rockstar." The way he said my nickname...it was a test. He was feeling out how I'd react.

Remembering the deal I'd made with him to have a good time, I softened. "See you losers up there." I smiled and winked and was slightly relieved to see one side of Colter's lips quirk up before I turned and headed up through the hatch.

The view was as breathtaking as I'd hoped. More so, actually. There wasn't a cloud to mar the sky, and the wind was a welcome caress against the island's sunbaked heat. The faint bash of the sea against the breakwater below was only lesser to the thrumming buzz of Javier's drone as it circled the lighthouse's peak.

Cam had come up through the hatch after me and had made his way over to Alan without a moment's hesitation. From the other side of the lighthouse's circular platform and through the windows that housed the lamp, I peered warmly at my friends. I watched as Cam affectionately wrapped his arm around Alan's waist, pulling him in close and planting a kiss to his temple. My heart swelled at the sweet moment.

The giddy smile I wore was for them as I turned my attention fully to the cerulean ocean beyond. The water was briskly clear and free of any boats. Down the shoreline I could make out what looked like a thatched roof of a large structure along with canopy shaded areas that I was curious to discover what was underneath.

I knew it was Colter who'd come up beside me, resting his elbows atop the circular railing. I could pick out his mere presence in a crowd. A petty part of me didn't want him to get away with speaking first, so I beat him to it.

"Have you ever seen anything like it?" I asked the question without holding back the true awe I had for it. I wondered if views like these ever became stagnant to those who were lucky enough to gaze upon them at any time they wished.

"No," Colter replied after a short pause. "Beautiful," he added.

Finding the remark a bit sentimental for Colter, I turned to examine him and was taken aback to find him gazing at me.

My gut had me wondering if he'd meant to say that about me. I narrowed my eyes on him, feeling him out, but as he held my gaze, and his relaxed smile turned ever so serious, I realized with a chest tightening clench that it indeed wasn't the ocean he was referring to.

I blinked and whipped my head back toward the ocean breeze. After everything that'd happened today, for the first time, I finally admitted to myself that maybe sometimes it was the best practice to keep my mouth shut. So, I just ignored his compliment, pretending as though it was in fact directed toward the scenic overlook set before us.

Even as I hid the shy smile that slipped onto my lips behind my curtain of hair.

On the climb back down, I kept to myself as Alan and Cam led the way. Colter was at my side but let me be as he jumped in and out of the other men's conversation. I'd kept my tone and my facial expressions friendly as we traversed further into the park where there was an outdoor buffet-style restaurant and Tequileria. We'd met back up with Ben and Gracie for lunch and our first alcoholic beverages of the day, and I'd made a show of toasting to the newly engaged couple, which spurred a wave of toasts in congratulations throughout the whole restaurant and even all the way to the beachgoers beyond. I was pretty certain Ben and Gracie were going to be showered with free drinks for the remainder of our stay.

The canopy covered structures I'd noticed while atop the lighthouse turned out to be shaded hammock areas. I'd happily planted my ass into one at the first moment possible, sipping a Sex on the Beach as Cam jumped into one on my left and Colter into the one on my right. They each were sipping on their own drinks. The three of us had a really good time as we let Gracie and the twins enjoy their newfound family bonding time as they snorkeled in the reef close to the shore.

At one point I was pretty sure I'd dozed off, only to regain full consciousness enough to realize it was Colter who had reached out his hand and was softly swinging me as I napped. I peeked at him through the wide weave of my hammock. He hadn't noticed me spying on him as he and Cam chatted about pirates and the odds of the two of them surviving a mythological sirens call. It was no competition. Especially since Cam was obviously into dudes. Colter admitted his likely probable weakness and I covertly agreed behind my closed eyelids, smiling to myself.

ELEVEN

We'd made it back to the resort just as a storm was rolling in. The thick dark cloud that inched nearer with every minute flashed lightning, distant rumbles of thundering softly rolling.

"Perfect," Colter said with eyes full of delight as he parked the Jeep in line with the others. He leaned over the steering wheel to peer up at the clouds.

Unbeknownst to him, my low-level anxiety was slowly coming to life. "What is?"

"This thunderstorm as the background noise for the nap I'm about to go take." Colter turned to me with a cheeky smile. My lips twitched with the need to return it, but my body was not in a state of compliance, especially not when the first fat rain drop smacked into the windshield.

"You ready to make a run for it in the rain?" he chuckled.

No. Not really. Not when that rain was accompanied by thunder and lightning. I shivered.

"We better hurry."

Rain battered the windshield. *Plink. Plink, plink.*

We caught sight of Ben and Gracie as they hastily left their Jeep, taking off hand in hand in a bounding run straight through the covered lobby. It took no genius to assume where they were headed and how they intended to celebrate their engagement once they got there.

I twisted in my seat to investigate how Alan and Cam were managing. Unsurprisingly, the two of them took a leaf out of Ben and Gracie's book and had made a run for it together out of their Jeep, too. They'd left Colter and I to fend for ourselves and I had the sinking feeling it would be a long while before he and I saw either couple again.

"Let's get you wet," Colter teased. I snapped my head to him at his words. For a brief moment, my brain focused on nothing more than those words and his mouth as he'd said them. Something animalistic was slithering its way around my bones at an innuendo that Colter surely wasn't even sending out, but my attention was picking up on anyway. He didn't wait for my reply after that, Colter winked and then jumped out of the car. To my surprise, he jauntily loped to my door and opened it for me. His expression was full of laughter as he offered his hand. "Come on, Rockstar. You won't melt."

Ignoring the overused term of phrase, I accepted his hand and bowed my face down at the first several heavy drops of the tropical rain. Lightning was still strobing through the clouds but to my relief it seemed the worst of the storm was still miles away. Colter closed my door, and I was pulling on his hand, silently insisting he hurry but he'd curled his fingers into my mine and forced me to slow, forced me to submit to the rain.

"Hurry!" I raised my voice over the sound of the rain smacking into everything around us like a chorus of applause.

"Take it easy, Molls!" Colter's tone was easy, relaxed. He led me straight through the rain as he took the long way around the lobby, giving us only a few seconds of relief from the downpour as we popped under one corner of the roof to get to the pathway that lead to our building.

"We're getting absolutely soaked," I pointed out as I hugged my sling bag to my body, hoping and praying it was water-resistant enough.

Colter nodded and raindrops collected and slipped off locks of his hair as he took a casual pace toward our stairwell. "Just enjoy the feel of it." He shrugged. "It'll still be months before we know what the warm rain feels like again."

I raised my eyebrows at the ground as I took in what he'd said. Colter was right. Back home in Michigan, it'd be a long, long while before we got to enjoy something like this again…and suddenly I understood. Colter didn't want to take this moment for granted. Here he was so easily bending to the will of nature so he could just experience it. Live it. So, yes, while it felt incredibly silly to be walking through the rain while everyone else we passed on the way were ducking and covering, racing and dodging, I just smiled and turned my face up to the rain. I closed my eyes and savored the feel of it as I let Colter guide me.

By the time we'd entered our room, our sandals were a squelchy beat to the music of our laughter. We'd not left any lights on when we'd left but the floor-to-ceiling sliding glass door that served as our only window had the curtain pulled back, either by Colter before we'd left or housekeeping, who'd obviously come through at some point earlier in the day; Colter's bed was made and a chocolate lay atop the pillows. Given the storm, the daylight was drowned out and the bedroom was cast in a grayish ambience. The AC had been cranked and being as wet as we were the feeling of the chilled air iced over my skin.

I sucked in a sharp breath and wrapped my arms around myself. "Oh wow, it's freezing in here."

Colter, who I hadn't realized had already disappeared into the dark bathroom, reappeared with fresh towels. He shook one out and handed it to me as I thanked him through chattering teeth. I'd immediately wrapped the fluffy white towel around my shoulders like a twelve year old at a pool party and I eyed Colter as he ran his towel through his hair and crossed the room to adjust the temperature on the AC unit. I kicked off my sandals and left them at the door.

I didn't want to get my bed wet, so I just stood in the middle of the room and used the corners of the towel I was fisting in my hands to wipe my face down. When I finished, I opened my eyes to see Colter standing before me, an unreadable expression on his face.

"You want to go first?" Colter asked softly as he tossed the towel to the corner of his bed.

I couldn't stop the way my brows furrowed at his question, nor the way my eyes about popped out of my head as he unceremoniously reached down and pulled his clinging wet shirt up. The wet material stuck to his biceps as he'd struggled with it over his head. The way his muscles flexed and worked as he undressed, the way the sheen of rainwater coated every inch on his chest, abdomen, and then his back as he turned away from me, walking to the balcony...I was fully, unabashedly staring now and I couldn't stop it.

"I'm sorry?" I managed to get out without it sounding like I was a complete airhead.

"Do you want to use the bathroom first?" he said as he slid the door open with one firm hand. "Unless you want to stay in those wet clothes and turn yourself into a tequila infused popsicle."

I blinked. "I only had two Sex on the Beach drinks. And those are made with vodka, by the way." I called out after him as he promptly threw his shirt over the rail of the balcony to dry...in the rain.

He flashed me a mischievous half grin over his muscled shoulder. "Oh no, Rockstar. I'm not talking about that alcohol." Slowly, Colter turned and slipped through the door, sliding it closed but leaving it opened just a small crack. To listen to the rain, I realized.

I shivered, but it was entirely because of my wet clothes. Entirely. "What do you mean?"

"I won a bottle of tequila with my winnings from the casino night. If we're stuck in the room for a while, might as well get drunk." Colter stepped to my luggage bag and tossed it onto my untouched bed, unzipping it and flipping back the lid.

"What are you doing?" I asked carefully.

"I'm finding you something dry to wear since it seems you're both literally and figuratively frozen to the spot," he teased as he rifled through my belongings. "What," Colter breathed as a wicked grin appeared on his full lips, "is *this*? Should I have coined you Pornstar instead of Rockstar?"

The thin gossamer he dangled before his face made my stomach drop.

"Put that down," I gasped as I recognized the brand-new, babydoll lingerie set I'd bought specifically for this trip.

"Do you sleep in this thing?" Colter ignored me as he used both hands to drape the material wide, examining it. "This looks wildly uncomfortable."

Finally—*finally*—my frozen feet peeled off the floor as I shot out, snatching the lingerie from his long fingers that had seemed to increasingly dwarf the scrap of material. "You *know* it's not meant to sleep in," I murmured, softly nudging him out of the way so I could finish his task myself. I tucked the material into a hidden pocket in the lid, hoping to never see it again. I'd bought it in Eric's favorite color. Cobalt blue.

Colter laughed as he stepped around me and busied himself with his own luggage, presumably searching out a new set of clothes for himself. I snagged an old, weathered tie dye t-shirt from my high school days and paired it with a new pair of black sleep shorts considering my other ones were sitting in a corner with a layer of sand still on them.

By the time I turned around, Colter was standing there with his dry, warm clothes balled in his hands, waiting.

"You can go first," he said with a shrug of his shoulder. The look in his eyes had me wondering if he was offering it by way of an apology for embarrassing me with my lingerie. I stared at him for a moment. Felt what oddly enough seemed like vulnerability coming from him. Under my gaze, Colter tensed, the muscles in his stomach going taut. My heart leapt in response. For a heat-flushed moment I thought about maybe offering—

Like the crack of a whip a thunderclap ripped through the sky beyond the balcony, and I jumped. "That one was close." Colter whistled as he looked over his shoulder.

Flustered, I backed away, bumping into the corner of the bed as I went. "I'll be quick," I promised as he turned back to me just before I slipped behind the bathroom door. I took the quickest shower of my life as I tried to forget the fact that for a second there I'd almost entertained the idea of offering him an invitation to *join* me. We'd shared swim-suit showers after dips in his parent's hot tub before—it wouldn't have been that wild of a suggestion. It's just that after the way I'd been reacting to him all day…

I dressed quickly and then hurried to my bed, not looking up at Colter as I said, "It's all yours." I threw back the white linens of the bed and jumped in. By the time I'd grown the nerve to peak over the roll of covers I'd collected at my chin, he was gone.

Colter was fast, popping back out, freshly showered and in a pair of navy-blue boxer briefs and a fresh white tee. He looked like he could model a Hanes advertisement. I bit my lip, secretly watching him as he stepped to his bed and tore away the top blanket, climbing under nothing but the sheet. The storm outside was growing increasingly darker and wilder as rain beat down on the roof overhead.

We'd settled into a companionable quiet, entirely forgetting about the tequila. That, or Colter believed I was already asleep, so he remained silent. With each nearing rumble of thunder my anxiety built. I was wound up so tight—from the storm and from my own conflicting emotions—that when another bone-rattling crack of thunder ripped nearby I sat bolt upright in my bed and audibly gasped.

"You alright?" Colter asked, clearly still wide-awake.

"Storms," I breathed, schooling my inhales and exhales even. "They freak me out."

"How have I never known you were afraid of thunderstorms?" he asked as he rolled to his side, facing me. He propped his head up on a fist.

"I'm not." That wasn't exactly true, now was it? I turned to the ceiling. "Well, I *wasn't*. Not until last spring…"

Colter seemed to sense there was more to the story, and I looked back over at him as I heard him shifting in his bed. He had the sheet draped over his outstretched arm, creating a cavernous space, likely cozy and warm. An invitation. I hesitated.

But then a closer, louder thunderstrike shook the building and I was propelled straight across the room and into his embrace. Colter did not hesitate as he wrapped me up warmly against him, hugging me tight. I melted into him even as another rumble of thunder came crashing before the first one had even finished. I nuzzled into his heat, into his promise of safety, into the intoxication of his skin. His thumb made idle circles on my shoulder over my t-shirt.

I spoke, distracting myself from the way those little circles built a languid fire within, "I'd been shopping at Target after work one day and I hadn't realized a storm had rolled in until I was checking out." I paused, internally laughing at myself, surprised Colter wasn't. Target. How very basic of me. "When I stepped outside, I was pretty much the only car in the parking lot, and I'd parked far—I always do for the extra steps." He nodded as though this was something he already knew about me, his chin rubbing lightly into my hair. "Anyway, I made a run for it, not wanting to get my things wet. And, when I was just about to my car, a lightning bolt struck grass beyond the pavement like thirty feet away." Colter stilled. My cheeks heated at the retelling. "It was *so* jarring that I'd fallen flat onto my backside, earning myself quite the king of bruises on my ass. But what really freaked me out was the *sound* of it, y'know? The loudest thing I've ever heard in my life…it rang in my ears for what felt like the entire shaky drive home and then some. I get freaked out every time thunder nears ever since," I concluded with a heavy sigh.

Colter's hold tightened as he squeezed me. "I've never heard that story."

"I haven't told anyone about it. It's a little embarrassing," I laughed softly.

Colter didn't laugh, but I could hear the smile in his voice, "All of us have been afraid of a storm or two in our lives." I nodded, pressing my cheek into his chest. "But that does sound freaking terrifying. Sorry, Molls. I promise no big bad storm will hurt you here."

I wondered if he meant here in this resort hotel room or *here* in his arms. But I yawned, deciding it didn't matter. I could be in the most dangerous of storms in the world and know I was safe as long as I was in his arms.

~

I woke to the soothing rhythm of Colter's breathing mixed with the beat of his heart beneath my ear. The room was cast in darkness and as I lifted my head from my pillow—his chest—I realized he must've rolled onto his back at some point, taking me with him while we slept. Half of my body was sprawled on top of him, my arm draped over his waist, my leg tucked between his. Tingles erupted in all the areas we were pressed together. It was mind-bending how just the feel of him had me going molten. Surprised to find it so dark outside, I shifted up onto my elbow to look over my shoulder at the bedside clock and did not for one second miss the fact that my knee brushed right up and over the hardened length of his—

Colter's hand slid through the sheets and clamped down on my bare thigh, halting my movements. Colter was rock hard in his boxer briefs and with him pressed against the inside of my thigh like a branding iron, my body ran hot. Liquid heat pooled between my legs, the area flush against his thigh. The thin material of my sleep shorts the only thing between my throbbing center and his skin.

Colter's other arm wrapped around my shoulders, and he gripped me firmly as he grumbled out, "Don't move."

It was clear to me then that Colter had been more awake than I'd realized. I froze against him as my breathing turned into short, hot pants. I could feel him release a long and slow, deep breath as though he were diffusing a live bomb. In some ways I think he was. I squirmed restlessly against him, unable to keep myself still as he'd requested. He responded to my movement with a masculine rumble deep in his chest. My lips parted reflexively, and I turned my head to look down at him. Even in the dead of night I knew his blue-green eyes were searing into me.

Because I was doing the same to him.

The urge to lower my head and taste his lips punched my gut and I swallowed thickly. I'd always found the phrase *playing with fire* to be a bit dramatic, but now...now I understood. The *fire* was intoxicating, alluring. Like a moth drawn to a flame, my logic and reasoning lost to the tug-of-war with curiosity and raw desire.

Driven by instinctual need, I moved, angling myself an inch more above him, bringing the hardest part of him closer to the hottest, softest part of me. His hand on my thigh tensed, kneading my flesh with a delicious bite. A sharp, too-short breath caught in my throat and the sound was loud enough that it might as well have echoed through the room.

"Molly." He said my name like it both pleasured and pained him. A prayer. And a curse.

I couldn't speak—I didn't trust my voice to not shake with the trembling need I was battling against. *Losing* against. I slid the hand that had been flattened on his stomach around his waist and braced myself on the mattress as I dragged my body fully on top of him, hovering there on my hands and knees. His arm around me relaxed and his hand blazed a trail of fire as it caressed down my spine. My body responded, curving into him, brushing against him.

Then his hands were on my hips, and when he pulled me down hard against him a gasp rattled out of me. I dropped my forehead to his, my hair caging around his face. Colter tilted his head up as if to kiss me, and in a slice of clarity I pulled back just enough to keep from his reach.

I couldn't.

I couldn't *kiss* him.

It felt like it would be too world-shifting. It felt like it would be too much. Where this, the simplicity of our natural bodies together was just right. Just enough.

Not wanting him to think I was even close to wanting this to stop, I instead angled my head and dragged my lips down his stubbled jaw and planted a tentative kiss in the crook of his neck beneath his ear. I didn't know what the hell I was doing—but I didn't care to *question* what I was doing as he let out a breathy groan—I just knew I needed to do it. It'd been the first time I'd ever put my lips to anywhere on him that was not a platonic peck on his cheek.

He smelled divine, and I bet he tasted the same. So, I kissed him there again, darting my tongue against his skin, hoping to pull that sound from him once more. He didn't just reward me with it again—oh no—he jerked against me roughly between my legs and I squeaked at the bite of the seam of my shorts pressing into my very center. Unable to hold back, Colter gripped my hips and brought himself up and over me, flipping me onto my back. A desperate whimper of anticipation escaped me as he pressed his weight down onto me. He braced himself on one elbow beside my head as he went to reach for the light.

"Don't," I breathed, clamping down on his forearm mid-reach.

He paused. "Molly…there is no fucking way I'm going to do this with you and not be able to see your beautiful face through every fucking second of it."

A ball of emotion slammed into my wildly beating heart. "Colter…" I whispered into the space between us—the emotion, the fear of uncertainty, too strong to mask.

Colter dropped his elbow to the mattress and his hands cupped my cheeks as he rested his forehead against mine. "We can stop. Just…just say the word and I'll stop." I could hear—and feel—just how hard that would be for him, yet I knew if I said *stop* right this second he would.

But I didn't want him to. I didn't really know what I wanted.

"I don't want you to stop," I said softly. Colter shuddered above me as though he'd been waiting with bated breath for those exact words. I swallowed. "But…what are we doing? This…this is a bad idea."

"And here I was thinking this was the best idea we've ever had," he joked as he made to roll off of me, even as he placed a searing kiss to the side of my neck.

Forcing myself through the blissed fog *that* evoked, I brought my hands to his side, stopping him. I much preferred him right where he was. He obliged, settling over me once again, teasing me with a thrust of his hardness against my dampness. My breath caught and I licked my lips as I struggled to remember what I was planning on saying next.

"If…if we do this…what happens tomorrow?"

Solid question.

One of us needed to think through the repercussions before we detonated the explosion that could very likely obliterate our almost decades long friendship.

"We go for round two," he murmured against my ear, following it with a nip. My back bowed off the bed, bringing my chest to his, soaking in the feel of the chuckle that shook him and rattled me.

"*Colter*," I whined.

"What do you want, Molly?" His question wasn't pushy at all. It was sincere, curious, explorative.

The answer hit me so fast and so clear that I almost felt the need to pretend like I was taking time to consider my answer to save myself from the mortification of the indecency of it. But there was no way I could play with him like that. Not Colter. I couldn't pretend anything with him.

"I just…want to feel *you*. Your *touch*. All of it." My brain had begun to secrete the hormones that would have had me flushing with embarrassment at having admitted it out loud. But it was circumvented by the way my body instantly honed in on how Colter's hand slid behind my neck, into my hair, fisting it as he lifted my head off the mattress. He angled his mouth over mine, hovering there, and I *melted*.

"Whatever you need, Molly." His breath danced over my parted lips and I jerked my chin towards him reflexively, inviting him in without even meaning to. "Hm," he hummed, "I could have sworn you were avoiding my kiss just a moment ago." He teased a dip of his head, bringing his mouth near mine, forcing me to arch my neck to meet him, but then he pulled back like I'd done.

"I was." I was ready to sing like a canary for him. He could ask me anything and I would give him my unabashed, honest answer now.

"Why?" Colter briefly passed his lips over mine.

Just barely.

Not enough.

The action blew through my coherent thought like buckshot. "I…I…"

"Too slow," he growled, and then crashed his lips into mine.

TWELVE

The sound I made shocked me. Somewhere caught between a gasp and a whimper, it was purely animal, and it drove Colter wild as the fist in my hair tightened and his hips ground his cock against me roughly. I instantly rocketed into a level of lust I'd never known before, and I was both overwhelmed and crazed by it. Our energy and desires pushed and pulled, meeting the others' intensity.

Kissing Colter wasn't playing with fire, it was *being* fire. God, he kissed like a man starved for exactly what only I could give him. My back bowed and my chest lifted to his, the t-shirt fabric against my peaked nipples a frustrating aggravation. As if he knew exactly what I was thinking and feeling—what I was *needing*—his hand at my cheek lowered. His fingertips skimmed down my throat and over my collarbone at a torturous pace. My head fell back against the pillow, exposing my neck. He tore his mouth from mine and latched to my throat, pulling against my skin as his hand skimmed lower where it finally cupped my breast over my shirt.

I was already ready to scream his name at the sensations my body was being tossed through...and we still had our clothes on.

We moved against each other as his mouth explored the bit of skin he had access to, and like a punch to the gut I knew we both needed more.

I needed it all.

Everything.

All of him.

Consequences be damned.

I squirmed beneath him, my hands finding their way between us. He lifted just enough that I was able to snag the hem of his t-shirt, and I tugged, silently pleading. Colter let me go and sat up on his knees. In the shadow of night, I could make out his arm reach to the nape of his neck and pull his shirt off. Damn, did I ever wish I could see what that revealed. I had to admit, I wished I'd let him turn that damned light on because like he'd said, I didn't want to miss a fucking second of this.

Once the shirt was gone I heard it land in a whisper on the tile floor. My hands, having a mind of their own, reached out and touched him. I dragged my fingertips over every dip and crest of his stomach muscles, and I could feel them push back against me as he drew in a weighty, deep breath and then cinch tight on the exhale.

I moved then, lifting to my elbows as I tried to reach for the light switch that was still too far away. "The light," I whispered. "Turn on the light. Please."

"Thank fuck," Colter sighed.

My small laugh was stifled by the sheer fluster of his body as he leaned forward, caging me in, to reach the switch.

It was *thrilling*.

The light was buttery soft as it washed over us in a flash. I looked up into his blue-green eyes, and he made to sit back up, but I wasn't going to let him go that easily. My hands flew up to his shoulder blades and I dug the tips of my fingers into his flesh, nailing him there against me. Colter, using the regained closeness, reclaimed my mouth with his. This time he drove the kiss deeper, and I opened for him. His tongue sent bolts of pleasure straight to my core as he tasted me—devoured me. I moaned into his mouth, and he growled with approval.

All too soon, Colter lifted off me and my body physically lurched after him as though it were tethered. My eyes flared as I willed them to focus so I could consume him with my eyes the way he was doing to me as he sat there, staring down with hunger.

Impossibly tan, tantalizingly well formed...

Colter was a god.

My thighs squeezed reflexively around him.

He bit down on his lower lip and his eyes just about rolled into the back of his head as he leaned forward, his forehead against mine once again. I moved towards him as though I was going to steal another kiss. "I don't think I've ever wanted anything this much in my life, Rockstar," he said against my mouth.

I traced my fingers down his arm, over each bulge and vein until I hit his wrist and I brought his hand to my breast again. "Then take it."

Colter did not need to be told twice.

He ripped his arm from my grasp as he moved to bracket my waist, pushing up and sliding his calloused hands under my shirt. He didn't right away go for my bare breasts, instead he paused right before he exposed me. His blue-green fired eyes hit mine, making damn sure he had my permission. I hadn't even finished nodding when he pulled the shirt up and over my heavy breasts. The rush of cool air against my sensitive skin made me shudder.

Before I could even take a breath, he was on me, and the moan I let out was guttural as he drew my nipple into his hot mouth. I gushed between my legs, nearly going blind with need. Colter rose, pulling my shirt clear off and he wasted no time moving on to rid me of my shorts. I lifted my ass off the bed, helping him as he tore away the soaked material.

He sat up to look down at me. His eyes roved over every inch of my body and the eroticism of being completely exposed to him stole my breath. I'd have thought I'd be shy, thought I'd be compelled to hide myself. But I knew that was impossible now, not when it was Colter above me. There was no man on the planet I trusted more. I felt on fire with a feminine energy that propelled me to reach between my legs to grab his thick length through his boxer briefs. He jerked into my hand at the contact but kept himself composed as his eyes continued eating me alive. "You're beautiful, Molly. Fucking *perfect*."

The tightening in my chest at words I'd never thought I'd ever hear come from his mouth almost hurt. I hooked my fingers into the band of his boxer briefs, and he let me pull them down. He sprang free and I breathed, "Oh my God..."

I'd already known he was *gifted*—it hadn't only been a running joke among the rest of the boys since they began sharing the locker room in junior high—but I'd felt him through the fabric of his boxers enough tonight to anticipate the thrill. And *wow* my imagination hadn't done it justice.

A god, indeed.

I wetted my lips, biting down on the bottom one as I finally tore my eyes away from his almost intimidatingly large, throbbing hard-on. The way he watched me as I looked at him was heavy. Colter began to pull his briefs off, and I was so eager to get him as completely naked as I, that I helped him pull them down his legs with my foot, kicking them to the floor with the remainder of our clothes.

We paused then, to just...stare at each other. I lay there, propped onto my elbows and so wet that I could feel it dripping down into my—

"Oh *fuck*," I cried, dropping my head back in ecstasy as Colter fisted himself and dipped it into my arousal, pulling it up through my folds until he hit my clit and circled it with his tip. That was damn near the dirtiest thing I'd ever seen—*felt*.

"Look at how wet you are. *Damn, Molly*." Colter's voice was strained with uncontrollable need.

"Colter," I moaned, rocking my hips forward. The movement caught him, and he slipped into me just an inch. I could've wept at the forbidden pleasure. "Take. It." I'd meant it to sound more demanding, but it came out a keening whine.

And then he did.

Colter pushed into me at a perfect soul-snatching pace, and this time I did weep. Tears pricked at my eyes that I couldn't explain, but then he was there, laying over me, our bodies flush and he kissed me with more tenderness than I realized he was

CALLEY CLOVER

capable of. My heart squeezed in my chest, and I kissed him back fervently, silently begging him to never stop. I was beginning to think I could happily live the rest of my life with him fully seated inside me as he sunk to the hilt.

Colter buried his face into my neck, his breathing and his body trembling as he began to pump in and out. My hips matched his rhythm, slowly increasing in pace and intensity as we both stoked this wildfire. Colter kissed me again, delving his tongue into my mouth so hungrily he might as well have been in competition with his cock for how far he could get himself inside me. It ripped another moan from me, and he swallowed the sound with his kiss.

Just when I thought I was going to burn alive right there beneath him, Colter moved to my breasts once again sucking, nipping and kissing. I grasped for his hair, holding him to me as I panted in time to each of his deep, claiming thrusts. I felt so incredibly *full*. That realization alone was pushing me further along to a too-soon climax.

My hands were frantic as I kneaded the muscles in his back, sliding down until I was able to sink my claws into the flesh of his toned ass. Greedy, desperate, and beyond horny I helped push him deeper into me and he immediately took over from there. Colter slammed into me so hard that it actually tore a delirious scream of approval from my chest.

"*Yes, yes, yes*," I breathed into his ear. He lifted his head to kiss me again, planting his lips to mine as he rattled my sense of reality.

For the love of all things holy, somehow Colter managed to find it in himself to fuck me even deeper and harder and I couldn't hold back any longer as I was being rushed right up over the edge. Right before I was about to come I could feel him meeting me with his own push to climax, so I did the only reasonable thing in that moment; I locked him in with my hands and heels on his ass. I shattered into a wave of raw pleasure and starbursts, his name falling from my lips in a strangled cry. And then a second wave hit me all over again as I felt him pulsing and spilling inside me with his own release and somehow that made it all the more...*hotter*.

Colter claimed my mouth, pinning me to the mattress as the last throbbing waves of his pleasure left him and pooled in me. My toes curled; my fingers raked up his back muscles. He broke the kiss, resting his forehead to mine as we both took a breath, slowly coming back to earth. I'd been prepared for him to collapse his weight onto me—I'd been craving it. But instead, Colter placed a quick kiss to my swollen lips and then slid out of me as he sat back. The pull of him leaving me made me jerk, conjuring a feeling of emptiness in its wake.

My heart lurched in my chest.

In the light of the bedside table lamp I scanned his face, unsure of what expression I'd find there. He stared, hawk-eyed directly between my legs where I could now feel his release slipping. A muscle ticked in his clenched jaw. I reflexively clenched my sex and made to close my knees, feeling vulnerable, indecent, and honestly a bit embarrassed. As soon as the muscles fired in my legs, Colter sensed it and he brought his hands up to my knees, keeping them pried open. The look on his face had me about ready to panic. The realization that we'd just had unprotected sex—and he had *not* pulled out— hit me like a brick.

"I'm on birth control—"

Colter shook his head. "I know. That's not...that's not it." I snapped my mouth shut. Stark anticipation burned like coals in my veins. I'd opened my mouth, somehow having enough nerve to ask him what it was then, but he beat me to it. "Molly, I never thought I'd ever get to see the sight of my cum dripping from your pretty pussy. Just...give me a moment."

Well, fuck me sideways.

My lips parted on a sharp inhale. He hadn't been eyeing me in concern; he'd been eying me in...awe. My apprehension was obliterated. In its place a welcome, weighty feeling washed over me. It was a natural, heady connection I was feeling to him now. A small, bitter part of me thought I ought to be ashamed for everything that had just happened, especially on the tailwind of the crashing and burning that was my not-so-distant year long relationship with someone else, but...

Colter, seemingly having looked his fill, leaned down and placed a kiss to the inside of my left knee then flicked his eyes to mine with a boyish smile. My chest tightened. "I'll be right back."

I watched with utter astonishment as Colter crossed the hotel room to the bathroom, admiring his toned backside the whole way. Finally alone with my thoughts, I dropped my head to the mattress and mouthed *Oh my god* to the ceiling. My eyes closed as I turned inward.

Sure, doubt and self-loathing were waiting to pounce in the shadows of my subconsciousness, but they could not hold a candle to the other emotions I was processing through: bliss, satisfaction, connection, excitement as I imagined recreating the entire scenario all over again as soon as we could. Because I wanted to. So badly, I wanted to have Colter again. I wanted him to take me, claim me, again and again until I had nothing left.

The soft tapping of his feet on the tile alerted me to his advance. My eyes opened and immediately drank him in. His naked body before me sent a rush through my blood. I fixated on the way the muscles in his upper thighs worked on each step—an area I'd never been given access to until now. Before I could collect myself and correct my gaze Colter was beside me, a damp washcloth in his hand.

I looked up into his eyes and he held my gaze as he reached down, cupping me with the cloth. My hands shot down, clasping his wrist so I could take over, but he swatted me away as he wiped up the evidence of our blatant line-crossing from my still-throbbing center.

I stiffened with nervousness and didn't know why—it wasn't the first time a lover had had the decency to provide aftercare, but it was the first time that lover had previously been a *friend*. I'd shared bathrooms with this man for nearly my entire life; it wasn't like he didn't have a familiarity with the wide array of human biological functions. And yet here he was treating me with a lover's tenderness. I almost wished he'd stop it. Almost.

With the last swipe of the cloth, he bent to kiss me again slowly. Languidly. Like he was draining me, sapping me of any fight I might harbor against...*this*.

He disappeared into the bathroom again, and as he did so, I turned to my side and scooted up to rest my head on his pillow. I pulled the sheet up and over my body, fisting the fabric in my hand nestled against my pounding chest. I closed my eyes, fighting back the nerves that threatened to scare me out of his bed and back into mine. I took a deep breath, and then another, my heart rate slowly calming as I processed everything.

I'd been so deep in my warring thoughts that I hadn't heard Colter return to the bed until I'd felt the mattress shift with his weight. My eyes snapped open, and for a second, I thought that I just might leap back into my own bed. That maybe he didn't intend for me to stay with him after what we'd just done.

But I was frozen. Frozen with fear and confusion.

My eyes caught the time on the bedside alarm clock. 1:35 a.m. We'd slept through the whole evening and we'd both likely have a load of missed text messages from our friends who'd been wondering what we'd been doing all evening. That thought struck a chord of apprehension. Our *friends*. What would they think?

"Molly." Colter's voice rippled through me, instantly halting my downward spiral of thoughts. "Molly, look at me."

I couldn't. I needed to get out of this bed. I rose to my elbow, unsure of what to say because *thank you* didn't seem appropriate but neither did silence. "I'll let you sleep," I said with overt politeness as I made to stand.

Colter's hand snatched out, cuffing my wrist firmly. "Where the hell do you think you're going?"

I spun on him with wide eyes. His tone was purely male; authoritative and somehow grounding. Firm but gentle. It commanded my attention—attention that my traitorous body yearned to give him. I swallowed. "I was going back to bed."

Colter's head tilted as he analyzed me, his eyes unnaturally probing yet tender. "I can see the wheels turning in your head. If you don't want to sleep with me—and I hope that's not the case—then fine, Moll. Whatever you need." His honesty rattled me. "I know what just happened here is no small thing. We just did something we can't take back and that's its own thing we'll have to figure out, but for now..." He shrugged. "For now, just get your ass back here. Stay."

So, I did.

THIRTEEN

I sat on the beach watching Colter as he swam effortlessly through the rolling waves. My body was deliciously sore in ways I hadn't felt in a long while. Just thinking about it had me soaking in my already ocean-soaked swim bottoms. I dug my bare toes into the sand and chewed on my lip as I recounted the way we'd spent the early hours of this morning.

Even though I'd been three seconds away from bolting from the bed last night, by the time I'd settled back down with my body pressed into his in a rather intimate embrace—his dick nestled in against my backside—it had taken only a few more seconds to fully submit to his calm. I'd been exhausted with a mix of post sex bliss and overthinking. He eventually slipped the hand of the arm around my waist up until he cupped a breast, pulling me tighter against his chest, making my eyes roll back in my head with comfortable peace and ease unlike any I'd ever known.

We fell asleep like that and hadn't moved another muscle until I woke to the light of the early morning filling our still-open window. I could feel him against me, warm and full of a wicked promise I now knew he was capable of. Still half asleep, I'd arched my back, pushing into him and it did the trick. I'd listened to the way his breath hitched as he woke to me grinding my bare ass against his swiftly hardening cock. When he thrust himself against me, I was already slickening with my own instantaneous arousal.

Colter had distracted me with alternating nips and kisses in the crook of my neck and had me panting by the time he pressed his hard length inside me. I'd let out a breathy moan, throwing my head back and to the side so I could look up at him. Colter had looked so intoxicating in his masculine beauty that I'd parted and licked my lips, begging for him to kiss me.

And he did.

He'd taken that hand that had held my breast and wrapped it around my throat and jaw, bringing my face up to meet his and it undid me. I'd bucked against him, whimpering a *please* that pleaded him to take me harder and faster, and he did not disappoint. For the second time in the span of one night, Colter had taken me and spilled himself inside me. I reveled in the eroticism of it. I was quickly becoming an animal for it.

By the time we'd finally dragged our sated, naked asses out of bed he'd convinced me to head to the beach with him. I'd joined him in the water at first, stealing private moments where we'd hold each other or brush against one another teasingly. I'd even snuck a quick kiss or two for reasons beyond what I was capable of thinking deeply about. But he'd kissed me back every time.

I'd told him I'd had enough of the water after twenty minutes of groping torture because I was only a few more teasing touches away from asking him to take me right there in the ocean—which looked nice in movies, but I figured would not bode well in reality. Besides that, more and more early risers were making their way onto the shore, and I didn't want an audience...especially if there was a chance it could hold one of our friends who, surprisingly, hadn't even tried to call or text yesterday evening.

The sun behind me had just peeked over the tree line and was kissing my shoulders as Colter headed my way. The waves lapped at his waist as he waded and he ran his hands down his face to shuck off the ocean water, then combed his fingers through his hair, swiping the wet strands away. The sunshine hit his hair, then his eyes, lighting them both up so he looked like he was glowing with godlike intensity. He landed those bright eyes on me in a wild look that let me know he was as ready for me again as much as I was ready for him and I wasn't sure what to make of it.

We hadn't talked yet about what this seemingly newfound *hobby* of ours meant. I'd never fucked a friend before and I wasn't sure how to navigate it, but something about being on a tropical island made thoughts of reality fly out the window.

I was tempted to stay in our play-pretend forever.

He crossed the sand and swiped up his towel, and I watched him as he dried off at the same time my mouth watered with the urge to taste him. It was becoming embarrassingly clear that I had possibly been suppressing secret attraction to Colter for longer than I cared to admit given the feral intensity I felt for him now that the walls had come tumbling down. A wall, I realized, I'd put up after that day I'd heard him make that nasty comment to that rough group of friends all those years ago.

I'd written him off then, only to fold so, so easily. Too easily. But I was already too far gone, if Colter and I were going to blow up our happy little group of friends, I was going to have fun while doing it.

"Careful, Rockstar. Keep looking at me like that and I'm going to spread your legs right here on this beach and take what's mine." He reached for my hand, and I gave it to him, letting him pull me up into his arms. "Because I know you're wet right now. And I know it's for me."

I swayed, leaning into his strength as I willed my legs not to tremble. "I am. It is."

Colter smirked. Such a confident asshole he could be sometimes. "I was going to suggest we head to breakfast but I'm thinking I should take you back to the room and eat you instead."

I audibly squeaked out an *oh* and squirmed in his hold. Colter dipped his head to claim my mouth—

"Molly?"

Colter and I froze halfway to each other's lips. That voice in my ears at this exact moment was like having a bucket of ice water dumped onto your head. I went to push out of

Colter's grasp, but he doubled down, pulling me tighter in his protective, if not possessive, hold.

"Eric," I replied by way of greeting. Just seeing him was stoking a coalbed in my gut. I eyed him. And then eyed the bikini-clad redhead he was with. The broad had the nerve to eyeball Colter. An ugly beast inside me reared its head. I wanted to lunge at her. Not because she was on Eric's arm. But because the trollop had the nerve to stand hand-in-hand with one man while eye-fucking another.

Another who happened to be *mine*.

Eric's mouth was working into a smirk and scowl combination that made him look particularly unattractive at this moment. "That didn't take long," he muttered, glaring at Colter. My brows furrowed in anger, and I stole a glance at Colter noting how a muscle in his jaw ticked as Colter met and held Eric's glare.

Slowly, I turned my eyes back to Eric. I was starting to see red. "Excuse me?"

"I knew you two would be fucking before the end of the week, just thought it'd take another couple of days. You two wasted no time at all, did you?"

"You've got a lot of fucking nerve." My tone dripped with warning. A mad chuckle worked its way up my throat as I turned my eyes to the redhead whose eyes were practically disrobing Colter while she held Eric's hand. *This has got to be a fucking joke.* "Tell me," I said, grabbing her attention finally. "Do you know you're number four for this asshole this week?" I pointed a damning finger at Eric.

The redhead's attention on Colter vanished and she shot a look up to Eric. "Well, she's got it all wrong, doesn't she, Eric?" I stilled with a prick of confusion. The girl's face went sinister as she turned back to me. "The other woman we left in bed was technically number four. So that'd make me number five."

Oh. This. Bitch.

I opened my mouth ready to spew an onslaught of expletives as she leaned towards me, her eyes flashing in a way that said *bring it*. Eric let out a nervous laugh, like he hadn't expected the girl to rise to his defense. "Alright, Sasha." He pulled her behind him. "That's enough."

"Why? I was just starting to have some fun." She set a malicious grin on me. "I like to fuck *with* women as much as I like to *fuck* them."

If anyone had enough, it was me. For the first time in my life, I lunged at a woman. I'd broken Colter's hold and sprang right at her. She'd cackled and danced on her feet behind Eric's shoulder as I felt Colter clamp his arms around me. He lifted me clear up and off the sand as he spun and put me down so that he stood between me and the two spawns of Satan.

Colter whirled on Eric. "I know we're stuck together at this resort for the remainder of the week, but if you make one more nasty comment to Molly, I will lay you *the fuck* out. I don't want to see your face again, do you understand? If you see us, you turn the fuck around and start heading the other way. And you." He drew his attention to Sasha as I rounded his shoulder to get a better view. Sasha taunted him with a wink that sent my blood boiling. "Not in your wildest fucking dreams."

With that, Colter turned snatching my hand as he guided us off the beach and toward our hotel room. I fumed the whole silent walk back, imaging how satisfying it would have been to have landed one on the redhead's stupid, pretty face. But the way Colter had spoken to them…the way he'd put Eric in his place—and he had, because I'd watched the way Eric's eyes widened with fear at the threat—and the way he dismissed Sasha…*not in your wildest fucking dreams.* Animalistic pride ripped through me. That poor, dumb little bitch.

When we entered our room the sun was fully up in the sky, greeting the day. I stomped into the center, flexing and unflexing my hands.

"Are you okay?" The question was thoughtful, but I knew Colter was barely containing a hedging temper of his own. The question threw me. Because I didn't really know. I was angry, that was for fucking sure. I was humiliated, too, if I was being honest with myself. Evidentially my hesitancy concerned Colter. "Molly, talk to me. What are you thinking right now?"

"I…I'm wondering what was so wrong with me that my boyfriend of a year decided it was necessary to throw me away so he could fuck his way through every woman in the resort in the span of a week."

There. I said it. The crux of what was deep down strangling me. It was only ever drowned out when Colter was fucking my brains out and a pang of shame hit me as I wondered if I was guilty of using him as an escape.

When it felt like Colter wasn't going to say anything, I looked up at him, the heat in my cheeks burning. Colter was watching me, and he looked dark. Angered and hardened…primal.

Before either of us could say one more thing he stepped toward me, picking up his pace so quickly that I braced for him, knowing he was coming to crash into me, and I welcomed it. He cupped my face and kissed me hard, lips and teeth gnashing. I lit up with desire. It flooded my brain and my senses. Then, faster than I could process, Colter spun me and pulled my back to his front so forcefully it pushed a gasp out of my lungs. His hand was on my waist, and he slid it up between my breasts, up until he grasped my jaw, forcing my head back so he could speak directly into my ear as I panted.

"You need to listen, and listen real good, Moll." The low, dark tone he spoke to me in was entirely new and had my heart pounding with thrill and anticipation, he didn't wait for a reply as he nudged me forward with his knee. I walked until my knees hit the edge of our bed. *Our* bed. *When did I start considering it our bed?*

"Eric is a fucking idiot. I knew it the moment you brought him to meet the group. Do not waste a second of your time worrying about his beyond fucked choices. There is not a damn thing wrong with you. Do you hear me?" He craned his neck around and forced me to look into his eyes. I nodded as I melted into him. Muscles low in my belly clenched at how he was handling me, the words he was saying to me. "Say it out loud, Rockstar. Do. You. Hear. Me?"

"Yes," I whispered, my breaths too short and barely hitting my lungs enough to keep my head from going dizzy with savage lust for him. Like he'd inadvertently flipped a kink-switch in my brain, I caught his wild eyes, and the side of my mouth twitched with a smirk, as I added, "Sir."

"Fuck," he growled as he ground his forehead into my temple. My eyes closed in languid pleasure from what that little word seemed to give him. "I want to fuck you right now. I want to fuck you fast and hard, so that I know you believe my words. But I know you've got to be sore. So, I'm going to let you go. And I'm going to remove myself from this room until I get control of myself. Okay?"

Colter's grip went to loosen, but I sank my nails into his forearms. "I do believe you. I am sore," I panted. "But you're not leaving this room."

"Molly," he warned, but he betrayed himself as he planted a hot wet kiss to my shoulder.

"Fuck me, Colter," I breathed the plea as I arched into him. "Fuck me hard and fast."

A dark, low chuckle rippled through his chest and into my back, and the muscles in my core tensed. "Do you know what you're asking for, Rockstar?"

"Yes. No," I admitted, but I didn't care. I needed it now. "I want to know."

"You trust me?" Colter asked and then nipped my ear.

My knees went weak. "Yes." And I knew right then and there that that truth was my first-class ticket to Fucksville.

Colter let me go but as soon as his hands left me, they reappeared in the band of my swim bottoms. He tore them down to my thighs, revealing my ass, but before I could back myself up against him, one hand bit into my hipbone while the other raked up my spine, his callouses grating against my skin.

With a force I hadn't been prepared for, Colter fisted the hair at the nape of my neck and bent me over until the side of my face was plastered to the unmade blankets of the bed we'd tousled in last night and again this morning.

The jolt of his handling me so forcibly was something I had never experienced before. I had what I always thought was a healthy appetite for control in the bedroom, and all my past lovers had happily accepted it, but this…*this* was making me hotter, wetter, hungrier.

I never knew Colter had it in him.

But my body responded as my cunt flooded with my wetness, anticipating the eye-rolling feel of his cock that I was sure he was poised to slam into me. But it wasn't his cock. It was his fingers, and I cried out into the mattress as he fucked me like that just as he'd promised; hard and fast.

My hands came up beside my head to fist the sheets for traction, so I could push back against his onslaught. Guttural moans ripped from me to the rhythm of his fingers.

"That's it," he praised. "You're taking it so good." *Holy fuck.* I was going to rip apart with the orgasm he was launching me toward. "I want to feel you cum on my fingers."

Yep, that'll fucking do it right there.

I screamed in ecstasy as I came, my walls fluttering around his fingers. *Had he slipped in a third?* Like everything else, my orgasm was hard and fast, but it was perfectly mind-melting. I went to lift myself up off the bed to get my mouth on his, because I needed it, but his fist in my hair tightened and he shoved me back down. An oomph left my chest.

"I'm not done with you." That sinful voice of his had my eyes rolling in the back of my head.

The breath I drew in was shaky, my toes curled, my core throbbed. I felt him as his weight came down over me, caging me in as he pinned me down. His face came into view and I watched as he brought his fingers—yes, it was *three*—to his mouth to suck off my wetness. "Like candy."

My eyes widened with sheer, raw shock of his sexual fearlessness. "Oh, fuck," I whined as we locked eyes.

Colter smirked. "Yeah, baby. *Oh, fuck.*"

And he slammed into me, filling me up to the hilt and I shouted again, the pleasure spiking through my body beyond what I was sure I could handle. Colter readjusted his grip, leaving my hair so he could wrap his dominant hand around the back of my neck, holding me down while he went wild behind me. The delirious cries of *yes* and *don't stop* that fell from my mouth were one hundred percent mine, but at the same time I didn't feel like I'd used any one of my obliterated brains cells to conjure them up.

On another forceful thrust in, Colter forced me up onto the bed fully. I planted my knees to the mattress for support, tipping myself further toward him and Colter ate up every inch I submitted. His growl of approval at my offering elicited goosebumps all along my skin. Orgasm number two was already gearing up. I let go of the blankets, hungry to touch him while he fucked me to oblivion. Reaching back, I found his thighs and bit my fingers into flesh and muscle.

His hands worked together as the one on my hip slid to my lower belly and the one on my neck slipped down and around until he snaked it between my breasts, and then he lifted. Colter lifted me clear off the bed as he plastered me to his front and my fingers dug into his forearms. Changing the angle and the position, Colter effectively threw me into the orgasm unexpectedly as he groaned, "Fucking. Perfect." in time with two remarkably hard thrusts that had me screaming before his hand could slip up my throat to my mouth to smother it. I could feel him inside me as he came right along after me.

The fact that Colter had spilled himself inside me *three* times in the span of less than eight hours had me near delirious with feral craze. How the fuck was it so hot?

Colter dropped us to the bed, making sure to support me as my limp limbs uselessly lay beside my sated body. He kept himself inside me as he hovered over me, his chest lightly touching my back with each calming breath he took as he placed kisses all along my shoulders and the back of my neck. Somehow I was still capable of breathy little moans at the sweet sensations those kisses drew out of me.

A knock on our door followed by Gracie's voice calling for us both had us freezing and holding our breath. My heart rate, still wild from the sex, was sent soaring again as I realized what we'd just done and how we were supposed to greet out friends while I wouldn't be surprised if our hotel room reeked of sex.

"Is everything okay in there? I thought I heard screaming." There was definitely an edge of worry to Gracie's tone. I blushed, remembering the scream she was referring to.

"Shit," I breathed as Colter's low chuckle rumbled against my sweat-slicked back. "It's not funny," I laughed.

"It's kinda funny," he countered, then kissed my cheek. "Ready?"

I gave him a silent nod in response, and he pulled out. Quickly, I scooted off the bed, my toes finding the chilly tile floor. As I stood up straight, Colter's release immediately slid down my leg, another blush-inducing reminder. I was about to reach for the box of tissues on the dresser behind me, but Colter had beat me to it as he snatched out three quickly and tossed them to me.

"Guys?" Gracie called from the door with another frantic knock.

As Colter delved into his suitcase for something to throw on, I hastily cleaned up and skittered to the door while I yanked up my swimsuit bottoms. I'd planned on throwing the used tissue into the trash bin that should have been near the door—that's where it had been in my previous room—but one wasn't there. I panicked as Gracie began another round of knocks and opened the door, hiding the ball of tissues behind my back.

"About damn time," she playfully huffed as she crossed her arms. "What were you doing in there that took you so long? I heard you scream, are you okay?"

In my momentary silence as I wracked my brain for a reasonable excuse, Gracie took the time to eye me up and down as though double checking my physical wellbeing for herself.

"I'm fine," I laughed lightly. "I slipped. In the bathroom. But I caught myself before I did any damage. There was some water on the floor." Gracie peeked into the room over my shoulder, and I wasn't sure if Colter was decent or not, so thinking quickly I redirected her attention. "I was just in there cleaning it up." I presented the tissues. "Didn't hear you knocking with the bathroom door closed." Lies. Before she could get a good look, I hastily hid the tissues behind my back once again.

"And Colter?" she asked. Something apparent in her voice let me know she wasn't completely buying my story.

"I *was* sleeping," Colter said as he suddenly appeared behind me, pressing himself to my back, closer than I thought was necessary. Then I felt his fingers at my hand. Realized he was sneaking the tissues from me.

"Oh." Gracie's eyes caught on something, and I followed her gaze down to my hip...where the band of my swimsuit bottom was rolled over itself from having pulled it up so quickly. Gracie looked back up to me shaking away whatever thoughts or suspicions had been circling in her head. She schooled her face into a smile. "We're having brunch in the main dining room. A little post engagement celebratory meal. And then..." Her grin turned mischievous, "it's time to go spend a day snorkeling and drinking piña coladas at the beachside tiki bar."

"Sounds great!" I exclaimed at the same time Colter said, "We'll be there." He and I shared a glance and then quickly looked back to Gracie.

"Damn right!" She actually bounced with excitement. And fortunately, she didn't see me almost jump as Colter snuck his fingers into the band of my swim bottoms, correcting the material. His nimble fingers were out of her sight by the time Gracie sobered, and they now rested on the small of my back. Chills ran up my spine.

"Let's do it!" Gracie made to turn down the hall.

"I'm just going to change out of this wet suit." And use the damn bathroom.

"Okay! Come on Colter, let's go." Gracie beamed at him expectantly.

Colter's hand on my lower back flexed. "I just have to grab my phone. I'll be a step behind ya."

Appeased, Gracie trotted off and thankfully Ben opened their door down the hall at the same time, taking all her attention as Colter reached over my head to close the door.

I let out a slow exhale through pursed lips. "That was close—*Colter*!" He'd grabbed my hips and pulled me against him as he trailed a path of kisses down my neck and over my shoulder. My body responded immediately, ready as if he hadn't already had me shaking and begging seconds ago. "You're insatiable," I laughed as he kissed that trail back up to my ear.

"I wouldn't be...if you weren't...so damn appetizing." Colter nipped my ear, and I shuddered.

"Colter we've got to slow this down," I panted, my body betraying me as I arched into him. Colter paused. His mouth left me and the grip on my hips loosened. His silence ratcheted a gut-twisting sensation that had me wishing I hadn't said that. "I just mean that…if you keep doing that we're never going to get out of this room…" But it was too late, he'd already dropped his hands from my hips, and I spun around to watch him as he walked away to the bedside table, reaching for his phone.

"No—I know," Colter said casually. "You're right." He sent me mischievous wink, but something about it didn't seem entirely authentic. "Besides, I told Gracie I'd meet her and Ben on the walk down."

With unblinking eyes, I watched my best friend slip his phone into his pocket and walk towards me with a trained saunter I'd seen before. My chest tightened in response. I hadn't meant to, but I'd definitely drove a spike of reality right through our blissful veil of tropical fantasy.

Colter passed me and reached for the door, opening it with a nonchalance that had my heart racing with hurt and confusion. I couldn't explain why but I was almost upset he hadn't kissed me as he made to exit. A bolt of something akin to determination went through me and I reached out, snatching his hand before he disappeared behind the door—a door that seemed like the beginning of something or the end of something. Final.

A tenseness in his shoulders melted away at my touch—a tenseness that I would not have noticed had I not reached for him. I didn't need to plead with him to turn to me, he yielded easily. "I just want to make myself clear," I started low and quiet, considering we had the door open to the open-air hallway. "I said slow. Not stop." Testing the water, I tugged on his hand, pulling him closer. Blue-green eyes that had gone hard at some point eased into a somber softness.

For a fraction of a second, I thought I detected a flinch…a wince as though something crossed his mind that had caused him physical pain, but it was gone before I could place it, and then he was leaning in. I parted my lips on a soft inhale right before his lips found mine.

Of all the kisses we'd shared, this one…this one was *different*. Soft and slow at first. I wasn't going weak like I'd done with his demanding kisses. No, I was strengthening—fortifying—with this one. Growing in my trust, my devotion to our friendship. Because this was a kiss of love, not a kiss of lust. I just wasn't entirely sure what kind of love it was.

His mouth parted mine and our tongues explored one another's—easy, languid. Natural. I could feel my skin all over coming to life as my brain shot a concoction of chemicals straight through to all of my nerve endings. My hands crept up to his chest and I felt the muscles—the heartbeat—under the shirt he'd chosen today; navy blue. Colter's hands snaked around my back, holding me firmly against him—twin bands of safety and security.

A sensation I couldn't place bubbled up in my chest and I tensed up, unnerved by it. Colter didn't seem to notice but he pulled away from the kiss and then slowly removed his arms, his hands caressing down over my backside where he finished with a firm squeeze to each cheek.

"Get changed and I'll see you down there," he promised as he grabbed the door behind his back. I offered him a small smile and nodded my head. When he was gone and the door had latched shut, I sighed, forcing my shoulders to relax. I headed straight for what *had* been *my* bed where my suitcase was now propped open and I busied my brain with making a choice for my brunch attire. I focused entirely on that one task—because if I didn't, then I'd have to think about the fact that that kiss had been stirring up something inside me that was more than just having some wicked fun with my supposed *friend*.

FOURTEEN

I'd arrived at brunch in my white bikini with an equally white crocheted cover-up, my flip flops smacking on the polished stone floor. As I passed the buffet line swarmed by the bustling bridal party I realized I could have easily been mistaken for the bride. My cheeks grew warm. And then I remembered this was the exact same bachelorette group that Eric had his first dalliance with. My jaw clenched with distaste, and I scanned the crowded tables.

His eyes caught me in their glare and immediately my tension eased. He'd been looking for me. Colter raised his hand lazily as a signal, a well-contained intensity in his eyes that made my skin pebble with goosebumps.

Fuck that bachelorette party. Fuck Eric.

Forcing my face to remain cool and calm, I blinked slowly with all the cool, confident energy I could muster. I breezed by the group of girls, brushing my shoulder with the bride's and murmured, "Congratulations."

Her brown eyes were wide and bright with elation as she turned to me. "Thank you!"

All the rest of the girls rang out a chorus of whoops and hollers. All except one, who held a white-knuckled grip on her half-full plate of food. Her smile strained. I'd bet all of that casino night's chips on her being the one who'd fallen for

Eric's charm. Good for fucking her. She didn't have to worry about me. Any fight I had in me had been snuffed out entirely by Colter's actions.

Even with the little experience I had with Colter over the last several hours, I knew I'd wound up with the sweeter, hotter, better end of the deal—when it came to mine and Colter's sexual chemistry...Eric could not compare.

Free. I felt free as I approached my friend's table. A smile broke over my lips, full and wide. I found Colter's face again, and he, too, quirked his lips into a knowing grin. The only spot left at the round table was directly across from Colter. I ignored the teensy-tiny part of me that was a little disappointed I wouldn't be right beside him. But he was sitting between his best friends—Ben on one side, Alan on the other. And I was happily squeezed in between Gracie and Cam.

"I ordered you a mimosa!" Gracie slid the crystal glass toward me, sending bubbles racing to the top of the liquid. "You're going to have to catch up. I've already had two."

"Damn girl," I breathed as I sat down in the seat, pulling myself up to the table. "Are we all starting early this morning?"

"I'm up for a day of straight day-drinking on the beach," Cam said as he gave a wink and twisted off the cap of a pint whiskey bottle. He dumped the contents into his *black* coffee. Absolute savage.

"Al? Care to join?" Cam wagged an enticing eyebrow at his lover.

"I've been waiting all week for you to ask," Alan replied coyly, offering his own mug of coffee, already laden with creamer—like a *normal* human being.

Down the line, the little bottle of whiskey was passed. Everyone poured a good dollop into their hot coffees and when it finally hit me—no coffee yet to pour it into—I hesitated.

"*Game of Life*," Alan coughed under his breath.

I popped my eyes wide in astonishment at him. Inspecting the bottle, sure enough, there were no markings to make it safe from our age-old drinking game. The table went still, barely contained grins on everyone's faces. I peered at the contents of the bottle. Probably about two shots worth remaining.

151

When I looked back up at Alan he held me in his glare, a wild dare dangling there.

"Oh, come on." Gracie swooped in to save me. "She doesn't even have a chaser. That wasn't fair, Alan."

"Life's not fair." He waved her off. He leaned in closer across the table toward me. "Game. Of. Life."

"This isn't even my bottle," I threw out there.

Alan shrugged. "It's in your hands, isn't it?"

"You'll be sorry when you're stuck carrying my ass back up to bed by two in the afternoon," I warned, not breaking eye contact as I brought the bottle to my lips, ignoring the pungent sting of alcohol as its fumes already burned my nostrils. I tipped back and chugged.

"I'm sure Colter will take care of that for me," Alan whispered to me.

As I chugged, eyes burning, throat stinging, I was close enough to Alan that I found his shin with my foot under the table...and kicked. He barked a laugh and settled back into his seat, ignoring the look of confusion on Cam's face. When Cam's eyes turned to me for clarification, I subtly shook my head, rolling my eyes as I forced myself to finish off the last of the bottle.

Smacking the empty bottle to the table, Gracie—ever the caretaker—held my mimosa out before me. An offering to chase down the burn. I appreciatively sipped on it, welcoming the fruity flavor that combated the harsh whiskey.

"Well, I guess you don't have to catch up now," Gracie sniggered, eyeing me as I set my mimosa back down.

"No." I cleared my throat. "But I need food now. Or the Rockstar will emerge before it's even eleven o' clock in the morning. Then you'll *all* be sorry." I gave a pointed glance to Colter, who hid his smirk behind his coffee cup as he drank.

I hadn't realized how ravenous I'd become, but as I remembered the amount of energy Colter and I had been expending, remembered how we'd slept right through dinner last night, my hunger became painfully obvious. I'd followed behind Gracie, second in line in our group of friends, as we hit the buffet line. Colter, somehow, had worked his way up behind me. Maybe it was the whiskey, maybe it was our never-ending supply of hormones barreling through our bloodstreams—likely a combination of both—but any chance he got to reach for food in front of me, he pressed himself against my back in a way that had me subtly arching my ass right back into him. By the time we made it back to the table I was starving in more ways than one.

I'd had half a mind to accept the offer for another round of drinks when the server stopped by halfway through our gorging to check in on our table. But if we truly were having a day-drinking excursion, I'd need to pace myself. I chugged a bottle of water instead.

"So now that we've all had a bit of sustenance," Ben started from Colter's right side. Everyone at the table looked up from their plates as we waited for him to continue, "Gracie and I have an announcement to make—"

"Oh my God, you're pregnant!" Alan jumped in, smacking his hands on the table obnoxiously. I might have to take charge of Alan's drinking pace today, too.

Gracie scoffed. "Shut up, Al." But she smiled at him in a way I could only describe as sisterly fondness. "We figured," she continued, taking a dramatic pause to look into each and every one of our eyes, finally landing on Ben's as he smiled, "that since everyone we love is present and we're in such a beautiful place—" My palms began to sweat. I already knew where this was going. I prepared to jump out of my seat. "—that Ben and I should just get married here. Now. Well, *Friday*." She giggled as the table sparked with excitement and shock.

"I freaking knew it!" I bounced in my seat, pointing my finger at the two lovebirds as they happily clung to one another soaking up the celebration and love everyone at the table showered them. "Yes! This is so exciting!"

"I didn't think I'd come to Mexico and leave with a sister." Alan was actually crying. My mouth dropped agape as I witnessed it. Tears pricked my own eyes at his show of emotion. Across the table, Ben cleared his throat for the same reason.

"We've already spoke with Javier and he's going to help us throw this wedding together in the next two days," Gracie explained, reaching for her mimosa as though her nerves needed an outlet. Then, swallowing a lump of emotion, she turned to me. "Will you be my Maid of Honor?"

I pretended to recoil with offense. "Ugh—well, *duh*."

Gracie's laugh was joyous, thrilling. Contagious. I joined her and leaned over to wrap her tightly in my arms. She shook with emotion as we swayed in the embrace.

Ben's voice carried across the table, "Alan—"

"Don't even ask," Alan interrupted. "We all already know I'm the Best Man."

Everyone else joined in the mirth. Taking a leaf out of the book from the bachelorette party, I raised my mimosa into the air and announced to the room, "My best friend's getting married!"

The breakfast-goers cheered.

~

The beachside tiki bar was already a riot as we stumbled to the swing seats that lined the entire horseshoe bar beneath the thatched roof. The two bartenders working the bar were young and lively, keeping up expertly with the demand of the clientele. Miguel and Juanita—their names we quickly learned—worked in tandem as though they'd been doing this together for years. There'd only been four swings available so Alan, Cam, Gracie and I sat down, while Ben stood behind Gracie, holding the ropes of her swing as he gently rocked her, and Colter faced down the line of us as he rested an elbow on the bar top beside me.

Piña coladas were the first thing ordered for the entire lot of us. I'd been halfway through sucking mine down when a thought occurred to me. "Hey, aren't we supposed to be drinking out of coconuts?"

Juanita overheard me and shot me a grin. I watched as she leaned back to whisper to Miguel who was helping the other side of the bar. He whipped his head over to look at me and smiled. My brows rose with curiosity. Before I could ask what that was all about, Miguel set his customer's drinks on the table and snuck out from behind the bar. I watched until he disappeared down the beach.

"Was it something I said?" I asked no one in particular.

"Maybe you made him mad." Colter shrugged, having seemingly watched the whole ordeal. "Probably gets that a lot." My smile fell as I looked up at him. Colter's eyes widened. "I'm kidding."

"You're going to make me feel bad." I stuck out my bottom lip in a pout.

Stunning me, Colter reached up with two fingers and pressed my pout away. "I will make sure you feel much better by the end of this day."

I stared at him and swallowed. Heat swamped me, muscles low in my belly clenched. One side of his handsome mouth tipped up in a smirk as his eyes swarmed with promise. Effectively speechless, I broke eye contact as I turned to face the bar and took a much-needed sip from my cool, refreshing drink.

It went on like that for some time as drinks were passed and laughter was shared. Colter and I did our best to remain an innocent part of the party, but any chance he could sneak his hand to my thigh, he did. And each time he inched it closer to the throbbing area at the apex of my legs. I'd pulled my swinging chair in with my elbows up to the bar to hide his touch, so close that I barely had room for my ribs to expand to take a breath—though breaths were few and far between as they had been consistently stolen from me each time Colter whispered some wicked little thing into my ear when no one was paying attention.

I'd been worked up enough that a flush had crept onto my chest, hardly visible in the shade of the tiki bar roof and easily passed off as a reaction to the alcohol that was being consumed, but Colter and I both knew better.

Finally overwrought with enough tension to burst like Mentos in a bottle of Coke, I damned the consequences and adjusted my position in the swing so I could face him. "Stop teasing me," I warned in a low voice.

Heat flared in his eyes—a challenge. "Why?"

It was my turn to make him squirm. I leaned in, brushing my lips to his ear, my breasts pressing into his chest. "Because this piña colada is tasting like I need to drop to my knees right here at this bar and suck you dry."

I could feel him tense. Smirking slyly, I leaned back just enough that we could see each other's eyes, mouths inches apart. A muscle feathered in his jaw.

Catching something behind my shoulder, Colter schooled his face relaxed and raised his brows. "Miguel's back."

I spun in my seat to look at the same time I secretively reached down, cupping and squeezing Colter's package in a silent promise. He choked on a laugh.

Miguel had indeed returned, a bag of coconuts and pineapples slung over his shoulder. My mouth dropped open in surprise. "Miguel!" Everyone turned to look at me at my outburst. "Did you seriously go get coconuts?"

Miguel flashed a smile and shared a glance with Juanita. "Climbed the tree myself."

Shocked and impressed, I gushed, "Did you really?"

Juanita shook with silent laughter. Miguel shook his head, smiling smugly. "No, senorita. There's a market down the road."

I wagged my finger at him. "You got me."

Miguel swung the bag up onto the lower prep bar in front of me. "There is an extra cost to getting your drink in a coconut, though." His eyes narrowed on me, questioning whether I'd take the bait. Even Juanita paused her drink mixing to walk to Miguel's side, eyeing me suspiciously.

I was no pansy. Bring it on. "And that would be?"

Juanita supplied the answer this time, "Body shots."

Our entire group perked up. My brow raised and Miguel chimed in, "And seeing as you were the one to make the request. You're first."

"Hell yes!" Gracie shouted as she stood right up on the bar's footrest.

I sucked on a tooth and narrowed my eyes on Miguel. Then Juanita. "First to take the shot or first to *be* the shot?"

"Be the shot! Be the shot!" Gracie chanted.

Miguel smacked his palms to the bar top. "And who will be the first to take?"

Gracie nearly toppled out of her swing as she made to climb down. "Me!"

I barked a laugh, as did everyone else.

"Here we go," Ben muttered, his gaze going skyward as though offering up a prayer. Or a plea.

Closing one of his hands into a fist, Miguel knocked on the bar top. "Climb aboard."

With bated breath, everyone waited to see what I would do. I looked at Gracie first and she scrunched up her face excitedly at me. Then I swung my head to Colter. He had his bottom lip pinned between his teeth, still lazily resting his elbow on the bar top. His eyes were hooded, as though he just couldn't wait to see this.

With my eyes, I asked the silent question, *You're alright with this?*

Colter left my gaze to scan the bar. Seemingly at ease with the slim scattering of bargoers who were not even paying attention, he brought his eyes back to mine and winked his affirmation, *Have fun.*

I rolled out my neck. "Alright," I sighed as I stood to the sounds of my friend's whoops and claps. I raised my voice over the din of their revelry, "But I'm telling you now! This moment right here? This is where the rest of this day either turns into a shitshow or the best day of our vacation."

"Likely both," Miguel quipped as he bent to retrieve a fresh bottle of tequila from the stocks.

Immediately Juanita began clearing the drinks off the bar top to make room. Standing on my own two feet, preparing to haul myself up, I swayed a little—the mornings beverages catching up with me. Colter was there, pushing off the bar and reaching for my hips. In a swift motion that took my breath away he hoisted my butt right up onto the counter. I wondered if anyone else noticed how his fingers had tightened briefly before letting me go.

We were treading dangerous waters, but the waters were mixed with rum, whiskey, and soon-to-be tequila, so any inhibitions were scarce and dwindling quickly.

As Juanita retrieved a saltshaker and a bowl of limes, it was Miguel who offered his hand to help me lie back. I extended my legs and crossed my ankles as I wiggled myself comfortable as much as possible on the unforgiving hardwood bar. I lifted my head to collect my hair and caught sight of Colter staring between my legs, still biting on that lip of his. I clenched my thighs at the rush that brought on.

Gracie grasped my shoulder as she sidled up next to me. "Just like college, am I right?"

I dropped my hair over the edge of the bar and cackled, "Just like college."

"Here is your salt," Miguel said, passing it over my belly to Gracie. She grabbed it and then the bowl of limes he then passed.

Gracie leaned her elbows on the table to look down at me. Her hair fell forward tickling my arm as she did so, and I squirmed a bit as she looked me in the eye and asked, "Where we putting the salt?"

I snorted. "Surprise me."

"Shitshow," Ben said from above my head somewhere. I tipped back to eye him and giggled as he closed his eyes and shook his head. Alan chuckled and clapped a supportive hand to his brother's shoulder as Ben clarified, "This is going to turn into a shitshow."

"Chest it is," Gracie said as I felt the tickle of salt crystals dropping to my skin.

Down the line of my upside-down vision, I saw Cam wriggle as though uneasy, and I had the distinct feeling he was remembering the incident from a few days ago when nearly every single one of my friends almost saw my breasts. "Don't worry Cam!" I assured. "Clothes stay on for these kinds of things." Jokingly, I looked back to Miguel who was pouring tequila into a shot glass. "Right?"

"Ah," Miguel started as he set down the bottle and lined the shot up to my belly button. "Clothes stay very much on. If clothes come off, I lose my job." He winked down at me. My stomach muscles tensed as the cool glass hit my belly.

"Alright, no one make her laugh, or we waste this precious tequila!" Gracie's order rose above all other voices and laughter. I clenched my jaw tight to smother how much that alone made me want to laugh. Everyone quieted to watch. I heard the sound of a phone unlocking and looked back up to see Ben with his phone out to capture the moment. I stuck my tongue out at him. Still staring at the scene through his screen he stuck his tongue back out at me.

"Ready babes?" Gracie sang.

"Party on Garth." I grinned.

"Party on Wayne!" She hollered, joining in our inside joke. Then she collected her hair and bent over me to lick the salt that collected at my collar bone. At the initial contact I gave an excited yelp. Gracie moved fast, clamping the shot glass in her lips and throwing it back expertly. I closed my eyes and heard the clink of the empty shot glass on the bar top and opened one eye to watch her bite her lime.

Everyone watching let out another round of cheers as I finally broke out into a fit of laughter. I made to sit up, believing my time was done and I ought to now be rewarded with my coconut cup, but Miguel beside me raised the bottle and shouted, "Who's next?!"

"I'll go," Ben piped up as he dropped his phone.

In disturbing unison, Colter, Gracie, and myself all looked to him at the same time said, "No, you won't."

Miguel and Juanita howled with laughter, and a blush hit Ben's cheeks as he said, "No, I won't."

Juanita was the one to point at Alan and Cam, "Either of you?"

Alan smiled sweetly as he leaned over the bar, pointing with his thumb between himself and Cam. "Not really our thing," he joked, winking. Though, I did catch Cam give a playful look of consideration that earned him a whack to the chest from Alan. I giggled as I watched Cam mouth, *Kidding.*

I caught the swift peck of forgiveness Alan gave Cam's smiling lips as Miguel commanded attention, saying, "That leaves you, amigo." Miguel was pouring a second shot glass and using his pointer finger of the hand holding it to point at Colter.

My whole body flushed, and I locked eyes with Colter, heart pounding in my ears. He took his time as he perused my body from head to toe. "Alright. I'll bite." When his eyes found mine again, I squirmed.

The volume level that ratcheted up as everyone again cheered made me jump. Miguel reached out to place the shot glass onto my belly once more, but Colter met him halfway and took it from his grasp. Miguel obliged and stepped back, letting the man do his work.

I swallowed again, my skin crawling with excited anticipation. And nervousness.

Colter was about to lick me.

In public.

And I wasn't exactly sure what kind of reaction that would pull from me.

Colter held my gaze as he dipped a finger into that tequila and then painted the alcohol in a thin line up the top of my thigh, trailing ever so suspiciously towards where it joined the other.

"Oh shit," Gracie giggled under her breath.

"What are you doing?" I breathed, my eyes going wide as Colter shook the salt onto the wet track he'd created. Salt crystals that hadn't caught in the slickness danced along my thigh, whispering down into the crevice between my legs. I bit my lip.

"I'm taking a body shot," Colter purred, low and slow. Then something wicked flashed in his eyes as he tipped the shot glass. I gasped through my nose as the tequila pooled directly into my belly button.

"Oh shit!" Gracie repeated, louder.

Someone down our line of friends whistled. My hands flexed and unflexed at my sides as I applied more pressure to my lip, praying for some kind of release soon because this was edging on near erotic.

"You up for this, Rockstar?" he whispered as he fished out a lime wedge from the bowl on my other side, just out of my sight. Still biting into my lip, I smiled and nodded my head. He nodded once in approval and then flicked me under my chin. "Open for me."

"*Colter Evans!*" Gracie hissed in fake reprimand.

"What is going on here?" That was Alan, his voice full of cautious amusement.

Oh, I opened for him, alright. More out of sheer shock than obedience. Colter wasted no time in placing that lime between my lips. I applied light pressure with my teeth, holding it there for easy access when he was ready to take it.

I couldn't help it anymore. I was strung as tight as a bow. I let out a squeal of excitement that made Colter chuckle darkly.

"Girl, what did you just get yourself into?" Gracie laughed as she appeared in my view. She looked excitedly astounded. "Blink twice if you need help. Blink once if you need me to back the fuck off and let the man cook."

A laugh bubbled up my throat and I gave her *one* deliberate blink.

Her eyes just about popped out of her head and she looked to Colter, amazement dripping from her tone as she said, "Shoot your shot, you lucky bastard." Then she was out of sight.

Colter replaced her and he was suddenly there at my ear. "I told you I'd make you feel better," he half-growled half-whispered, as I felt his hand grip my thigh, right below where the salt was laid. "Stay still, Rockstar."

I stifled the shudder that threatened to wrack my body and held my breath as Colter, keeping himself hovering low over my body, slunk down out of sight.

"Oh. My. God," Alan laughed with disbelief. "I'll ask again, what the *hell* is going on here?"

"Hush, Al!" Gracie's voice rang out excitedly right before I felt Colter's hot breath at my thigh.

I tensed and then lost the air from my lungs as Colter's tongue pressed flat to my thigh and skated up, up, up to nearly my swimsuit line. I squeezed my eyes shut as I knew what was coming next and sure enough the feeling of him plunging his tongue into the tequila pooled in my belly button caused me to lift my back right up off the bar.

I could hear the shock of our friends as they watched the debauchery playing out before them, but Colter wasn't done. On his way up to my mouth he placed one teasing kiss to my sternum that made me growl from behind the lime, but immediately his mouth was there, swallowing the sound as his teeth snatched the lime, his lips pressing into mine.

Possessed with the need to take him, I pressed my lips back, lifting my head right off the bar, the tase of salt, lime, tequila, and Colter filling my mouth. The sounds of the shouts and claps of our friends and the bartenders who'd instigated the whole thing was drowned out by the rush in my ears.

Colter's hands grasped my shoulders—his lips, not for one second leaving mine—and pulled me up, spinning me to sit upright on the bar top. He settled himself between my legs and the sound of both of our laughter, muffled in the kiss, joined that of the uproar of our friends. Colter broke away to pull out the lime from his mouth and then his hand delved into the hair at the nape of my neck as he pulled me back in for a deeper, fiery kiss that had me clawing his back.

"OH MY GOD!" I could hear Alan over the chaos.

The secret was out now. The alcohol was burning away the last thread of mystery as we damn near ravaged each other for the world to see.

"Hey, hey!" Miguel playfully shouted. "Remember I said clothes. Stay. On."

Finding my senses, I planted my palm to Colter's sternum and pushed him away enough to break the kiss. Colter looked like he'd just won the lottery—eyes bright, face flushed with excitement, a smug smirk on his swollen lips. I shook my head softly at him, but I gave him a wide smile as I heaved in a deep breath. "That was torture."

He wagged his eyebrows at me, and I cackled as I finally got the strength to really push him away. Hopping off the bar, I readjusted my swimsuit and crossed my arms over my chest knowing damn well my nipples were twin, stiff peaks poking through the thin material. I surveyed our friends and found an interesting sight.

Gracie had both her hands clamped over her mouth, eyes popped in shock. Ben's eyebrows were nearly to his hairline as he bit down on the inside of his lips. Alan had taken off and was running a lap down the beach unable to physically contain his surprise. Cam, dumbfounded, had his mouth hanging wide open, amusement danced in his eyes.

"Wait a minute now!" Miguel said from behind the bar. Everyone looked at him. "Are these two *not* a couple? You all look very scandalized."

I couldn't vocalize my answer. I just smiled and shook my head no. Gracie dropped her hands as she barked out, "No!" She pointed a finger between me and Colter. "This has never happened before—they're *supposed to be* just *friends!*"

Miguel turned wide eyes to us. "*Amigos* don't take body shots like that."

"No," I agreed as I sat up into my swing once more. I felt Colter's teasing hand on my thigh and playfully shoved it off as I shot him a look. "No, they don't."

Colter threw his head back in a laugh as he placed a hand to the small of my back and leaned in to kiss my cheek. Blushing, I pushed him away again. "Go!" I pointed to ocean behind us. "Go and cool the hell down, *Evans.*"

"Whatever you need, Rockstar." Colter winked, ripping off his shirt, tossed it to me, and then took off at a backwards jog towards the shore. Just as he was passing a still racing Alan, he turned, met up with the twin and the two of them raced to the water. Alan clapped a hand to Colter's back as they hit the ocean and Colter was the first to dive headfirst in, Alan following suit seconds after.

Wiping the goofy smile off my face, I finally turned back to the bar, pinning Miguel with a look. I slapped a hand to the bar top. "Where's my damn piña colada in a coconut?"

Miguel bowed his head. "Coming right up, *jefa.*"

Gracie was out of her swing and nearly jumping onto my back in a bear hug. "What was *that* all about—Spill, *now.*"

I held up a silencing finger as I watched Miguel work on my coconut. Only once he'd popped a paper umbrella into it and handed it over, did I finally turn to Gracie, take a very large and very needed swig of the rum drink, and open my mouth to start with, "Well…"

FIFTEEN

I didn't give her all the details, only a snapshot of the little events that led to the Body Shot Incident. Gracie sucked on her piña colada—in a pineapple—and listened with a captivated focus I didn't realize she'd been capable of. Where was that level of attentiveness in high school? Regardless, I did not fess up to Colter and I actually having sex. That was something neither of us had discussed telling anyone and I thought it best to keep it to myself, especially considering Gracie didn't seem urged to question it further.

When we'd had enough of our coconut and pineapple cups, we moved on to one of the pools at the resort we'd not been in yet. Shaped as a generic rectangle, it was a pool that was small and completely free of other resort guests. Which meant it was the perfect spot for our rowdy group. The single bartender that was manning the swim up bar looked at us with relief now that he realized he wouldn't have to sit here alone any longer. And he'd have access to tips. And after the morning's drinkscapades we were gracious with our tipping.

By the time he started pouring liquor directly into mouths, I knew things were only going to get wilder from there. The hours felt like they were flying by as we danced to the music over the bar speakers and played pool games. Colter and I dominated in Chicken until Alan got on top of Cam's shoulders and then wiped the floor with us.

The sun had already set by the time our little party gained attention. The small pool became packed as guests of the resort started to join in the fun. Javier eventually showed up. With a foam machine. And strobing lights. Without having even meant to, we'd somehow started an all-out pool party.

Colter and I had kept our hands pretty much to ourselves since the body shot make-out session, only getting handsy when we could sneak it in. Instead, we turned the focus onto Ben and Gracie as we all announced to anyone in the pool who'd listen, that they were getting married in two freaking days.

Alternating between chewing and sucking on the straw in my gin and tonic, I lifted one hand into the air and spun around to the music in my small little spot of the pool, swaying my hips to the left and right to the beat I sang the lyrics to Khalid's *OTW*—

I was silenced as I felt someone press into my back, their hands on my hips guiding me as our bodies melded in sync to the music.

The lyrics wended into my mind as I closed my eyes, lost in the dance. Thinking about being put into drive, coasting like there's no tomorrow, making sense of the past week, moving too fast.

Eric passed through my inebriated thoughts, a sharp pang flitting in my chest. As soon as it'd come it was gone, replaced by thoughts of Colter. Colter today at the bar. Colter last night as we finally crossed that line. Colter before he left for Tennessee. Colter when he lost his mom. That pang turned into a festering ache as I remembered his grief, his pain.

It'd been rough. Her death had come on so quickly—an aneurysm. He'd spoken to her on the phone that morning. By the time he'd left work, he'd received the heartbreaking call. She'd passed before he had time to make it to the hospital.

By now I'd stopped dancing, stopped swaying. A heavy sense of melancholy hit me, and the joy of the party had worn off. Realizing someone was still behind me, I broke into a moment of clarity. *Was this even Colter?*

My eyes flashed open, and I spun around to face my dance partner; a stranger. I balked, taking several steps back until I ran into someone else's back, spilling a bit of my drink into the pool water.

"Hey, where you going?" the man said, reaching out for me as the song came to an end, a new one quickly starting, more upbeat and livelier. "We were just getting started!"

"I don't know you!" I shouted over the music. Matter of fact, I didn't know anyone around me. Where had my friends disappeared to? Where was Colter?

Stranger Danger reached out for me again, this time he caught my wrist. I tried to shout over the noise of the party for him to let me go, but he just smiled, ignoring the way I tried to pull free from his grip. Frantically looking around, I tried to find a familiar face, tried to find the edge of the pool, but bodies were moving and pushing and swaying and churning the foamed surface of the water. Something akin to real fear began to eat away at my stomach.

Colter. Where was Colter? Where were Gracie and Ben, and Alan and Cam—

A flash of blonde and pink whizzed past me and barreled into my aggressor. "Let her go!" The feisty thing snapped over the din. To my shock, it worked. The man released his hold on me and backed away into the throng of people with his hands up and a look on his face that said, *Not worth the trouble.*

Gracie whirled to me. "Molly! Are you okay?" Her pretty eyes were wide with concern.

"Thank God!" I breathed as I fell into her, my arms wrapping tightly around her neck. "I lost everyone!"

"Molly, the boys are out smoking a joint someone sold them." Gracie hung on my arms, pulling away enough to look me in the eyes. "Don't you remember? They all asked if you wanted to join, but you said no." I blinked at her dumbly. She sighed, "You said you wanted to stay and dance. So, I stayed back with you? You said you wanted another drink? I left you alone for like two minutes—three tops!"

I didn't remember any of it. Not a damn second of it. I shook my head slowly, a frown pulling at my lips.

"Hon, I think you're blacking out," she said, smoothing back a stray lock of hair from my eyes. Gracie gave me a grim smile as my shoulders sagged. "I think maybe we should call it a night."

"I just wanted to dance," I said quietly as I dropped my head and frowned at the drink I clutched to my chest.

"I know, babe," she cooed as she wrapped an arm around my shoulders, leading me to the pool stairs. "I know."

Stepping away from the lights and the noise of the mini pool party, we entered into the night's darkness and made our way down to the beach, Gracie saying she wanted and expected to find Colter there for the room key he'd zipped in his swim shorts pocket.

We stumbled through the dark, tripping over an obstacle course of hidden lounge chairs as Gracie called for Ben, for Alan, for any one of the boys. Where they had run off to, she wasn't sure.

"Are we..." I hiccupped. "Lost?"

Gracie, who'd resorted to linking her arm in mine so she could tug me along beside her, scoffed. "We're not lost. The resort is lit up like a Christmas tree back there. We'll find our way back."

I hummed, shaking my head slowly. "I mean them. Are they lost?"

We crashed into a stand of snorkeling equipment, sending the thing toppling over.

"Shit!" Gracie hissed, releasing me as she dropped to her hands and knees to re-erect the thing. Several of the snorkels and goggle sets were still strewn about the sand. I bent at the waist to help but the motion sent my drunk addled head into the spins. I shot back up quickly, managing to hook at least one set of the snorkels into my fingers on the way.

Once again upright, the world settled into its normal drunk waviness, and I examined the goggles in my hands. "I haven't got to snork yet."

Gracie laughed as she stood up with the rest of the snorkels in her arms. "It's snorkel, you dumbass."

"Yeah." I rolled my eyes. Instantly regretted it. "That's what I said."

Gracie ignored me as she began hanging the equipment back up. Stretching out the band on the goggles, I brought them over my head. I made the rookie mistake of breathing through my nose and completely fogged out the goggles.

I laughed at the idiocy of it. "Oh no. Where'd you go?" I brought up my arms like Frankenstein and snorted a giggle at how stupid my voice sounded while wearing the damn thing.

"Oh, my word, Mol," Grace half-sighed half-laughed. "You are a real piece of work tonight."

"You know who's a real piece of work?" I replied, attempting and failing to pull off the goggles, the suction stronger than I'd anticipated.

"Who would that be?" she indulged me as she stuck a finger into the rim of the goggles, breaking the seal. Gracie helped pull them off my head and then helped when my snarled hair got caught in the strap.

"Fucking. Eric," I spat.

"Surprise, surprise," she mumbled, turning her back to me to hang up the snorkel set with the rest of them.

"But!" My voice pitched higher at the excitement. "He's not my problem anymore!"

Gracie laughed as she once again linked into my arm, tugging me along. We both went silent for a moment and then, tentatively, Gracie asked, "So...*Colter*..."

I didn't realize I was smiling until I had to talk through it, "He's an entirely different piece of work. Piece of Grecian God...mmmasterpiece."

"Whoa there, Molls. Don't go all poetic on me now," she snickered.

"Oh, but it's true. Grace...I don't know how I didn't see it before," I admitted, gazing up at the sliver of moon above the ocean.

"I don't think you've ever let yourself." She paused. "I don't think he ever let himself either, though."

"What do you mean?" My nose scrunched as I fought to make my alcohol-muddled brain understand.

A flash of light hit us from behind, sending our shadows sprawling out in dark streaks before us. "Hey you two! Everything alright?"

It wasn't a voice I recognized right off the bat. Gracie and I both spun around towards the wielder of the megawatt flashlight, nearly blinded against its lumens.

"Just looking for our friends!" Gracie called back, squinting against the glare.

"Would you put that thing down!" I scolded, shielding my eyes with my hand.

"Pardon," the man said as he lowered the bobbing light to the sand. He approached and stopped close enough that I could finally make out who it was. And he the same. "What are you two ladies doing out here all by yourselves?"

"Javier! If it isn't my favorite Director of Fun." I reached out a floppy, welcoming hand in his direction.

"How'd you find us?" Gracie inquired, her tone back to its normal friendliness.

Javier threw his head back in a laugh. "A guest was complaining about a couple of ladies disturbing the peace on the beach. Also said they'd been catching whiffs of what suspiciously smelled like marijuana. Which, I know could not be you two," he said with teasing reprimand, "as it is quite illegal to smoke it on the premises."

Quoting the great Shaggy, I threw up my hands in surrender, "Wasn't me."

"Didn't think so," Javier replied, though the way he eyed us implied differently. "Can I help you ladies find your way back to the resort? A few more steps and you'd have stumbled onto private property." Javier flicked the light up to flash the direction we'd been heading.

"Oof." I frowned. "Sorry, Dad."

Gracie snorted a laugh.

Javier, however, gave us a tight-lipped smile. "Ha... Let's go muchachas." His tone left no room for any more of our antics, and he did not wait for us to respond before he turned and began a brisk walk back to the resort.

"Now look what you've done," I teased Gracie as we stumbled after the fading light. "You went and got us in trouble."

"No," she argued. "Those damn boys got us in trouble. Wherever the hell they went..."

"I can't believe they didn't invite me to smoke. I love a moonlit waltz with the Mary Jane every now and then." I kicked at a piece of driftwood on the beach. Missed.

"Are you for real right now?" Gracie gaped. I grimaced at her. I couldn't really see her eyes, but I just knew she'd rolled them at me. "They *did* invite you, remember? You declined the offer."

"Really?"

"Really."

"Lame."

"Smart, honestly. Given your…condition."

I scrunched my nose. "That sounds like an insult."

"It wasn't a compliment," She sang.

"*Vamonos*, ladies!" Javier called out from far ahead of us.

Gracie and I laughed and broke out into a rather pathetic run.

~

"No!" I launched across the bed as Gracie appeared with a cup of water she'd filled from the bathroom sink after Javier let us into mine and Colter's room. Once we'd walked into the fresh chill of the room she'd beelined it to the bathroom stating she wanted to make me some coffee to offset my intoxication. I, on the other hand, had immediately kicked off my flip flops, leaving them strewn in front of the door and dragged my feet as I face planted into Colter's pillow until she'd stumbled out of the bathroom, stopping and staring at me on alert now. "You can't use the tap water. The bottled stuff. In the fridge."

"Oh, shit. Good call. Maybe you're not as useless as I thought you were." Gracie turned on her heels and disappeared into the bathroom right before the pillow I'd thrown at her could reach its target. "Missed!" she cackled as I heard her dump the water.

"Bitch," I mumbled jokingly under my breath.

"I heard that!" she yelled back. Then I looked up as I heard her open the fridge and twist the cap off a water bottle. I watched as she fished through the options beside the coffee maker. "Breakfast blend or bold?"

"Doubt I'd even be able to tell the difference right now," I said as I nuzzled into the scent of Colter's pillow. Him. God, it was him and I suddenly ached with need to have him here with me now.

"You're probably right," she mused and then paused—paused her speaking and her coffee making.

Alarmed, I rose to my elbows and looked over my shoulder at her.

Gracie was staring at the other bed. At the nearly perfectly made, seemingly untouched bed. Slowly her eyes moved to the bed I was on now. The one that was unkempt. The one surrounded by both mine *and* Colter's belongings. Hard eyes met mine. I swallowed.

"It's not what it looks like." The stupidest excuse in all of history.

"Oh really?" Refastening the water bottle cap, she crossed her arms. "Because it looks like you and Colter are sharing more than just some one-off body shot kiss. It looks like you and Colter are sharing a *bed*. And by the way you're blushing right now I'm pretty sure you're not sharing it just to *sleep*."

"I…" My drunk brain hadn't even begun to come up with an explanation.

"*Molly*," she hissed sharply. I winced. "Colter's your friend—*our* friend. What *the fuck* are you doing?" Gracie paced the floor and didn't even let me respond as she continued, "For fuck's sake you *just* broke up with Eric after he cheated on you—do you know how bad this looks?" She set the water bottle beside the coffee pot, not missing a step in her pacing. "Damnit Colter. Damnit *you*." She shot me a disapproving look. It was enough to snuff out the guilt and shame and ignite a bit of anger inside me. I rose up to sitting, my eyes narrowing. She went on, "Wait…how long has this been going on? No—you know what—that doesn't matter. Either way, this is stupid. Reckless and stupid."

"Hey!" I rose up onto my feet. "Colter and I are not stupid. And *you*," I lifted a finger at her, "you are being mean."

"No, Molly. You are most definitely being stupid. How could you do that to your friendship? You're still hurting Molls, barely two days off a messy break up. You're either using Colter or Colter's taking advantage of you. Don't you see that? This…" She winced as she looked away and raked her fingers into her hair. "This could end badly—blow up the friendship. The whole group."

"Excuse me!" This time I did not hold back my bite. Her words had sliced something deep in my chest. "That's jumping to conclusions don't you think? You're telling me it was all fine and dandy for you and Ben to move from friends to more—for Alan and Cam to move from friends to more—but God forbid if Molly and Colter—"

"You and Colter are not *in love*, Molly!" she shouted over me, silencing me. Something inside cracked open and I sagged at the weight of it, dropping my ass back to the bed. "Ben and I are getting *married*. Alan and Cam are *lifelong* lovers. You and Colter are…I don't even know what this is…fuck buddies?"

My jaw clenched so hard it hurt. Her line of questioning was not uncalled for if I was being honest with myself. Colter and I loved one another, that much was obvious—but had either of us indicated that there was a possibility that we could be *in love* with one another? I wasn't even certain he was open to such an idea. We had gone from zero to a hundred in practically a handful of hours.

I felt the blood leave my face.

"Molly?" Gracie's tone softened.

My stomach lurched and I clapped a hand to it. "I think…I think I'm going to be sick."

"Shit," Gracie cussed.

I shot up and raced past her to the bathroom, sliding on the rug in front of the bathroom sink as I lunged for the toilet. I crashed into it just in time to heave up all the drinks I'd downed earlier today. Cool hands were at my forehead, at my neck, collecting my hair and tying it off into a loose bun. I had only enough time to wipe the tears from my eyes before another round hit me.

Gracie rubbed my back and spoke softly as she encouraged me to get it all out, promising I'd feel better once it was all over. As the real vomit ebbed, the word vomit flowed, "Gracie?"

"Yeah babe?"

"I don't know what we're doing." Colter and me. "But…I do know…he feels like home." A sob shook me and I white-knuckled the toilet, willing myself to go on and literally get it all out. "He's been there. He's *always* been there. I don't want to blow up the friendship, but he feels like home. And the sex…" I paused to clear my throat and sniffle. Gracie's hand stilled. "It's…unbelievable. The little we've had—it's incredible. Best sex of my life." It damn near hurt to admit that out loud. "I never showed him any interest because I didn't think he wanted *me*. I didn't think he ever saw me as more than a friend."

Gracie's sigh was loud as it rang through the small, tiled bathroom, but she didn't stop me as I went on, "I don't know for certain if I'm in love with him right now—I know I'm still fragile from the mess with Eric. But Grace… It's Colter. It's different. It's so damn different. And it's scary and exhilarating all at the same time. And I think…I think I could fall in love with him."

Finished with my spiel—and my spew—I rested my cheek on my arm and breathed and breathed. Gracie let me stay there until she was certain I was done upchucking, and then she pulled me up from under my arms. Neither of us said a word as she brought me to the sink and helped me get my toothbrush ready. She didn't even look up at me through the reflection until she'd left and returned with another water bottle, then handed over my brush, toothpaste already on it. Like a parent and a toddler. I gave her a brief weak smile of thanks and brushed my teeth as she then took care of cleaning any mess I'd left behind.

Teeth brushed, face washed, and changed into a fresh pair of pjs, Gracie had stayed to help me climb into bed. *Not* Colter and I's bed. Apparently she didn't deem it appropriate to put me in the one I'd obviously been using. Probably another signal from her that she did not approve of what was going on here.

When I was comfortable, I looked at her as she sat at the edge of the bed, staring at her hands. At her ring.

"Can I ask you something?" she finally said after a few too quiet moments.

"I think you've earned the right," I weakly quipped.

"Did you love Eric?"

I refrained from rolling my eyes at his name. I knew the answer immediately. "I *thought* I did. But now? I'm not so sure..."

Gracie just nodded her head quietly and rose, slowly making her way toward the door.

"Can I ask you something?" I countered, sheepishly.

She paused and waved her hand, gesturing for me to go ahead.

I swallowed back the dryness in my throat. "What did falling in love with Ben feel like?"

Looking as though she were debating sharing her answer, she sighed, then finally looked up at me, opening her mouth to speak. Before she could say a word, a raucousness outside the door filled the hallway. Laughter and rowdy voices echoed off the walls. My ears picked up on Alan first—always such a loudmouth. Gracie seemed to pick up Ben as she whipped her face to the door, the twin second loudest after his brother. And then I froze, holding my breath as I heard Colter.

"They're back," Gracie stated. "Get some sleep, Mol. Talk to Colter tomorrow okay?"

Disappointment began to creep into my chest as I thought she was going to leave without even so much as a goodbye, but she stopped before she opened the door and turned to me as if forgetting something.

"Home," she suddenly said, at first confusing me. "Falling in love with Ben felt like coming home."

My mouth parted on a soft breath as she opened the door and disappeared. Immediately, the volume of the boys outside diminished. I could tell at least some were still out there as my ears picked up hushed voices. There was a silent pause and then I nearly jumped out of my skin as I heard the hotel knob beep, the door softly pushing open then quietly latching shut.

I briefly thought about pretending to be asleep, but he was there at the foot of the bed staring at me, catching my eyes before I could make the decision.

"She knows," was all I said.

"I know," he replied, eyeing me as though I was a skittish animal and a flight risk. He took a deep breath and withdrew his analyzing gaze as he set to work getting ready for bed. It took a handful of minutes for him in the bathroom to freshen up before he was back in the bedroom, shucking off his swim shorts and rifling through his suitcase for something to wear.

Evidently, he wasn't afraid of being stark naked in front of me whatsoever anymore. I tried not to, but I was still a weak, red-blooded female, and I stared at his perfect ass as he searched. Finding whatever it was he was looking for, he turned to me, and it was then that I finally averted my gaze. I listened to his footsteps as he came to the side of the bed, simultaneously stepping into a pair of black boxer briefs. Listened to the soft flick of him shutting off the bedside lamp.

I couldn't even begin to wonder why my heart was racing, my thoughts going about a mile a minute through my mind. But all thoughts were blasted to smithereens as I felt the mattress shift under his weight. Colter pulled back my covers and I felt him slide his arms beneath me. Flooded with excitement—and relief—I wrapped my arms around his neck, helping him as he lifted me and brought me tight to his chest. Without a word, he carried me back to our bed and settled himself behind me, pulling me into him warmly. My chest tightened as the rest of my body relaxed at the touch, at the realization that whatever Gracie had confronted him with in the hallway, it hadn't scared him away. I swallowed the lump of raw emotion in my throat and then forced myself to speak, "What happens now?"

A beat.

Then I felt him move, felt his lips press gentle kisses at my temple, my jaw, my cheek, before they brushed my ear. "Now...we sleep."

Good.

We were still good. Relief poured into me.

Before I let sleep drag me under, I nuzzled into him just a little bit closer. I reveled in the way he responded by tightening his grip around me.

Home.

SIXTEEN

The morning sun shone in through the sliding glass door with a fury, lighting the room with its bright yellow glow. It hurt my eyes.

Hoping to hide from it, I turned my face into the pillow and nuzzled in. An arm that'd been wrapped around my waist lifted, found its way to the back of my head, smoothing away stray strands. My hair must've tickled his face.

Colter.

My heart was instantaneously throwing itself against my ribcage.

It took everything in me not to move as Colter's arm found its place around me once more, this time his hand cupping my breast. Squeezing. I dragged in a silent gasp, stomach muscles clenching.

A few moments of stillness passed. Enough that I was certain he was completely asleep again. Though my breasts were heavy with arousal, I relaxed, softening back into the mattress as I listened to Colter's breathing—his breath softly blowing the baby hairs on my neck behind my ear.

We'd woken up similarly this way yesterday morning. It had brought on the same onslaught of sensations then and I was struggling to control them now.

His touch, his skin, his breath, his presence. It was all too much and not enough. I suddenly couldn't deny the thought that screamed I wanted this right here, every morning. Forever. Emotion, raw and heavy crawled through every nerve ending.

Home home home

And with that the fractured memories of last night funneled in like a bad dream. Gracie and I's argument. The words she'd said.

You're either using Colter, or Colter is taking advantage of you.

I squeezed my eyes shut as tears threatened to spill. Was she right? Was that what was happening here? Because if that was the case then surely this carried a real and true risk of blowing up our friendship—blowing up the group friendship.

Was I using Colter? I had most definitely climbed from one man's bed and into another with breakneck speed. I had barely had time to thoroughly process the heartbreak and humiliation accompanying a breakup like mine—but that had been the deal Colter and I had made. To save the tears and the worry for later, enjoy our time here. It had been his idea.

So…was he taking advantage of me?

Colter…who has always been there for me in the past. Colter, who had never once until this week even made a pass at me. Colter, who at twelve exclaimed to his friends that he wouldn't touch me with a ten-foot pole. I conceded to myself that maybe that wasn't the best excuse, after all that had been twelve years ago. We'd been children.

And while some in high school would agree he'd been a bit of a man-whore, they did not know him like I know him. They did not see the sweet boy underneath it all—the good man he'd grown to be underneath it all.

I couldn't bring myself to reconcile all the differences. I couldn't say for certain that I was using him or he was taking advantage of me. That uncertainty made me…scared. Terrified. I suddenly felt as though my heart was breaking. And it had nothing to do with Eric.

My heart lurched, highlighting the fact that I was breathing fast. Uneven. With Colter's hand at my breast, it was possible he'd feel it. I couldn't bear him waking up to me behaving like this. I needed to hide. I needed to get away—

I didn't give myself another moment to think about it. Hoping against hope that I didn't wake him, I quickly but gently removed his hand, setting it gingerly against his own hip and slipped out from the bed. I paused, standing there, my feet cold on the tile floor, and fretted over where to go. What to do.

Before I really knew it, I was out the door. Down the stairwell. Across the hotel and past the pool. Still so early in the morning it was like a ghost town. I did not see a single soul until I'd hit the beach and spotted someone preparing the tiki bar.

A bar. A *drink*. I needed a drink.

Still in my pajama camisole and shorts, I made my way through the sand and up to the bar, recognizing the man behind it immediately.

"Miguel!" I breathed a bit crazily as I hoisted myself up into a swing.

"*Buenos dias!*" He beamed, setting down the rag he'd been polishing a glass with.

"Tequila," I demanded, then winced as I watched Miguel's eyes widen in surprise. I smoothed it over with an apologetic smile. "Please."

"Of course, *senorita*." He inclined his head, but I could see the hesitancy in his eyes.

Feeling out of sorts, I bounced my leg on the footrest and rapped my knuckles softly on the bar top. My eyes kept scanning the premises as though Gracie were hiding in the bushes just counting down the seconds before she'd pop up and begin her scolding once again.

"Tequila for celebration or tequila for nerves?" Miguel's voice suddenly broke me from my worry, and I tore my eyes from the palm trees to look at him. He placed the shot on the counter and slid it toward me.

I stopped my fidgeting. "I look nervous, don't I?"

"Well…you don't look celebratory."

I sighed through my nose and brought the tequila closer, staring into it as though it were some magic 8 Ball that would tell me my future—tell me what was true and real and right.

"Do you want to talk about it?"

I looked up at Miguel again, and though his words were friendly, the look on his face told me he wasn't actually prepared to play bartender-counselor at this time of the morning. This wasn't that kind of bar. And I wasn't that kind of girl.

"Not at all," I said gently, smiling a bit.

Relief hit his brow and he nodded once and then let me be, continuing his work on prepping for the day. I closed my eyes, took the shot—no salt, no lime—and savored the bite of the alcohol. As I clacked the empty glass to the bar top I opened my eyes and froze.

For right across the bar, a wad of clothing in his hands and wearing a pair of crooked sunglasses, was Eric. Looking for all intents and purposes as if he were on a morning walk of shame. The derisive snort of laughter I let out immediately snagged his attention. And I mentally cursed and kicked myself, as he suddenly turned and headed my way.

"Miguel—I'm going to need another," I quickly whispered, my leg beginning to bounce again.

Miguel popped up from the ice trough he'd been scrubbing and looked at me and then looked to where I was staring. "You got it," he said, swiftly pouring a second into the same glass I'd used before. I tipped it back just as Eric entered beneath the lip of the tiki roof.

"Good morning," Eric drawled as he slowed his pace as though cautious of approaching me all the way.

"Hi," I snipped out, spinning my empty shot glass in front of me. Apparently taking my curt greeting as a good sign, Eric dared to seat himself in the swing beside me. Reflexively, I leaned away in my swing.

In my peripheral I could see him plop his wad of clothes onto the counter. It appeared to be a hoodie, and a t-shirt wrapped up into a ball.

And something white with a satiny sheen.

I narrowed my eyes on it, ignoring as Eric ordered whatever I was drinking. Miguel had poured him a shot of tequila, and I thought maybe he'd then been staring at me as though waiting for me to look up and assess whether I wanted this strange man here beside me. But I was too busy burning a hole in the satin strip I was looking at.

"What is that?"

Eric, having only just tipped back his shot, still holding the liquor in his mouth looked to me and then the clothes. I watched as he brought up his hand as though he were about to slide the pile away, further out of my sight, but I was quicker. I reached out and snagged a finger on the material. What I pulled out stunned me.

A satin, white *Bride* sash.

I dangled it between the two of us and Eric cussed softly. Disgust, pure and rampant, flooded me.

"It's not what it looks like," Eric mumbled with annoyance.

The same sorry line I'd given Gracie last night. I barked out a rather unattractive laugh that made Eric recoil. "Oh, of course not. It never is."

"Molly—"

"You know something, Eric?" I harshly butted in. "I never—not once—pictured wearing one of these for *you*."

Eric's mouth snapped shut in bewilderment.

It was true. It had been a revelation when I'd been admiring the older couple walking hand-in-hand on the beach days ago. The truth of if now suddenly snapped free something that had been constricted deep in my bones. It was so liberating that I could have almost cried. But I was not going to be that kind of girl, either. Not right now.

"I'm sorry. For everything," was all he said.

Noticing then that Miguel had left the bottle of tequila on the bar top, I poured myself and Eric another shot. He glared at me as I took mine, then glared at his own as he hesitated to join.

"Well, I'm not. Goodbye, asshole." I pulled the sash open. I brought it over his head, dropping it around his neck, and lightly patted his cheek twice.

Rising from the swing, I waved goodbye to Miguel and turned to find Colter standing there, his jaw set and his eyes hardened.

The shot of adrenaline that ran through me stole the breath from my lungs. It took a fraction of a second to realize he wasn't looking at me with such disdain—he was looking at Eric.

Daring a glance over my shoulder, Eric had turned to watch me go and was now holding Colter's glare.

"I always knew you'd be there waiting to pick her up right where I left her," Eric jabbed, finally taking his shot of tequila.

A blur whizzed past me and before I could realize what was happening, Colter had reached Eric and clocked him right in his eye.

I clapped a hand over my shriek of surprise.

Miguel had nearly jumped across the bar and put his hands up between the two men as though he could separate them when it was clear both Eric and Colter had a whole head of height on him. "*None of that here amigos!*" Miguel snapped.

Colter was already taking a jaunty step away, shaking out his fist. "It's all good." The fake tone of friendliness made my skin prickle. "I got in what I needed to."

"The *fuck* dude!" Eric growled as he brought the heel of his hand to his eye.

Colter was already walking backwards towards me, but he lifted a damning finger at Eric. "I warned you."

Eric's only response was to flip us off. Colter turned and he stopped abruptly before me.

My hand was still on my mouth, my eyes as wide as saucers. We stared at each other as Colter worked to steady his breathing. I watched the way his anger melted away, giving way to acceptance—not quite shame or regret—just maybe disappointment.

In himself or Eric or me…I didn't know.

Opening the hand he'd hit Eric with to me, he tentatively asked, "Are you with me?"

Perhaps it was the tequila, the adrenaline of what just happened, or the realization I'd just shared with Eric not even a few moments ago, but I slowly dropped my hand. I smiled, unable to contain my humor and laughed softly as tears pricked my eyes.

"I'm with you," I breathed, sliding my hand into his bruised one.

Colter wasted no time flashing me a smile and pulling me away from the tiki bar, away from Eric, and back towards our room.

"How did you know where to find me?" I asked, clutching his hand in both of mine.

"Javier," he answered as he tugged on me to prevent me from walking off the sidewalk I wasn't paying attention to as we left the beach. "Gracie had sent the resorts concierge on a shopping trip for all of us yesterday at some point. He stopped by all our rooms this·morning to drop off a couple of outfit options for you and me both for the wedding. Said he'd seen you heading this way appearing...frazzled."

My brows shot up. Wow, Gracie had wasted no time. And Javier had hawk eyes. And loose lips.

I was about to say as much when Colter suddenly pulled me off in a different direction than what would take us back to our room. "Where are we going?"

"Breakfast. Just you and I," he stated simply. At my quietness, he peeked down at me. "After last night, you need food."

"What exactly did Gracie tell you?" I could feel the warmth accumulating on my cheeks.

"Enough to know you need something in your belly. Especially since you thought it was a good idea to start shooting tequila at..." He slipped his phone out of his shorts pocket enough to view the time, "seven-forty in the morning."

Oof. Colter was right.

I didn't question him on it any further. Not until we sat down at a small table for two along the ocean-view windows of the breakfast area with plates full of food.

"Did I wake you when I left this morning?" I asked after a bite of toast.

Colter was mid-sip on his coffee. He swallowed and set the mug down. "I'd already been awake before you."

A jolt went through me. So, the handsy boob-grab had been a conscious effort. Got it. I tried not to think about how my breasts felt heavy now at the memory.

"Why did you leave?" His question was soft but firm. "Without a word. Without your phone."

I blinked at him, finding myself suddenly unable to answer. I couldn't talk to him about what had been going through my mind, what had prompted me to run. Not here, not right now. Pathetically, my only response was to shrug.

His eyes narrowed on me as he nodded once and picked up his coffee for another drink. Hoping to soothe over my declining to answer, I pleaded with my eyes, *Later. I'll explain later.*

I thought it'd be easier to talk about this once we had privacy back at the room, but after we'd finished our breakfast and shared a quiet walk through the resort, I stepped into our quiet room, Colter holding the door and stepping in behind me, and went still with nerves.

"I just need a second," I blurted out as I slunk away into the bathroom. That, at least, was true. I needed to relieve myself considering I hadn't given myself the chance to when I'd bolted from the room early this morning.

When I'd finished, I looked at myself in the mirror. Disheveled hair, wrinkled pajamas, sad eyes and all. God, I didn't want to feel sad for a second longer. I didn't want to feel the shame, the guilt, the hurt. I wanted to feel the rush, the pleasure, the *ecstasy* that was Colter. I wanted to feel home.

I caught sight of the shower behind me in the mirror. I could use one—especially since I spent all day in a pool yesterday and hadn't taken one before bed...but I didn't want to leave Colter hanging for too much longer.

The idea hit me fast and hard and with a rush of excitement.

When I'd finally worked up the nerve, I exited into the main room and found Colter had plopped himself on his back on our bed, waiting with his hands behind his head. He smiled at me, though it didn't reach his eyes. In that position, his shirt was pulled up to reveal that tantalizing strip of tanned skin.

I pulled my lips between my teeth as they tingled with the need to taste him there.

He might not have said as much, but it didn't take a leap of logic to see that my escaping out the door this morning without a word, only to find me throwing back tequila with my ex had not bode well for Colter's spirits.

Colter was put out—even if he'd been able to ease *some* of his aggression with a fist to Eric's face.

We needed to talk, we *so* needed to sit down and have a real talk. Especially after everything Gracie had said last night, but I just…I couldn't yet. Not as I gazed upon him lying there, looking relaxed and dangerously delicious.

I'd originally come out here to ask him if he'd like to join me for a shower, but a better idea came to mind now.

My heart rate pounded through me as I took a step toward him, my courage igniting and gradually increasing with each step. Something about my advance piqued his interest and he tensed as I stopped at the foot of the bed, standing there between his knees, his feet still flat on the floor.

A sensual energy slipped over me, and I let it guide me, hooking my thumb into the strap of my camisole and guiding it over my shoulder. I did the same to the other. Then I slipped the camisole down over my hips and took my pajama shorts and panties with it. The items pooled on the floor at my feet.

Colter's eyes had churned into a burning fire of blues and greens as I did so. He untucked his arms from behind his head and made to sit up, but I planted my knee to the mattress between his legs, and with a firm hand on his chest I pushed him back down. A muscle feathered in his jaw as his eyes flared, taking in the sight of me naked above him. I took my time as I glided my fingers across that strip of skin above his waistband, his muscles there flexing in response.

Desire bolted through me.

I tugged on his shirt, and he obliged me, sitting up enough for me to slip it up and off of him. I tossed it to the floor with the rest of my clothes. Our gazes locked and I could see the carnal need there. I had his full attention, and I loved it. His chest rose and fell with bated breath as he stilled, observing what I was going to do next. Slowly, I perused his body. His broad shoulders, sculpted pecs. Even those nipples.

A small smile hit my lips. By the time I was to his abdomen I couldn't stop myself from reaching out to touch him—to feel *those* muscles bunch under my fingertips again.

"What are you doing, Rockstar?" he asked with a low, sultry voice. I flicked my gaze up to his and silently shushed him with a soft shake of my head.

By the time I reached the soft patch of hair that would lead me to the promised land beyond the band of his boxers, my mouth was watering.

I leaned forward, wetting my lips and pressed a kiss just below his navel. His hips jerked up at the contact and a low, purring laugh wended up my throat. Using the opportunity, I snagged my fingers into his bottoms and tugged one side down then the other, slowly and teasingly pulling and pulling—my arousal ramping up as I heard his sharp intake of breath, realizing where this was headed—and I freed him of the remainder of his clothing, those too joining my pile on the floor.

I looked down at him, hard and throbbing, and shuddered.

This was new territory—obviously—for us. A different level of intimacy. Yet, looking down on him now…I was not afraid.

I was exhilarated.

There was no time for teasing now, not when I so desperately needed to take him—taste him. I wrapped my hand around him and again he bucked, a cuss hissing past his lips. I lowered, lining him up with my opening mouth, my body strung tight with anticipation—

Colter's hand brushed my hair behind my ear and then his fingers trailed to my jaw, cupping beneath and lifting my eyes up to his. I panted through my mouth, hot and heady, as he looked down at me with an untamed intensity.

"I don't want you doing this out of pity." His voice betrayed him; he was hoarse with desire.

I was too far down the lust spiral to take offense to the comment. Pity was the farthest thing from my mind anyway. I tightened my grip around him so he knew I wasn't playing around. That muscle feathered in his jaw again.

"I am not doing this out of pity. I'm not even doing this as an apology." I pulled my face free from his grasp and quickly placed a kiss to his tip, catching a bead of his arousal on my lip, the taste of it making me close my eyes against the pleasure-induced eyeroll that it elicited. Colter shook as a masculine groan rumbled in his chest.

"I'm doing this," I said, flicking my heavy, hooded eyes back to his, "because I *want* to. Because I *need* to. Let me do this. Please."

Colter sat up then, reclaiming my jaw in his hand. He kissed me, hungrily and fiercely, knocking the wind from my lungs. He nipped and licked at my lip as though he could taste himself there, and then pulled away to look me straight in the eye. "Whatever you need, Molly."

He settled back down onto his elbows, his head tipped back slightly, watching, waiting. Eagerness blasted through me now that I had free reign. Releasing the hook of my thumb on him, I flattened my tongue against his base and then dragged it along the sensitive skin of his underside until I reached the head, circled the tip with my tongue, and then dove ravenously, taking him in.

"*Fuck.*" The word was filthy rolling off his tongue. He jerked up again, his cock meeting the back of my throat with a force that only served to throw me into an even more desperate craze. His size—his *taste*—flooded my senses, pulled me right out of reality and tossed me directly into a dizzying state of need and frenzy. I moaned around him, dragging my lips up to the rim of his head, circling it with my tongue again and then coming back down, eyes watering at the sensation of him in my mouth. At my throat.

I worked him, mouth and hand in unison as my other hand kneaded the flesh of his thigh. I hadn't thought to tie back my hair and every couple of seconds I had to bat it out of my way. By the third time, Colter had caught on and his fingers raked into my hair, collecting it at the back of my head in a fist that gently tugged me along with my movements.

Liquid heat pooled between my legs, and I clenched my thighs reflexively creating a mess that caught the cool air, the sensation sending me into a whirlwind.

I don't know if he'd been watching me squirm or if he just couldn't hold himself back any longer either, but he moved, sitting up. I kept my pace all the while, up until I felt his hand reach around my backside—until I felt his fingers skim through my wetness.

The sensation was blinding and entirely unexpected. The cry I let out was muffled by his cock and it somehow made it all the hotter. I pressed back against his fingers without even meaning to. Taking it as an invitation, Colter plunged his fingers inside me, and I forced him all the way to the back of my throat, my eyes squeezing shut against the need to scream, in delirious pleasure.

"You're so fucking wet," he said in a near growl.

His fingers thrusted in and out quickly and then disappeared with a whimper from me. I still worked him, sucking and sliding tongue and lips against him with sheer, brutal need. I heard him groan and the words he said next had me quivering as I realized what he'd done with those fingers that had gone MIA, "Taste so fucking good." His hand returned this time for a biting squeeze to my ass cheek. "I need more, Molls."

Thinking he was talking about what I was already giving, I doubled down, eager to please. But his hand in my hair gently tugged me to a stop. I released him and looked up, the cool air catching on the tears in the corners of my eyes as I panted and locked gazes with him.

"Come here," he softly commanded. I didn't understand at first, but then he laid down onto his back and waved at his face. "Here. Now."

I stilled, heart pounding in my chest. Of all the times to suddenly go bashful...

Truth be told, I did not let something like this happen very often. Eric had been the only person on the planet I'd grown comfortable enough with to let him have that kind of access. The idea of Colter's head between my legs now had me clamming up.

"I…" I swallowed back the trembling in my voice that was sure to give me away. "I'm fine—"

"I'm not asking, Rockstar," Colter countered, suddenly reaching down for me.

Sensing my shyness, he clasped my upper arms and pulled me into a heated kiss. He devoured me in that way only he can, in that way that obliterated my thought process. Colter gently tugged me up as he laid back down all the while, enough so, that I crawled up his body to keep the kiss connected. When he finally dropped fully onto his back, pulling my weight down on top of him too, I was straddling his abdomen, my wet heat coating his stomach.

When he broke from the kiss, I panted above him, completely transported and burning like a five-alarm fire. His hands found their way to my ass again, and my core instinctively clenched as his hands pulled me apart, exposing me to the chilled air of our room. "You're going to spin around and sit your pretty little self right onto my face. Do you understand?"

I locked gazes with him and my eyes went wide with shock and desire. I'd taken too long to respond. Colter lanced a sharp smack to my ass cheek and demanded again, "Do you understand."

Dragging in air to replenish the breath that had been stolen from my lungs, I quickly nodded. "Yes. Yes, sir."

"Good," he growled as his hands slid to my hips and lifted, starting me off. I took over, taking on my weight and did as he'd instructed. I swung a leg over his head and climbed back over him, trembling at the realization my ass was inches from his face. His hands were at my hips again, fierce and perfect as he all but lifted me back those last few inches to line his mouth beneath me. I scooted back to help and then hovered there, bracing myself with one hand on his hip, the other finding its home around his glistening length once again. Hoping to distract myself, I stroked him. Once. Twice. Before his hand shot out to my wrist, stopping me.

"I said sit. Not hover."

Fuck me.

I was so out of my league here. But I couldn't resist. I couldn't tell him no. My *body* couldn't tell him no. I sat and threw my head back in a silent gasp as he sliced through me with his tongue. I jerked against him, drawing out an even greater sensation. His fingers clenched into my hips, keeping me pinned against his hot mouth as though he was a starved man clutching his last meal. Every flick and swirl of his tongue, every suckle, every graze of his teeth had me writhing on top of him.

It only took a handful of seconds to damn the nervousness of what we were doing—because what we were doing was unbelievable. What Colter was doing was effectively shattering my previous experiences. His cock, still in my grasp, jerked with need and I snapped back into myself. He worked me and I jumped right back into working him. I lowered, taking him all the way into my mouth again, enthralled with the new angle and the new depth.

He rumbled a groan against me, and I couldn't stop the way my body reacted by riding his face. His hold tightened more as he followed my movements enthusiastically. Each grind against him, each hotter and wetter pull of him in my mouth incited a chorus of whimpers and moans from me. Pressure built in my core, hot, languid and promising a punch that would have me half in a daze the rest of the day.

I felt the buildup in my skin first, along my arms and my thighs. It sparked tingles at the back of my neck and then barreled down my spine, the sensation stringing me tighter, driving me up that hill. Sensing my climax, Colter kept his pace steady. He thrust into my mouth again and I knew he was there too.

Mouth full, I let out one long cry around him as it hit me, blinding me with a flood of flashing white and black behind my eyelids. I rocked on Colter's face, completely giving in to my body, letting it take over. I forced his cock as far back in my throat as I could take him—just because I absolutely fucking needed to—and marveled as I felt him pulse and burst, thick and hot into the back of my throat.

I quaked above him as he lapped at me straight through the aftermath. I brought my mouth down around him and applied pressure as I sucked, drawing every last bit out of him as I pulled up and finally released him. He bucked at the sensation. I braced myself on either side of his hips and hung my head, panting.

Colter, though, apparently wasn't finished. He cut lazy strokes against me, making me jerk with each pass.

"That's enough," I giggled. He bore me down tighter against him again, drawing a shriek from me. Reaching back, I swatted the side his head. "That's *enough*."

He chuckled against me before finally relinquishing me. My legs were nearly useless as I swung myself off him, flopping onto my back, my head at the foot of the bed. I rested my cheek against his thigh and closed my eyes as I tried to calm my breathing.

Colter reached a hand over his chest and softly stroked the top of my thigh which was still half on top of him. I don't know how it was possible, but my brain still registered the sensation, still made my skin pebble at the touch.

"That was..." He paused to breathe and kiss my knee.

My chest tightened and I supplied the rest, "Incredible." He hummed his agreement. "I didn't know it...could be like that."

"You don't get that often, do you?" Colter's voice was cautious, as though he was uncertain if he should bring it up.

Too blissed out to be shy about it now, I simply asked, "Why do you say that?"

"Because when a man tells you to sit on his face, we mean *sit* on our face," he laughed softly.

I laughed, too. "I've never been asked to sit on someone's face. I've never had someone so...*eager* to be down there at all, really. Not without me having to ask."

It didn't feel appropriate to use Eric's name, even if he was the *someone* I was referring to.

Colter's sudden silence sent a bolt of worry through me. Had I said something wrong?

"Then you've only been with losers," he finally replied, pushing my leg off him so he could sit up, bracing himself above me. Colter's other hand brushed the side of my face as he pushed his fingers into my hair. His fingers delved until he cupped the back of my head and then lifted me until I was inches from his mouth. "Did you enjoy it? Sitting on my face," he whispered above me, his breath skating over my mouth. My lids felt heavy again, my breath suddenly disappeared again. I nodded and the corner of his lips quirked into a lazy half-smile. "Stick with me and you'll never have to ask for it again. You can *live* there if you want to."

Holy shit...

Colter tilted his head and nipped at my jaw, and I gasped in his ear.

"I don't think I'll ever get enough of you, Rockstar." he said, and then he kissed me shamelessly.

SEVENTEEN

My pandemonium of parrots was scattered throughout the trees as the sun began to slink its way behind a big dark stretch of cloud over the sky. Here and there some would flutter their wings for a takeoff while others would swoop effortlessly in for a landing to take cover from the rainstorm surely about to begin any moment. Graceful and beautiful.

"What is it about the birds?" Colter asked through the hold of the smoke in his lungs, reaching over to pass me the joint as he observed me watching them.

I dabbed my fingers dry on the towel we'd set beside the tub, and I reached over to take it. A small huff of a laugh left me. "Honestly, I don't know. It started with the two that are always hanging out in the stairwell. I like to pretend they're a pair of lovebirds and I just think it's...cute."

A creeping, handsome smile hit his lips as I took a hit off the joint.

It'd taken about fifteen minutes for either of us to move after we'd finished devouring each other. I'd made a joke that I'd meant to come out and ask him if he'd like to shower with me, not go straight into a 69 session, and at that he'd said he had a better idea.

And boy, was he right.

We were finally putting the balcony tub to use, and Colter had presented to me a joint he'd saved from the boys' adventures from last night.

So, we soaked and smoked.

As I blew out my smoke, I kept the joint. I eyed it and then eyed Colter, who didn't seem displeased that I was taking my time with it. "Is this triggering?" I asked, curious as to how our *no cigarettes* deal was going for him.

Colter's took on a look of deep thought as he mulled it over. "Surprisingly no. I'm getting a fix in other ways." He winked.

Tingles shot down my neck. "Oh, are you now?" I allowed myself a second puff on the joint before I relinquished it back to him. "Should I be worried you're starting a sex addiction in replacement of a nicotine addiction?"

"That depends." His eyes went dark with that intensity of his. "Are we talking sex in general—" Colter brought the joint close to his mouth but didn't wrap his lips around it, not yet,. "—or sex with *you*." My heart leapt in my chest. "I haven't even thought of a cigarette since the moment you climbed into bed with me. Take that as you will." He finally drew his hit, then rested his arm outside the tub.

I could feel a blush working its way to my face. "I wouldn't say I climbed into bed with you—"

"No, you're right. More like jumped into bed with me. Pole vaulted into bed with me. Catapulted—"

"Alright now! That had more to do with the thunderstorm than anything and you know it," I said, splashing a small wave toward him.

"Do I?" The chuckle that emanated from him made my toes curl.

I couldn't understand it. I couldn't begin to understand how on earth he could make me feel so turned on all the time, seemingly out of nowhere. A blurred memory wended its way into my mind then. One of Gracie and I as we stumbled along that dark beach last night.

'I don't think you've ever let yourself. I don't think he ever let himself either, though.'

Now was a good time as any to begin our talk. Especially as a soft downpour of rain finally released from the clouds above. Other than drinking away the time, there wasn't much to do other than sit and talk until the rain passed.

"I'm sorry about this morning." The words came out a little fast, but the softness and sincerity were there and that's all I cared about getting across, really.

A somber half smile from him. "I know."

"I didn't go looking for Eric. He found me." Those words rubbed me the wrong way, but they were the truth.

Colter inclined his head. "I know." My brow furrowed as I watched him take another hit off the quickly dwindling joint. "I watched him approach you."

My mouth dropped open. "You were there the whole time? Why didn't Miguel say anything…"

"Miguel's my guy," Colter laughed and handed over the last remaining length of the joint. "Who do you think sold us the weed?"

"No shit?" I plucked the joint from the pinch of his thumb and forefinger and Colter nodded as he relaxed into the back of his side of the tub.

"So," I paused for a toke, "you heard…?"

"Everything."

My stomach tightened at the realization. Colter had heard me proclaim how I'd never even thought of Eric being in consideration for marriage. It made me a bit embarrassed for reasons I couldn't understand.

"Why were you even with him it that was the case?" he questioned casually.

I balked. Why was I even with him? I drew another hit to buy myself time to think it over. The joint was as good as gone, so I snuffed it out with a hiss into a puddle of water collected on the tub's tiled edge and set it down. "I…don't know. He was nice. I didn't want to be alone. He could be funny. Pick any one of the usual multiple-choice options."

"I was told once that if you didn't see yourself being with someone for the rest of your life there was no point in even wasting each other's time."

I supposed I could see appeal to that argument, though it sounded lonely. "Is that why you never have serious girlfriends?"

He shrugged in answer.

"What about—what was her name—*Sophie*!" I grinned as he cringed. "You seemed to have a more serious thing with her."

"Sophie's a good girl," he mused. I had to force myself to ignore the curl in my belly of something akin to jealousy which that little statement elicited. "But after some time, I just knew."

"Knew what?" I asked, my voice a bit breathy.

"It wasn't going anywhere." Colter's blue-green eyes flicked up to me, demanding my attention. "She wasn't the one."

I sunk into the water until it kissed the bridge of my nose. Colter flashed his teeth in a beautiful smile as he averted his eyes, staring out toward the hunkered down birds.

Released from his intense gaze, I slowly rose back up out of the water. A few seconds of companionable quiet passed before I got the nerve to ask, "Who told you that? The whole *seeing someone for the rest of your life* thing."

Still looking out at the jungle expanse, Colter pursed his lips and nodded his head for a moment before he quietly answered, "My mom."

I went still. It was more than he'd ever given me since she'd passed. Sure, during the initial week and through the funeral he'd been able to grieve as he should. I'd spent a lot of that time by his side—as did the rest of our crew, obviously—but he'd seemed to collect himself in the days after fairly quickly and he went on with life per usual. Three months later he'd run off to Tennessee.

A niggle of hope hit me.

"I miss her," I offered sincerely. "I see so much of her in you." This could be dangerous, but I had a feeling that perhaps he was ready to hear it. "Especially your humor."

To my great relief Colter smiled toward the trees and even briefly shook with a bit of silent laughter. "Yeah she was pretty hilarious. She was…a great mom."

Seeing him talking about her now made me want to cry happy tears. But I did my damnedest to hold myself together.

Until a memory hit me like a force of nature.

"She really was, Colter. You know, she was more proud of me when I started my first period than my own mom." I couldn't fathom looking at him while I regaled the story, so I too gazed at the birds. "My mom had just shrugged it off like the normal and natural thing it was, but when she'd called your mom to let her know for that time I stayed at your house for the weekend after it started, your mom she...she pulled me aside and gave me just...the *biggest* bear hug and she cried and said I was a woman now and that she was proud of me and if I ever needed anything to let her know and..." Tears were nearly ready to fall. "I'll never forget that. I didn't realize how much I needed that at the time."

Maybe a TMI story, though Colter's been tasked with having to run into stores to buy me tampons before so there was no illusion here. Alan, too, much to his dismay, had to do it once. But that's the sort of thing that happens every now and then when your best friends are guys throughout childhood and adolescence. Yet, when I finally worked up the nerve to peek at Colter I found him looking at me with welling eyes.

"Makes sense now," he said simply.

"What does?" I sniffed back the tears that I refused to let escape.

"Why she always kept tampons and shit in the house even after her hysterectomy." A pause. "They were for you. The daughter she always wished she'd had."

That'll do it right there. One tear slipped, and then another. I quickly reached up wet hands to ineffectively wipe them away. "I'm sorry. I didn't mean to turn this into a cry session."

Colter laughed. "Don't worry about it. I like this. Learning new things about her. About you."

I gave him a waterworks frown of a smile and then shook myself right.

"You know, Alan told me not too long ago that she caught him smoking a cigarette when he was fifteen," he started. I smirked at that and settled in for him to continue. "He'd left school early that day and walked to my house to wait for me to drive home and he didn't know she was home early that day for a dentist appointment or something like that. But he'd lit one up on the front porch. Said he about shit himself when the door opened and she sat down beside him. Told him to hand over his pack and the one he'd lit up. She apparently snuffed out the cigarette and then made him follow her inside where she proceeded to tear up the whole pack right before his eyes into the trash. Told him she wouldn't tell his parents if he promised never to do that shit again."

I perked up. "Oh my God—and he never did!"

"He never did," Colter agreed with a soft chuckle.

I remembered Alan's brief dalliance with cigarettes. He'd claimed he'd tried them and that they just *weren't for him*. It had been Helene Evans' intervention all along.

Again, peaceful silence fell between us. I brought my elbows up to rest on the sides and laid my cheek to my left arm. "I'll bet she was thrilled to hear you'd taken up the nasty habit at eighteen."

"Oh, I would never hear the end of it from her." His eyes widened with playful annoyance at the memory. "Every holiday. Every time I went to see them for dinner. Every *phone call*. She never did let it go."

"That's what moms do," I noted sleepily.

"You're the same way."

I gave him a look. "I, too, will never let you hear the end of it, so get used to it."

"Well, you've got me to quit so far."

"Yes, but as we discussed we may have alleviated one addiction with another."

The joke fell flat. Or at least I thought it did, until I looked over to see Colter had somehow so effortlessly slipped back into his sinfully heated gaze, his laid-back, sensual demeanor. I swallowed thickly.

He dropped an arm into the water then. In seconds I felt his hand at my calf, stroking gently. A battle of nervous energy for the fact that I hadn't shaved today, and was probably stubbly, hit me at the same time a wave of excitement washed over me. Then my worries were affirmed as a teasing smile graced his lips and he said, "Prickly."

I let out a humph of humored aggravation and slipped my leg from his grasp, bringing it up to the water's surface to kick another splash his way. "I haven't been able to shave yet, you jerk."

"Where's your razor?" he asked through a laugh.

I scoffed. "What—are you going to shave me now?"

I was met with silence. I gaped at him.

"You've shaved me before." Colter shrugged.

A man's face seemed wildly different than a woman's legs, yet…

Now more interested to see if he'd follow through, I took the bait. "In the toiletry bag on the bathroom counter."

He was up and out of the bath with a teasing splash of his own at me in the fraction of a second. Colter was gone and back before I had time to reconsider his offer. I squirmed in his touch as he settled back into the water, wrapping his hand around my calf and placing my foot directly on his chest. I bit my lip as he ran his hand over me to make sure I was slick with soap before he carefully started.

He'd made three clean strokes with the razor before I giggled, "Is this weird?"

Colter, head still bowed over my leg in concentration, lifted his eyes at me from beneath his lashes for just a breath as he said, "Weirder to you than sitting on my face?"

This time when my toes curled, they curled right into his chest. The action did not go unnoticed as Colter smirked and carried on with his task.

The rain continued to shower as silence fell between us. Completely relaxed in his touch and surely in part due to the weed, I laid my head back on the edge of the tub and closed my eyes.

I didn't open them again until he got close to the center of my thighs and I had to force myself to remain still even though my body ached to move. As he alternated razor and hand all along my thighs my breathing began to quicken, shorten. Colter was somehow turning a mundane task into something sensual, and I didn't know if it was on purpose or just in my own damn head.

On purpose—definitely.

Because not a moment later his knuckles brushed right up through my center, teasing my clit. I drew in a deep inhale that made my breasts poke out of the water.

"Sorry." I could hear his smile in his low voice.

Staring at the ceiling of the balcony I rolled my eyes. "No, you're not."

"No. I'm not."

I bit down on my lip to keep from smiling. Didn't want to encourage him too much, there was still one half of a leg to finish.

By the time he finished, setting the razor down on the tub's edge, the rain began to ease to a dappled drizzle and the bath water was going lukewarm.

Slowly, I pulled my leg out of his grasp to sit upright. We locked eyes and the sexual tension was a third entity in the tub. It dawned on me then that we still hadn't really talked about us…not really.

"I'm hungry," Colter suddenly stated.

Amusement lit inside me. "Munchies starting to take hold on you?"

"Something like that."

Now that he mentioned it, my own stomach tightened as though reminding me I too could use something to eat for lunch.

Or maybe it was the marijuana talking.

Who knew.

I made the decision and rose to standing in the tub, water cascading down my body in rivulets back to the soap-murky surface of what was once our lavish bubble bath. Colter's hands gripped the edges of the tub tightly, and while his stomach may be empty, his eyes gobbled down the sight of me wet and naked before him—as if he hadn't already been freely given such views over the last couple of days.

He had to stop looking at me like that…

"Colter—"

"Molly."

"What are we doing?"

There. I said it. It was out there in the open between us.

Looking mischievous, Colter stood up beside me in the tub. "Well, we just finished a bath and now we're about to go on the hunt for some food."

I leveled him with a wry look. "You know that's not what I meant."

He huffed a laugh through his nose as he stepped out of the tub and onto the balcony. He reached to the chair where we'd set down towels and shook both of them out, handing one to me. Unease attempted to settle into me as I wrapped the towel around myself, watching him do the same.

"We," he began, offering up a hand to help me step out. I took it and looked away, unable to look him in the eyes as I prepared for his answer, "are enjoying—really, really enjoying—each other's company."

Close. But not enough.

"To what end." A boulder sat on my chest.

"What do you want?"

I couldn't hold back the small twinge of irritation. "An answer."

"Whatever you need." Colter led me into our room, his words unafraid and unashamed. It was an answer and yet it left me with more questions.

He kept saying that phrase over and over, throughout our life, but more so over the span of this trip than any other time.

"Gracie thinks we're making a huge mistake."

"I don't give a shit what Gracie thinks." Colter's words struck like a viper; shockingly quick and thoroughly honest. My brows shot up in surprise. "And I understand if you do…but she's wrong."

"How can you say that? She's your friend. You should care what she thinks."

Colter dropped my hand as he sat down on our bed right beside a spread of dress clothes for him and me that Gracie had chosen, and Javier had delivered this morning. "Gracie is not my friend. She's your friend, and my best friend's girl. She doesn't really know a damn thing about me."

Shock. I was in absolute shock at the truth to his words. It had never occurred to me that perhaps others might feel this way. I for one took what all of my friends said to heart. Though, I could admit that Gracie was more my friend than anyone else's since I'm the one that introduced her in the beginning. Still…

"She said I'm either using you or…" I hesitated to even say it as Colter looked at me expectantly and patiently. "Or you're taking advantage of me." Colter kept his face straight, but I caught it—the hurt that flashed through his eyes.

"Is that what you think this is?" The way his voice nearly broke, cracked something deep in my chest. I regretted even saying it out loud. "Do you think I'm taking advantage of you?" I watched his hand that he'd braced himself on the bed with curl into a fist around the sheets and around several choices of neckties that had been laying on top of it.

Hearing that question falling from his lips ripped at me, tore my very soul. My face crumpled with guilt. "No. No, Colter. I don't think that at all."

Colter stared at me, analyzing me as though he needed a visual confirmation of my words. Then he looked down at his fist, and the three ties he now clutched. He took those ties, wrapping them around his hand and then stood. I had to back up a step to give him the room, but when I tried he reached out for me. With surprising ease, he had one arm around my back and the other behind my knees, whisking me up into his arms.

The act was enough to pull me out of my funk. I shrieked, laughing "What are you doing?"

"Proving something very important to you," he said, hiking me up higher into his grasp as he rounded our bed and stepped towards the unused one. A trill of anticipation traveled through me as I noted the sultry promise in his tone. My heart rate kicked up a notch when he laid me on the bed and pulled off my towel. As he straightened I watched with widening eyes as he unraveled those ties from his fist.

"Our little excursion to the nautical museum was not for naught," he quipped as he dropped his own towel from his waist. I huffed a laugh at the word play but immediately forgot it as he climbed on top of me, straddling me at my waist. "Learned a few things...about knots."

I sucked in a shaky breath as he slipped out one necktie and gathered my hands, pinning them together. I knew where this was headed and lightning quick strikes of arousal darted through my body, directly into my chest and all the way down to between my legs, the muscles clenching reflexively in anticipation.

Colter created a loop on the end of the tie and slipped it over my joined hands, then tugged, pulling it tight. I gasped at the pleasant pressure. Then he leaned over above me, his rippling abs just inches from my face as he proceeded to fasten the other end of the tie to the headboard. Feverish with need for him, I lifted my head off the mattress and drew my tongue against his stomach, ending the trail with a kiss. Colter jerked above me as he finished and lowered back down over me. He grasped my jaw in his hand and tilted my head back, bringing his mouth just above mine.

The look he gave me was decadently sinful and I pressed my thighs together in response to the ache it caused in my center. The brush of his lips on mine was featherlight, teasing. Torture. But he soothed over the tension as he released my face and dropped a trail of wet kisses down my throat, between my breasts, against my lower belly.

Finding the other two ties he'd left somewhere beside me, Colter dragged his calloused hand down the outside length of my right leg, curling his fingers at last around my ankle. A heady mix of trepidation and craving had me simultaneously squeezing my legs tighter together and flooding my center with slick heat. A breathy whimper left me, making me blush.

"Open for me," Colter said, his grip on my ankle tightening but making no move to physically pry me open himself.

I hesitated, apprehension and desire warring. "I don't know if I can do this. I-I've never done this...been *restrained*."

"Me neither." He paused to look up at me then, his eyes full of honesty and heat and longing. "Earlier you begged me to let you have your way with me. Let me do this for you now. *Try* this with you. Trust me?"

The rebuttal on the tip of my tongue that he wound up getting his way with that particular outcome died as he bent and placed a kiss on the top of my foot. Besides...I did trust him. I trusted him more than I sometimes trusted myself. I'd never had a bondage kink in the past but if there was anyone I felt compelled to explore it with...it was Colter.

I answered by relaxing my legs. Colter's responding grin alone was worth it.

I did my best to control my panting breaths to keep myself semi-sane as he tied down one ankle to one corner of the bed, but lost myself as he pulled the other leg equally as wide, tying it down to the other corner of the bed. I trembled with want as he stood back to admire his work.

Colter's chest rose and fell in great breaths that enthralled me. His eyes took me in with an almost predatory concentration. "You are a goddess."

My back bowed off the bed as a sleeping tiger within peeped one eye open. Exhilaration rippled through me as I realized...

I may very much enjoy this.

EIGHTEEN

Colter's mouth was the catalyst that wrenched a strangled cry from my lungs. He'd dove in, wasting not another second, seemingly needing to quell the ache he could see he'd built up in me. I lifted my head to watch as he feasted, as his large hands splayed me open, his thumbs teasing my entrance.

"*Oh fuck*," I whined, brow furrowing. Without missing a beat, his heated eyes looked up at me, and I could see his working mouth quirk up into a satisfied smirk. I laughed as I dropped my head back, utterly uninhibited.

And then...I couldn't stop the laughing. But it wasn't humorous laughter. It was wild, blow-your-mind, blinded with pleasure laughter.

His tongue worked hard and fast, unrelenting. My laughter warped into a rhythmic pattern of short, breathy moans with each pass of his tongue, and I rocked greedily against his mouth.

What neither of us had accounted for in this position was that there was *nothing* to muffle the sounds I was making, and heaven knew I was beyond helpless to control it myself.

And I'd never been so fucking vocal in my life.

"*Colterrrrrr*," I groaned through clenched teeth as he slipped a finger inside me. He pulled out and then swiftly returned with a second. I tightened around his fingers, and he growled hungrily in response.

His fingers curled inside me, and I squeezed my eyes shut, my mouth opening on a silent scream of pleasure as he hit *that* spot. His tongue competed with his fingers as he licked and then sucked with fervor.

My whole body tensed, the ties biting into my wrists and ankles as I tugged, bracing against their hold.

I knew right then and there that I was hooked.

Colter could tie me down six ways to Sunday any time he fucking damn well pleased.

"*Oh my God.*" The words fell out of my mouth of their own accord, fierce and guttural.

When Colter added a third finger to the mix I shot my head back up on a choked cry of delirium. He lifted his head just enough to pin me with a look, commanding, "I want you to sing for me, Rockstar."

My mouth snapped shut, nostrils flaring. My breasts, tips tightly peaked, bobbed on each heavy breath in and out through my nose as I nodded enthusiastically in obedience. Colter raked his teeth over his bottom lip before he delved back in, burying his face.

I thrashed my head back as another "Fuck!" tore from me.

With the way he worked on me, Colter was not playing games. He pounded his fingers into me as he coaxed me toward the edge of oblivion. My whimpers and moans weren't short bursts anymore, they were long drawn-out cries as I braced myself for impact.

In the back of my consciousness, I thought I heard a knock on the door. But there was no way we were stopping. Colter's free hand splayed against my lower belly and slid its way up to my breasts. The satisfying stimulation to my nipple slingshot me further and a low moan started.

And it didn't stop.

The closer I came to release the louder my moan grew, the higher it pitched until it turned into a keening wail—a sound I'd never before made in all my life. Didn't realize I was capable of.

That damn knock went off again, but it was a barely registered annoyance as I *snapped*.

I arched nearly clear off the bed, Colter's hand slipping up my throat and over my mouth, as I screamed through wave after debilitating wave of an orgasm unlike any I'd ever felt before. Tears crested the corners of my eyes as I jerked with each continuous burst. His hand released my face, and he brought it thoughtfully to the other breast so it would not go neglected. But I needed to come down now, I was drained completely of strength and breath, yet Colter...

He kept going.

I bucked against him, stuttering out the words, "D-Done. *Colter.* I'm done." But he was no longer man. He was animal. My muscles felt like they would snap at the relentless onslaught of sensation I wasn't used to battling, "*I-I can't!*"

Colter replaced his tongue with his thumb as he broke away. "You can. You will."

At his encouragement—and as his mouth took back control once again—I handed it over.

I handed over my sanity, my body, mind, and soul. It was his. It was all his. It was always his.

I gulped down air right before the next wave hit me. Then I seized under its command, the neckties snapping tight as I pulled. The faint sound of a stitch tearing in one or maybe all of them was drowned out as my blood rushed through my ears. I came again so fiercely, so potently, that it stole my very air. I faintly noticed the rush of something pooling beneath me. Water from the bath? Sweat? *Fuck.*

Colter pulled his mouth away from me as I collapsed to the bed like a sack of bricks. My limbs were useless, lifeless things attached to my absolutely wrecked body. His fingers remained inside me, softly pumping slower and slower until my muscles released him. I couldn't lift my head, but I looked down at him as best I could manage and blinked as I saw him panting above me, his face slick with my arousal.

"Fucking. Glorious," he breathed, his eyes closing as they rolled into the back of his head. Shuddering, I swallowed as I watched him bring those three fingers to his mouth and suck like he hadn't already been feasting on me for what now felt like hours. Tears were still slipping out of the corners of my eyes as he rose up and over me, planting soul-healing kisses here and there as he went.

When his mouth finally found mine, I let out another whimper. A sound that actually made my heart ache even through the post-orgasm bliss. Sensing my need, Colter put a hand under my head to lift my useless neck for a better, deeper angle. Tasting myself on his mouth was downright filthy and utterly decadent.

The words flashed through my head then. Foreign ones. New ones. Right ones. True ones. I'd almost been stupid enough to pull away from his kiss and let them go free from my tongue, but my phone pinged somewhere on the bedside table, ripping Colter and I both back into reality.

He pulled away to look in the direction of the phone with a playfully aggravated sort of look, then turned back down to me, slipping back into our own little world of Fuck N' Fun. "That was the sexiest thing I've ever seen in my life." Colter quickly stole another kiss, causing another pathetic little gasp out of me. He reached up to release the knot at my wrists, and as I was freed, he said, "You squirted."

I bolted up to my elbows, nearly knocking into him as he sat back on his haunches, still straddled over me.

"What?!" I felt the blood drain from my face. I'd never done such a thing. Heard of it, yes. But...

One of his brows inched up pulling a corner of his lips with it in a smug smile. "Why do you think I tied you down to *this* bed?"

I registered the feeling then, remembered the pool of liquid that I'd mistaken for bathwater or sweat. Embarrassment tore through me like a rabid animal. "Oh my god. I'm so sorry," I breathed as I straightened to sitting.

Colter, seemingly unfazed, scooted down off the bed as he reached for one ankle, freeing it, and then going for the other, "Why the fuck would you be sorry."

"Because?" I didn't want to have to say it out loud. I was nearly mortified already.

I stifled a shriek as Colter clasped behind my knees and tugged me down to the edge of the bed in one swift movement. I grasped his sweat glistened shoulders to steady myself as he knelt there between my legs.

"Molly Connors," he said, amusement riddling his tone. "Do not for one second feel embarrassed." Colter reached up to brush my hair behind my shoulders, dragging the tips of his fingers down each side of my spine as he leaned in to press his lips to my collar bone. "What happened right here," he said, pausing to angle his head to kiss the other side of my collar bone, "was fucking mind-blowing incredible. And it *won't* be the last time."

I was putty in his hands all over again. God, he rearranged my very world. And I couldn't get enough of it.

My hands—finally free of restraints—found each side of his face and I brought my mouth to his greedily and hungrily. I broke away, planting kisses along his jaw, down his neck, nipping where I felt the need to, trailing my tongue up from his collar bone to the crook under his ear.

He let me play, let me kiss and let me touch, his own breath hitching as I did so. My hands roamed voraciously over his shoulders, down his arms, across his stomach and around his waist to his back where I dug my nails in for good measure as I pulled him closer to me. His head had dropped back as I pulled on the skin of his throat with my mouth, crazed for his touch and his taste. When my fingers wrapped around his cock, more rock hard than I think it had ever been yet, he snagged my wrist.

"This was supposed to be all about you," Colter stated, his voice hoarse, as he pulled my hand away.

I yanked out of his grip and reattached my hand to its home, lining him up before my still soaking center. "Shut up and get inside me."

He obeyed without hesitation.

NINETEEN

I sat in the spa chair beside Gracie, sharing a bottle of wine as we each received a foot massage, giddy with anticipation. It was her text message that had pinged from my phone earlier when Colter and I were still in the throes of swapping body fluids. The way he'd taken me after he'd untied my restraints, the way he'd latched onto my neck, his hands delving into my hair and pulling—*hard*...

"So did you try on any of the dresses I had sent to you?" Gracie asked into her wine glass.

I opened my eyes and rolled my head towards her, mentally giggling at how silly she looked with the green facemask on and her hair wrapped up in a tall, fluffy towel. I had no doubt I looked equally silly donning the same.

After Colter and I had finally finished our afternoon delight, we'd shared that shower together and headed down to the Mexican restaurant for tacos and a pitcher of margaritas by ourselves.

While there, Javier passed through, stopping by our table as I flagged him down and requested his assistance in a top-secret mission. Surprisingly, none of our friends but Gracie had messaged me and it was to let me know she'd booked us a girls' spa evening starting a few hours after Colter and I had finished lunch.

"Not yet," I replied a bit sheepishly. We'd obviously been a little busy. "But Colter did try the ties." I sipped my wine as I internally snickered at my own little joke, Gracie completely—and forever to remain—unawares.

"Yeah?" She was pleased to hear that much. "Which one did he settle on?"

Ah, shit.

I'd been a little too preoccupied to notice the different patterns. I was shaping up to be a real shit Maid of Honor, but I would change that here soon.

I took a stab in the dark. "The blue one." A safe, manly tie option.

Gracie nodded with a satisfied smile. "Yeah, that was a nice one. Well, that's good. Another step in the right direction." She craned her neck to check the clock on the wall. "Because we have twenty-four hours until I'm Mrs. Campbell!" Her sentence had ended in shrill excitement.

I scrunched up excitedly too and offered her a *woo-hoo.* I reached my wine glass to her, initiating a cheers which she happily obliged.

"I wanted to apologize, y'know. For kind of crapping all over you when I found out about you and Colter." She sighed as she settled back into her chair.

I tensed, my wine glass going still before it reached my mouth. A part of me had been hoping to pretend like last night had never even happened, not when I was still so thoroughly sated from Colter's efforts earlier today. But I could see an olive branch when one was being extended to me, so I softly smiled at her. "Thank you."

"It's just scary. When things change like that," Gracie went on. I humbled myself and let her speak her mind. "What you and Colter decide to do in your private time is none of my business—though I could hear you getting your brains fucked out of you when I went to knock on your door earlier. I just hope that you're being careful."

"That was you?!" I snorted into my wine. "And you know I'm on birth control."

"That's not when I meant," Gracie said with a quick shake of her head. "It's just…like I said, you just went through a messy breakup. I don't want to see you get hurt again."

"You think Colter will hurt me?" All pleasant intonations vanished. My pulse skittered.

"No!" Gracie turned her torso to me. "I just mean…Oh, I don't know. He's always been a bit of a wild child and well you're…*you*."

"I don't understand."

Gracie's shoulders rose and dropped with a deep breath as though she knew she'd made some mistake and was frustrated with herself as she tried to figure out how to fix it. "Colter's always been a bit of a free agent. A rolling stone. A ramblin' man." With each fancy title my brows ticked higher. "And you," she exclaimed with a heartfelt smile. "You're our sweet, do-good, girl-next-door Molly." My brows slammed down.

"I was letting y'all take body shots off me yesterday, what are you talking about?" A stupid excuse, but I was snatching for anything that would prove her wrong.

"Yeah. *Me*," she emphasized, as though it made her point. "And Colter, but now I know why."

"I would've let someone else take a body shot off me—a stranger. I *could* have done it." I weakly argued.

Gracie snorted. "Okay, sure. Even if you would have been comfortable enough to do that…Colter damn sure wouldn't have been."

Awareness zinged through me. Why would Gracie assume it would be up to him? It was my body, it was my choice… But I had subtly asked *his* permission, didn't I? I'd looked right to him for his approval before conceding to it. He'd also pulled me down as soon as his turn was finished, preventing any other takers from getting a chance, not that I thought there were any takers, but still. And the way he'd stopped me on our first night here from fondling myself in public. *He'd* stepped in when no one else had. And it was *Colter's* comfort I yearned for when we even made the initial takeoff from Gerald R. Ford airport. I was always seeking Colter.

I had an entire life's worth of examples just like those that were flashing through my head now. It had been Colter who'd secretly taken the time to help me learn how to drive in the pre-built subdivisions in high school. It had been Colter who I had asked what he thought if I got my belly button pierced when I'd turned seventeen. It was Colter who I'd talked to when I decided to change my major from education to administrative assisting. It was Colter who'd been there to take me to junior prom when my date backed out three days before. It was Colter. It was always Colter. And I...I was a fool for him in every good and bad sense of the word.

But he was mine. And Gracie...she had it wrong. He'd even said it himself; *'Gracie is not my friend. She doesn't really know a damn thing about me.'*

"You're wrong about him," I suddenly said quietly, twirling the wine in the bulbous glass. "You don't know him like I know him. He'd never hurt me."

"I sure hope he'd never hurt you. But I do know him, Mol. He's a player. Always has been. You're just too dickwhipped to see it right now—"

"What's his favorite color?" I challenged, knowing it was a stupid question, but I figured I'd start small.

"Seriously?" She set me under a look of incredulity and when I held my stern face to her, she rolled her eyes, giving in. "Fine. Um...his Jeep is orange. So...orange."

"Forest green," I supplied. In the same breath I moved on to the next question. "Where does he work?"

"Some electrical company? I don't know..."

"Trident Electrical Services. He'll have been there four years this spring," I smiled wryly. "Do you know that little mark on his arm?"

"His birthmark?"

"His *scar*," I corrected. "He likes to let people believe it's a birthmark, because he got it when he was eight after he fell off of his scooter and nearly impaled himself on a garden stake and it embarrasses him."

Gracie winced. Winced in solidarity with the pain he'd must've felt or perhaps because she realized how wrong she was. I'd forever tell myself it was the latter.

"Still doesn't smooth over his track record," she spitefully added as she downed the remainder of her wine.

"He doesn't waste his time with women he doesn't see a future with." A part of me knew I shouldn't have said it. It had been something his mother had imprinted on him, and he'd told me that in confidence. But the other part of me needed Gracie to just understand him.

"And you think he sees a future with you?" The derisive laugh she let out sliced me deep.

"That's not what I'm saying—"

"You've already fallen for him, haven't you?" Gracie's eyes narrowed as she leaned deeply on her chair's armrest toward me. "Tell me, Molly...has he *told* you he has *feelings* for you?"

I stilled, an ember of anger burning through me. But her question had me filing back through the scenarios that had played out over the last week. And while there were plenty of instances where Colter was eager to tell me I was beautiful and perfect and even glorious...he'd never said anything about how he was feeling.

"Oh my God, Molly. I'm so sorry. I didn't mean to throw this in your face. Shit." Gracie smacked a hand to her green forehead. It was the gentle apology, the pity in her tone that rocked me. She'd played her last card, and she'd watched me fold into myself as I could not call her bet. She'd witness it firsthand.

Scooping out any dignity I had left, I waved her off as nonchalantly as I could muster. "It's fine. I'm fine. This is all so silly anyway. I never expected Colter to be anything more than—what did you call it? A *fuck buddy*. Let's just," I finally looked her in her sorrowed eyes, "have a good time. Okay? You're getting married!"

Gracie smiled at my forced enthusiasm, but her eyes still held an air of wariness that told me she knew she'd hurt me somehow, somewhere deep.

By this time, we'd realized both our masseuses had finished their half-hour and had silently and discreetly left the room. I stared at the cracked open door and listened as Gracie poured the remainder of the wine bottle into both our glasses.

"Here," she said, holding out my filled-to-the-brim wine glass. A peace offering.

I laughed through my nose and accepted it. When we both raised our glasses to drink, neither of us dropped them back down until we'd emptied the entire contents.

~

With Colter at my side once again, the world seemed right. The weightiness that had settled over me after another heated discussion with Gracie had lifted as soon as I'd returned to our hotel room and I found Colter in the bathroom, finishing up a shave.

He'd reached out to me as I tried to pass him and tugged me into his arms for a hug and a knee-buckling kiss that left me having to wipe off shaving cream from my freshly pampered face.

I'd let him talk, going over everything he and the boys did while Gracie and I had parted to have our girl time. The boys had found jet ski rentals and spent the afternoon annoying sailors and fisherman alike beyond the break.

As I'd gotten ready, choosing one of the three dresses Gracie had sent up that I was certain I was not wearing to the wedding tomorrow, I listened to Colter, smiling like a fool through it all.

Now, I stood in the resorts high-end personal dining suite I'd booked for the evening. Its walls were lined with floor-to-ceiling windows of sunset ocean views separated by floor-to-ceiling shelves of wine. The table was long and rectangular with a seating space for up to ten people.

Javier had had Imelda arrange a lovely place setting for six, and while even the thought of her made my stomach flip, I had to admit she had a talent for such things. I'd shocked myself when I had realized that mention of her had rubbed me raw not because of her time with Eric...but because of her time with Colter on day one of our trip. I forced myself to forget about it, focusing rather on the gorgeous oranges of the sky now visible outside.

"You look beautiful," he said as his hands slid onto my hips from behind. Before I could turn, Colter placed a kiss to the exposed skin at the crook of my neck and shoulder. I shivered at the pleasant contact.

"Thank you," I replied, tipping my head back to rest it on his shoulder. "You look *very* handsome, yourself."

"I know." His air of arrogance made me bust out into an all-out grin. "I saw the way you looked at me as we left the hotel room. You can't wait to get me back to bed."

"Colter Evans, your conceitedness knows no bounds," I teased, reaching up to plant a kiss to the corner of his mouth.

He was too late to turn and steal the kiss back, but he feigned a patronized look as he said, "I think you mispronounced *confidence*."

I barked out a laugh to which his grip on my hips tightened, pulling my backside firmly against his groin.

"You do look beautiful though," Colter's tone had turned serious for a moment. "Glowing."

He was buttering me up big time. I hooded my eyes as I demanded his gaze. "Probably because you've been filling me up all week with your c—"

Colter choked a cough at the same time voices suddenly carried into the room.

"Hola amigos!" That was Gracie.

"Oh snap, this place is *fancy*!" Alan chimed in.

Colter and I both turned around to welcome our arriving friends. I pulled out of Colter's grasp before anyone had a second to look away from the beauty of the room and look at us. I hurried over to Gracie and Ben as I said, "Surprise! Welcome to your rehearsal dinner!"

"Oh, my goodness!" Gracie beamed. "You are the best."

"Wow, thank you, Molls. This is really incredible," Ben added, still gawking at the space.

Both bride- and groom-to-be stepped in to give me hugs and I tried not to cry through the makeup I'd applied before I'd arrived. We'd have all day tomorrow for waterworks.

As we settled into our seats, Ben at the head of the table with Gracie to his right, I secretively tugged on Colter's hand to make sure he followed and sat beside me as I plopped down to Gracie's right. Alan sat on his brother's left, Cam next to him. I wondered if maybe I should feel bad for forcing him so far away from his friends, but once we'd pulled our chairs in and I felt his large hand slip onto my thigh with a teasing squeeze, I knew I'd made the right decision.

The extent of his groping remained fairly PG given I was in a floor-length lilac dress—though, he wouldn't know it until I surprised him later, that I'd forgone wearing panties altogether.

Javier had done an excellent job with selecting an Italian inspired menu for the night and even enlisted the help of our new friend, Miguel, to wait on us—something he must've picked up on when he'd overheard Colter and I talking about him endearingly when we'd spoken at lunch. I made a mental note to tip him generously for giving up his time behind the bar tonight.

Colter had treated himself to a Delmonico steak and I settled on a very adult version of basically macaroni and cheese, fancifully titled Cacio e Pepe. But the real star of the show was a ball of cheese-filled risotto that was fried and served on a bed of tomato sauce and doused with spinach aioli. Absolute bliss.

Despite the tensions that had sprung on between Gracie and I, the night went wonderfully. Everyone had taken a chance to go around the room and share a favorite memory of the happy couple and my favorite was a story that Alan had shared of how Gracie had peed herself laughing so hard at a family reunion and Ben had had to discreetly sneak her out of there to run back home so she could change. They'd successfully duped everyone. Well, everyone but Alan who seemed set on never letting Gracie live that down for the rest of her natural born life.

I'd been cliche and settled on the night that Ben finally asked Gracie to be his girlfriend. It had been at his grad party just a month after our graduation. He'd asked in front of everyone, and she'd about jumped to the moon as she said yes.

~

Hours later, I stood in Colter and I's room as I created a stack of clothes for overnight. Wanting to go the traditional route, Gracie had asked over dinner that I sleep with her tonight and let Ben room with Colter since he had a free bed and all.

I blushed even thinking about the bed now. But Colter and I had stripped the bed of the linens and housekeeping had swooped in to cart away all the evidence and remake the bed, it looked more pristine than before I'd even attempted to sleep in it. I thought maybe we should offer him the other bed, but we'd had plenty of sex in that one too, so…

Besides, if Gracie knew Colter and I were sleeping together, I had no doubt Ben already knew what he was getting into.

"How was your spa day?" Colter asked as he launched himself onto our bed. He leaned his temple on his fist as he watched me. He'd been so enthralled in his earlier sharing of his own day that we hadn't much discussed mine.

"Oh, you know," I replied jauntily, "relaxing."

Lies.

"Gracie didn't have anything more to say about you and me?"

Shocked he'd even go there, I paused my packing and turned to him. "Why do you ask that?"

Colter gave me a dry look. "Because she basically pretended like I didn't exist tonight and kept a hawk's eye on you as though you needed a chaperone."

"Are you implying that she set up this sleeping arrangement to separate us?" I cautiously inquired.

Colter's brows shot up. "No, not at all. But now that you mention it—"

"Oh, stop it." I laughed as I picked up my pillow and tossed it at his face. Colter was wicked fast as his hand swung out to catch it easily before it made impact. That frustrated the ever-living crap out of me, and he could see it on my face.

"Sorry. Do you want to try again?" he teased, holding out the pillow to me.

"Yes." I snatched it back, but then thinking better of it, plopped it back into its usual spot. "No."

"I'm going to miss you tonight."

The words stunned me, and I was embarrassed to admit that I swayed on my feet a little bit at them. And it had nothing to do with the wine I'd sipped on at dinner. Truth be told, I wasn't exactly excited to be apart from him for the night either. I'd grown rather accustomed to his body beside mine, his breath at my neck, his hand always holding my right breast.

So, I said as much. "I'm going to miss you, too."

Wagging his brow mischievously, he leaned in toward me. "We could just lock the door. Not let Ben in."

"Yeah!" I cackled. "I don't think that will earn me any brownie points with my best friend. Though, I'd bet Ben would agree with you. I'm sure he's crestfallen that he won't be getting any nookie tonight."

"Same," Colter mumbled under his breath.

"What's that?" I probed innocently.

"I said, have fun." Colter winked. But I gave him a look that told him I knew better.

All jokes and smiles vanished as a knock hit the door. I couldn't explain the gut-twisting feeling that it produced. Colter was already jumping up from the bed, stepping to my side.

I faced him suddenly unsure of what to say, what to do. Did we kiss goodbye? That seemed like a wildly couple-y thing to do, and a couple, we were not. Did we shake hands—no, of fucking course not. I was being an idiot.

"Promise me one thing." Colter broke me out of my thoughts as he reached up and tucked my hair behind my ear. My heart raced.

"What?" It was hardly even a whisper on my lips.

"Don't let her get in your head." His eyes dropped to my mouth for a fraction of a second but then he was looking into my eyes once again. "She seems to think she has her reasons to not like whatever this is between us, but..." He seemed to struggle to find the rest of his words, but I was still hung up on what he'd already said.

Nearly shaking with nerves, I took advantage of his pause and cut in. "What *is this* between us?"

Colter looked away as his throat worked on a swallow. I began to feel the first stages of panic. Until he looked up at me and posed a question that only stumped me further. "What do you want it to be?"

Well, damn.

He just flipped that shit right on me. Now I was the one looking away, my brain unable to comprehend the magnitude of what was going on. Somehow this was harder than giving in to sex with him. Though, *that* had turned out spectacularly for me...

The knock sounded through the room again making me jump. I closed my eyes, breathing to steady my nerves as Ben's voice carried under the door, "Hello? Anybody home?"

Colter then dropped his forehead to mine. "Think on it," he whispered in the space between our mouths.

I opened my mouth to say what, I didn't know. But then he brushed his lips to mine, there and gone before I could even kiss him back. I all but lurched after him as he backed away, turning to the door and shoving his fingers through his hair. I stared at his back with a gaping mouth as he answered the door.

TWENTY

Music played on one of our phones still sitting on the bedside table inside Gracie and Ben's hotel room after our girl's night of karaoke at the poolside bar.

With the door cracked open, we sat in her empty balcony tub in our pajamas as we shared a bottle of wine we'd smuggled from the stash at dinner. Sitting the short way in the tub side by side, our legs hung out, our feet bouncing along to the beat of the music.

"So how does it feel to spend your last night as a free woman?" I winked, sipping right from the bottle.

Handing it over, Gracie pretended to think deeply on the subject before taking a mouthful. "Hm. It feels..." She turned lively eyes to me, "wonderful."

"What do you think your families are going to think about this?"

Gracie shrugged. "Don't care. We'll arrange a reception party after we get home. Maybe something in the spring."

"That would be nice! Then I could actually help do Maid of Honor duty things." I knew this would likely be my one and only shot of playing this role considering Gracie was my closest and only girlfriend. I wanted to do right by her, which was hard to do when I'd only had a handful of days' notice in advance.

"My mother will be thrilled with that." Gracie snorted.

"Oh, Mama Storteboom and I are going to plan something real fun."

Gracie tipped her head back onto the tub edge and groaned. "Oh, thank God I finally get to rid myself of that godawful name."

I feigned offense. "What? Grace Jo Storteboom is a beautiful name. How dare you."

"Wrong," Gracie countered. "Grace Jo Campbell is a beautiful name."

"It is nice," I conceded, accepting the wine as she offered it back to me. I took a sip, smacking my lips and giggled as something hit me, "Campbell. Like the soup. I'm gonna call you Ol' Soup Lady. O-S-L. I'm making a shirt."

Gracie let out a dramatic sigh. "Only you could manage to somehow ruin it for me."

I sniggered behind the wine bottle. "I sorry."

"No, you're not, you little a-hole." She rolled her eyes and snatched the bottle from my hands, taking a hefty swig. Gracie swallowed and then settled down again, softly asking out of nowhere, "How is it to finally spend a night away from Colter?"

Maybe any other night that question would have thrown me off, but I was always a fun wine-drunk, so I playfully placed the back of my hand to my forehead. "Oh, I'm devasted can't you tell?"

"Oh yes, *I'm* certainly horrible company by comparison." She snorted, loving the fact I was ready to play.

"Yeah…you really are shite." I nudged her shoulder with mine. "Actually, I think I'm going to have to fire you."

"I mean, I don't see how you have any other option."

I squeezed an open hand between us. "Thank you for your time."

Gracie took my hand and shook it. "It has *not* been a pleasure."

Below us we heard the purposefully loud opening and closing of the sliding door to the balcony of the suite beneath us, someone muttering annoyedly under their breath.

Gracie frowned at me. "Was it something I said?"

I lost it then, breaking out into a fit of laughter, dragging Gracie down with me.

"How much do you think they heard?" I squealed through welling tears.

"I hope not all of it, I got pretty detailed on my story about my horrible gas on the first night here!" I choked on my laughter and Gracie handed me the bottle of wine. "Here, take a sip." She clapped me on my back.

I indeed partook in another nip and then breathed until we grew quiet once again. Noting an off taste to the wine, I lifted the bottle and examined it. "I don't think this is really meant to be drank warm."

"I'm out of ice," Gracie said as she pulled herself up and onto the rim of the tub. "If you want to get more to chill it, the ice maker on this floor is broken, so you have to go to the second floor. I have to pee. So, I'll be back!"

She padded across the tiled floor and out of sight. I sniffed the bottle and cringed. Yes. It needed to be chilled. I wasn't going to waste it—it was an expensive fancy bottle. I hauled myself out of the tub and closed the door behind me as I entered my room for the night. My phone was the one playing music, so I opted to leave it there as I crossed to the door, exchanging the wine for the ice bucket off the kitchenette counter as I went. "I'm going to go get that ice Grace! I'll be right back!"

"Don't get lost!" She hollered through the door.

"Don't send a search party if I do—just say something nice at my funeral and play *Baby Got Back* as the processional."

"Godspeed!"

I exited out into the hallway, softly closing the door behind me. Immediately I could hear the laughter and banter of all of the boys back in Colter and I's room. And smell the weed that a breeze must've been catching and funneling back into the hallway from their balcony. I was gazing at the door to the room with a goofy smile on my face and almost didn't see the rope that was strung across the stairwell with a sign that said *Please Use Elevator or A Different Stairwell.* On the landing at the foot of the first flight was a yellow *Wet Floor* warning sign. The steps glistened in the hall lights.

Again, any other night and I'd have maybe pouted, but I was in good spirits, so I shrugged and spun on my heels to head down the long length of hallway to where the elevators I had yet to use would be. The resort seemed to be fairly quiet for a Thursday night, though I really had no idea what time it was. It couldn't be too late, I know Gracie had said she wanted to get a good night's sleep. Though, when on vacation one could set their wake-up time for 10 a.m. so, who knew.

By the time I reached the elevator and pressed the button for down, a yawn was taking me over. The elevator was there in seconds, opening wide to reveal nothing but cool air and pleasant Caribbean music inside. Pressing floor two on the panel, the ride was laughably short. Thankfully, the ice machine on the second floor was directly across from the elevator's opening. I filled up the bucket, swaying to the elevator music already stuck in my head.

When I hit the elevator to go up, it took longer this time to reach me. I closed my eyes and cracked my neck both ways as I heard the ding and the gliding of the doors opening. Putting a foot over the threshold, I opened my eyes and froze.

Eric stood there with his arm around yet another strange woman.

An obnoxious laugh bubbled up out of me and Eric grimaced. The girl with him curled into his side, a look of concern on her face, as though I was the thing in the night to steer clear of.

"I'll get tha next onnnne." My speech suddenly seemed more slurred than before.

"Molly, it's fine, just get inside so the doors will close." Eric sounded exasperated.

The strange woman blinked up at him. "You know her?"

"She's my—"

"I'm noone," I said with a long, drawn out wave of my hand. "No. One. But you must be—six?" I placed a finger to my chin as I pretended to think on it. "I mean you only brought a pack of ten, Eric, so it's not like she's eleven."

"Molly," Eric growled.

"What the hell is she saying?" Six asked, her brows furrowing as she leaned away from Eric's hold.

"Oops." It was obvious now that that was a very rude, very unfunny joke. I hadn't actually meant to hurt anyone's feelings by it.

"Just shut up and get in," he snapped.

I bit down on the inside of my lips and slipped in, leaning against the farthest wall away from the two of them. I didn't need to press the third-floor button. Eric had already obviously done so. Thankfully the trip was short. And quiet. But it was a very awkward walk back to our rooms. I wasn't sure if I should walk next to them—cringey for several reasons—or, walk behind them—also a poor option. So, I picked up my pace and walked in front, hoping to gain some distance between us.

I could hear Six whispering something to Eric, could hear him speak low and soft in return. The exchange made me feel fidgety, but I held my head high and walked with purpose back to Gracie's door. I stopped before it, realizing I hadn't brought the key with me, so I nonchalantly knocked on the door and waited. And waited.

Eric and Six reached the door beside Gracie's, and I looked at them as Eric used the key to open his door for her. I gave them both a tightlipped smile and looked away, knocking again on Gracie's door. A prickle of tension hit me as I could still see Eric in my peripheral waiting at his door, watching.

"Everything okay?" he asked tentatively.

I knocked again. "Just fine."

Nothing from the other side.

"Did they know you were coming?"

"I'm sleeping here tonight, so yeah, I'd say so."

"Hm."

"Good night, Eric," I said as sweetly as I could manage.

"I think they're asleep," he noted uselessly.

I suppressed my eye roll. "You...might be right."

"Do you need me to call the front desk?"

Like a beacon in the night, I heard Colter's laughter emanating from behind our hotel room door down the hall. My shoulders dropped as tension released. The smile I wore now was genuine as I turned to Eric and started to walk

225

backwards toward Colter's voice. "No, thank you. I'm actually all good. Night, Eric."

He didn't return the sentiment as he watched me bounce on my feet, practically skipping to Colter's door.

I rapped my knuckles against it and didn't have to wait more than two breaths before the door swung open and Cam was there, holding a beer and a hand of cards, rather impressively, all in the fingers of one hand.

"Sorry sister," He flashed a teasing grin, "it's boys' night, tonight."

"I know, I just need Ben. I got locked out of the room and I think Gracie fell asleep on me." I lifted the full ice bucket before me by way of explanation.

Cam's grin turned sympathetic. "Alright, alright."

He opened the door for me to pass under his arm and as I stepped into the room my eyes widened. The boys had pulled the desk into the space between the beds and had dragged the outdoor chairs inside to set around it for a makeshift poker table.

Alan, who'd chosen a bed as his seating arrangement of choice, was laid out long with his back to me and his cards held up so Cam and I could see them. Ben sat in one of the outdoor chairs facing me but was completely enthralled with whatever card he was deciding to play next.

Colter was in the desk chair, leaning far back with his hands laced behind his head, smirking at the table as though he'd just made the play of the night.

Cam let out a whistle and all of them looked up. I waved dumbly.

"Caught a stray out wandering the halls," Cam quipped.

I shot him a wry look. "I got locked out of the room."

"Hey Rockstar," Colter rang out, his chair wheels clacking over the tiles as he pushed away from the table to stand.

"Here we go," Alan murmured, tossing his hand to the table face down as though the game was indefinitely paused.

Cam eased past me and then Colter as Colter closed the distance between us. I tipped my head back to look up at him as he wrapped his hands around my upper arms and began to gently push me back into the darkness of the bathroom. My pulse rocketed as he flicked on the light and shut the door behind us. Locking it.

"I'm so happy you decided to stop by," he purred, as he leaned a hip against the counter.

I gave a breathy laugh. "I got locked out. I just came for the room key."

"That's a shame," he said as he lifted his hands. An offering to take the ice bucket. Curious, I handed it over.

"Indeed," I replied, eyeing him with playful wariness. He set the bucket on the counter beside his hip and then pushed to standing. The breath I dragged in seemed to go nowhere as Colter swaggered up to me. "What are you doing?"

Colter grabbed my hips, pulling me into him so that my pelvis ground against his front. My hands flew up to his chest, fingers lightly curling into the shirt he wore.

"Stealing a moment of your time," he answered, placing a kiss to the jaw I'd exposed as I tipped my head back for him.

"Colter." His name a cautious warning on my lips, though my body betrayed me as I rocked against him.

"Say it again," he growled, placing another kiss below my ear.

It slipped out as a half moan, *"Colter."*

He gave a gravelly hum of satisfaction as he grazed his teeth over my earlobe.

"You're insatiable." And it thrilled me.

His chuckle was dark as he leaned back to look me in the eyes. "You bring it out in me."

I shook my head in amazed disbelief, looking up at him. *"How?"*

Colter's playful expression fell for just a brief second. "Is that a serious question?"

Was it? I paused as I reflected on it.

"Kinda," I admitted, my smile wobbling as I felt the vulnerability to that truth.

Colter's eyes narrowed, studying me even through the haze of his obvious high. He sighed through his nose and then snaked his hand between us. Capturing my jaw gently, he twisted my face toward the mirror. My eyes went wide in the reflection as I stared at the two of us, seeing us in a way I hadn't ever before.

His eyes blazed as he looked at me through the mirror. "You're the only person I know who's as beautiful on the outside as they are on the inside, Rockstar."

My chest brushed against his with each shaky breath I drew in, my veins thrumming. A nervous laugh got stuck in my throat.

"That's not how you made it seem all those years ago." I couldn't stop it as the train of thought that had been riding on my back nearly half of my life came barreling out of me. "You'd said you wouldn't touch me with a ten-foot pole."

"What?" Colter's voice went serious, flabbergasted. He turned my face back to his to look at me directly and dropped his hand to meet the other he'd snaked behind my back. "I would *never* say that—"

"But you did." My voice had gone incredibly quiet. "To that group of friends you'd started hanging out with in the junior high. What were their names? Colby, and JT and AJ Crews. I overheard you under the bleachers at a football game."

Colter's eyes went distant as he looked away, searching for the memory. His brows furrowed with the struggle to conjure it. The realization of what I'd just stirred up hit me and I instantly felt hot and clammy. My breath hitched as I waited.

"A football game with those guys…" He suddenly paused as though it came flooding back to him. "I remember that game. I…I remember that conversation." Colter's eyes slowly slid back to mine. Hesitant. Wary. "You heard that?"

I nodded pitifully.

"Did you happen to hear the whole conversation? Which, I'd like to point out was said between idiot thirteen-year-olds—how you even remember it, surprises me."

"I remember it because it stung like a bitch." *There* was my voice, sturdier and louder. Colter flinched and I caught myself, softening as I finished answering his question, "And no. I didn't hear the whole conversation, but it hadn't seemed to matter to me then. I walked up just as you were saying it. I turned on my heel and never spoke of it to anyone."

His eyes closed as though he were frustrated but by the time they reopened they'd gone earnest. "If you had been there just a few minutes earlier...you'd have heard them saying wildly inappropriate things about you—especially for as young as we were. Those kids were rough. And I could see their wheels turning even back then. I couldn't stand the idea of any one of them making a play at you, so I did what I did hoping to throw them off your trail."

Silence, thick and heavy fell between us.

His jaw clenched as his eyes scanned my face. "But you know what...if there was any part of that conversation that you did overhear I'm glad it was only that. The shit they were saying..." Colter's hand drifted up my spine, slid up my neck and cupped the back of my head as he tugged me into an embrace. I heard his next words directly from his chest against my ear. "I hovered in that group for months after, until I knew for sure they'd moved on—forgotten about you."

At thirteen he'd had the sense to protect me, to look out for me. Maturity beyond his years. I felt at the same time tingly and numb, but I clung to him as I processed his words. The remark that set me on the path of keeping Colter at an arm's length away had been his last-ditch effort to guard me from what he'd deemed a potential threat. Something perhaps he never truly felt but said because he thought he needed to. Something I should have never overheard, should have never even known, should have never believed or taken to heart. But for me, at twelve years old...that is a fragile age for anyone.

My arms around his neck, I squeezed tighter as I whispered, "Thank you."

There was a lot more I could say. Would say. But not now. Not while I was wine-drunk, not while he was high. This was not the time, but there would be another.

"I'm sorry," he replied, burying his face into my neck. "I wish you'd have said something to me about it sooner."

"Me, too."

But there was no changing that now. There was only today. And the future. I pulled away, finding his gaze before I looked at his lips just inches from mine.

I kissed him. He kissed me back. And this kiss…it was different from all the others. It was heart shattering. It was the kiss I'd been afraid of experiencing when we'd first had sex because this kiss was world altering—breaking down who we were and building us back up into something else entirely. My hands came up to the sides of his face, his delved into my hair as though both of us intended to hold each other there for eternity.

I opened for him at the same time he'd made to deepen the kiss and as his tongue delved into my mouth a breathy moan eased out of me. The sound ramped up his ferocity, sending my heart into overdrive as he grabbed my hips, turned me and set me upon the bathroom counter. I let go of him to brace a hand on the sink behind me as his lips left mine and attached to my neck possessively. My hand slipped as he pushed against me wildly and I knocked the ice bucket into the sink basin, the sound of it and the ice a clattering echo through the tiled bathroom.

"Hey!" a voice called out from the main room. "This is supposed to be a night of abstinence!"

It was Alan—*of course* it was Alan who would have the balls to interrupt what was obviously something very heated. And private.

Though riding high and completely enjoying ourselves, Alan's interjection had sufficed in making Colter and I dial down the intensity of our kiss. Our shared laughter was muffled by one another's mouths, and slowly, finally, we stilled. When we finally broke away, Colter tipped his forehead against mine breathing heavily as my hands caressed his face.

"Waitin' on you, Evans!" This time it was Cam who spoke up. Probably egged on by Alan.

"I should," I started, pausing as Colter stole a peck, "probably," – a second stolen kiss – "go."

He pressed his mouth to mine, a lazy, drawn-out sip from my lips that left me feeling thankful I was sitting down because it would've likely knocked my legs out from beneath me had I been standing.

"If you don't, I'm going to take you on this bathroom counter, and while I do think the use of this mirror would be *a lot* fun," His lips quirked up into a devilishly handsome half smile, "I don't need all of our friends as an audience on the other side of this door."

"Yeah. No, thank you," I giggled softly.

Colter backed away, his hands dropping and flexing at his sides as though physically releasing me was difficult. And I knew the feeling. Shaking out my hands and my riled-up nerves, I hopped off the counter.

I'd stepped up to Colter who had already reached the door, unlocking it, waiting with his hand on the knob. He turned to me, a ghost of a smile flashing over his mouth before he reached up and raked his fingers through my hair, fixing whatever he'd likely disheveled. I felt heat rise in my cheeks and chest.

"Let's go," he said, his voice going cool and calm. I pressed my lips together in a secretive smile and nodded as we exited.

"Oh wow, you two got your clothes back on in record timing," Alan jibed as Colter and I reappeared. Ben was gone.

I snorted and gave him an eye roll. "Shut up, Al."

"While you two were making babies, Ben ran off to go check that Gracie wasn't passed out on the floor. He's been gone as long as you two have been, so either they're *also* making babies, or she really did pass out on the floor and he's still working on getting her to bed," Cam said, holding his hand of cards and rearranging them into his preferred order.

"Oof. I should probably go help." I winced as I shot a look at Colter. Turning back to the other two hooligans I gave a soft wave. "Good night you two. Remember…it's a night of abstinence." I winked as I backed toward the door.

Cam didn't even bother to look up, his mouth just twitched into a smirk that told me he would most definitely *not* be participating in that little prewedding tradition with the rest of us. And Alan…

Well, he just flipped me off, classy guy that he was.

Colter kicked out a foot and spun to follow me to the door. "Can I walk you home?"

I chuckled. "Are you worried about my safety on the—" I opened the door and investigated the length of space from our door to Gracie and Ben's, "—five steps it will take me to get there?"

"I have my reasons to believe you've been drinking tonight, ma'am. I'd only be doing my due diligence to ensure you make it back safely," Colter joked, his voice carrying a playful, policelike authority that struck a chord of pleasure in me.

"Thank you, but I think I can handle it. *Sir.*"

Colter's eyes flashed and I got out of there quickly before he pounced on me again, but he had reached out and smacked my ass before I was able to get out of his range. I stifled a squeal of excitement and shot him a wink over my shoulder. He rested his head against the door and watched me go, biting down on his lip the way I wished I could be doing instead.

Ben had propped the door open by flipping the stop-lock, so I didn't think he was in there getting frisky with Gracie. And as I tested a listening ear and softly knocked on the door I could hear him call out with equal softness, "Come in."

What I saw when I entered pulled at my heartstrings. Ben had Gracie cradled in his arms against his chest as he sat on the bed against the headboard.

"She'd passed out. In the *tub.*" He raised a reproachful brow at me and my lips twitched into a grin. "When I picked her up she just…snuggled into me." He looked back down at her, and indeed she'd pressed her cheek to his chest and even had gripped the front of his shirt in her sleep, still clutching it with a fury. "I was just savoring it. Waiting for you to return."

"I wish I could take a picture."

"Don't you dare."

"But this is so cute!" I whisper-yelled.

"Molls," he sighed.

"Fine."

Ben took it as his cue to head out. So, he gently stood and turned, gingerly setting her down in the bed. I tiptoed to his side, smothering a giggle as I watched him have to individually pry her fingers off his stretched-out shirt.

"She's like a baby," I joked.

Ben huffed a laugh. "I love her."

I whipped my face to him, tears gathering in my eyes. "She loves you too."

"I don't know how I got so lucky."

I sighed through my nose as I looked at him, looked at Gracie, and then looked up at my reflection in the sliding glass door. "I don't know how we all go so lucky."

TWENTY-ONE

Gracie sat across the small table from me, a forkful of scrambled eggs frozen halfway to her gaping mouth, her eyes as wide as saucers. "You called her *what?*"

"Six." I winced as I bit down on my lip.

"Molly! You're such a bitch," she laughed, dropping her fork to her plate. "Hilarious. But a bitch."

"Shit. I know." My nose scrunched in shame as I hid behind a sip of coffee. "I just—I don't know—I was tipsy. And spiteful."

"I don't know how Eric—or even this girl—didn't wallop you." Her hand that rested on the table curled into a fist. "Lord knows I would have if I'd been them."

"I highly doubt the nature of their relationship is so serious that either would have felt warranted to do so."

"Still," she snickered. "God, I love you."

"Don't encourage me," I snipped good-humoredly.

Gracie resumed eating her breakfast after that.

Earlier, once we'd woken up to the mid-morning light creeping into our room, I'd pushed through my slight hangover to jump up on the bed and announce to the entire resort that my best friend was getting married today. Gracie had promptly blasted a pillow in my face, and we'd shared a good laugh as she finally caught on to my excitement and joined in.

I'd received a text message from Ben that he and the boys had decided to try out a breakfast restaurant off the resort that they'd marked on the drive in from the airport, so Gracie and I ventured down to breakfast together alone. They'd planned to spend the day apart so that the first time they would see each other on their wedding day was as Gracie began her walk down the aisle. Or beach, rather.

A beach wedding, one Gracie said was part of a selection of wedding packages offered by the resort. She'd been just so lucky enough that there hadn't already been a wedding scheduled for this particular Friday night. The wedding would begin just before sunset and included a private dinner on a docked sailboat off the resort's pier.

I'd also received a text message from Colter. A *Good morning beautiful* text that had my heart fluttering and my head spinning. I wasn't sure how to feel about the fact that I was spending nearly an entire day of my vacation separated from the one I'd like to spend every waking second with, but I supposed as the saying goes, distance makes the heart grow fonder. I had a sinking feeling I'd be wound up tight by the time I was able to lay eyes on Colter once again.

"I know tomorrow's our last full day here and I know we intended for this vacation to be spent together but since it's technically the day after my wedding I'd like to spend it alone with Ben. Like a micro-honeymoon."

I focused my attention back to Gracie. "As you should!"

"Yeah?"

"Of course!" I gushed, reaching to place a hand on top of hers. "If you didn't I'd be concerned."

She tossed her blonde locks over her shoulder and laughed with relief. "Oh, good." Then her smile turned a bit mischievous. "I'm sure you and Colter can find something to do." At the look I gave her, she feigned innocence and continued, "Though, I know Alan and Cam are renting the Jeeps to do another tour. Mayan ruins, a tequila tasting, and then hitting the flea market if you care to join."

I gave her a refined smile. "Sounds like fun."

She shrugged and smirked knowingly as she sipped her coffee.

~

Miguel, of all people, stood beneath the palm-adorned white arbor, waiting with a pamphlet in his hands that he had clasped in front of him, looking ever the proper and patient officiant. There was no music for the processional and no other attendees than the six of us that were lined up waiting for Javier's instruction.

Colter stood shoulder to shoulder with me as I twirled the single blue hibiscus flower in my fingers. It matched the flowy blue sundress I'd chosen from Gracie's selections. And Colter's tie…

Ben and Cam were the first ones down the aisle, and as the groom sidled up before Miguel, Cam stepped off to Gracie's side as a bridesman. Gracie had insisted on keeping things even and Cam was happy to appease the bride by whatever means necessary.

"Ready, Rockstar?" Colter said quietly as he offered his arm, smiling at me charmingly.

My pulse quickened as I threaded my arm through his, returning the smile. "Let's do this."

To nothing more than the music of the ocean waves beyond, Colter and I walked down the aisle.

The thought briefly, teasingly, harmlessly flashed through my mind…if this is what it would be like if Colter and I ever did such a thing ourselves. With someone else. Or together. I killed the thought before it could go any farther, before it could do any more damage to my already racing heart. This moment right here wasn't about me or Colter.

Ben, who'd been given strict instructions to keep faced forward while we'd gathered here, was rolling out his shoulders. I smirked and then looked at Cam who, shockingly, looked as though he may be close to tears.

As Colter and I reached the end of the aisle and made our separate ways, I reached out to Cam who grabbed my hand and squeezed. We shared watery smiles and then I turned, taking up my position and then just about blubbered as Gracie, escorted down the aisle by Alan, made her debut.

A part of me had been a bit angry with her that we wouldn't ever get to do the whole Say Yes to the Dress rite of passage together, but I had to admit, looking at her now, it didn't matter. She'd found the dress in the short handful of days since the proposal and it was perfect.

A spaghetti strap that eased into a deeply cut neckline that almost hit her navel, and panels of white chiffon that exposed her legs underneath the folds...Gracie was a veritable goddess in that dress as she floated down the aisle. She'd left her hair down in beachy waves that danced in the soft ocean breeze, and as I looked to Ben who'd been given the OK to turn, I swore the man was about ready to kneel at the sight of her.

Stunning. My best friend was *stunning*.

The ceremony was short and sweet—the best kind—and was timed almost perfectly to the grand farewell of the setting sun, a backdrop of deep oranges that complimented the glow of the newly married couple. And at the first ever declaration of Mr. and Mrs. Benjamin and Grace Campbell, I looked over and caught Colter's eyes.

The smile on his face was warm. The look in his eyes was one of peace. He looked like a man sure of himself. When his eyes turned to the happy couple, they lit with genuine joy for them. I was near bursting with delight.

~

The sailboat was docked at the end of the resort's pier. The sails were furled, and strung all along the masts were fairy lights that lit the boat in a starry glow. The meal, the stars, the company. It was perfect. I had half a mind to copy Gracie's wedding if I ever tied the knot myself. Small, intimate, and with the closest people I loved the most. It was perfect.

I sipped crisp white wine and peeked at Colter beside me. His face was flush from the wine and he was sharing a laugh with Ben who sat across the table about something they remembered from band in high school. Thoroughly engaged, I set my wine down, propped my elbows onto the table and rested my chin in my hands.

Maybe it was the post-bliss of the day, the lulling rocking of the sailboat on the ocean waves or the beginnings of being wine-tipsy settling in, but Colter was, for lack of a better word, mesmerizing. I noted each and every time his lips found themselves tugging into a smile, my own mouth mirroring his behind my knuckles. I observed the way the fairy lights caught in his eyes. I even noticed the perfect tousling of his hair by the briny breeze every time he subtly tilted his head one way, then tilted it the other mid-conversation as he looked to whoever was speaking next.

When his large, warm hand slipped its way onto my thigh I knew then that he had noticed I'd been ogling him. For likely the entire time, given the way he gave my flesh a delicious squeeze. I perked up in my seat a bit and folded my arms politely onto the table.

Finally looking away, it was Gracie who captured my gaze. She had a smile on her face and a raised brow as though she too had caught me in the act and then noticed the way Colter's arm was angled toward me under the table. I didn't even pretend to hide it. I just simply smiled. And she did too. And suddenly I got the feeling that she just might stop giving me such a hard time over Colter and I's exploration of…whatever this was. I supposed your wedding night might soften a heart some.

I was just about to pick up my wine glass when I noticed the flash across the sky in the not-too-distant horizon. Checking around the table, it appeared no one else caught it. I tried to tell myself that maybe it had been a trick of the lights or my imagination, but as my eyes kept darting to the distance I noticed something I hadn't before.

Like a black curtain sliding closed, there was a definitive line across the sky where the stars turned pitch black. Clouds. Even in the dark of night I could make out their opaque bulkiness. I knew what was headed our way for certain when another flash dappled the sky off to the left.

Leaning in toward Colter, I reached under the table and placed my hand on top of his. "I think another storm may be rolling in."

And just as I said it, before Colter could even look up to observe it himself, the wind picked up, catching the flame of the tealights spread across the small table, sending them flickering wildly, if not extinguishing them entirely.

"I think you may be right," Colter replied as he craned his neck to peer out into the horizon.

Just then, Javier approached from the darkness of the pier. "Hey amigos! Nothing to fear, but I did just check the radar, and it appears a quick but strong rainstorm is headed this way. You're welcome to take shelter belowdecks until it passes, or if you wish, you can cut your dinner short and take your desserts back up to the shelter of the tiki bar or poolside pavilion."

"Actually," Gracie announced to the table, biting her lip as she gave Ben a sidelong glance, "I think I'm ready to call it a night."

"And that's my cue," Ben said as he eagerly slid out of his seat. "I'll take that dessert to go, my man." He reached out to Javier and shook his hand, giving him a clap on the back, as we all laughed.

As the waitstaff packaged up our desserts-to-go, everyone went around giving hugs and then goodnights and see-you-tomorrows. We all let the newlyweds disembark first, giving whoops and applause as Ben whisked Gracie up into his arms to carry her off.

Colter and I were the last ones off the sailboat and as he stepped onto the dock, he turned and offered his free hand to me. His other hand held the precious to-go container of Mexican Wedding Cookies. Thankful that I'd been able to wear my nice sandals and not a pair of high heels on the rocking boat, I took Colter's hand and easily stepped down onto the pier.

Evidently love was in the air, for Ben carried Gracie down the entire length of the pier, while Alan and Cam walked after them with their arms wrapped around one another, Alan's head resting on Cam's much taller shoulder. Even Colter didn't let go of my hand as we made our way down the boardwalk.

"Bar, pavilion, or bed?" Colter asked as we stepped off the pier and onto the beach. My mind was certainly playing in the gutter at that last option, but Colter hadn't put any innuendo in it which made me believe he was genuinely up for whatever I wanted to do. Happy to just be together.

"Hm," I pondered, eyeing the resort as people also noticed the incoming rain and moved to shelter. The pool pavilion bar was absolutely packed so I didn't necessarily want to head there, not after such a lovely, relaxing evening. Ben and Gracie had already disappeared, and it seemed Alan and Cam were set on heading back to their room too as they headed off in that direction.

That left...

"The tiki bar," I answered, flashing a smile. "Maybe we can find a swing and just, I don't know, watch the storm roll in."

"And here I thought you were afraid of storms," Colter teasingly whispered, inclining his head to me.

I was. But with Colter, I was growing more open to pushing against the confines of my comfort zone. So, I looked up at Colter and sheepishly smiling said, "Me too."

Colter gave one curt nod and a look of something like pride and led us off in the direction of the bar, lit up on the beach with festoon lighting I hadn't noticed during our previous day drinking.

The tiki bar was also packed, which was a given, so we only managed to find one open swing, but it was at least oceanside and offered a perfect view. Colter had offered up the swing to me, but I just shook my head, smiled coyly, and suggested I sit in his lap.

Trying and failing to hide his roguish grin to that little suggestion as he sat down made me laugh under my breath. A bartender we hadn't met yet approached us to ask if we'd like anything to drink.

Colter just gave me a questioning look, letting me take the lead. I thought about it. Thought I might continue to fuel the pleasant buzz I had begun with the wine. But as I looked at Colter I felt content just as I was.

"Y'know what...I'm all set, thank you," I told the young man behind the counter.

"I'm all good as well, thanks," Colter agreed. His arms, wrapped around my waist, tightened briefly. His chin then rested on my shoulder, and we swung softly. As the wind picked up and the storm grew closer, goosebumps pebbled my skin for a multitude of reasons. All of them good.

It took maybe all of two minutes before the rain started. A tiny spike of anxiety prodded at me, so I focused entirely on everything good: on Colter here with me, on the beautiful wedding we'd been a part of, on the Mexican Wedding Cookies Colter had sat down on the bar yet awaiting me.

"Do you ever see yourself getting married?" Out of nowhere, that question fell from my lips all too easily. My pulse picked up as I realized how it came off sounding.

Answering as easily as I'd asked, Colter replied with a smile in his voice, "That depends."

I didn't dare ask what it depended on. Because the answer either included me or it didn't. And neither answer was one I was anywhere near ready to confront during a rainstorm in a tiki bar. So...why had I even asked?

Like a small mercy, the rain flipped a switch suddenly and turned into an all-out downpour, commanding Colter and I's attention. The wind was still increasing, sending the rain sideways into the bar.

"Oh boy," I exclaimed, pressing back into Colter as my dress started to soak.

Colter chuckled. "Here, hop down," he said as he made to stand. I obeyed and he too hopped off the swing as everyone on our side of the bar did the same. I pressed myself against the edge of the bar top trying to get out of the rain as much as possible, my veins buzzing. Colter even put himself between me and the onslaught, but the wind and rain was its own force as it seemed to double down, soaking everything. At this point my heartrate was beginning to edge on frantic.

"Javier meant it when he said the rain would come in quick and strong!" Colter raised his voice over the sound of the rain. I nodded and looked around the bar, hoping for any place that might offer a bit dryer shelter but it was no use. It was filled to the brim. The only option left was up. I gripped the bar top and hefted myself up onto it even though rainwater was already pooling on it.

"This is crazy!" I said, pulling Colter nearer.

"Maybe we should have—" Colter had braced his hands on either side of me when he'd immediately cut himself off. Startling me, his hands were at my hips. "Get down, now." I didn't even have time to process what he'd said before he was pulling me back down to the sand himself.

"What is it? What's wrong?" I asked as he wrapped his arms around me, turning me away from the bar.

"You didn't feel that?" Colter sounded a bit in disbelief as his hands stroked my back.

"Feel what?"

"The bar. It's not grounded." he said into my ear as he hugged me to him. "We just got shocked."

"*What?*" I hadn't noticed anything. Had I? "I thought I was just feeling tingly from the wine from dinner!"

He barked a laugh and pulled back to look at me, brushing wet hair that stuck to my forehead out of my face. "No, babe. That's not what that was."

My heart jumped in my chest at him calling me *babe*. Such a simple little pet name and yet it wasn't something he'd ever referred to me as before. Another first checked off the ever-growing list between us.

"Shouldn't we tell someone?"

One side of Colter's lips quirked into a half smile. "No one's over here anymore."

I hadn't even realized it. Somewhere between me hopping up onto the bar and him calling me babe, the customers on our side of the bar had made a run for it. The other side of the bar still had partygoers, still dry and enjoying themselves as the lone bartender braved the rain to dutifully man his post.

We'd decided to head back to our room after that. If there was a tell-tale sign that the night's festivities should end before things got out of hand, I was thinking an electrical shock, albeit a mild one, was a good place to stop. Colter had passed along his two cents to the bartender who only half listened to what he was saying.

We hit the stairwell just as the quick tropical rainstorm died down, leaving behind a dappling of fat rain drops on the pavement of the walkway we'd left behind. Colter kept a soft but firm hold on my hip as we ascended toward the third floor, him telling me more about the day he'd shared with the boys while he and I had been separated.

My parrots were nowhere to be seen as we hit the landing, probably somewhere still hunkering against the last of the rain. I frowned inwardly and then looked up the last flight of stairs to find Imelda.

TWENTY-TWO

She appeared to be off duty in a flowy navy-blue dress with a dainty pink floral design. Her hair was down like it usually was but didn't have the flower she usually wore tucked in her ear.

She froze as she blinked at Colter and I, and while in another life I may too have frozen at what perhaps should have been an unsettling encounter, I forced myself to keep a steady gait.

"*Buenas noches,*" I said politely with a tip of my head.

Her eyes widened as she looked between Colter and I, a smile finally forcing its way onto her face. "*Buenas noches.*"

I could feel Colter's hand at my hip as though he intended to slow us down so that we'd all have time to step out of each other's way, but I carried on...forcing Imelda to turn and flatten herself to the wall. At the way her mouth dropped open as I breezed past her, I smirked, somehow feeling like I'd won.

Imelda wasn't my enemy. Not really. In fact, if someone was so petty as to keep score, we were on equal grounds considering she and I had both slept with the same two men in the span of one week. But at least mine was still by my side. Even if she was on her way out from Eric's room, it seemed she'd be leaving by herself tonight.

I kept myself together even as we safely found ourselves on the other side of our closed and locked hotel room door.

"I saw what you did there," Colter said a tad bit chidingly, tossing the room key onto the dresser.

I placed a hand to the wall as I worked to unclasp my sandal at the ankle, focusing on it intensely. "I don't know what you're talking about."

Colter walked up behind me, placing his hands on my hips as he breathed against my neck. "Felt to me like you were asserting dominance back there." I dropped my chin to my shoulder, bringing my mouth closer to his as he placed a kiss to my bare skin there. "You have nothing to worry about with her, Rockstar."

My eyes flicked up into the floor length mirror on the opposite wall that captured Colter and I like a framed picture. I could see the way he held me, watched as he placed another kiss to my shoulder. It made me equal parts hot and cold.

"What reason would I have to need to worry about her anyway, Colter?" The question came out all wrong. Crueler than I'd ever intended. Not sure how to smooth that one over I added, "You were with her before we…" I stopped there, realizing my mistake.

A part of me wanted to just leave it at that. Brush it off and continue with what had been a spectacular day. The other part, well, it screamed at me to just say it, to finally have that conversation we so desperately needed to have because I knew that for me…there was no going back.

Not after that way Colter had claimed me. Multiple times. Not after he shattered what my idea of what safety and security was. Not after he dismantled what—up until him—had been what I thought was a decent sex life.

"I didn't sleep with her."

I hadn't realized how still we'd both gone until he said those words. Confusion hit me, nearly sending me reeling back into him. "You didn't?"

"No." Colter's hands disappeared, and I internally shuddered at the loss of contact. "I mean, I was *going* to. But…I stopped." Colter's eyes found mine in the mirror and I quickly looked away as a dull ache settled in my chest at his confession. Something about going from not really knowing one way or another to now knowing it indeed *almost* happened—had been well on its way to happening—sat bitter in my belly.

"Why?" None of my business, and yet my mouth asked it anyway.

Colter stepped around me and walked further into the room. He stopped at the foot of our bed and loosened his tie—the tie he'd used to bind my wrists as he feasted on me only a day ago. My blood ran hot in my veins at the reminder.

He was quiet long enough that I wondered if he hadn't heard me, but my nerves glued me to the spot, sealed my throat so I was unable to speak. I couldn't move. I kept one hand on the wall, my tether to reality.

"Molly." Colter turned to me then, a determined look in his eyes. "You know why."

The room felt like it swayed, and I *really* begged to differ. All at the same time, I did and did not know why, and it absolutely terrified me.

"Because…I interrupted you?" My voice was barely above a whisper as I cautiously stepped forward.

Colter's jaw clenched. Then he laid himself bare. "Because you interrupted me, yes. And because you got in my head. Because you've always been in my head. Because I am in love with you."

I felt the energy in the room change, felt the tingles erupt over the bare skin of my arms, felt the thrum of my pulse in my ears as it spiked, the hitch in my breathing.

"How." I shook my head slowly in awe.

"What do you mean *how*?" he asked, his tone incredulous at my unexpected response.

"How can you love *me*?"

Colter tensed as he went quiet. His eyes narrowed as he studied me and under his scrutiny I could feel myself cowering, closing in on myself as I was nearly suffocating in vulnerability. And shame.

"You think you somehow don't deserve it," he stated.

I sucked on my teeth and looked away, unable to hide the tears that pricked my eyes, tears I couldn't stand to have him watch fall. "I've used you all week."

"Don't," Colter warned.

I swallowed thickly and dared to face him once more, captivated by his darkening eyes. "I've used you my whole life."

"That's really what you think our relationship has been?" The pain in his voice cracked something in my chest.

Yes. No.

"Molly," Colter sighed my name and brought a hand to his face as he massaged the tension out of his expression. "There's a lot of bad choices we've made in our lives when it comes to one another. But you and I? We're still here. We still care for each other. I may have not realized what I was feeling for you until it was too late, but I know now that I've always loved you. I've loved you at different levels at different stages throughout our whole life. And I think you've always loved me too. That's what this is, Moll. That's why we continue to fall into one another, why we thrash, why we fight, why we fuck— make *love*. I love you because you see and accept me for exactly who I am and always have."

"I'm not the same person I was when we were kids, Colter—"

"And thank fuck for that," he laughed wryly. "And you won't continue to be the woman you are standing in front of me today. We are going to change like we always have. The one constant that has always been in our lives is each other."

That was true. Through heartbreaks, and regrets, through ups and downs we'd always been there for each other. I'd seen him at his worst and he mine. He'd been on the receiving end of my disdain; I'd been on the receiving end of his disrespect in years past. Our friendship had always survived, somehow stronger for it.

"Eric and I only just broke up days ago." I was hardly feeling any pain in regards to that anymore, but at this point my heart was racing so badly with hesitant fear at what could happen if this thing between us didn't work out that I was reaching for any excuse.

"I don't care," he said it so simply.

I dragged in a shaky inhale through my nose and looked up to the ceiling as though the heavens could give me strength. "You should."

"I don't," he emphasized. *Damnit, Colter.* "You're mine, Molly. I love you. And I know," Colter took a cautious step toward me, "you love me too. So, I don't care if you don't say it back right now. I already know."

Surety. Confidence. Authority. He carried it all as he took the risk I was so pathetically too weak to take. And then his eyes closed, his face falling just a fraction as though the weight of what was transpiring was unbearable.

What the hell was I doing? What was I fighting? How could I still be holding back? The words were ones that I had been suppressing for half of my life. They were the words I'd wanted to say when I'd sought him out the night of the football game all those years ago. They were the words I'd wanted to say when he'd been there to teach me to drive, take me to prom, buy a stupid box of tampons for me, watch my back as I peed in the woods in the middle of the night, offer me the extra bed in his hotel room. They were the words I'd wanted to say when he'd fucked me into admitting to myself that, deep down, I was his.

The anxiety gripping me was solely based on the risk of things going wrong between us—I would never survive losing him. Except there was another risk I hadn't been paying enough attention to…

What *we* could lose if we didn't give this a chance; a reward that would far outweigh the risk of things not working out.

I shattered through the fear of the unknown.

"I do love you. I love you, Colter." My heart spoke for itself, saying the words it needed to before the moment passed. My lungs drew in a sharp breath as his eyes reopened with a churning, molten desire in them.

It changed that quickly, my body and my behavior. I needed only to say those words, have him give me that look, and the fight in me was gone.

As though breaking free from half a life's worth of invisible restraints we'd put on ourselves, we hurried to one another, bodies and mouths clashing as my fingers dug into his shoulder blades, and his grasped my face.

The kiss was urgent and thorough, drawing me to the tips of my toes with the need for more. Colter kissed me like I was his, kissed me like he'd said...like he loved me. While there was an ungodly amount of desire spiraling between us it was also so much more. It was consuming. It was binding.

"I need you, I need all of you. Please," I said, screwing my eyes shut tight as I panted into the space between us.

"Don't you ever beg," he said, capturing my mouth with his again, this time rougher, needier.

His hands dropped to my shoulders, pulling the straps of my dress down as he freed my breasts. Hooking his thumbs into the material he pushed it down over my hips, snagging my panties along the way as I in turn reached up and broke away from the kiss to tear the loosened tie up and over his head. His hands gripped my ass, fingers biting deliciously as he peppered kisses to my face while I swiftly undid the buttons of his shirt.

On fire, I gripped his belt and yanked fiercely, pulling him forward as he dipped his head to kiss my neck, his hands freely roaming and kneading all over my body. A breathy moan escaped me when he palmed my heavy breast. He sunk his teeth into the flesh between my neck and shoulder and my eyes popped open in carnal surprise. A throaty laugh bubbled out of me as I finished undressing him and then...

Colter took a step away.

Not to stop. To *savor.*

Our chests rose and fell raggedly as we took a moment to breathe and just gaze upon one another.

Completely bare and completely vulnerable and completely in love.

"I love you," he said, again.

I wasn't sure how I could feel any more weightless. "I love *you.*"

Colter's hand reached out and took mine, tugging softly. "There's no going back after this. If I make love to you now, you're mine and I'm yours. Do you understand me?"

Feeling a bit dizzy at the wash of connection to him that pulsated through me I nodded my consent.

"Say it. Out loud."

"I'm yours," I said, watching as his eyes flared. The next words had me wanting to actually shout, but I contained myself. "And you're mine."

"Come here," he growled as he closed the space between us.

Lifting me up, he spread my legs, and I wrapped them around his waist, shuddering as his tip pressed against my entrance already slick with stark arousal. He walked us to the side of the bed, kissing me deeply and a sound escaped me as I sucked in a sharp breath through my nose when he pushed himself in by just an inch. I rocked against him to bring us together, but he was already pulling out as he bent over, one hand bracing us as the other held my back to ease me down gently to the bed.

I writhed beneath him, needing more, and then whimpered as he lay his weight against me fully. His hands were in my hair again, tipping my head back as he delved into my mouth and stroked his tongue against mine possessively. I raked my nails down his back softly, at first. Then as I crested the curve of his ass, I bit my nails into him with feral intensity.

Gratifying me—and himself—he finally lined up with me and then slowly thrust into me at a toe-curling, eye-rolling pace. My back arched off the bed, pressing my chest against his tightly as he held there, grinding down into me like he intended to punch us right through the mattress. A guttural moan shook me as the near-painful pleasure spasmed out and into my limbs.

His name fell from my lips and then I couldn't speak as he pulled back and pumped forward deeply. My body responded to each pump with a rhythmic rolling grace. Between us, there was a natural connection, a fluid dance. It was tantric and soul shifting.

At this pace we could go all night.

So, we did.

There was no rush, no savage need to hit the already promised finish line. This was a giving and a taking of everything a body had to offer. Colter braced his knees wide under mine and lifted me upright in his hold so that I was seated to the hilt, straddling him. I dug my fingers into his hair as my head fell back, forcing my breasts up to him. He claimed the plump flesh, the tightened peaks, into his mouth affectionately. A languid hum of pleasure rumbled both our chests and a smile cracked my swollen lips at the sound.

Colter laid me back down but didn't follow, he braced himself on straight arms over me so he could look down at me, his eyes hooded, as he drove in and out. I held his gaze and bit my lip as he angled himself against a spot that sent a short burst of heightened pleasure through me. His eyes dropped to my breasts, and I knew he was enjoying the way they jostled with each movement we made. I too stole the opportunity to look down between us and a switch flipped in me as I watched him pull back, gleaming with my wetness, and then sink into me.

I bit my lip again, stifling the cussword that didn't deserve a place here in the beauty we were wrapped in. The deep sigh that shook Colter above me caught my attention and I flicked my eyes up to his, seeing that we were nearing a threshold that would send us into savagery. We both knew what I was conveying when I suddenly nodded.

I was there and ready and I needed him to take it.

Colter wrapped a hand under my knee and hooked my leg over his shoulder. I let out a cry of pleasure at the new angle, kicking my head back. I stewed in the new, delicious sensation until it cracked my composure. When I looked back at him I gave him the full fire of my siren eyes.

Colter snapped, shedding his self-control, and pounded into me, hiking my other leg up onto his other shoulder. I wrapped one hand around his thigh, the other around his forearm, hanging on for dear life as he sent me barreling into oblivion on an unleashed cry, my orgasm pulsing through me on crashing waves.

He came tumbling into bliss after me, forcing his forehead into mine and I could hear his breathing ripping in and out of him, swearing I could almost hear his teeth grinding. He trembled as he kept thrusting in and out, pushing himself past his own capability as though he was dead set on giving me even just a few more seconds of ecstasy. I reveled in the way I could feel him throbbing inside me as we both floated back down to earth through a haze of bliss.

We shared a quick look of satedness and then he collapsed his weight onto me—a decadent sensation in its own right.

I could forever live my life happily beneath him. My legs splayed wide, allowing him to adjust his arms out from under them and he brought his hands to the top of my head as he buried his face in my neck.

As our breathing slowed and deepened, I traced idle circles all over his back with soft fingertips.

A wicked smile crept onto my lips as he jerked every time I neared the sides of his waist; a ticklish spot. One I was already familiar with because I knew Colter—and he knew me—in all the ways a person could possibly know another.

I wiggled happily as he suddenly moved, placing a trail of kisses up my neck until they stopped at my mouth, the kiss soft but firm. A lover's sip.

"I love you," Colter said once again.

I beamed with a full smile, my eyes pricking with happy tears as I replied, truly and honestly, "I love you, too.

TWENTY-THREE

The sun filtered through my eyelids; the veil of skin lit up in a reddish tint. Laying on my belly, I ignored the stickiness of my cheek plastered against my forearm as I relaxed my fingers just a hair and was rewarded with the slinky kiss of rushing ocean water wending through them.

A sigh left my body and relaxation seeped into its place.

This was the life.

A seagull's cry rang out in the distance. A boats engine revved somewhere even farther out to sea. A gust of ocean breeze caught the sail of our mini catamaran and flapped it vigorously. I heard movement as the sail was righted.

Then I felt a warm hand settle on the back of my calf.

A small smile pulled at my lips. I sucked in a sharp breath through my nose, tingles shooting up my leg as the hand slowly caressed up behind my knee, up onto the back of my thigh. It veered down into the space between my legs as it crept higher. All the muscles in my core snapped to attention as fingertips teased the scant swimsuit material that covered the area that ached for his touch the most.

"Colter," I warned in a throaty voice. His responding chuckle finally forced a full smile onto my mouth. "We're in public."

"Technically, we're out to sea," he countered as his fingers slipped into my bottoms.

"We're in the wide open in broad daylight." I opened my eyes and was met with miles of lulling blue ocean. I squelched a moan as his fingers circled my clit.

"No one is paying attention to us." Colter's voice had slipped into that sinfully low tenor that fried my braincells. I turned and bit into my arm to stifle a groan as he slid a finger inside. "From this far away it just looks like I'm giving you a massage."

"Yeah, a massage of my inner walls," I laughed breathlessly. The laughter died as he pulled his finger out and focused his efforts back to my clit, circling, pressing, teasing. It was taking everything in me to stay still. If I started pressing against his hand I was afraid it would look like we were...doing exactly what we were doing.

This was wholly indecent. And absolutely exhilarating.

Me from a week ago would have been scandalized.

A squeak escaped my throat, and I screwed my eyes shut as release drew near.

"Quiet now, Rockstar," Colter crooned, picking up his pace.

My hips inched back and up, lifting my pelvis clear off the mini catamaran which Colter and I signed out for the hour. I panted through my nose as I smashed my mouth against my arm to do as he'd said, *keep quiet*.

"*Fuck*." I garbled out as I snapped, a bright, fierce orgasm seizing my body.

It'd started and ended so fast that I was pretty sure my brain was scrambled. Colter slipped out of my swim bottoms and I lifted my head, peeking over my shoulder as he did what he always did—sucked my arousal clean off his fingers.

"You're absolutely *wicked*," I playfully seethed, half in a daze.

"You're absolutely *delicious*." His deviously handsome smirk had me wanting to reach up and kiss it right off his face.

Slowly gathering my senses, I flipped onto my back to sun my front and cupped a hand over my brow, shielding the sun, as I admired the man sitting with his back to the mast. He winked at me before he closed his eyes and tipped his head back.

Everything in me demanded I crawl between his legs and take him in my mouth. His cock, half-erect beneath his swim trunks, was *beckoning* me. My mouth watered.

"You will not be able to keep it discreet if you try what's on your mind," Colter advised, eyes still closed. I narrowed my eyes on him. *How did he know what I was thinking?*

"How do you know? I can be very discreet," I said, reaching over and raking my nails over his crossed shins.

He opened one eye. "Okay...*I* will not be discreet."

I clapped the hand that had been shielding the sun down over my eyes as I bit my lip to contain my smile.

Indiscreet is just how I liked him.

"Duly noted." Appeased, he closed the one eye again. And wickedly, I added, "I'll get you back later, then."

Both his blue-green eyes opened and bore down on me intensely. "I have no doubt."

~

I placed a hand onto the ancient stone, mesmerized.

The tour guide, who'd been rambling off historical facts raised his voice, "These sites were primarily where Mayan women would pay tribute to the goddess of love," — a stupid smile hit my lips — "and fertility."

I yanked my hand away as if the stone were red-hot.

Alan, who'd been sneakily watching me snickered. I shot him a *shut the heck up* look that made him laugh even harder. Thankfully this all went unnoticed by Colter and Cam.

"What?" He stage-whispered. "Like you're not interested in having Colter's babies? We all know you two are fucking like rabbits now...you *do* know what happens when a man and a woman—"

I halted his speech as I reached up and inconspicuously dug my nails into the back of his neck. "Al, I swear to God..."

From an outsider, it would look like I was placing a friendly hand on my pals back as we carried on a hushed conversation.

He choked a laugh. "You mean you swear to the *Goddess* of Love and Fer—*ah!*" I'd dug deeper. "Okay, okay. Claws off me, you harpy," Al hissed.

I released the nails, but kept my hand on his upper back as I patted him innocently. "What did we learn?"

"That Colter must have skin like steel if he has to deal with those talons."

That earned him a swift smack to the back of the head that caught some other tourists' attention. I smiled sweetly at them and they immediately turned back around to minding their own business. "You're a real piece of work, Connors."

"You started it," I said through a toothy smile.

Al slunk out from under my touch and backtracked to Cam's side, joining in *his* beau's conversation with *my* beau. Seeing his opportunity, Colter picked up his pace and sidled up to me as our group carried on with the tour.

"What was that about?" he asked, faking casualness as he stuck his hands in his pockets.

"Like you didn't hear," I play-scoffed, crossing my arms over my chest.

Colter hung his head and chuckled in defeat. "Is having my babies that repulsive to you?"

Was it? My kneejerk reaction was to shout *yes*. Not that I'd be repulsed if it was *Colter's* child but because…because, damn, I was not in a place to be thinking about kids. I stole a sidelong glance at Colter who still smiled at the ground.

"Isn't it to you?" I tested.

Colter looked up straight ahead, squinting against the midday sun. "I have every intention to put a baby in you someday."

I tripped over my feet, but Colter threw an arm around my waist, steadying me. *Well, damn.* I shot a nervous glance over my shoulder, wondering if Alan and Cam heard. Given their wide-eyed stares, I'd say yes, yes they did hear. Loud and clear. Alan weaved his head tauntingly and mouthed, *I fucking told you so.* I slipped my arm around Colter's waist and flipped Al off.

When I looked back up at Colter, realizing he'd directed his attention to me now, I perked.

"Don't you want babies? *My* babies?" he emphasized.

My stomach dropped. When he looked at me like that, I lost all common sense, but this was a serious topic of conversation and I shook away his effect on me.

"Babies? Someday. *Your* babies, specifically? Absolutely. But talking about it right this second—in the Mayan ruins of fertility, no less—is a little nerve-wracking, okay? Let's just add this to the five-year plan."

Colter's hand on my hip tightened, drawing me to a stop as he slowed. Alan and Cam had to break apart to walk around either side of us so they didn't collide directly into us. The rest of the tour group faded away as Colter cradled my face with his free hand, forcing my eyes to his.

"I'm not kidding, Molly." His voice held no amount of amusement. Colter was all seriousness. So much so, I lost my breath. "I've never really imagined having kids before. But with you...I'd put a baby in you right now if you gave me the green light." He kissed me fiercely, bursting something in my chest. "I want it all with you."

It was his absolute fearlessness at the thought of such a life-changing, important thing that put a fissure in a wall that had never been tested before. Of course, I dreamed of marriage and children, but up until this exact moment it had never been in the realm of true possibility. But looking into Colter's eyes, a portal to a world of new opportunities opened.

~

The tequila tasting was the last point of me remaining on my best behavior.

Since Cam and Colter had volunteered to drive the Jeep rentals and were limited on the alcohol intake, it left Alan and I to the important job of tasting the tequila.

And taste, we did.

The employees at the tequila farm zeroed in on Al and I like a farmer plumping up a pig for the Christmas ham. Originally we'd been told we'd get *three mini shots per person.* But...

Our tequila guide kept coming back to Al and I. And coming back. And pouring more. The shots were tiny; no bigger than a splash but when I stopped counting at ten of them, I was already feeling it in my toes. And neck. And face. And other areas...

After we left, I finally paid Colter back for his little escapade on the mini catamaran from the morning. It was my first time giving road-head and it was in a foreign country. I had Colter hissing and vocalizing so much that I was about ready to call *him* Rockstar.

When we ended our Jeep day at the Saturday flea market in town, I began to suspect they organized the tour to go shopping *after* drinking on purpose. I was too tipsy to keep a poker face and let my desires for all kinds of goods and souvenirs show all over my face.

We'd stopped to admire a street painter as he finished up a piece of a beach sunset. I gave him my regards as we passed, to which he gave me an appreciative nod in return. I was rubbernecking as we continued down the sidewalk, still caught up in admiring the artwork, but Colter's arm around my waist kept me from stumbling or veering into oncoming pedestrian traffic.

Colter had to pull me off my high horse a few times:

Where are you going to put up a coconut bird house? You live in a basement apartment.

You already bought one blanket, how many more blankets do you need?

Do you have space in your luggage to take home a fire-glazed clay serving platter?

One of us had to be the voice of reason.

I walked away with one blanket, a hand-painted wooden bowl, and a Cozumel magnet for my fridge. After a half hour of perusing the tables and tents, Colter left me in Cam and Al's capable hands to find a restroom.

Al was cradling a pile of goods of his own.

"Ooh, what ya got there?" I sang as I craned my neck to see.

Al snickered. "I'm bringing Mexico home with me."

He proceeded to point out all his belongings; an authentic sombrero, a *Cozumel* graphic tee, that damn serving platter I'd been eyeballing, and another hand-woven blanket.

Al and I were more alike than I realized sometimes.

"He can't tell me no." Alan shrugged as he tipsily beamed up at Cam.

"There's plenty you can't tell me no to too, love." Cam gave Alan a subtle wink that sent Al into a flushed tizzy, nearly dropping the precious platter.

I let out a pathetic excuse of a wolf whistle—that was likely the first time I'd ever heard Cam drop an innuendo. And the first time witnessing Alan fluster. I loved it.

"Have you two always been like this and I just never noticed?" I smiled as I pointed a finger back and forth between the two of them.

"Welcome to the Couples Club," Cam teased, squeezing my upper arm.

My brow pinched. "Wait a minute, I've been a part of plenty of couples and haven't been given insights into your relationship dynamics before…"

Alan snorted. "We've never cared for your boyfriends before—" He was cut off as Cam reached behind him, likely pinching him…somewhere.

I let that one slide. After the mess with Eric, I could see why.

Minutes dragged on and eventually the three of us sat down on the curb of the parking lot where the flea market was held, waiting for our fourth wheel so we could get this show on the road. I needed food.

"So…speaking of couples…" I'd have expected this from Alan, but it was Cam opening up this can of worms. "Are you and Colt a serious thing now or is this some hot vacation fling?"

I had to give it to him…the man had some balls.

My mind immediately went to work dissecting my answer. It was the first time since our confession last night that I had a moment to really think about what this meant for Colter and I's future. We'd proclaimed our love for one another. And he'd said *There's no going back after this. If I make love to you now, you're mine and I'm yours.* And just earlier today he'd claimed he wanted it all with me; a future—marriage and babies?

The weight of it all pressed against my chest. I realized that my world was truly shifting and suddenly that fear of change and the unknown tried it's damnedest to pull me back under.

It was all bliss here in paradise, but what happened when we left for home tomorrow?

And then a thrill bolted through me at the thought of Colter coming over to my apartment on a regular basis, being able to spend more time with him, alone and otherwise. I hadn't realized how much I'd missed him during his stint in Tennessee. I knew before this trip he'd been planning on getting his certification and then leaving the state but what of his plans *now*? I had no intention of ever leaving Michigan— no matter how brutal the winters could be. I was a die-hard Michigander.

This was all too heavy a topic to be tackling on a Saturday night, tequila-tipsy on a street curb in Mexico. So I sent Cam and Alan a genuine, sweet smile and simply said, "Yes."

Because it was both.

Colter found us shortly after.

~

Sometime later back at the resort, the four of us closed our time together with snorkeling at the beach. Finally. By the time we were heading out, I'd almost been too tired to notice Eric laying on a beach chair looking particularly burnt out.

Alone and appearing as exhausted as I felt, I looked at him, not with disdain but…indifference. He didn't seem to notice the four of us as we passed. He had an arm slung over his eyes as he baked in the late afternoon sun.

Al and Cam didn't say a word or mention Eric. Colter simply placed a supportive hand on the small of my back. I kept a curious eye on Eric, wondering why he was deciding to spend his last night here alone. For the first time this week, something akin to pity hit my chest for him. Whether or not he'd had a different woman warming his bed every night this past week…he'd be arriving in Michigan alone tomorrow. While I would be surrounded by friends and love.

TWENTY-FOUR

It totally wasn't weird taking a plane ride home with your current and ex-boyfriend at the same time. It totally wasn't weird for Ben and Gracie or Alan and Cam as they each took turns sitting in the same row with him on each separate flight so that Colter and I wouldn't have to. I'd tried to tell them it wasn't necessary—we were all adults and I could handle it. But it seemed they wanted to avoid our cringey confrontation as much as, if not more than, I did.

"We are about twenty minutes out from Gerald R Ford. We will be landing in a bit of a snowstorm—it appears Grand Rapids saw eighteen inches over the last two days. It's currently twenty-one degrees and snowing." The pilot relayed the weather report as I reached up and slid open my window. It was dark beyond the wings.

I felt Colter's hand grasp my knee, and it was only then that I realized I'd been bouncing it.

"It's going to be just fine," he said in a hushed voice.

I wrapped my hand around his. "I know." I didn't, though.

Closing my eyes, I tried my best to focus solely on my breathing. *In. Hold. Out. Hold.* Colter still held onto my leg but allowed me peace and quiet to go inward.

I'd been shocked that our flight hadn't been cancelled. We were delayed in Atlanta and Colter had noticed my anxiety beginning shortly after I learned of the weather here at home. He'd distracted me by pulling me into an alcove to kiss me silly. Ben had to break it off before we got too carried away. I almost wished Colter could distract me right now—

The plane banked as the pilot neared the airport, readying to line up for landing. My back stiffened and my grip on Colter increased enough that I felt him flex his hand beneath mine.

"Pilots fly in this every day," he said comfortingly.

After a small eternity, the airport came. And then went.

The pilot leveled out and banked again. And again.

Panic was sealing up my throat. It was obvious to everyone on the flight that we were not being cleared for landing for whatever air-traffic-control reason.

"He can't land, can he?" I whispered, leaning in to Colter's side with my eyes closed.

I heard him let out a trapped breath and then he kissed my temple, his lips brushing my ear. "It'll be fine, Molls."

Then we were descending. And my heart rate was ascending.

I opened my eyes, daring to take a peek out of the window and saw the airport runway nearing at a shocking speed. It all seemed so fast. Too fast. What if there was ice? What if we slid? What if—

The wheels touched down on a harsh screech as Colter grabbed my face and kissed me. My hands clutched him, hanging on for dear life as the plane pulled left and then corrected to the right, jostling us passengers roughly on the way. Colter kissed me through the whole thing, until the plane slowed to a steady taxiing before curving off the runway. Several passengers applauded in gratitude and relief.

Colter rested his forehead against mine as he broke away to breathe, "See. Told you."

I swatted his chest, but it lacked any oomph. "You did. Foolish of me to doubt you."

"As long as you recognize that," he chuckled, patting my thigh.

Playfully rolling my eyes, I pulled away to gaze into his and found something there I wasn't expecting. Apprehension.

"You were scared too, weren't you?" I asked as the plane taxied to the gate.

"I will admit no such thing," Colter said, leaning back into his seat, avoiding eye contact with a small smile on his face.

My mouth twisted to the side. "You're not denying it either." His face was stoic. But he winked. I dropped my head onto his shoulder as my heart swelled. "Thank you."

For distracting me. For supporting me. For loving me. For just sitting here with me.

Colter dropped a kiss to the top of my head. "Whatever you need, Molls."

I couldn't've stopped my smile if I'd tried.

~

It also wasn't weird standing on the opposite side of the baggage claim conveyor from Eric. Apparently, like Colter, he was still waiting to see his suitcase come funneling out of the special little hidey-hole. I could feel his eyes on Colter and me.

Assessing? Judging? Fuming? It was hard to tell from this far away, but he seemed very interested in us.

I turned my back on Eric, and wrapped myself around Colter's waist, burying my face into his shirt and scent. "I'm so tired."

It was ten past eleven at night. There was still a drive home to make, and I'd been the idiot who hadn't taken my Monday after a vacation off. I had to be at work at 8:45 a.m. tomorrow morning.

Colter stroked my spine. "I'll get you to bed soon enough, Rockstar."

It wasn't laced with any sexual intention, but my body still responded like it was. I warmed in his hold and looked up at him, my chin resting against his sternum. "Will you stay with me tonight?"

He was still looking at the baggage claim, but I watched a dimple appear at this angle that I'd never noticed as he smiled. His hand stroked lower, stopping at the curve of my backside. "Whatever you need, Molls."

I squirmed happily in his arms and then blinked as a thought struck me. "Why do you say that all the time?"

"What?" He finally looked down at me, mild confusion distorting that smile and his dimple disappearing.

"*Whatever you need.*" I tried to mimic his voice. Pathetically. "To everything. It's like your go-to response."

He shrugged and looked away as though he wasn't going to answer. But then his chest rose beneath my chin as he took a deep breath. "It's just...something I grew up hearing all the time. My Dad," Colter paused to swallow as he scratched the back of his neck, "always said it to my Mom."

I froze. Stopped breathing. My heart constricted.

"I don't know," Colter continued, laughing softly. "I think it was kind of his way of saying he loved her. He wanted to give her the world. Give her whatever she needed to be happy."

We were quiet for a moment as I took in those words. A sort of replay went through my head of the past week and of each time he'd said those words to me. But beyond that, he'd been sneaking that phrase to me our whole lives.

A memory flooded me then.

Of us as kids. Playing on the playground after school before summer break. We usually were some of the last kids picked up so it was typically us two left as Cam rode the bus, and Ben and Alan's mom didn't work and often was waiting at the door for them when the bell rang.

I'd started down the slide, forgetting that it'd rained earlier in the day. A puddle of rainwater had pooled at the bottom of the slide and in the mud pit below it. I'd been able to press my hands and feet into the sides to stop myself, but I couldn't get back up. Colter had been right behind me, prepared to follow me down. I'd looked up over my shoulder asking for help up.

He'd reached down, saying, "Sure, Mol. Whatever you need."

Colter had helped me then. He'd been helping from the sidelines my whole life. He was helping me to this day, right now. Part of me wanted to grieve the fact that it took us this long to get here. But I couldn't deny that being here now, especially in his arms like this—even standing in the middle of the airport baggage claim—I was so incredibly grateful.

"I love you." I needed to say it.

That is what made me happy. *That* is what made me feel on top of the world.

Colter's hand on my back rose into my hair, cradling my head as he lowered his mouth and kissed me. "I love you, too."

~

If I thought the flights and waiting at baggage claim were weird it was nothing compared to the walk to our cars. It was Eric's Malibu and Colter's Wrangler left on the roof of the parking ramp, and it appeared that our friends had been kind enough to shovel snow off of Colter's car...but left Eric's buried.

As Colter and I neared his Jeep, both of us shivering in the night's cold, I could hear Eric behind us dragging his feet and cussing. This was exactly the nightmare that had turned his mood for the worse when we'd parked up here last week.

I wasn't sure why, but a pang of guilt gripped my insides.

Colter brought me to his passenger seat door and opened it for me, but I hesitated. He shuffled on his feet, trying to stave off the cold. "What's wrong?"

I looked up at him and then at Eric over my shoulder, who was rifling through his trunk, probably looking for a snowbrush he had yet to use this season. When I caught Colter's eye again, I didn't have to explain. He already knew.

"I'll help him," Colter grumbled as he went to open his backseat, looking for his own snowbrush.

"Actually..." I spun and took the door handle myself. "I'll do it."

Colter looked at me like I was crazy. Maybe I was. "I'm not letting you freeze out here. *I'll* help him.

"No, Colter." I shook my head and gave him a pleading look. "I need to do it. He and I need closure now that you and I are going to start down this road. Just—can you please give us a moment?"

I could see his jaw clenching, the muscle flickering. He was silent for a moment as his eyes bore into me. Then all at once, he moved, producing his snow brush out of his back seat and handed it over to me.

"Try to make it quick," he said, his tone clipped in the cold. That pang in my insides ratcheted up now that it was obvious I was hurting Colter in some way. I understood his displeasure with my choice, but he seemed willing to let me do what I needed to do. Whatever I needed, right?

"Sure." I nodded once as I wrung the brush handle.

Colter rounded to the driver's side and hopped in. The music he'd been listening to when he'd parked blared to life and his hand shot out to silence it, but then he cranked his heat, letting a new sound take over the atmosphere of the car. "I'll be here." *Watching and waiting*, he didn't need to say.

"Thank you," I whispered as I shut the door.

I took a deep, frigid breath and then turned and headed toward Eric who'd found his brush and was already working away at the snow on his back window. He didn't seem to notice my advance until I started on his driver's side.

"Mol?" Eric straightened, and it was as if the blood drained from his face. In the foreground of the blustery winter night, he looked pale. Frail.

"Hey." I brushed in long sweeping strokes, being careful not to bury my feet.

Eric was slow to start his brushing again, and his eyes darted to Colter's running Jeep. Our breaths, and the exhausts of the cars, fogged the snowy air around us. "What are you doing?"

"Helping."

"You don't have to do this," he said with an air of defeat.

I looked into his eyes. "I know."

His eyes were bloodshot. From crying? From exhaustion after such an action-packed week? Eric cleared his throat and moved on to the passenger side as I moved to the hood, the cold beginning to sting my exposed skin.

"Colter and I didn't start anything until after…" I trailed off then, because I didn't want to say it out loud. For some reason this didn't seem the time or place to throw his infidelity in his face.

"I know," he said as he used the sleeve of his shirt to wipe under his reddening nose. "You don't have to explain yourself, Mol. It's fine. I'm fine."

At his shockingly accepting words, I paused to study him. For a moment I thought about all the good times over the past year we'd shared together. He was so starkly different right now that I suddenly found myself narrowing my eyes on him, my brow furrowing. Eric kept cleaning off the piles of snow, not noticing that I'd halted my work.

His arms shook but I got the feeling that it wasn't from the cold. It was a bone deep shaking that, frankly, rattled me.

"Eric."

He didn't stop or look up at me. Deafening internal silence was seizing my thoughts.

"*Eric.*"

He looked up briefly. Flinched.

Attempted to carry on. Failed.

I slowly made my way over to him, cautious he might actually faint. "Eric, are you okay?"

He forced a laugh as he brought his brush up to finish the windshield I'd abandoned. "I'm fine, Molly. Thanks for your help, you should go. With Colter." He nodded his head to the Jeep and flinched again.

"Tell me what's wrong," I demanded calmly. I let him know in my tone that I would not be leaving without an explanation.

"Nothing's wrong—"

"Don't lie to me." I closed this distance between us and snagged his snow brush before he dropped it into the snow piled on the pavement. "Eric—you're not well, I can *see* that."

Eric's eyes closed and he sucked in a shaky breath through his nose. "I need to sit."

I jumped into action, ripping open the passenger door and helping him sit before he fell. I straightened and was about to shout to Colter for help when Eric reached for my hand and pulled me down, stopping me. "Don't," he begged.

"What do you mean, *don't?*" I helped him put his legs into the vehicle. "You can't drive like this. You need help."

Eric dropped his head to the head rest, eyes still closed, and shook his head. "Please, Molly. *Don't.* Just give me a *goddamn* minute."

I froze at the harshness of his words. He'd done more cussing at me in the last week than he had in all of our year-long relationship combined.

"Not unless you tell me what is going on. Right now. This isn't some chronic hangover…"

He was quiet for a moment, licking his lips and swallowing, just breathing as he worked up the nerve to talk to me. I reached in and placed my hand on his forehead to feel his temperature as I stole a glance up at Colter's Jeep, wondering if he had been watching and was seeing what was going down.

Eric pushed my hand away. "I'm not that kind of sick."

I crouched in the door, my pulse pounding. "What do you mean—"

"I'm dying, Mol," he said softly, eyes opening and pinning me frozen to the spot.

Stomach roiling, my kneejerk reaction was to ask him if this was some kind of sick joke. But his eyes held every ounce of seriousness and genuine acceptance that could only mean one thing…

Eric was dying.

And he'd somehow come to terms with it.

"What?" I breathed, my knees knocking as I shook with more than just cold.

He huffed one dry laugh, and his speech was brittle as he explained, "Brain cancer. Stage four. It's…aggressive."

We were both shaking so violently that I found it hard to speak. "How…how aggres-s-s-ssive?"

"Aggressive enough for me to trash my relationship and spend a week in Mexico making all kinds of fucked up decisions." His harsh joke fell flat. And absolutely shattered my heart.

Tears were running down my cheek, going cold before they could drop from my jaw and into the snow. "Why?" I squeaked, my fingers going stiff on the car door and roof as I supported myself. Anger bubbled up out of nowhere inside me. "Why would you do that?!"

"Molly. Stop. Please. Will you," he paused to cuss under his breath, teeth chattering. "Will you get in the fucking car?"

I clenched my jaw and screwed my eyes shut, squeezing out tears that were blurring my vision. "I'll be right back," I snapped before I shut his passenger seat door.

My steps were clumsy as I waded through snow to Colter's Jeep, my mind going a mile a minute. I opened the door, jump-scaring him as I did so.

"Hey—whoa. Molly what's wrong?" Colter set his phone in his lap and braced a hand on the shoulder of the passenger seat as he leaned in toward me. I didn't get in.

"Please don't hate me. I will explain everything, but right now, I need to take Eric home." It was the hardest thing I'd ever had to say to Colter. And my heart broke watching the way his face fell into disappointment.

"You're going with *him?*" The look in his eyes...he was wounded. In disbelief.

"Colter, please," I begged as more tears slipped out. "It's not what you think. I love you—Colter, *look at me.*" He'd averted his gaze as I'd said I loved him. He slowly slid his eyes back to me, a look of wariness behind them. "*I love you.* But Eric..." How much could I say right now? I didn't know the proper etiquette for this situation, "is not well right now. I don't trust him to drive. I'm taking him home. I will call you and explain everything. I promise you. Can you trust me on this?"

Colter was white-knuckling his steering wheel, but after a breath he shifted into gear. "Whatever you need, Molly." But the sentiment didn't hold its usual weight. Something about it this time lacked feeling.

I didn't feel like I had the time to tackle that issue, so I just nodded. "Thank you. Colter, thank you. Please, please, please, drive safe," I pleaded.

He crossed the passenger seat, grasping me by the back of my head to plant a fierce kiss to my lips. As he backed away, he gave me a hard look. "*You* drive safe, too."

I nodded and then stepped back, closing the door. He was already backing out before I could change my mind. And the look he gave me out his window as he drove away drove a blunt stake through my chest.

He hadn't said I love you back. Everything felt wrong. Broken.

Distraught, I trudged to Eric's driver's side and let myself in, frozen muscles relaxing only a fraction as I was met with heat.

"Where is he going?" Eric asked, craning his head as he watched Colter's Jeep retreat. "Molly...you should have gone with him."

"And leave you here?"

"My episodes only last a few minutes." Eric paused, swallowing thickly. "I'll be fine to drive any second now..." he trailed off.

"Well, we're stuck together now."

It was pointless now anyway. I waited for a moment, letting my limbs thaw before I even attempted to drive in this shitstorm. When I'd finally gained enough composure, I shifted into reverse and looked at him, carefully saying, "Eric...tell me everything."

~

Eric had a rapidly spreading brain tumor that was deadly. He had explained surgery was out of the option—too risky. And he'd calmly and calculatingly explained that he had made the decision not to undergo treatment. That, even with treatment, survival rate was low. Really low. Twelve to fifteen months at best.

Without treatment...four.

I couldn't help but fight when he'd admitted he'd decided to forgo treatment. We argued. Brutally. He was young and fit and deserved to live—why not fight for more time? But he was all too formal as he explained the life he'd be living if he accepted treatment; he didn't want to spend the last moments of his life adding on the difficulties that it could bring.

270

My heart completely shattered when I'd asked how long he'd known, how long he'd been keeping it from me.

Three months.

Three out of his four months prognosis, he'd lied. He'd carried this weight. I started to think back on our time together and I couldn't understand how I'd never seen the signs. When guilt and shame started eating away at me, Eric picked up on it and snuffed it out.

"I didn't want you to have to deal with this...any of this." He'd cried as we drove through the storm on the way to his house. "It's why...I did what I did."

"So, you thought it was best to blow up our relationship by cheating left and right behind my back?"

"No. I had every intention to break up with you and *then* go buck wild. But...that first day...I was actually sick, Moll. I couldn't get out of bed. I was exhausted and yeah, I'd had plans to meet up with Imelda." He looked absolutely disgusted with himself and my insides warred with equal parts repulsion and heartbreak. "She knew. I told her. I was so scared and I needed someone."

"You had me," I whispered helplessly. "Damnit, Eric. You had me. I was the person you were supposed to lean on—"

"No," he argued. "I couldn't do that to you. This isn't what I wanted for you."

"I would've helped. I would've seen this through—"

"I know. I know!" His voice rose. "That's why I needed to let you go. I needed to see and know you were happy and safe before I was gone. That you'd be taken care of."

Happy and safe.

"Did...did you want Colter and I to wind up together?" My voice had gone eerily quiet at the realization.

"I've always known he had feelings for you," Eric said as he curled over in his seat, dropping his head into his hands. "I knew he'd be there for you. I knew this vacation would be the perfect opportunity for you two..."

I couldn't breathe. I groped the steering wheel as if it were a lifeline to reality.

This whole time, Eric had schemed and planned for me to wind up falling into Colter. Because he didn't want to leave me behind to crash and burn after he...he...

"You're dying," I sobbed. The words finally hitting home. Eric didn't respond to that. Maybe he knew I just needed to vocalize it, because *fuck*.

The last week played over in my head. When I thought he'd been glaring at my friends with disdain in the parking ramp on our way to Mexico...had he really been grieving the fact that he'd never have a real place in the group? Every time I'd seen him looking tired and upset as he moped around the resort, had he been dealing with his symptoms? Colter had punched him for fuck's sake. I'd gone off on him; telling him I'd never seriously considered marrying him, that I wasn't sorry we'd broken up. I'd absolutely *trashed* him.

I was so appalled with myself that I was sick. I clapped my hand over my mouth as I hunched over his steering wheel, doing my best to drive while falling apart at the same time.

Eric groaned, "Molly. Don't do that, please don't do that."

"Don't what?"

"I can see you beating yourself up over it." He sighed, reaching over to pull my hand away from my mouth. "I don't blame you or hate you for anything that's happened this week."

"I was despicable to you," I whispered into the cab of his car.

"You were hurt. Understandably so. I don't fault you for any of it."

"I'm so sorry. Eric," I turned to him briefly, I couldn't take my eyes off the road for long, but I needed him to see it, feel it, "I am so, *so* sorry."

"I know." His voice wobbled a bit. "Me too."

Forty minutes later we pulled into his apartment building's parking lot and I parked his Malibu in his carport. I helped him take his suitcase inside. Helped him to bed, all the while feeling my heart chipping away bit by bit.

"Should I stay?" I asked as he closed his eyes. He hadn't even changed out of his airplane clothes he was so exhausted.

"No," Eric snapped. "No, I don't want Colter hating me— or you—for this. You can take my car."

I scoffed. "Don't be silly. I'll get an Uber."

He opened one eye. "You really think you're going to find one at this time of night in this shit weather?"

I pulled out my phone and entered into the app, hoping against hope that there would be *someone*. "I'll be fine," I assured him. A heavy silence hit us then.

"I know you will be," he replied after some time.

I paused my efforts and looked down at him. My mind was still reeling in the background and yet one question kept nagging me. "Why would you not have just let me love you through this?"

Eric's smile lacked happiness as he took a minute to think that over. "Because I care for you, Molly—I do. But—and please don't take this the wrong way—you're not *the one*. When I got my diagnosis, believe me, I briefly considered falling into you and letting you hold me through to the end, but...I couldn't do that to you. Felt wrong. I needed to figure out how to let you down easy so that I could go spend whatever time I had left with my family on the eastside. I thought if I could nudge you toward Colter then...I don't know.

"I'd actually confronted Colter before he left for Tennessee. I'd overheard him talking to Ben about it at a bonfire. He'd said he knew it was a temporary job but that he was thinking about maybe staying down there when it was over. Find real work and move there. I told him it was a stupid idea when I had a moment alone with him later. I'd been about ready to beg him to come home so he'd be here for you when I was gone, but then Ben returned and kinda broke up our disagreement without even realizing it.

"We haven't talked about that confrontation since then. But I knew he would have to come home for this vacation we'd all planned and...I was hoping you two would find each other...even if it pissed me off to watch it happen."

I stared at him dumbfounded for a long time. I found it difficult to comprehend how he could follow through with this decision to orchestrate my life and his own so that we'd both deal with his passing in two completely separate ways.

Yet, I also somehow…understood. I wouldn't have wanted to drag someone else down a painful path, especially someone who I knew was never going to be *the one*. I supposed the end had a way of bringing out that kind of clarity in a person.

We'd talked a little while longer after that, until he could hardly seem to keep his eyes open. I'd let him know I was sorry, begged for his forgiveness. And he obliged on the one condition that I offer him the same. It had already long been granted.

We were only human.

We made choices, some of them good, some of them bad.

We held opinions, some of them good, some of them bad.

And that would likely forever be how things worked. None of it would stop life or death. But we could still have love in our hearts all the while. We could learn to forgive.

I'd found a stroke of luck when I was able to find an Uber that would pick up my ride request. I'd had to wait only fifteen minutes for them to show. In that time, Eric had fallen asleep and I just stared at him, heart deflating. Sure, he'd made questionable choices over the last week…

But he set Colter and I on a new path and I wasn't sure what to think of it. I told him I would check in with him tomorrow even though he was sleeping. And I left, feeling drained and weighed down.

The Uber ride felt like it lasted forever. My phone was nearly dead and my body was aching from a week's worth of alcohol and vigorous sex.

At least my tears had run dry…it would have been awkward to have a break down in the Uber driver's car.

It was only when I half-stumbled through my front door that I remembered all my things were in Colter's Jeep. I pulled my phone out of my bag and frowned when I realized it had died.

Dragging my feet through my apartment, I didn't even bother turning on lights as I went. Searching in my nightstand, I found an old charging cord, plugged my phone, and then pulled off my pants as I waited for it to charge enough to turn it on and let Colter know I'd made it home safely.

God, I missed him already.

In a t-shirt and panties, I slid into my too-cold sheets and huddled, reminding myself warmth would seep into my body in soon enough. What I wouldn't give for Colter's arms around me right now. I had a lot of explaining and making-up to do with him. But he would understand.

I *knew* he would understand.

I had so many thoughts trying to demand my attention but after some time my thoughts began meshing together into nonsense. And I fell asleep all too suddenly and deeply.

TWENTY-FIVE

Distant, frantic thumping. Knocking? No, *pounding*.

Someone was pounding on a door. Given the volume, that door was likely mine.

I sat upright as a bolt of adrenaline zinged through me. "What the——?"

I ripped my covers off and my hand blindly smacked around for my phone I'd plugged into the charger on my nightstand. Ripping the cord out, I stood and tried to check the time on the screen. It was off. That's right, I'd plugged it in when it was dead, and I must've fallen asleep before I could turn it back on.

Panic was springing sweat to my pits and palms as I raced on the tips of my toes to my bedroom door. The main living and kitchen area were still dark, the curtains having been drawn tight since before I'd even left for vacation a week ago.

The pounding was definitely at my front door.

My fingers twitched to the baseball bat I kept hidden behind the couch but then whoever it was outside spoke, "*MOLLY!* It's Gracie! Are you in there?! Open up!"

"Gracie?" I breathed. I raced to the door, checking the time on the stove as I whizzed by. 7:34 a.m.

Turning the lock, I yanked the door open. "Gracie! What the hell is going on—"

"*Oh my God!*" she cried, falling into me as she dragged me in for a hug. Tears spilled from her eyes. "Why *the hell* haven't you been answering your phone?!"

"It died! It's been on the charger all night—it's charged now, I just haven't turned it back on—"

"*Molly*," she sobbed, pulling away to look at me. "I've been trying to call you for the last half hour."

"Gracie—tell me what is going on."

My intuition knew—it spiked a blast of fear through me—something was wrong. Really, really wrong.

"Get some pants on. We have to go," was all she said, her voice shaky and clipped. She pushed past me into my dark apartment as she snagged the sling bag off my bistro table. She had it open and was rifling through the contents as though making sure all the necessities were there.

"Gracie—"

"Where's your phone?" Gracie looked at me, recognized the device in my white-knuckled grip, and then she shook with something akin to anger. "Why are you standing there—get some clothes on, now!"

"*Gracie!*" I shouted, almost feeling the need to stomp my foot.

Gracie stiffened at the rise of my voice—something I rarely ever did. "It's Colter," she said, her shoulders sagging. "Molly he was in an accident. He's at West Central Hospital. We have got. To. Go."

My stomach hollowed as I swayed on the spot. Gracie reached out like she was going to stabilize me, but I was already moving. I swatted her hand away as I raced back into my room, pulling on my dresser drawer so hard that I ripped it right out of the dresser, sending it crashing to the floor. I fisted the first pair of pants I could reach and stepped out of the room, toward the front door as I frantically and clumsily pulled them on.

"He's okay? Tell me he's okay!" I cried as she approached with my winter coat and bag draped over her arm. She grabbed my elbow as my foot caught in the sweatpants and I stumbled.

Guiding me into the blinding light of the hallway, the neighbors across the hall had their door open and were peering at me through the crack in their door, eavesdropping. I looked away, unable to even feign an apologetic look for having disturbed their morning.

She didn't answer as we raced down the hall and up the stairs to the main apartment door. "Gracie?!"

"I-I don't know," she admitted as she threw open the door, basking us in the frigid air, snowflakes swirling inside in a flurry.

"What do you mean you '*don't know*'?" I snapped as we both trudged through the snow, slipping on ice here and there as we went.

"We only just got the call a half an hour ago from Rick letting us know," she explained as she inclined her head against the icy wind. "We—we thought you were with Colter, so we asked where you were, and he said he didn't know—that Colter had been brought in alone. He alerted the police that there should have been a passenger, and they were on their way to recheck the crash site."

We parted ways as we neared her car and I half climbed over the hood as I made my way to the passenger seat. As we both fell into the vehicle, she resumed explaining, "Alan is there now aiding in the search—*for fuck's sake,* Molly. We've all been thinking you're dead and frozen in a ditch somewhere." Gracie heaved as though she were sick, distraught.

I clamped a hand to my mouth to muffle the sob that wracked me.

"Ben and I split so I could check your apartment, just in case. Ben should be arriving at the hospital now. I'm sure he'll be calling any minute to let me know what's going on. I texted and let him know I have you while you went to grab pants."

"*Fuck,*" I spat. "Did you call my parents?"

"*No.* I didn't want to freak them out without being sure."

Which was smart considering they lived on the other side of the country.

"Fuck!" I shouted again, as Gracie started the car and whipped out of the parking spot.

I buried my face in my hands.

What had I done? Had I made a huge mistake in not going with Colter last night? Should I not have gone with Eric? How could I have been so stupid, so reckless? I should have told Eric we could talk another night. I should have stayed with the one I love. I should be with the one I love.

"What happened last night, Mol? How did you get home?" Gracie asked as we hit the main road in the direction of the highway.

I squeezed my eyes tight with shame and tears fell. "I took Eric home..."

Stunned silence filled the frigid cabin of Gracie's SUV.

"He wasn't feeling well and there was so much we needed to say to each other and Colter let me go with him." Even saying it now disgusted me. Sure, Eric and I's conversation had been pivotal. But I would never forgive myself for having left with him if something happened to Colter.

Colter. Oh my God.

"I'm so sorry, Mol," Gracie said, much too quietly.

"Don't," I said, wiping the blur of tears from my eyes. "Don't apologize or say anything even like that. We don't know anything."

"You're right," she replied, her fists tightening on the steering wheel as she glared out at the snowy road ahead of us.

We listened to the screech of the windshield wipers and my leg bounced with a fury as I rested my clenched jaw in my hand. We made it to the exit for the hospital as Ben's call flooded through the vehicle's hands-free stereo system.

"Ben," Gracie said by way of greeting as she answered the call with a press to the dashboard touch screen.

"I just talked to Rick," Ben said, his tone grave. Serious. My stomach flipped and I pressed my forehead to the frozen window for a bit of relief.

"How is he?" Gracie replied.

"He's...stable." That news didn't give me the relief my body was seeking, because Ben was clearly troubled. "But he's...fuck, Gracie. He's unresponsive. Rick says he's on a breathing tube and the CT Scan shows he has a moderate traumatic brain injury. They're watching him for signs of brain bleeding and swelling."

Each word, every syllable ratcheted up the severity of my trembling as I listened to Ben speak. I pressed the tips of my fingers into my lips as though it would prevent the nausea stirring in my gut. This couldn't be happening. This *couldn't* be happening. I'd only been with him last night. Just *hours* ago. He was fine, safe and healthy.

I wept, tapping my forehead against the glass of the frigid window as though I might fall right through it and exit this nightmare.

"We're on our way. Maybe ten minutes out," Gracie said, her voice as calculated and composed as I'd ever heard it. She was putting on a brave face. For Ben? For me?

"Please, baby," he begged. "Drive safe."

I felt gutted as those words—the same ones Colter and I had shared last night—processed through my head.

"Of course. I love you," Grace gushed.

Ben's sniffle was audible over the speakers. "I love you, too."

Those last ten minutes of the drive were torture, thick and raw.

I felt like a trapped animal in that vehicle, and as Gracie pulled up to the ER visitor entrance she and I both burst out of it. She tossed her keys haphazardly to the valet who seemed entirely used to the sort of thing.

Reception pointed us down the hall to where the ICU waiting room was on the main floor. As we rounded the curving hall, Ben appeared, hearing our pounding footsteps. He ran to Gracie, a look of sheer relief on his face. When they embraced, I side-stepped them continuing my pace as I neared Rick—Colter's father.

Rick rose from his seat, his face gaunt, expression tense.

"Mr. Evans," I breathed as I slowed enough to stop from crashing into him. "Where is he? Can I see him? Tell me he's going to be alright."

Softly taking me by the upper arms, Rick pulled me aside, bringing me down into the chair beside his. My eyes darted all around him, gobbling down any bit of information I could glean from his appearance, his demeanor. My gut didn't like what I saw; a barely-held-together man, still riding the grief of his wife's passing only half a year ago, now struggling to reconcile the fact that his son...

Rick brought up a hand and his fingers and thumb dug into the sides of his temples as though he sought counterpressure to whatever thoughts were battering around inside his head. I swallowed but nothing was there in my throat, it'd gone dry and achy from having to stifle the urge not to cry.

"Colter's stable," he clipped out. I nodded, already knowing that much. Rick dropped his hand but wouldn't look me in the eyes. "He's being monitored for additional bleeding. Colter suffered a subdural hematoma in the accident. The docs say it is serious but improving—they're hopeful he won't require surgery to alleviate the pressure."

Okay. Okay, that sounded okay. Things could get worse, I knew that, but if doctors didn't think surgery was necessary...Hope sprouted in my chest.

"Can I see him?" The words were shaky as they came out of my tense mouth.

"Cam and Alan are in there now," Rick said, though he was nodding. "The hospital only allows two visitors at a time. As soon as they're out, I'll take you in there, Molly." For a moment, I was able to register the relief that Alan and Cam had made it to the hospital safe and sound. But then Rick reached up a warm hand, setting it on my shoulder. "But I have to tell you, sweetheart...Colter—he's in rough shape."

The hope in my chest faltered at the grave look in Rick's eyes.

Rick released me and stretched his neck restlessly. "He's still unconscious. They have him on a breathing tube to ensure he's getting the necessary oxygen to not place any further strain on the brain."

My eyes shut tightly against the distress which that thought ripped through me. I knew this. Ben had said as much but now here, in the hospital, sitting with Colter's dad, it was all too real. Too serious. Too much.

I sucked my bottom lip into my mouth and nodded. I could handle it. I didn't care what kind of contraptions they had him in. I needed to lay eyes on him. I needed to see his chest rise and fall, feel the heartbeat within him. My body shook with the need to confirm it; that he was alive.

"What happened? The accident, I mean." Gracie's voice suddenly pulled me out of my anxiety, and I shot her a quick glance before whipping my face back to Rick.

"He'd only made it a mile down the highway before he hit black ice." Rick pressed his palms flat onto his thighs as he leaned back into his seat as though stretching the tightness out of his back. "First responders say he must have rolled the Jeep at least three times." A humorless laugh shook the man. "Thank God he was wearing a seat belt. He would've been thrown from the vehicle if not." I was holding my breath as Rick carried on, "They're unsure how long he remained in the ditch like that. But dispatch got the call around midnight last night."

Our flight had landed at 10:38 p.m. and we'd probably taken a half hour to reclaim our luggage and then more to shovel off the snow and say our goodbyes. He'd likely been waiting for help for no longer than twenty minutes. Thinking about him injured in his mangled vehicle for *any* length of time tore my insides up.

The double doors to the ICU opened and I immediately shot out of my seat as I saw Alan first pass through the door Cam held open for him. Both men's faces were solemn and looking extremely fatigued. A hand rested on my shoulder and squeezed. I didn't know whose.

The way Alan's face crumpled as he took in the sight of me had me screwing up my face against the emotion that threatened to drag me under too. We stumbled toward one another and into a fierce hug.

"I'm so happy to see you're okay." There was none of his usual cheerfulness in his voice. That alone was enough to set me further on edge.

"I'm fine. I-I need to go see him," I said, cutting the hug short.

Alan released me instantly. "Go."

We shared a nod of solidarity and then I turned to Rick. "Please, take me to him."

Rick took the door from Cam's hold. "This way."

I reached out for Cam's hand as I passed, and he squeezed it reassuringly.

The rows of doors beyond was a bleak, white-washed journey of despair. We entered into a windowed room, the curtains completely drawn against the view of the hall. As Rick stepped out of the way, my hand shot out, snagging the sleeve of his henley as I tried to steady myself.

Air funneled out of my lungs on a silent whoosh.

I pressed the back of my hand against my mouth to smother the sob my body strained to release. Rick's arm that I'd snatched turned and reached up to lay his palm flat against my shoulder blade, a much-needed support.

"Colter." I knew he likely couldn't hear me, but I spoke his name out into the sounds of the machines working softly in the room. My chest constricted so hard it hurt. I could see a contusion peeking out from his hairline, see the wound over his eyebrow that had been cleaned up and secured with bandages. More bandaging closed several cuts all along the knuckles of both of his hands. The breathing tube was taped to his relatively peaceful face.

I hadn't recalled consciously making the decision to walk up to his side, but there I was, a shaky hand reaching out to hold his. I was careful of the IV that was taped into the back of his hand.

The warmth of his hand as I clasped it in mine was a small but heart-bursting blessing, and it devasted me.

I finally broke.

I didn't care if Rick was in the room. I cried, not bothering to hold back the pitiful sounds, the weeping, or the words as I proclaimed, "I am so sorry. I'm sorry, Colter. I should have never left you alone. I should have stayed. *Damnit*, I should have stayed with you." I blinked through the tears, determined not to let them blur my vision of him laying before me any more than they already had. Bringing his hand up to my face, I turned it over to place a kiss to his palm and flattened it to my cheek, whispering "I love you" into his wrist.

Rick gave me space as he sunk into the shadowed corner of the dimly lit room. I kept saying the words over and over again both inside my head and aloud. *I'm so sorry. I love you. Please wake up. I'm so sorry.*

Seconds, minutes, or hours later a knock was heard at the open door. I hesitated, then turned to see a doctor standing there, his fist still resting against the frame he'd rapped his knuckles against. Rick had pushed off the wall and came to meet the man with a handshake.

"Good morning," the doctor said in a cool, calm tone. "I am the new attendant on shift, I'll be taking over Colter's care for the day. My name is Doctor Greg Hale. I'd like to speak with whoever is next of kin."

"That's me. Rick Evans. Colter's father." Rick waited and watched as Dr. Hale sent a cautious look in my direction. My heart jumped. God bless him, Rick noticed Dr. Hale's hesitancy and cleared his throat. "Molly's fine to be here."

Dr. Hale nodded his head and procured a clipboard he'd had tucked under his arm. "Mr. Evans, I've reviewed the CT scan imagery and I have some things I need to discuss with you about Colter's prognosis." Rick and I both stiffened. Dr. Hale eased himself further into the room, coming to Colter's other side to take a brief overview of him.

"Alright," Rick stated by way of encouraging the doctor to continue. He also came up beside me and I side-stepped so he could get closer to his son. But I didn't leave Colter's side nor release his hand. I doubled down, threading my fingers through his limp ones. I ignored the ache in my chest, focused solely on whatever news the doctor brought.

"The good news," Dr. Hale flashed a brief smile. "Is that the bleeding seems to have subsided. Pressure is receding. This is good, great, even. He likely won't need surgery or any medical intervention once he's woken and can breathe strongly on his own—which, I have high hopes will be sometime today." My body shuddered with relief as I processed the words, but there was still a stitch of tension in my gut, because I could still hear the *but* in the doc's tone.

Dr. Hale peeked down at his clipboard and flipped a page over. Whatever he examined had him squaring his shoulders as he looked Rick directly in the eye and said, "The bad news is that, even with a moderate TBI, memory loss is possible.

Normal. *Likely.* The extent to which how much memory loss Colter will experience won't be known until he wakes."

I felt woozy, the walls of the room pulsated around me as I gazed down at Colter. My body went through the motions of breathing, but I didn't think air was going anywhere. I shifted on my feet, resting a hip against the hospital bed to keep myself from swaying again.

"Are we talking permanent memory loss?" Rick asked, voice hoarse even though I had noticed his body soften at the doctor's initial bit of information.

"Permanent or temporary, unrecoverable or recoverable, we just don't know until he comes back to us and we can evaluate him." The doctor said tenderly and matter-of-factly all at the same time.

Fine. It was fine. It would be okay. He was alive, expected to recover, likely to wake today. That was all that mattered. Colter could get through this—he *would* get through this. My heart somehow both seized and sped up at the prospect.

"Do you have any other questions for me at this time?" Dr. Hale asked, tucking that clipboard back under his arm.

"No, Doc. Thank...thank you." Rick sighed and placed a hand to Colter's shin. I thought maybe I'd seen it tremble, but I moved past that thought, looking back to Colter's face, willing him to wake up, willing him to remember...remember *everything* when he did.

Dr. Hale left then, leaving Rick and I alone. "The others will want to know the update."

I nodded my agreement, swallowing in hopes to moisten my ever dry, tight throat so that I could speak. I couldn't, though. So, I just settled on looking up at the man.

Rick looked haggard. Bags had formed under his blue-green eyes, so much like those of his son's. I could see the movement of muscle as he clenched and unclenched his jaw.

"How long have you been here?" I asked softly.

"I got the call around twelve-thirty last night." Rick's eyes closed as though it was painful to recall. When they opened he looked up at me apologetically. "I didn't want to call you kids until I knew more about his condition. It didn't make sense to call until visiting hours anyway. I did call you, y'know."

I looked away then, more tears gathering in my eyes. My voice was weak as I mumbled, "My phone was dead."

There was a silence that settled between us and then Rick removed his hand from Colter's leg. "I'll go talk to the others."

I angled toward him, not caring that my tone was more desperation than polite request. "Can I stay? Can I stay with him?"

"Stay as long as you wish, Molly," he said with a tired wave of his hand.

I smiled appreciatively and then he was gone, heading to wherever the others waited. I wasn't sure I'd be able to remember the way back there, but I didn't care. I'd been given the all clear to stay right here, and stay here was what I would do, even if I had to do it forever.

TWENTY-SIX

I'd already called in to work, letting them know I was going to use my additional personal time to clear myself for the next couple of days—the whole week, if needed. Unhappy as they were, I'd wandered off to a quiet alcove in the hospital halls and explained that my boyfriend had been in an accident and the nature of which we now waited to get more answers in regards to his recovery. They could fire me for all I cared. They wouldn't though, we were too short-staffed even on good days and I had the experience they so desperately needed.

I had also spoken to my parents who were both distraught to learn of Colter's accident. It had been...difficult to convey the entire story from the beginning all over again. I knew Mom had cried at the way her voice had gone thick and raw. I'd heard Dad in the background throw a soft curse to the wind, damning the fate that had brought this down on Colter.

Mom had cooed to me, shared her sympathies and her reassurance that everything would be okay. And to some degree, she was right. But what no one knew was that there was more to Colter and I's story now. We'd arrived in Mexico as one thing and returned home as something entirely different. And no one really understood that he and I were now hanging in limbo.

Everything we'd shared was threatened to be possibly completely wiped out for him from his injuries. I wasn't sure how to process it. I couldn't tell Mom this. Not while still pacing around the hospital, an air of weariness blanketing all of us who were able to remain.

With our promises to keep them updated, Gracie, Alan, and Cam had left to attend to their responsibilities they couldn't so easily walk away from. Ben, who worked from home as a computer service tech, had just screened calls to go to a call center and stayed with me. Rick was back at Colter's side after he left me with him for three hours as I watched, waited, and prayed, never taking a hand off him as I held, caressed, and inspected every inch of his hand.

Others had stopped in one-by-one to see him and say their see-you-laters to him. Gracie had looked almost in pain as she broke down when she saw him for the first time. She'd wrapped her arms around my shoulders, hugging herself to my back as she spewed apologies for having ever been hesitant to welcome our union. I'd patted her arm tenderly as she'd rocked behind me. I knew she was sorry. I knew she realized what she was seeing transpiring between Colter and I now.

Devotion. Adoration. Love. Heartbreak.

Ben was with me now in the café, grabbing a bite to eat before we rock-paper-scissored for who got to go sit in with Rick while the other bid their time in the waiting room. I pushed around a single corkscrew pasta around my plate with my fork.

"You need to eat more," Ben said as he forced a sip of his Coke.

Truth be told, I just didn't have the appetite or the energy to eat. I felt as though I'd left my body back in Colter's room and was now nothing more than a wraith as I moved through the hospital.

"I will." I likely wouldn't.

"We don't know when Colter will wake up, Mol," Ben grumbled, crinkling the can in his grip as he set it on the table between us. "You'll want the energy to talk to him when he does. Eat."

I stabbed the pasta hard enough to snap a tine from the plastic fork. I brought it to my mouth and ate, chewing slowly.

Ben sighed. "More," he instructed as his cell let out one solitary ring. I obeyed as I stabbed and ate a cube of cantaloupe with my three remaining tines. Ben read his message and slammed a hand onto the table, startling me. "It's Rick. Colter's awake. Molly—"

"Let's go." I was already up, prepared to bolt back to the room without bothering to clean up my tray.

We raced down the curved hallway, our reflection in the glass windows a blur. A nurse was just exiting the double doors of the ICU waiting area as we ran full bore at it.

"Hey!" she shouted, holding up an authoritative, halting hand. "Where are you two headed running like that?"

We both skidded to a stop, grabbing on to one another. "Colter Evans," I breathed, my fingers digging into Ben's forearm. "We're here for Colter."

She just shook her head and raised her brows at us like we were unhelpful.

"Room one-eighty-three," I shot out impatiently.

Realization hit her features. "Last I checked, he has one visitor already. He's only just woken up and there's a lot of people in there right now assessing him over. My best advice is to wait here until someone comes and gets you." With that, she breezed past us and through the waiting room as though she didn't just stomp out all the raging excitement that was its own entity between Ben and I.

"Fuck this," Ben said, ripping his phone out of his pocket. I was nearly bouncing on my feet as his fingers flew across the keyboard. "I'm texting Rick."

Determination slid over me like a well-worn cardigan. "You're right, Ben. Fuck this." I shot forward, throwing him an apologetic look as I took off through the doors and down the hall, leaving him standing there, mouth agape.

It was rude of me. But I didn't care. *He was awake. He was awake.* I honed my sights on the door of his room as I moved quickly, hope building as I neared. Doctors and nurses were funneling in and out of his room, many indeed. My breath was ragged in my throat. I hadn't sprinted like this in a long while.

I stopped short as Dr. Hale exited through the door and looked up to catch sight of me, his face stark with sorrow, eyes wearied. Recognizing me, Dr. Hale schooled his expression to calculated calm and approached me. "I'm sorry, I forget your name..."

"Molly—How is he? I was told he was awake. *How is he?*" I lifted to the balls of my feet, peering over the doctor's shoulders as he stepped into my line of sight.

Dr. Hale reached out a firm hand, grasping my arm and softly pulling me out of the middle of the hall. I gripped the cream handrail, preparing for the worst as I watched Dr. Hale's wheels turning inside his head, thinking about how to explain.

"What's wrong?" I hissed.

"He is awake. We've removed the endotracheal tube and he's doing well." There was more to it, so I briefly stomped my foot, silently demanding he get to it. "But as was expected he's suffered some extent of memory loss." He paused as his face screwed up in thought. "I take it your mother passed away not too long ago?"

My heart sank. Completely ignoring the doctor's familial ties mistake, I breathed, "Yes."

I'd take him thinking I was Colter's sister any day if it meant I got the direct details.

Dr. Hale nodded and said on an exhale, "I'm sorry for your loss... Colter asked for her once he'd had a moment to reunite with your dad."

My heart cracked. "What happened?"

"Your father's in there now explaining her loss." Dr. Hale slid his hand to my upper back, preparing to guide me to the room. "Colter is...relearning of it and...grieving."

My heart shattered. I maneuvered out of Dr. Hale's lead. "I'll...give them a minute."

Nodding his understanding, Dr. Hale patted my shoulder. "If you'll excuse me. I'll be back to reassess him after I make my rounds."

Alone, hanging onto the hospital handrail, fresh tears sprung to my eyes. My phone dinged—probably Ben—but I ignored it. I rolled until my back hit the wall and I dropped my head back with a satisfactory thud. The tears slipped out the corners of my eyes and into my ears.

He didn't remember at least as far back as *six months ago*. How much had he lost? Was there any possibility his memories could be recovered? I didn't dare think about what this meant for us, even if my body already knew, already was processing. It shook. It *ached*.

"Molly."

I opened my eyes and looked to the door where Rick poked his head out, his eyes bloodshot.

"I'm sorry, Mr. Evans," I whispered, suddenly feeling like I was intruding.

"Ben had texted me you were incoming." He frowned.

"I can come back later." Forcing myself off the wall, I took a step away.

"Hey. No, it's okay," Rick called out invitingly. "I asked Colter. He'd like to see you."

I sucked in a sharp breath through my nose and clasped my hands as I turned to face him.

"Are you sure?" The question was nearly likely too timid, too quiet for him to hear.

But Rick Evans reached out a hand and nodded encouragingly.

My steps felt jerky as I forced myself to walk at a normal, acceptable pace. But I placed my hand in Rick's and let him guide me into the room.

"Hey Rockstar."

I was grateful for Rick's hold on me as my knees went weak underneath me. Free of the tube, eyes dull and red from tears since wiped away but open and aware, Colter sat upright in his bed, looking tired and forlorn but half-smiling at me, nonetheless. The lines of his IV softly clacked against the rail of the bed as he opened his arms up to me.

Lurching forward, I was careful not to completely crash my weight into him as I fell into his arms. I sobbed and wept, staining his hospital gown with my tears as his hands soothingly caressed up and down my back.

"I'm fine, Molls," he whispered reassuringly; his voice gravelly from the damage done by the tube. He *was* fine. Thank

God, he was. But I wasn't sure if I could say the same about myself—something I tamped down, desiring to just enjoy the feel of him holding me once more instead.

"I didn't realize how much you cared," Colter teased. When I didn't share in the laughter, he softened, his hands gripping me tighter. "I'm fine. I'm okay." He buried his face into the crook of my neck, and I melted against him as something broken and guttural left me. "Hey. I'm here," Colter mumbled against my hair.

"I thought…" I shuddered against him. "I thought…"

"Molly. Stop. Breathe," He coached.

I was being so utterly stupid. I needed to pull myself together. He was the one who should be free to fall apart. He'd just relearned of his mother passing away only moments ago and here I was selfishly eating up all the room for anguish in the space between us. I nodded, my chin digging into his shoulder and I felt it drop away from me, heard the hitch in his breath. I'd hurt him.

I pulled back fiercely. "I'm sorry."

Colter laughed it off. "It's fine. My shoulder's a bit tender. I must've smacked it against the window. That and my head," he said, wincing as he brought a bandaged finger to the butterfly closures at his brow.

Reaching out, I stopped him from prodding and further hurting himself. "I'm so sorry," I reiterated. For more things than he realized.

"Sorry for what? You didn't roll my Jeep. I'm the idiot that did that." Always trying to diffuse the situation with humor.

The humor wasn't reaching my soul. I frowned and let my thoughts slip, "I should've stayed with you. I'm so sorry I left you."

His brow furrowed. "What do you mean?"

It was then that I realized I'd put my foot in my mouth. I wasn't sure what all he knew in regards to the accident and leading up to it, and I didn't think it was the time or place to info dump on him. I shot a look over my shoulder at Rick who leaned against the opposite wall, his scruffy face in his hand. Rick nodded his consent for me to continue.

So, I explained.

Explained the vacation we'd went on. The flight home. The snowstorm we'd landed smack dab into the middle off. Then I had to tiptoe around my reasoning for what I'd meant when I'd told him I was sorry I left him.

"You were supposed to drive me home," I ended on. "But I...went with Eric instead." Saying the words out loud to him, reliving the memory, gutted me. "If I'd have stayed with you, if I'd driven with *you*—"

"Then you could've been in the room next to mine, suffering from something similar or worse for all we know, Mol," he said, stopping me in my tracks. "*Thank God* you weren't with me. I'd have never forgiven myself if I'd have hurt you...or worse."

"He's actually right, Mol. The police said the passenger side caved in as the vehicle smashed into a tree—the only reason it stopped rolling. You'd have been crushed. Let's all be thankful everyone is walking away as lucky as you are right now," Rick added, the new bit of information slicing at me deeply.

I turned back to Colter, searching his face. He flinched as if in pain. "Don't look at me like that, Rockstar. I'm going to be fine—I mean I'm *devastated*," his eyes closed as he swallowed thickly, bringing a hand up to cover his face, "about...Mom." He took a deep breath, shaking his head softly. I rocked forward like I could wrap him in my arms and soothe the ache but stopped myself. Colter dropped his hand and opened his eyes to look over at his father who must've shared a look of something steeling as Colter regained his composure. "And I'm definitely pissed I don't remember anything about this tropical vacation I probably spent and arm and a leg on, but...I'll be okay."

He would. He was. That was all that mattered. That's what I told myself as I finally found it in me to leave his side so I could let Ben see his friend. That's what I told myself as Ben drove me home later that day after I'd said my goodbyes to Rick and Colter, with the promise I'd be back in the morning. They'd both said it wasn't necessary, especially in this weather—and maybe I should feel ashamed for forcing myself on them, but I just...I couldn't not be by his side. Not after everything.

It was Ben who I confided in as he walked me to my door.

He'd stayed and made me tea as I unloaded everything on him. Perhaps it would have made more sense to vent everything to a girlfriend—to Gracie. But besides Colter, Ben was my oldest friend. And he knew Colter and I in a way she didn't. And Ben took it all in stride, listening to me explain as I cried, and sobered, then cried again, and breathed through it.

I was plastered to my couch on my back, my feet on the armrest, the empty mug of tea dangling from my hooked finger as I threw my other arm over my aching eyes. "I don't know what to do."

Ben was quiet as he sat facing me at my bistro table, his elbows resting on his knees. "I don't know either, Molly," he admitted with an air of uncertainty that only served to scrape against my invisible wounds. "The doctors say there's a possibility that with he'll regain some of his memories."

"The last thing he remembers is the Saint Patrick's day bar hop we did last spring, Ben." I lifted my head to look at him. "That's ten months of his life just…gone."

"That's not true," Ben argued lifting his wrist and pulling back his sleeve. "He remembered giving me this watch for my birthday. He caught sight of it as I hugged him goodbye. That is as early as May. Some things are *already* coming back to him."

"Ben…" I whined. "The odds of him ever getting back his memories all the way to this last week are…well, I don't know. But something in my gut feels like it's telling me to brace for the real possibility he never will."

"Don't give up on him, Molly." The determination that flooded Ben's tone rattled me. I sat up onto my elbows, sensing a level of seriousness in him. "You've always been it for him. Before we even all became friends. He always spent every recess looking in your direction. Alan and I teased him to no end over it. A boy his age, already pining after a girl." Ben scoffed as though he was a child once again and he couldn't believe his friend would dare risk cooties from the shy girl who always stuck to herself, hanging upside down by her knees on the jungle gym. I kept my mouth shut but continued rising and shifting until I sat with my feet on the floor, transfixed by what Ben shared.

"I don't think he ever intended to follow through with ever going after you. I don't think he felt he was worthy of it." Ben rolled his eyes, and I felt as though I'd been sucker punched in the ribs. "But I know for a fact that you're why he's never settled down. Likely never will. Colter would go to the end of time always waiting for you. Honestly, I'm shocked you never knew. I always assumed you did but didn't share the feelings and just never chose to consider him an option. Granted, you seemed preoccupied with academics more than you did boys throughout school. Until you hit college and started dating." By this time, Ben was rising to his feet, pacing as he dredged up old memories.

"He drank himself stupid the night he overheard Gracie telling me about you losing your virginity to a one-night stand. Really fucking stupid of you, by the way. And yes, Grace tells me everything, Mol. Don't pretend like couples *don't* spill the tea to each other." He shot me a glance that I withered under. "Though, I think he'd been getting pushed to his limit when you brought Eric home. I think...I think he could see that there was the potential for something real there. We all did. It's why we accepted him even though we found him...abrasive. I hate that guy," He tacked on under his breath as though saying it to himself.

"You shouldn't," I whispered. I don't think Ben heard it, but I didn't care to elaborate. Not yet. There would be time to explain *that* whole situation—another doozy of heartbreaking info.

"Actually, I think Colter had been prepared to confront Eric one way or another, before..." He stopped suddenly, a thoughtful look passing over his features as though he was unsure he should share. My fingers curled over the edge of the couch cushion. "Before his mom passed away."

My mouth worked as I fought the urge to shout and cry. Ben continued, much to my bruising heart, "Eric and him did have a bit of an...argument later though. It was the weekend before he left for Tennessee. Eric saw it too—the way Colter always hovered around in your life, even if he'd made the decision to let you be. Love you from a distance."

"What do you mean?" I breathed, achingly enthralled.

"It was a night at our house. We were having a bonfire..." Ben eyes grew distant as though the memory was a bit of a struggle to search for. Considering most bonfires at Ben and Gracie's consisted of heavy drinking and smoking weed well into the late hours of the night, it made sense that the memory would be a bit fuzzy for him. I myself didn't remember the night he referred to. Too many weekends over the summer were spent exactly like that.

Ben crossed the space and sat down beside me. "You had gone inside to go to the bathroom, I think, with Gracie. Alan and Cam were doing what Alan and Cam do when they quietly sneak off for twenty minutes like they always do." I huffed a dry laugh at that. It was true. They were often known to slip out and then covertly slip back into the party relatively unnoticed. Stealthy, those two were. "I'd stepped away to grab more wood from the pile, leaving Colter and Eric alone. By the time I came back they were in each other's faces, a wild look in both their eyes."

I stilled. Stopped breathing altogether. Was this the night Eric had told me about?

"They chilled the fuck out once they noticed me throwing logs onto the fire. And when I confronted Colter about it later he brushed it off. He never did tell me what it was about, but I'd bet my left nut it all boiled back down to *you*." There was no humor in his joke. I frowned a smile, but Ben didn't look at me as he continued, "Colter's always been a hound for sniffing out bullshit from a mile away. I doubt he was in the wrong. Especially after what Eric did to you."

I nodded as I tried to take it all in.

My lips parted on a sharp inhale as I found the nerve to speak, "Why didn't anyone ever...*say* anything to me?"

If Colter had always felt this way about me, then there was an entire life's worth of opportunities for us to come together. But then, cruelly, life and fate had orchestrated our joining to a week before he'd lose all memory of us reaching that peak of truth? It seemed wrong. Unfair. Anger drilled into me, heady and rife. Anger at who? All of my friends that kept all of this to themselves? At Colter, for deciding for the both of us not to engage in a romantic relationship? At myself, for doing the same in my own way?

Fuck.

Fuck. Fuck. Fuck.

I wanted to scream.

"I don't tell you this to upset you," Ben whispered, sensing the rage bubbling in me. "I only tell you this because of what you shared with me. Colter…will flay me alive when he finds out about this—"

"He won't." The words left me without hesitation.

The decision in my mind had hit me fiercely as what Ben said cemented into me. Colter would never find out about this.

"Molly." Ben's voice was pleading and wary.

I looked at him, steeling myself. "He doesn't have any recollection of any of these things that led us together. It's possible he…never will." I sagged with the weight of that statement. "You said he'd wait til the end of time for me. I have to give him respect and do the same for him. If I confessed my love to him now who knows how it would play out? He wouldn't understand my sudden shift. Right now, he thinks I'm still happily involved with Eric. For God's sake, he just found out all over again for the first time that he lost his *mother*, Ben.

"He's probably severely struggling to cope with waking up not remembering a good chunk of his life, in general. I can't…add to that pile of shit he was handed." My hands came to my face, covering the way it crumpled with the pain of that alone. "You heard his doctors. We need to take things easy with him. Remind him of things slowly, in small doses. Give him the chance to come to things on his own, too. This…this is too much. He needs time. Space."

Looking like he wanted to argue, but remaining silent, Ben shook his head, biting his lip. His phone rang and he peeked at it, deeming whoever it was not as important as this conversation as he silenced it and slipped it back into his pocket. "I don't know the right path to take here, Molly. But that doesn't sound like the right one."

I looked away, nostrils flaring as I sighed through my nose crossly. "You don't understand. Mexico and the way it all played out between us was crucial to us tearing down our walls. *His...* They're back up, Ben. To do something on my end to pull them back down would be...manipulative."

Ben recoiled. "I wouldn't exactly call it that—"

"What would you call it?" I sniped.

His eyes flared with anger as he shot his gaze to mine. "I don't know—*I don't know*, okay?"

"Exactly!" I cried, voice breaking. I realized then that there was a good possibility this was the hardest thing I'd ever have to face in my life. Feeling like a husk of a person, I collapsed into the couch and went silent as the endless supply of tears fell, collecting in dark stains on my shirt.

At some point, Ben had risen, used the restroom, speaking softly to me all the while as he cleaned up the tiny mess he'd made when he'd heated a pot for tea.

He'd let me wallow until he prepared himself to leave, planting an out-of-character kiss to the top of my head. He walked out after saying something I didn't even register. Probably a generic farewell.

I didn't move from the couch. Not until the next day, when I woke with a kink in my neck, forced myself to shower, and left for the hospital.

No more progress had been made as far as Colter regaining his memories, but his prognosis was great. The doctors chalked it up to him being a spry, young man in his prime. He'd likely be able to go home by the end of the week as long as things kept looking up.

I, sadly, noted the way Colter had seemed pleasantly confused that I came back each and every day. Noted the way he seemed delighted that I'd continued to visit after he'd been taken home, even though there was a part of him perplexed by it.

The hardest part was receiving my stuff back from Rick after he'd visited the tow company's lot to empty out Colter's belongings. Rick had produced a wrapped painting, asking me if I knew who it was for.

It was a lighthouse. With sail boats in the water. And two Yucatan Amazons perched on the rocks of the breakwater. And baby alligators sunning themselves on the distant beach.

I knew instantly it was a painting done by the street artist at the flea market we'd visited. When Colter had disappeared he must have been requesting this. I warred with mixed emotions; humor at the inside joke and a heavy ache for the fact that it would no longer make any sense to him. I couldn't bring myself to take it home. I told Rick that Colter had bought it and he should hang it in his room. *Maybe* something about the peculiar piece would spark a memory for Colter.

~

Week after week passed and with it, so did Eric.

I'd been able to put my heartache aside attended the funeral with Gracie and Ben at my side—they too having found it in their hearts to not hold a grudge for the man once they'd come to an understanding. I was walking pain and anguish on all fronts, but I forced myself composed through it all.

Then months passed with no change other than Colter's increasing comfortability with me hanging around all the time. Even Rick had made a comment when he thought I wasn't within earshot as I cleared Colter's lunch tray I'd prepared for him one afternoon; Rick had told Colter he was lucky to have a friend like me.

A friend.

With time, that title didn't hurt so much anymore.

TWENTY-SEVEN

Six months later

Under the glow of the streetlamp, Gracie and Ben stood at the trunk of my car in the quiet dark hours of predawn. Gracie stared into it with a frown at all of my belongings stowed inside, and Ben rested his arm against the open hatch door. I still couldn't believe they'd woken up at this time to see me off.

"So, this is it?" Gracie asked softly. "You're all packed up and that's that?"

"That's that," I said on an exhale.

Her lower lip wobbled, and I had to look away before I started to lose it too. I knew she ached and wished things had turned out differently just as much as I did. I knew she was well aware why I was leaving and it angered her and Ben and the rest of them that I'd made this choice. But I couldn't stay here any longer. Eric was gone and Colter...

I'd spent the last six months hoping against all odds that something would change in my favor, biding my time and staying busy so the heartache of it all didn't suffocate me. But even after all this time, after all the memories Colter slowly regained, he still wasn't anywhere near to the time we'd shared midwinter in Mexico. And the doctor's believed the window of opportunity for him to ever retrieve those memories was undeniably coming to a close, if it hadn't already.

A car door slammed shut beyond us and I stepped away from my vehicle to look.

Parked across my apartment's parking lot, Colter's new forest green Wrangler gleamed almost black in the outer ring of the spotlight of the streetlamp closest to him. I could make out his figure as he swiped imaginary dirt off his hands and turned to us, heading our way.

I wiped my clammy hands on my yoga shorts and turned to face Colter as he approached, jumping a little as Ben shut my hatch for me with a bang.

Colter grimaced as he leaned his hip into the front fender of my Subaru. "We should head out soon if we want to make sure we arrive there by seven-thirty."

Because my first day at my new job in Chicago started today at 9 a.m. and we'd need time to quickly shove everything of mine now packed in Colter's Wrangler into the storage unit I'd rented until I could pay someone down there to move it all into my third-floor apartment.

"Right," I chirped, facing Ben for a goodbye first. Gracie had pressed her fingertips to her mouth and had stepped a few paces away into the shadows as though witnessing this was too hard for her. Turning my melancholy eyes on Ben's he gave me a sad smile that I returned. "It's only Chicago. A three-hour drive away—one hour by plane. It's not like I'm moving across oceans."

"You're the first one of us to spread your wings, Mol. It's difficult for all of us, but," Ben's eyes flashed behind my shoulder at Colter as his voice lowered. "We do get it. Why you need to do what you need to do."

I nodded, swallowing down the lump in my throat. It was when Ben came in for a hug, that the welling of the tears began. His hug was somehow unlike all the others I've ever felt from him before. Not the usual awkward squeeze, but a real, warm embrace and it poked at my bruised heart.

"I love you, please take care of Gracie for me, okay? Make sure she finds some new girlfriends. She's going to need some now that I'm leaving her all alone with you buffoons."

He laughed in my ear. "Yeah. She's actually already planned a dinner party with some girls from work, so I think she'll manage."

"Oh?" I sobbed. I hadn't known. She hadn't mentioned it. My heart cracked but I forced a smile so I didn't sound so weepy as I said, "Good. That's good. I'm glad." It was the truth, even though it rang bittersweet.

"Good luck, Molls," Ben said with a final squeeze before he pulled away.

"Thanks." It was all I could manage to squeak out. I wiped at the tears that were falling freely now as I heard Gracie, somewhere in the shadows of the apartment complex lawn, begin sniffling.

"Okay," I cry-laughed. "Where are you?"

"I'm here," She called back in a blubbering whimper.

I followed her voice and found her standing before a sapling pine tree, her shoulders shaking. "What are you doing?" I sighed with amusement.

"Luring you away so that I can whisk you off into the night so you can never leave me," she giggled through her tears.

I barked out a laugh that echoed through the quiet parking lot obnoxiously. She laughed, too, and before I knew it she pummeled into me, throwing her arms around my neck. "I'll never forgive you for this."

I squeezed her tightly. "Yes, you will."

Gracie breathed, "It's still hard."

"You're telling me."

Gracie pulled away a bit so she could try to view my face in the dark. My eyes had finally adjusted, and I could make out her hopeful expression. "You don't have to run, you know? What happens if one day he wakes up and remembers everything and you're not here or you've moved on? He'll never forgive us all for letting you go."

"I'm not running." My voice was weak as I tried to push through the pain her words were eliciting, but even I wasn't so sure that wasn't the case. I hadn't initially jumped for the job-opening when it was presented to me. But my manager had spent weeks nudging me in that direction, saying I was a perfect fit for the job and promising a world of new career possibilities if I just gave it a shot. But I had to admit, staying here knowing Colter would never know what we'd shared and what I was feeling…it'd started to take its toll. "You know the prognosis. If he hasn't remembered by now…he likely never will."

"But you know he still loves you deep down inside. Maybe if you stayed and spent more time with him—"

"Gracie," I whined, pulling away, but still clasping her hands in mine. I dropped my voice to a barely there whisper, "Colter and I's feelings for each other developed over a series of events that just can't be replicated. If I even tried to orchestrate something…it'd just feel wrong. *Forced.*"

We'd had this conversation before and I knew she understood this, but she was grasping at straws. Straws I, too, had held onto for some time before I realized I needed to…let go.

"I just don't understand how you can walk away from this."

"Because living through this is slowly killing me. Everywhere I go, everything I do, it…it always leads back to him. He's all I've ever really known and I'll spend the rest of my life wasting away if I don't go figure out what the world is like separate of him." A painful revelation even if I wasn't sure I agreed with it still. "Maybe Colter and I were in each other's lives to show one another what real love looks like so that we know what to look for…" Something my own mother had offered as an attempt to help me move on. Again, a hard and painful possibility.

"Or *maybe,*" Gracie began with a bit of forced hope, "you'll realize you miss us all too much and come home and by then you and Colter can reunite and spark something again naturally?"

What a wonderful thing that would be.

I shrugged as I nodded, tears falling onto my cheeks. "Maybe."

"I love you," she said, pulling me back into a soul-crushing hug.

"I love you, too."

"No goodbyes."

"Only see you laters," I agreed as we both finally let go of one another. We silently walked back to where Ben and Colter waited beside my driver's side door, wiping away the tracks of tears from our faces.

Ben opened his arms up for Gracie and she fell into him as though she'd been sapped of her ability to stay upright.

"Alan and Cam will be sorry they missed this," Ben said.

"Well, I understand that babies arrive on their own time," I conceded. "And I don't blame Cam for rushing off to meet his new niece one bit." Alan, obviously, had joined Cam on the last-minute flight to California to greet Cam's older sister's first child as she arrived into the world a whole two weeks ahead of schedule.

"Drive safe," Ben said with an incline of his head.

"And call us when you get there?" Gracie added.

"Of course." I backed away towards my door.

"You ready, Rockstar?" Colter's voice made goosebumps rise on my flesh.

I turned to him just as he opened my door. "Ready as I'll ever be."

"Then let's get you to the Windy City." He grinned, though there was a sheen to his eyes that caught the lamplight.

The gathering of tears that now blurred my vision as I lowered into the driver's seat was entirely for that look in Colter's eyes. Our goodbye would be later. And private, thank God.

"You sure you're up for the long drive?" I asked before he could close the door. Behind him I could already see Gracie and Ben heading towards their vehicle as if they wanted to give us space.

"Of course. Whatever you need, Mol. Always," he said leaning down as he rested his forearms on the edge of the door opening.

I had to look away because I couldn't stop the look of pain I knew was crumpling my face as he said those words. "Your doctors are sure this is okay?"

"I've been cleared to drive for two months now, Molls. Come on, you know this." Colter's laugh was easy, casual. "You worry like my mom used to."

The sound that came out of me was more of a sob than a laugh, but it easily passed for one. "Ha. Well, you know me."

"Come on," he said as he softly smacked the roof of my car. "Let's get through downtown before rush hour. Don't worry about me. I'll be right behind you. We'll keep an eye on each other the whole way down."

"Right," I agreed with a curt nod. We didn't say another word as Colter shut my door. I collapsed into my seat back and let myself go, crying freely as I watched him cross the parking lot at a jog, waving to Ben and Gracie as he went.

I blew out a long, therapeutic breath, reminding myself I had to get it together. "You can do this," I said aloud into the dark cabin of my car. "You can. You will."

I turned the ignition a second after Colter turned his. Checking one last time that my phone was plugged in to the charger, I pulled up the GPS directions on my phone, glanced up and waved at Ben and Gracie who still waited by their car one last time. And then I put the car in drive, and slowly pulled out.

"You will arrive at your destination at seven—"

"Ugh, shut up," I groaned, silencing the GPS voice as I pulled out onto the road. Glancing at my rearview I could see Colter's headlights bob as he followed me with all the things I couldn't fit into my car alone.

And so we were off.

~

Fifteen minutes into the drive and three very upbeat radio songs to lift my spirits later, I peered up through my windshield to catch an airplane gliding low over the highway as it came in for landing at the airport just beyond the trees.

"Wow, that seems way too low," I said to no one, gaping as I watched the airplane disappear over the top of the black tree line.

The song on the radio station ended and the distinct weather report jingle filled the car. Not bothering to hear the forecast for a city I was leaving, perhaps permanently, I fiddled with the scan buttons on the back of my steering wheel. I settled on an oldies station as I recognized the second half of the chorus of The Archie's *Sugar, Sugar.*

I hummed along as I neared a vehicle ahead of me crawling along ten miles under the speed limit. Checking my rearview and the fast lane I made sure there would be plenty of space for both Colter and I to pass and then flipped my blinker.

As I drifted into the left lane, my mirrors caught the glare of Colter's headlights.

"Damn," I murmured, reaching up to adjust my mirror so I wasn't blinded.

Colter was *close,* practically riding my ass. He flashed his brights at me and I stepped on the gas a little more. "What the…" I quickly passed the driver in the slow lane and kept up my speed to make sure Colter had enough room to slide in behind me.

Except he didn't do that.

Colter revved his engine and sidled up beside me. His overheard light was on, and I could see him pointing to the shoulder of the road mouthing *Pull over,* a frantic look in his eye.

Panicking, I checked all my mirrors and then turned on my blinker. I had no idea what was wrong, but something had him unnerved and it was tossing me into sudden alarm. Thankfully, there was an exit approaching so I pulled on the wheel and headed down it. The exit led to a rural road that wrapped around the back fields of the airport runways. It was vacant and dark.

I pulled to the shoulder, throwing the car into park and tossed open my door just as Colter was jumping out of his.

"What in the world is going on?" I hollered into the night.

Blinded by Colter's headlights, all I could see was his silhouette as he charged toward me at a swift, steady pace.

"*Colter?*"

He slowed as he passed my trunk.

"Do you love me?" he demanded, crossing into the stream of lights that flooded out of my car windows.

I could see him now. His eyes flared with an intensity that stole my breath, his jaw was set, his shoulders squared as though he were ready to confront something or someone. Me.

"What?" The word was hoarse off my tongue.

"Do you," He took a cautious step forward, "love me."

"Colter," I laughed nervously. "You know I do—"

"Are you still *in love* with me?" he clarified, his eyes squeezing shut on the words *in love*. When his eyes reopened they were rife with awareness. Clarity.

My chest seized. "I don't understand. Did someone call you just now? Was it Gracie? I swear to God, I'm gonna—"

"I remember." He'd said it at a perfectly normal volume, but my ears caught it as though he'd shouted it across the open expanse of airfield.

Everything went still. My senses honed, narrowing in to focus solely on him. My ears strained.

"You...remember..."

"Everything," Colter clipped. "I remember everything."

I blinked once.

And then I lurched forward reaching out a hand as he closed the space between us in one long stride as though he'd been ready, poised to jump in. As though he knew my legs would go weak beneath me.

"Molly?" Colter's voice was thick with emotion and concern as he wrapped an arm around me, his other hand splayed against the side of my face brushing my hair back so he could examine me. Make sure that I was breathing. Because I maybe wasn't.

Adrenaline pumped through me like buckshot. I brought my hands to his chest, pressed my forehead to his, my eyes closed briefly, blinking back tears. "You remember it all? *Everything?*"

"Yes," he breathed, both his hands coming up to the back of my head. "*Yes—*"

I don't know which one of us moved first. Probably both of us at the same time. Our lips were together before I could take a breath.

Colter. He was here, he was *all* here with me. And nothing else in the world mattered. I clawed my way up him, practically feral, and his hands came down to my thighs, lifting and spreading my legs to wrap them around his waist. My fingers delved into his hair, tugging and kneading desperately as his hands smoothed up and down my spine, one to the nape of my neck, the other to the curve of my behind.

"I love you," I said against his mouth just so it was out there before I dove back in for more. But as soon as his mouth crashed against mine I knew I needed to say it over and over again for all the times I'd had to suffocate it over the course of the last six months. I clasped his cheeks in my hands and still holding my lips to his as he panted, I repeated it, "I love you. I love you, Colter. Oh *God*, I love you." A sob rocked me on the last one and he stifled it as he captured my mouth again.

Colter was here, holding me, soothing me, caressing me any and everywhere his hands could reach. And I reveled in the truth that I...I could do the same to him.

His hand fisted into my hair as he broke away and planted a kiss to the side of my face before pulling me into a tight embrace. "I love you, Molly. I am so sorry. I am so damn sorry it took me so long."

"No," I cried, nuzzling into the side of his face as we clung to one another. "Don't be sorry. We're here now. It's alright." My words were cut off as he squeezed me tight enough that the air rushed out of my lungs.

But, oh God, it was the most exquisite of pains—to be held so fiercely by the one you love.

"You can't go." Colter's voice broke and I felt him tremble. "Please. Stay."

I gave a watery laugh and peppered kisses all along his temple, his cheek, and jaw. "*Whatever you need*, Colter."

"Fuck," he cried as he turned and leaned against my car as though his own legs would collapse under the sag of relief. "I love you," Colter repeated for good measure.

"I love you, too." I said, pulling away to look into his eyes.

He smiled, beamed. And seeing it there in his silver-lined eyes—the depth and truth of the love there—it cracked my heart and simultaneously built it back up in all the best and most meaningful ways. Colter claimed my lips again, this time achingly soft, as though he were memorizing the feel of mine against his, as though he were savoring it. As if he had all the time in the world to spend forever doing just this. Because now…now we'd have the chance.

The sound of a car approaching hadn't even registered. Not until the driver pounded repeatedly on their horn as they ripped by.

Colter and I broke apart as laughter rippled out of us. The sound a joyous ringing that threatened to drive my heart to implosion. "Think they enjoyed the show," he joked as his eyes scanned all over my face.

"Obviously," I whispered, a coy smile tugging at my swollen lips.

Seeing as we were still standing on the side of the road with our cars still running, I slowly unwrapped my legs from around him. Colter helped ease me to my feet but did not loosen his grip around me by even an inch. We could've stood there staring into each other's eyes for an eternity, but a thought struck me. "How? What made you remember?"

"The plane. The airport," he said, shaking his head slowly. "I remembered the takeoff first. Holding your hand." Colter looked down to where my chest still rose and fell with short, deep breaths. "And then it hit me, almost all at once. Everything came barreling in and it fucking took the wind of out me. I tried calling you. Three times."

My eyes popped wide. "I silenced my phone…I didn't want to listen to the GPS voice…"

Colter threw his head back with a silent laugh. "That explains it."

"I'm sorry," I said on a breathy giggle.

But Colter just shook his head as he looked down at me in…something akin to awe. In seconds, his face fell as something seemed to cross his mind.

"You were leaving." His eyes closed. "I was so close to losing you."

And the ache, the fear, returned for just a moment as I realized what he was saying.

Would his memories have returned if not for the plane flying overhead when it did? If we'd just been a few moments too late or too early. What if Colter had never bothered to offer to help me move in the first place?

I kissed him again as the weight of the decision I'd made to leave him behind slammed into me. "I'm sorry."

"*I'm* sorry," Colter said quickly, eating up any chance for me to grovel. "I should have told you how I felt years ago and bypass all of this...craziness. I could've lived with myself if you'd have rejected me. I could have tried again, and again, until maybe you changed your mind someday."

"You'd have likely driven me crazy," I laughed softly, raking my fingers through his hair, enjoying the feeling.

"Like I haven't been doing so my whole life anyway," he scoffed, burying his face in my neck again.

"I'm the one who is sorry." Truly I was, how stupid could I be to have let myself give up on us so easily. I was running. I was going to leave him behind. That was something that felt like I'd have trouble living with for the rest of my life now that Colter was with me now. "I was leaving—"

"Stop," Colter said shaking his head against mine. "I'd once been planning on doing the same, remember? I was going to get my license and—*fuck*—I was going to go as far as Tennessee, Mol."

He was right. But I couldn't find it in me to let it have any kind of hold on me whatsoever. Not when that would *not* be happening.

Ever.

I hugged him tighter and planted kisses up and down the column of his neck. "Take me home. Colter, *please* take me home."

"I told you once to never beg." His voice had gone low, sultry. He smacked my ass in playful reprimand. My heart rate spiked. Colter really did remember. God, he remembered everything and I...I was weightless.

Picking me back up into his arms, Colter headed to my open car door. He leaned in, careful not to smack my head against the roof and snatched my purse from the passenger seat, pulled my keys out of the ignition and shut the door as he stood. He walked the short distance to his Jeep, his heated eyes locked on mine the entire time, as he held up the key fob and the beep of my car lock blared endlessly through the fields.

I bit my lip, fire building within me as he rounded to the passenger side of his Jeep, opening the door with one hand.

Colter laughed as he started to pry my arms from around his neck as I only half-jokingly held on like a baby octopus. "Think you can drive with me in your lap?" I quipped.

"I don't think my doctors or law enforcement would appreciate that, but I'm willing to try, Rockstar," he challenged.

A throaty laugh left me, but I released him. Because I knew damn well he'd have tried if I'd been serious about it. He shut the door and hurried to the driver's side, hopping in with a briskness to him. "We'll pick up your car later. You're coming home with me," he said, starting the vehicle. I shivered with anticipation, thinking I might know exactly what he had in mind for us when we got there. Colter looked at me. "And I'm never letting you go.

EPILOGUE

A woman nearing retirement age sat in the aisle seat of a plane soon to head south. Her light brown hair was swept up into a low bun and her brown eyes were crisp with an antsy anticipation for the flight ahead. She gave polite smiles to each person that passed down the narrow aisle.

Coming down that aisle next, a young woman with dark hair looked down at the phone in her hand. Her blue eyes flicked up, reading the numbers above the older woman's head. The young woman gave a brief flash of straight white teeth and then tossed her chin over her shoulder.

"This is us," she said to someone behind her.

Realizing these were her row mates, the older woman quickly popped up out of her seat, side-stepped into the aisle, and watched as the young woman flicked her long brown hair over her shoulder, bending slightly at the waist to inch down into her seat. The person behind her was just finishing stowing his carry-on in the upper compartment, when the older woman got a good look at him.

Young and carrying an air of roguishness she thought looked familiar, the young man grinned at her.

"Hey there," he said politely as he followed the dark-haired beauty into the row.

The young woman settled into the window seat and held a small neck pillow tightly to her stomach. The young man sat down beside her, reached over and took one of her hands in his. "Everything will be just fine. You'll see. I'll get you a double shot of vodka when the beverage cart comes. It'll calm your nerves."

The older woman bit down on the inside of her lips to keep from smiling as she settled back into her aisle seat.

The young woman scoffed a laugh. "You're not just trying to liquor me up so you can talk me into sneaking off into the bathroom with you?"

"Well, that way I could definitely get your fear of flying out of your head, but no, that's not it, baby," he replied, bringing her hand to his mouth to plant a kiss upon the back of it.

The act made something in the older woman's chest squeeze. Taking the risk, the older woman turned to the both of them. "I find a drink helps. It's what I used to do, years and years ago."

"See?" The man said, his lips spreading into a wide smile. "She gets it." He offered the older woman his hand. "My name is Owen. This," Owen paused to eye the young woman next to him. "is my girlfriend, Hannah."

"Hi!" Hannah piped up, her cheeks going a bit red after realizing the older woman had heard their conversation.

"What's your name?" Owen asked politely.

"Molly. Molly Evans," she replied, an edge of pride in her voice.

"Nice to meet you, rowmate." Owen winked charmingly and Molly placed a hand on her chest, flattered.

"It's a pleasure." Molly inclined her head.

Molly Evans sat patiently as the rest of the passengers found their seats all the while listening to Owen and Hannah explain the reason for their flying with Northwestern Airlines this early February morning. A celebratory spur of the moment vacation to reward themselves for Hannah's graduating with her associate in marketing, and Owen passing his LSAT.

The plane began taxiing, turning to the left as it positioned itself at the foot of the runway, waiting to be cleared for takeoff.

Molly had grown quiet, clutching onto the aisle armrest, reminding herself as she usually did, that it would be alright. She didn't have a fear of takeoff and landing like she'd once had many, many years ago, but she couldn't outright pretend it didn't get her heart rate going from time to time still.

The sound of the plane engines revving made her suck in a breath. Across the aisle, a passenger took the earbuds out of his ear canals, pocketed them in his jacket, and reached across the aisle to place his hand on top of Molly's.

At the contact, Molly jumped. She looked up over into the blue-green eyes she knew all too well which belonged to the passenger and smiled lovingly.

"I'm fine," she reassured him.

"I know you are," he said, his voice floating above the increasing din of the loud engines. But his hand still tightened around hers. She was grateful for the affection. Molly smiled at him.

Her son.

Her adult son, Logan, who was headed down to Cozumel.

To Coral Rojo Resort, to be exact. Headed there for his destination wedding to the petite blonde sitting next to him, her five-year-old son from a previous marriage in the window seat, peering out at the tarmac with mouth hanging open in awe. Serena and Kaden. Molly's soon-to-be daughter-in-law and grandson-in-law. Though for all Kaden knew, Molly was the only grandma he'd ever known. She would make sure he knew she was a true grandma, nonetheless. She loved the little boy with all her heart. Like she knew she'd love her future grandbabies her son and Serena would hopefully make together someday. Soon.

Her heart ached as she wished her husband could see the sight of the three of them now. A happy little family soon to start an entirely new adventure. One she knew well herself. She had spent her whole life in love with her husband—a love she knew not everyone was lucky in life to share.

The plane took off without a hitch. And the same went for all takeoffs and landings as they touched down in the airport on the island of Cozumel she hardly recognized. It had gone through a series of renovations and remodeling in the thirty-four years since she'd been here.

She and her husband had always said they'd make their way back to the island someday to reminisce. And here she was. Her heart beat wildly with excitement for the week ahead.

Giggling to herself as her son griped and moaned about the stuffiness of the shuttle ride to the resort, Molly exited the front seat of the vehicle, having happily spent the ride in the chill, albeit weak, flow of the shuttles air conditioning system. It must not have reached Logan who'd been relegated to the very back. They'd needed to arrange a special shuttle that had been equipped with a booster seat for Kaden.

Logan had already taken Molly's luggage out from the back and wheeled it over to her as Serena unbuckled Kaden. "You want to go check in with us or do you want to wander?"

"You guys go on ahead," Molly replied, grateful Logan understood her need to run off. "We'll catch up later for dinner?"

"El Sombrero," Logan confirmed with a kiss to Molly's cheek. "Love you, Mom."

"Love you, too," she said, then turned to the opened shuttle. "And you, too!"

"See ya later, Mom!" Serena huffed through the strands of hair that fell into her face as she struggled with Kaden's buckle.

"Buh-bye, Nana!" Kaden chirped from his seat, accidentally kicking his mother in the arm.

As Molly waved them off, she took in the sight of the lobby before her. She walked through it, absorbing all the differences that had been made over the several years since she'd walked through this place. The lobby was no longer open to the outdoors. Glass walls with beautiful frond etchings had been erected, probably to hold off hard rains like those she'd experienced the night of Ben and Gracie's wedding.

Oh, Gracie.

At one time, her closest friend and confidant, Gracie had left Michigan after her divorce from Ben. That had been ages and ages ago, and the two women had slowly drifted apart over the years. The marriage between her and Ben had fizzled out in the first two years, and it perhaps had broken the hearts of their friends more than it had the two of them. Through her ongoing friendship with Ben, she was well aware that he and Grace still talked to each other regularly to this day given they shared a daughter just two years older than Logan. Both had happily remarried; Grace now on her third husband.

Molly didn't judge. Never had, never would. She'd seen just how complicated love could be.

She still kept in touch with Alan and Cam who were living in California after their daughter had landed a teaching job there three years ago and to also be closer to Cam's side of the family. Molly enjoyed the pictures the happily married couple shared to their social medias—the two of them having sprung up a sort of fanbase to their tomfoolery and travel activities that still followed them to this day.

She wheeled her luggage to the edge of the paved sidewalk that met the beach. Looking up out onto the churning ocean beyond the sand she smiled.

Rising from the water was a man aged like fine wine. His hair was beginning to gray, but his blue-green eyes were sparkling as they took in the sight of her. Her heart fluttered as she watched him shake the water out of his hair, wipe it from his face. He was still built well, taller and bulkier than he had been at twenty-four somehow. She'd forever tell herself he looked so healthy because of the deal he'd made with her on this very beach long ago; to quit his smoking habit.

Both of them had kept their side of the deal. She never again let herself wallow over her break-up. He never did have another cigarette. Neither of them had needed to.

The man crossed the beach, bending to pick up a towel and shake it out, using it to collect water from his chest, the back of his neck. He was as handsome as ever, she had to admit.

"Hey there, Rockstar," Colter crooned as he stepped up before his wife, reaching around the back of her head to pull her hair out of the bun.

"I've missed you," she said, right before he pressed his lips to hers.

Indeed, it'd been four days since she'd last seen her husband. Colter had arrived early to prepare everything for the wedding happening in two days. Molly would have come along, but she'd had to stay at work to button up a few loose ends. Because after this week, Molly and Colter would be heading to Seattle to finally embark on an Alaskan cruise they'd gifted each other for their thirty-second wedding anniversary.

Colter, having started his own electrical company at age thirty-six, wasn't tied down to such requirements these days. He'd simply handed everything off to his second-in-command and flew off.

He pulled her back gently by the fistful of her hair to look her in the eyes. "I've missed you, too."

She was putty in his hands like she'd been since they day he'd first kissed her.

"Come here, I want to show you something." Colter stepped around her, still holding her hand and clutching her luggage in the other.

She'd happily let him lead her to the edge of the world...but they were not headed toward their beachside bungalow they'd reserved ten months ago. "Where are we going?"

Looking down into her brown eyes, Colter wagged his brow at her. "You'll see. Trust me."

Always.

She faintly remembered the walk. Things were a bit different. New trees, maybe? New landscaping. The walls of the resort had been repainted in different shades of vibrant red. But as he guided her to a stairwell, she immediately remembered.

The wrought iron enclosure that wrapped around the open stairwell was still the same. Molly craned her neck to view it, but Colter gently pulled her along to the first step, collapsing the luggage handle and picking it up by its side grip.

"This isn't—"

"It is." Colter couldn't contain his smile.

Molly lit up with a whirl of emotions, remembering just how close he'd come to forgetting all about these things. Things she'd already almost forgotten with time and age. They hit the landing between the second and third floor and Molly had to stifle her gasp so as not to spook them off.

The two Yucatan Amazon parrots that sat perched on the decorative iron.

She couldn't explain the tears that sprung to her eyes. "Can we just...watch them? For a little bit."

Colter wrapped his arms around his wife's waist placing a kiss to her cheek, the smile evident in his voice as he whispered in her ear, "Whatever you need, Molls."

ACKNOWLEDGEMNTS

First and foremost, I have to say thank you to my husband, Tyler, for being my number one cheerleader in taking my hobby, and actually bringing it from a document on the laptop he gifted me for my birthday, into an actual fully written book. Without his constant support this never would have come to life.

And Lindsey—for helping me make this book make some sense. You were a bigger part of this getting out into the world than you know. Thank you.

Next, a huge dollop of gratitude is bestowed on my longest friend, Cady. As the first person to ever read my first draft of Midwinter in Mexico, she was another pillar in my foundation that prompted me to make something more of the stories in my head.

And to my parents, Chris and Dave, who have always loved and supported me for the creativity I've always sought in life, whether it be writing, voice lessons, guitar, dance, pole fitness, and musical theater. If my acting career had ever taken off, my mother would've been an excellent Mom-ager.

ABOUT THE AUTHOR

Calley has enjoyed writing recreationally since she was in high school. That love of writing, and most definitely reading, has followed her into adulthood. She is a caffeine addict, typically has four books in progress (reading and writing) at any given time, and lives on her farm in Michigan with her husband, two kids, and her goodest boy, a chocolate lab named Maverick. Midwinter in Mexico is her first novel.

www.ingramcontent.com/pod-product-compliance
Lightning Source LLC
Chambersburg PA
CBHW051954240626
47153CB00005B/1751